Praise for Li

'Page-turning and c

'The story was full of twists an
A fantastic start to an intriguin

'A harrowing and suspenseful page turner that
perfectly encapsulates "Northern Noir". This is how
a police procedural is done' **Nadine Matheson**

'Dark, disturbing and compelling' **Neil Lancaster**

'Gritty and gutsy, with assured writing and a
stellar plot. I loved it' **Ruth Dugdall**

'A superbly-crafted story with writing so vivid the
atmosphere floats from the pages. A compelling
launch in a terrific new series' **Rick Mofina**

'The first in a promising new series featuring
the inspired pairing of Scottish female cops
Solanki and McQueen . . .' ***Choice***

'Packed with humour and grit, *The Revenge Pact* is a fantastic
thriller told at a breakneck pace. Liz Mistry is fast becoming
one of my favourite authors, and the Jazz Queens might
just be my favourite new detective duo' **Tom Mead**

'Riveting' ***The Post***

LIZ MISTRY moved to West Yorkshire in the late 1980s. Her gritty crime fiction police procedural novels set in Bradford embrace the city she describes as 'Warm, rich and fearless' whilst exploring the darkness that lurks beneath. Yet, her heart remains in Scotland, where childhood tales of bogey men, Bible John and grey lady ghosts fed her imagination.

Her latest work, The Solanki and McQueen crime series is set around West Lothian, where she uses the distinctive landscape, historic heritage and Scottish culture as a backdrop to her hard-hitting yet often humorous stories.

Struggling with clinical depression and anxiety for many years, Liz often includes mental health themes in her writing. She credits her MA in Creative Writing from Leeds Trinity University with helping her find a way of using her writing to navigate her ongoing mental health struggles. The synergy between creative and academic writing led Liz to complete a doctorate in creative writing researching the importance of representation of marginalised groups within the genre she loves.

Her husband, three children and huge extended British Indian family are a constant support to her. In her spare time, Liz loves visiting the varied Scottish and Yorkshire landscape, travelling, listening to music, reading and blogging about all things crime fiction on her website blog, The Crime Warp.

You can connect with Liz here:

Website: lizmistry.com
X: (Twitter): LizMistryAuthor
Facebook: https://www.facebook.com/LizMistrybooks
Instagram: @lizmistryauthor

Also by Liz Mistry

Last Request
Broken Silence
Dark Memories
Blood Games
Dying Breath
End Game

The Solanki and McQueen Crime Series
The Blood Promise
The Revenge Pact

Deadly Reckoning

LIZ MISTRY

ONE PLACE. MANY STORIES

HQ
An imprint of HarperCollins*Publishers* Ltd
1 London Bridge Street
London SE1 9GF

www.harpercollins.co.uk

HarperCollins*Publishers*
Macken House, 39/40 Mayor Street Upper,
Dublin 1 D01 C9W8
This edition 2025

1

First published in Great Britain by HQ,
an imprint of HarperCollins*Publishers* Ltd 2025

Copyright © Liz Mistry 2025

Emoji(s) © Shutterstock.com

Liz Mistry asserts the moral right to be identified as the author of this work.
A catalogue record for this book is available from the British Library.

ISBN: 9780008686512

This novel is entirely a work of fiction. The names, characters and incidents
portrayed in it are the work of the author's imagination. Any resemblance to
actual persons, living or dead, events or localities is entirely coincidental.

All rights reserved. No part of this publication may be reproduced, stored
in a retrieval system, or transmitted, in any form or by any means,
electronic, mechanical, photocopying, recording or otherwise,
without the prior permission of the publishers.

Without limiting the author's and publisher's exclusive rights, any unauthorised
use of this publication to train generative artificial intelligence (AI) technologies
is expressly prohibited. HarperCollins also exercise their rights under Article
4(3) of the Digital Single Market Directive 2019/790 and expressly reserve this
publication from the text and data mining exception.

Printed and bound in the UK using 100% Renewable
Electricity by CPI Group (UK) Ltd

This book contains FSC™ certified paper and other controlled sources
to ensure responsible forest management.

For more information visit: www.harpercollins.co.uk/green

As well as being dedicated to my ever-growing extended family and my brilliant husband & children, Deadly Reckoning *is also dedicated to Kath, my niece Jaina's guide dog who very sadly passed away this year. Such a beautiful, gentle dog and wonderful companion to Jaina, she will never be forgotten.*

Prologue

May
Mhairi

With the salty water lashing my face, its stinging droplets like acid on my flesh, and the wind tugging mercilessly at my hair hard enough to yank it right out, I stand with my back to the receding island and look to the future. My future. A future that might constitute my end game or equally a new beginning. Either way, I'm up for the challenge, ready to march onwards like the soldiers I so like to taunt. I've enjoyed shocking their sensibilities these past weeks, but although for now they're scratching their heads in perplexed confusion, I'm savvy enough to accept that a bit of hair dye, body-fattening disguises and the like won't protect me for much longer. But *c'est la vie.*

I pull my jacket tighter round my body, savouring the push and pull pounding my bones as the freezing squall buffets me – an inconsequential piece of flotsam in the ebb and flow of life. But at least I'm alive. These last months have been trying – not the end of the world, I agree – after all, living here, albeit in a basic cottage, beats being tossed in the nick. Although it's not been pleasant, on a positive note, it has been safe – well, safer for me. That's what comes of having a muddied past – it's hard for them to follow all the interwoven threads that might have led them here.

I mean, who would ever link me to a step-great-grandad from Skye who was as canny as me when it came to putting things down on paper? No, the auld bugger, on his death bed, just slipped me

1

the key when I was twelve. My adoptive mum – totally lame bitch that she was – had moaned and groaned about trekking up there. The only reason she made the hike, I reckon, was because she thought the auld bugger would leave her something in his will. No, that was a bit harsh. Deep down she probably cared for him. He didn't though – leave her a sodding thing that is – and boy, did it piss her off. Instead, he left it in trust to the community, with the proviso that his step-great-grandchild (no name ever stated) had the key and was entitled to use it for their lifetime.

Like I said, the auld yin was well canny and with the locals viewing both him and his land with fear, augmented by the multitude of creepy bogeyman stories that circulated for years, they kept well clear, allowing it to slip into disuse, only to be awakened on my infrequent visits. This was the only thing that belonged just to me. Not even Simon knew about it, and as for Jazzy? Well, it was all the more special to me because she hadn't tainted it with her presence.

Course, I never told anyone about my windfall, not even the cowbag, and it's come in handy over the years. A bolthole to escape to when I needed it and no passport or ID necessary; although, I managed to get a fake ID using his name – McCullough – just in case, and I kept up with the utilities over the years, so no one had any cause to gripe. Besides, I doubt anyone in the 'community' really wanted a battered – little more than a bothy – hovel in the middle of nowhere. Not even the village kids thought to use it for their illicit drinking or weed smoking seshes. Too far to trek to when you're high and besides, I think fear of the ghost of my cantankerous auld step-great-grandad Stuart McCullough was enough to frighten them off.

Every time I visited over the years, I made sure to be in disguise. I value the importance of forward planning, and even at that young age I realised that there would come a time when that hideaway would be of use. But now it's time to leave the safety of the island and return to the limelight. It's time to put an end to this once and for all. Thankfully my network of acquaintances, apostles and hangers-on have been helpful and the use of satellite phones for communication purpose has decreased the chances of detection. I know sister dearest has been excluded from the investigation and that fills me with joy. She'll hate being on the sidelines but it only serves her right; besides, she won't be on the outside looking in for very much longer. She's got a lot to answer for, has my sister – such a lot, but her time has come, so she better watch out, for this is a duel to the end.

On a whim, I raise my arms to shoulder height and stretch them out to my sides and, channelling my inner Kate Winslet, I yell into the waves, 'I'm coming for you, Jazzy Solanki. I'm coming for you!'

Chapter 1

Tuesday

Jazzy

The seaside town of Portobello was lovely at this time of year. The promenade alive but not yet heaving because it was a school day. The calm before the storm, which would soon arrive when the summer holidays freed local teenagers and families to indulge in hours of beach entertainment intensified by the inevitable advent of holidaymakers. It was heading from spring jacket wear to lighter layers – not quite 'taps aff' weather, but getting there – and DS Jazzy Solanki was happy to be off duty for once. She inhaled, savouring the way the briny scent wrapped her up in a homey, *I belong* blanket. She needed it. The past few months had been hard emotionally, mentally and physically.

She walked along with her mother, Lillie, while Jazzy's young friends, Benjy and Ivor, strolled ahead, the sea breeze gently caressing their faces. Beside Jazzy and Lillie trotted Crumble, Lillie's guide dog. Their pace was leisurely and, as they strolled, Jazzy studied the teenagers. They'd both been through the mill before Christmas. Ivor had been abducted by Jazzy's serial-killing siblings and had very nearly lost her life. Benjy had watched as his cousin's blood drained from her throat and even now, over six months later, the haunted look hadn't left his eyes. His frail nervousness and the way his eyes darted around as if always on the alert for attack concerned Jazzy the most.

Since those devastating events, Jazzy had become their friend – maybe an honorary big sister. Their shared experiences had forged an unbreakable bond between the three and it haunted her to see Benjy so diminished. By contrast, through her artwork, Ivor had discovered a way to process her trauma and, despite her weight loss and being a little less exuberant, occasional glimmers of the old Ivor surfaced. Jazzy was sure the teen would regain her spirit. Benjy, on the other hand, floundered. He was fading away before her eyes. The entire Stùrrach community was at their wits' end so, through a tangled sense of guilt and affection, Jazzy spent as much time with them as her job allowed. When Crumble wasn't working, Benjy enjoyed spending time with the dog who, seemingly sensing the boy's distress, had taken to sitting near him, watching over him.

Perceptive as ever to her daughter's mood, Lillie squeezed Jazzy's arm. 'How is he?'

Jazzy knew her mum didn't have to see the boy to know he was in pain. When he spoke, his affect seemed laboured, his movements lethargic, his responses slow. Jazzy sighed and took a moment before replying. In Benjy, she saw traces of herself as a tortured child before her aunt Lillie and maternal uncle had adopted her when she was twelve. All the echoes of her childhood of abuse and neglect by her birth mum, Hansa – her adopted dad's sister – the horror of Hansa's subsequent death and the ultimate trauma of being wrenched away from her two younger siblings for whom she'd been a de facto carer since they were babies.

Echoing her mum's quiet tone, Jazzy frowned. 'He's fading away, Mum. Not eating and judging by the bags under his eyes, not sleeping either. None of us can convince him to have therapy. It's almost as if he wants to . . .' Her voice hitched and she couldn't finish her sentence. She swallowed the lump in her throat and blinked away her tears. Her mum gripped her arm tighter. 'Everyone's watching out for him, sweetheart. It's early days, you know that. These things take time.'

As Jazzy watched him keep pace with his cousin, she saw his hand creep into his pocket, just for a moment, and she smiled. 'I gave both Benjy and Ivor a miniature Lord Ganesh figure similar to the one you gave me when I first moved in with you and Dad. It made me feel safe, grounded. I hoped it would do the same for them. He hasn't told me, but I know he carries it with him everywhere, Mum. They both do. He's got his in his jeans now.'

'Aye well, it's worked before on a child whose world had imploded. A little faith, and a symbol of love from someone you respect, has healing properties. I've seen it work wonders before now. I don't think seventeen years old is too old to start. You did a good thing there, Jazzy, and I'm sure it'll work equally well on those two.'

Jazzy grinned and gave her mum a quick hug. 'Yes, I'm never without mine either.'

Her mum's smile widened and, as she lifted her face up to the sun, she changed the subject. 'Can you see Inchkeith, Jasmine?'

With her fingers caressing the small Ganesh statuette she kept in her own pocket, Jazzy gazed across the sea towards Fife and smiled. On their last walk, it had been foggy and the huge rock had been all but hidden from view. But today, the island sat proud in the tranquil blue sea, its white lighthouse reflecting the sun's rays.

Lillie tilted her head towards it. 'So many stories about that place, Jasmine. There's that one about the two wee bairns left there with their deaf and dumb nanny as an experiment by James IV to determine how they would communicate with each other. And the fact that syphilis sufferers were quarantined there in the 1400s. Disregard for human wellbeing isn't a new thing, hen. Not by a long chalk.'

She'd shared these observations with Jazzy on countless

occasions since visiting the island, but Jazzy didn't mind hearing them again. Centuries of history layered one on top of the other had spoken to Lillie and, as Jazzy watched her, the older woman, a frown marring her forehead, shuddered. Jazzy hooked her arm through her mum's, desperate to wipe that worried look from her face. Over the past six months, her happy disposition had been tainted by anxiety and worry over Jazzy's wellbeing, and Jazzy had done everything she could to alleviate it. For now, though, she had no words to combat the current cause of her mum's concern.

They continued to stroll along, Crumble knowing exactly where they were heading. First the Shrimp Wreck restaurant on the promenade to feed the humans and then on to Harry's Gourmet Treats – a shop specialising in handmade dog goodies – to feed her. Jazzy already knew what their order would be – a shrimp bun each. They were to die for and, with the weather being so nice, they'd be able to sit outdoors and savour the treat by the beach rather than scurrying home with their gourmet loot to eat at her mum's kitchen table, sheltered from the wind and pelting rain they'd had just a month earlier.

They arrived at the Shrimp Wreck, ordered their food along with steaming takeaway hot drinks, and as they waited for their order to be prepared, Ivor insisted they pose for a selfie, first with Crumble and Jazzy's mum and then the three of them on their own, Jazzy in the middle. It had seemed like a rare flash of normality and, seeing the slight smile on Benjy's lips and Ivor's pout, Jazzy flung her head back and laughed. This was a good day!

Food in hand, the four of them settled on their usual benches opposite the wooden groynes that jutted into the sea. The teens sat in companionable silence on one with Jazzy and her mum on the other. Jazzy's heart contracted as she saw Ivor unwrap Benjy's sandwich and place it in his hand. His gaze was blank as he stared into the distance, his face a mask. *Where have you gone, Benjy? Please come back to us. Please let us help you.* The desire to wrap him in her arms and hold him tight was almost overwhelming, but Benjy would resent that. He'd shrug her off and turn more into himself than ever.

For a few seconds more, Jazzy watched Ivor scoff her bun, whilst Benjy's skinny fingers picked at his, flicking bits of bread onto the ground and popping the odd prawn into his mouth, his expression tortured, lacking enjoyment. Maybe her mum would have more luck convincing him to seek help. Maybe she could use her magic tranquillity to tease out some of the thoughts that troubled the boy. But for now, she'd savour the time with her mum. Jazzy had worn her long hair down for once and now wished she hadn't because the breeze, though soft, made eating without getting food in it impossible.

Her mum nudged her gently. 'You okay, Jasmine?'

Jazzy risked a glance at the older woman. She didn't want to worry her mum, but the woman was far too perceptive to be fobbed off with platitudes. Despite Jazzy's efforts, she had clearly picked up on the tension that plagued her, and that wasn't fair. Her mum and dad worried about her as much, if not more, than she worried about them. The three of them couldn't forget that one half of Jazzy's serial-killing half-siblings, Simon, had threatened Lillie in their home. Whilst Jazzy and her team had apprehended him before Christmas, his twin sister Mhairi had escaped. The pair had wreaked so much havoc and killed so many innocent people, and the knock-on effects of their violent actions still affected so many people. Having a serial killer in their house must have brought the reality of their daughter's job home to them and Jazzy hated her siblings for causing anguish to the two people she cared most about in the entire world.

When she'd got the phone call the previous week to notify her that Simon had somehow managed to take his own life, it had felt like a battering ram had hit her. The mixed emotions about her siblings that she tried so hard to control rushed over her like a tidal wave and for days she'd been unable to function. Then she'd discovered that he'd requested that Jazzy organise his funeral and her world had imploded again. For her, there had never been any doubt that she would do it. Simon wasn't only a serial killer to her – he was her baby half-brother. The little boy who, along with his twin, she'd let down. She'd been the one to break the blood promise that they'd shared so seriously as children. She'd promised that she would never leave them, never let them be split up.

They were only babies really. Four years old and so defenceless. She'd been their mother, their protector, their comfort through all the chaos of their rancid home life. She was the one who allowed them to be separated and she was the one who'd walked away from Simon earlier in the year, and she wasn't sure she'd ever forgive herself for letting them down – no matter what they'd become. So, if organising his funeral was her penance, then so be it.

However, her decision impacted her loved ones and her parents deserved better from her. They'd sacrificed so much when they took her in. Jazzy's birth mum Hansa had become estranged from her parents when she married a Muslim and, always a wild child, she'd hated them until the day she died and, as Jazzy later found out, the feeling was mutual – her grandparents disowned Hansa and they hated her offspring – the half-Muslim elder grandchild and the 'half-caste' twins. Hansa's brother, Jiten, and his wife Lillie had fostered Jazzy, despite the huge unresolved rift it caused between them and the grandfather Jazzy had never met, but who hated her with such fervour. They'd taken her in when she was a traumatised kid, showered her with love, given her the security her birth mother's addictions had denied her and finally managed to adopt her.

Jazzy would do anything to protect them, including presenting a brave face and concealing her concerns over her half-sister, Mhairi, a serial killer on the run from murder charges. 'I'm fine. Just tired. Worrying about Benjy and with the funeral arrangements and all that.'

Her mum tutted. 'You didn't have to take that on, Jasmine.

9

That man made your life hell throughout your last investigation *and* afterwards, too. If I could have got my hands on the bugger, I'd have rung his bloody neck. It isn't your job to arrange a funeral that nobody will attend for someone who conspired to kill you. Nobody gives two hoots about that monster. Besides, it's no wonder that poor wee laddie's in a state. He's not daft. He knows that Simon's death might mean that woman will come back. He's right to be scared. Maybe you should be, too.'

A sad smile twitched Jazzy's lips. Her mum was right about so many things and the feeling was mutual. No one else had stepped forward to claim Simon's remains and, at the behest of Operation Birchtree, the task force responsible for locating Mhairi, Jazzy had swallowed her misgivings and agreed to organise it in the hope that it might lure Mhairi back. Her relationship with Operation Birchtree was strained at the best of times, because, despite all the intel they had, they had failed to locate her sister and had refused to allow her input to their strategising.

Despite the pain he and Mhairi had inflicted, Jazzy couldn't forget the simple truth – he was her brother and, at one time, she would have died for him. She'd never forgive him for the things he'd done, but her mind was made up. Her work partner, Queenie, had been vociferous in her objections, pinpointing what she considered the crux of the matter. Her words still rang in Jazzy's ears. *'You think he's still your responsibility, but he's not. It's guilt making you take this on, hen, and you've sod all to be guilty about. You need to let it go. Let the bastard rot in hell and don't look back.'*

Yet, how could she *not* look back? How could she allow strangers to dispose of her brother when she'd known him as a cute baby and adorable toddler? Besides, taking the woes of the world on her shoulders was her thing. That's why she'd become a copper in the first place, and self-flagellation was her middle name. Her therapist described it as behavioural dysregulation – a form of self-harm – which she continued to work on overcoming.

Her memories kept her up at night, when four-year-old Simon visited her and sat on the edge of her bed, his deep blue eyes punishing her with their judgement and pain. The intrusive memory flashes of him entering her birth mum's bedroom, the snippets of cruelty she'd seen but put down to him being a child vied with those of him giggling when she tickled him or told him jokes that weren't funny or his scrunched-up face when she helped him with his reading. But those were nothing to the conflicting ones she ruminated over, courtesy of her sister. It wasn't Simon she should have been more aware of. It should have been his twin she kept an eye on.

Then there was their blood promise – the one Jazzy had broken – she had a permanent reminder of that. Lost in retrospection, she ran her fingers over the small scar that remained on her palm. Since being forcibly separated from her siblings, she experienced their loss as an acute stabbing in her heart. Believing they were in better places, she'd come to terms with that. How wrong could she have been?

Well, she discovered that when she'd been dragged into the nightmare of their revenge and everything she'd believed about her siblings – every pleasant, happy memory she'd kept safe – had been tarnished and drenched in blood. That's when grief had injected itself into Jazzy's heart and a heavy boulder had taken up permanent residence deep inside her. It pressed against her internal organs, making her gasp for breath in the night, making her fear her heart would explode when the nightmares took hold. She'd carried that sorrow through their next major investigation into a seemingly mega turf war between Glasgow and Edinburgh gangs that had somehow spilled over into Lothian – and she still carried it now.

True to form, Simon had held the cards even at the end. Whilst Jazzy had assumed he'd want a Hindu cremation – after all, he had often waxed lyrical about the importance of their shared heritage, their blood bond and their Hindu roots – she was wrong. Although he'd spent time every morning and evening in contemplative meditation, reciting mantras from memory, even in death, he'd foiled her. His will stated his wish to be buried under an engraved headstone in a local cemetery. With delusions of his own grandeur, he thought that it would be a fitting monument for his acolytes to converge on in his honour.

For the task force, though, the possibility of luring Mhairi to attend was the biggest driver.

'He's my brother, Mum. Who else is going to do it?'

'Hmph. He doesn't des . . .'

Jazzy balled up the wrapper her bun had come in and lobbed it into the bin beside them. 'I know he doesn't. I'm not doing it for him, Ma, I'm doing it for me.'

Lillie chewed a shrimp from her bun. Her face softened, the lines across her brow fading as she ate. When she finished, she handed her rubbish to Jazzy and nodded. 'About time you did something for you, Jasmine Solanki. Too often everyone else comes first. If this is for you, then that's fine. In fact, your dad and I will come too, to support you.'

The boulder in Jazzy's gut shifted and a wave of nausea hit her. 'No, Mum. No chance.' She hadn't wanted to frighten her, but she'd been pushed into this situation. 'You and Dad can't come. It's too dangerous.'

Her frown returned and even Crumble, sensing something was amiss with his owner, whimpered and nudged Lillie's leg with her snout. 'Dangerous . . .? How is a funeral dangerous?'

Jazzy groaned inwardly. Once more, her career choice was frightening the people she loved most. Crumble laid her head on Lillie's leg and looked at Jazzy, her big brown eyes reproachful. *For goodness' sake, not you too, Crumble!*

'There, there, sweetie. I'm all right. No need to fret, my wee love.' Switching to her 'everything's all right in the world' sing-song tone, Lillie stroked Crumble's ears, but the look she threw Jazzy was pointed. 'Explain.'

'We're taking precautions, that's all . . . in case Mhairi turns up.' She slung her arm round her mum's shoulders and squeezed. 'It's routine and . . .' as she uttered the lie, Jazzy faltered, unused to deceiving her mum '. . . we doubt she'll have the nerve to show. I mean, why would she? She's stayed under the radar for so long. Why would she take the risk now?'

Lillie shook her head, a rueful smile drawing one corner of her mouth upward. 'Oh, Jasmine, you're a rubbish liar. It's *exactly* the sort of thing she would do. Simon's not only her brother – he was also her *twin*. The pull may well be too strong for her to resist. Besides, this is another opportunity for her to drag you through hell – she won't pass up on that chance. Not that bitch.'

Her smile faded and she straightened her shoulders as if bracing herself against every instinct – maternal and human – that she possessed. Her tone became low and harsh. 'Just promise me one thing, Jasmine. If she does turn up, you end it. I don't care how you do it, just end it, because being in limbo like this is destroying you. You've got too skinny . . .'

Jazzy blinked. She should have realised her mum would feel her weight loss when they hugged. 'Your shoulders are tense and I could sense you scoping out the area as we walked.' She gripped Jazzy's arm tightly. 'Get this finished with. Do that for yourself. You need to move on. Maybe even get another job. I mean, you're bright, you could easily . . .'

Jazzy sighed. She wasn't overly inclined to continue this conversation. Not after such a lovely walk in the early summer sunshine. Not when this was their special together time. Inevitably, they went round and round in circles – usually with her dad mediating – but he wasn't here today. It came from love, but that didn't lessen Jazzy's frustration nor – because it also stemmed from fear and concern – her guilt. Her outstanding performance on various investigations had secured her early promotions and so at the ripe old age of 27 she was one of the youngest detective sergeants in Police Scotland.

Of course, her dedication to duty meant she had little time

for anything other than work, but that suited Jazzy. It gave her purpose. Her dad seemed to understand that. His own childhood had been less than ideal. His father ran the house with a tight fist and a leather belt and his mother, with no relatives to support her, had little option but to obey her husband. He'd only spoken about it to Jazzy once, yet that secret, offered reluctantly, gave her valuable insight into her birth mother's behaviour. Perhaps that young woman – faced with a constant threat of violence at home, a fearful mother, and a brother who was always favoured – believed that her only recourse was to leave. Jazzy often wondered whether her birth mum's choice of a Muslim partner had been down to love – she might ask her biological father one day – or down to a desire to stick it in her father's face and let him know that he wasn't the boss of her. Unfortunately, everyone knew how *that* had ended.

However, her birth mum's motivations didn't concern Jazzy as much as her adoptive parents' very real fears for her safety. They were at a stalemate. Jazzy couldn't give up her job. Despite everything – the exhausting physical and emotional trauma she'd been through, the issues that sometimes reared their ugly head around her ethnicity, the frequency with which she and the chief super were paraded out to show the world how inclusive Police Scotland was, when in reality there was still work to do – none of it made her regret her decision. She wanted to be part of the evolving Police Scotland. The one that was inclusive, that didn't racially stereotype, the one that addressed their biases and moved forward stronger and fairer as a result. Policing was her life, and she was damn good at it.

'Aw, Mum.' She kept her tone light as she pulled her mum to her for a brief hug. 'You can't keep bringing this up. I'm not going to pack in a job that – despite its trials – I love and replace it with one that could never match up to it. We can't keep revisiting this. We just can't. You need to let it go.'

Lillie stiffened for a moment, but then relaxed and gave a

small shrug. 'Okay, Jasmine. I can't promise not to bring this up again, but I can promise to try. How's that?'

It was enough. Jazzy knew how hard it was for her mum. That was one of the reasons she'd increased her WhatsApps and FaceTimes to their wee family group and kept up with her weekly visits whenever possible. Previously, she had to admit they'd been a bit hit and miss, but she was making the effort and her parents appreciated it. 'Come on, let's get Crumble's treats for her.'

The wee dog looked up at Jazzy for a second, her brown eyes alive with anticipation, as if she understood every word.

'Ready?' Ivor gathered her and Benjy's litter together and looked from Jazzy to her mum, clearly having earwigged most of their conversation. 'All okay?'

Lillie got up, smiling, and Crumble, back in work mode, waited by her side. 'Of course, we're okay – just a wee family spat, but nothing for you two to worry about. What about you, Benjy? You enjoy the shrimp?'

Momentarily startled out of introspection, Benjy blinked. 'Aye, Lillie. Best I've tasted in a long time.'

Lillie moved closer to him, linked her arm with his and, as per their usual route, the little entourage set off towards the Portobello bottle kilns where they would circle up Bridge Street to the high street before dropping in to Harry's Gourmet Treats.

As she stood up, Jazzy met the gaze of an old man who overtook them heading towards the kilns. He smiled at her and for a second, she frowned wondering if she knew him. Perhaps he was one of her mother's neighbours, but as she joined her little troupe of friends, she dismissed the thought as unlikely.

Chapter 2

Mhairi

I wonder if she realises that she wears the scars of the last few months like a cloak. It's in the way she moves. How her head darts furtively around as if expecting a monster to jump out at her yelling 'Boo!' at the top of its voice. It's even in the slump of her shoulders, followed by the quick spring to attention, as if she'd momentarily relaxed her vigilance and was telling herself off for her lapse. As for those two kids, it still niggles me that we didn't manage to kill them when we had the chance. Of course, I blame Simon for that.

Heart pounding with excitement at the thought of being this close to her, I edge even closer. What a thrill to be so close to her yet she doesn't even notice me. That's power – real power! I'm certain that my disguise will withhold even Jazzy Solanki's scrutiny. That's the beauty of body padding, wigs, heels, make-up and the ability to blend into my surroundings. I'm right. She doesn't register my presence, so engrossed is she in some argument with her mother. The dog glares at me, though. Clearly Crumble's senses are much more attuned than either its owner's or her daughter's. Her baleful eyes are glued on me as I turn round, having supposedly taken my fill of the view, and use the movement to scrutinise my sister.

This is the closest I've been to her since I nearly killed her, and it's revealing. However, as the dog's hackles raise slightly, perhaps confused by my altered appearance, but not enough for the two women to notice – just another elderly man taking in the early summer sun, I saunter past. I'm not about to linger in case the dog decides to take issue with me and bark. No point in attracting Jazzy's attention. Not till I'm good and ready, anyway.

She's lost weight. Huge bruises hang unattractively under her eyes and her cheeks are concave. Even her luxurious dark hair looks matte and dull, and that fills me with joy, glad that I'm not the only one who's been suffering. Is she losing it, perhaps? Has the strain been too much for her, nudging her off her game, making her careless? The Jazzy I know wouldn't follow the same routine, especially not when she feels under threat. *Really, Jazzy, sweetie, you need to be a bit less predictable.* I'd have thought her training would have taught her that, but maybe she's exhausted.

I take the same path the women will soon follow and, anticipating the upcoming events, I smile. A woman with a toddler coming towards me smiles back, her eyes uncertain, her nod tentative as she gently steers her child past me and speeds up. Perhaps she can sense what lurks in the depths of my soul. My smile widens – she's probably just one of those overprotective mums, who mistrusts everyone they meet; not a bad philosophy to have if you ask me. It would certainly make my job a lot harder if everyone became less trusting. Would definitely up the ante. Let's face it, months of near isolation, constantly in disguise – not this particular one, of course – and having to behave myself on the beautiful but harsh Isle of Skye have left me feeling up for the challenge.

Humming 'Over the Sea to Skye' under my breath, I plod on, forcing myself to move slowly, almost cumbersomely, whilst inside me excitement churns my gut like bubbles of champagne at a birthday party.

Chapter 3

Jazzy

The Portobello bottle kilns always reminded Jazzy of two over-sized beehives and, although the chimneys had been capped a long time ago, she half expected swarms of bees to fly through the sky and take up residence inside. Their presence here was a nod to the town's once thriving pottery industry. She appreciated them as a relic of bygone days, reminding her that the world and society was an ever-evolving entity.

As they strolled through the car park towards the iconic structures, her mum chatting about everything and nothing with Benjy and Ivor, a young uniformed police officer leaned, fingers splayed, against the wall that offered a degree of privacy to the flats with their sea view that separated the kilns from the promenade. His face was drained of colour and head bowed, legs bent, he vomited loudly and copiously onto the brickwork. Unless he'd taken ill all of a sudden – which, to Jazzy's suspicious mind, seemed unlikely – something was very wrong.

On high alert, her stomach tightened as she scanned the area, making a mental note of the passers-by. Some sidled past giving the heaving constable a wide berth, whilst others loitered a few feet away, ogling him and sharing light-hearted comments about 'tax dollars at work' and the like. A few of this group had their phones out and were busy filming the oblivious officer's plight. Poor sod! Last thing a new officer wanted was to go viral on social media, throwing his load. Jazzy could almost hear the jibes from his colleagues and the kid would no doubt be landed with some vomit-related nickname that no matter how hard he tried, he'd be unable to live down. A few of the less callous gathering crowd stepped closer, offering tentative words of concern. One even offered a half-drunk bottle of water.

Jazzy's gaze was drawn to Benjy, who had stopped dead just in front of her, his fingers clenching and unclenching by his sides, his eyes everywhere, head moving in jerky movements, his breathing audible. Beside him, Ivor clutched her cousin's arm. She too looked around, but unlike Benjy, her actions were measured, yet fluid, although her face had paled, either in response to Benjy's reaction or to some inner warning system of her own.

'What's up, Jasmine? Why are there so many people hanging around here and . . .' Lillie, head tilted towards the heavily breathing officer, frowned as the unmistakable sound of retching filled the air. 'Is that someone being sick? Shouldn't we help them?'

Jazzy turned to her mum. 'Mum, it's a police officer. I need to stay here and help him for a bit.'

She glanced at the teenagers. Benjy had become paler and was shaking now, the strangeness of the scene putting him on edge. Ivor pulled him closer to her, attempting to calm him, but his terror was contagious. Her eyes also darted around, as if searching for any possible threats. Jazzy squeezed her mum's arm and, maintaining as matter-of-fact a tone as possible, she guided the teens to either side of her mum, saying, 'There's nothing to worry about, but I'm going to help these officers. Go back to the benches with my mum and Crumble. I'll meet you there in a short time.'

Benjy, still shaking, met her gaze and with a single nod, moved closer to Lillie. Ivor smiled at Jazzy. 'I've got my phone if we need you. We'll head over to the Shrimp Wreck, where it's busy.'

Then Lillie began to retrace her steps. 'If you get held up, your dad can collect us.' She paused, swallowed hard and, her voice a little gruff, said, 'Look after yourself.'

Jazzy hugged her. 'I will, Mum, but it'll be okay. It'll be something minor.'

Even as she uttered the words, Jazzy suspected that she was wrong. She watched them walk away for a moment and then strode towards the sick officer. Another officer walked from the side of the other bottle kiln, her shoulders flung back, and her lips tight. Despite her rosy cheeks, the officer had a worried frown on her face and was heading straight for her partner. With her ID out, Jazzy approached *Rosy Cheeks*, smiling in what she hoped was a reassuring way. 'I'm DS Jazzy Solanki from Lothian and Borders MIT. I know this isn't my jurisdiction, but it looks pretty much like something untoward has happened here. Do you need my help till backup comes?'

Rosy Cheeks slapped a hand on her forehead, took a deep swallow and nodded. 'Backup! Christ, I've not even radioed it in yet. We've only just seen it. Thought it was kids messing around and then . . .' Her florid cheeks paled and she shook her head as if to dislodge the memory of whatever she'd found inside from her mind. With a tremulous smile, she held up a finger to indicate that Jazzy should wait, and she radioed for assistance.

Aware that a group of people were collecting round Mr Sicky and still unsure of the severity of the incident, Jazzy listened in as *Rosy Cheeks* gave her badge number and, mindful of the earwigging loiterers, made her request for backup. 'PC Dornan and I found a dead body inside one of the Portobello bottle kilns. Yes, I'm sure he's really dead. Assist needed.' *Rosy Cheeks* swallowed and straightened her shoulders before adding, her voice muted so the gathering crowd wouldn't hear, 'It's a murder, so we need the works.'

As she ended her call, Jazzy, eyeing the accumulating spectators, their eyes flitting avariciously over the area, stepped closer. 'You should move these people on and establish an outer and inner cordon. If this proves to be a murder as you said, then we also need to take footage of all these spectators, so body cam on, eh? You know the old adage about criminals returning to the scene of the crime? Well, sometimes they do. I'll get your partner on that. Now, what's your name?'

Rosy Cheeks exhaled and took a beat. 'PC Brown.' She glanced over at Mr Sicky, then 'He's PC Dornan. Yes, of course. That's what I should do. I'm on it.'

Jazzy, voice still low, gestured to the second bottle kiln. 'In there?'

PC Brown shuddered, but managed a brisk nod.

'Okay, move this lot back to the car park over there. As soon as extra officers arrive, we need to block off both ends of Bridge Street redirecting traffic up Pipe Lane at this end and William Jameson Place at the other. From now on, no one goes within ten metres of those kilns, okay? Oh, and whilst you're doing that, get contact details for as many of the bystanders as you can. I'll deal with your partner.'

With a quick nod, PC Brown headed over to the group closest to the kiln and began to direct them away from the area. Jazzy was pleased to see she was already jotting down names and contact details. That would prove useful to the investigation team when they arrived. The second officer who, having finished puking, still visibly shaken, stood with one hand on the wall as if to ground himself. The crime scene investigators would be pissed off with him for the mess he'd made, but what could you do? The only saving grace was that his puking was restricted to the outskirts of the scene and would have little impact on evidence gathering.

'I'm DS Jazzy Solanki and although I'm with Lothian and

Borders, you'll have to make do with me till someone from Edinburgh division gets here. You okay to help your partner, Constable Dornan?'

To give him his due, despite his now overly flushed face and shaking hands, he pushed himself away from the wall, straightened up and tugged the bottom of his hi-vis vest down as if presenting himself for inspection. When he exhaled, his acrid breath rolled over Jazzy, causing her throat to spasm, but she didn't flinch as he responded, 'Yes. I'm good. As long as I don't have to go back in there.'

He gestured towards the small four foot by two foot rectangular entrance, which provided access to the bottle kiln – traditionally so it could be filled with items ready to be fired. Jazzy followed his gaze, wondering what the officers had discovered inside. Although the doorway was only partially visible from here, its makeshift metal door was lying discarded on the floor nearby. For years now, the entrance had been barricaded off to prevent anyone gaining access and vandalising the kilns, so clearly someone had removed this one. 'Was the cover ripped off when you arrived, or did you do that?'

'After the anonymous call came in, we were sent to investigate. We found it just like that.' He grimaced and pursed his lips. 'We thought we'd find evidence of some teenage drinking. You know, empty voddy bottles and the like, maybe a few Rizlas and some old spliffs. Never imagined we'd find that . . .'

He exhaled again and averted his eyes from the kiln entrance, closing them briefly as if he expected that would banish whatever memory was lodged in his head. Jazzy knew from personal experience how hard it was to erase this sort of unpleasant scene from your mind, but the best therapy right now for PC Dornan was to be busy. 'Okay, your partner's clearing the area – moving the spectators back, but I need you to switch your body cam on to record the faces of everyone who is hanging about. Hold it together and your efficiency from here on in will be what people remember.'

23

Blinking rapidly, the young officer offered an uncertain nod before joining his partner. Jazzy's eyes trailed over the accumulated crowd and spotted one or two of the people she'd passed on their earlier walk – the old couple with their fat corgi, the old man who'd smiled at her and the ruddy-cheeked mother with the pushchair. She doubted any of them were complicit in whatever had happened in the kilns, but best to err on the side of caution. Although it wasn't her jurisdiction and it certainly wasn't her case, the desire to see whatever was inside the kiln was overpowering. Standing on the outskirts of an investigation was frustrating for Jazzy, but there was nothing she could do about that. Quite rightly, if she took her size sixes and plodded all over the crime scene, the senior investigating officer, whoever that may be, would be pissed off. She sighed then swivelled on her heel and began helping to clear the cordon area as they waited for backup to come with tape and other paraphernalia that would keep the scene as pristine as was possible.

Hopefully the officers hadn't disturbed too much evidence inside the kilns, especially Mr Sicky Dornan, for there was no way he'd get off lightly if he'd vomited near the body – but they were duty-bound to investigate and then to establish that life was extinct. Apart from the upchucking, they had both rallied and, despite their inexperience, were doing their best to control the area. Jazzy would have a word with their boss to make sure they knew that.

It was twenty minutes before the cavalry arrived and Jazzy, after repeating what she'd instructed the two young officers to do regarding establishing cordons and moving the loiterers away from the area, was glad to hand over the baton. Out of curiosity, she observed the suited and booted CSIs and the SIO for another twenty minutes until they entered the kiln. It would take time to process the interior, and despite her desire to find out the specifics of the incident, Jazzy shrugged and backed away. It wasn't her business and she should get back to her mum, Ivor and Benjy.

She'd just reached the promenade when the voice of the officer she'd updated earlier, called her. 'DS Solanki. Not so fast. I think you'd better come here.' He was a bit of a smooth talker and Jazzy had been relieved to get away from DI Clive Shanks earlier. Now here he was calling her back.

Chapter 4

Mhairi

I get a chill up my spine when I see Jazzy spring into action. The puking police officer is an added bonus. Shows me I've done my job properly. Of course, my period in exile provided ample opportunity to plan how to punish Jazzy. Such an abundance of time to work out all the little twists and turns I can create to keep her off kilter. So, I made my plans and then reached out to my network, to help me set events in motion. I'm going to keep her on the hop. She'll be bombarded with so many different clues at once that she'll feel as dizzy as a whirling dervish and I savour it. Misdirection, confusion and uncertainty are my new mantras.

No, DS Jazzy Solanki won't know what's hit her by the time I'm finished. She'll be damaged beyond repair – destroyed, annihilated, obliterated, eviscerated. Oh, I've learned a multitude of words with similar meanings, but they're irrelevant because what I have in store for her is more debauched, more depraved than even her wildest imaginings. Her unawareness of my true potential is what truly satisfies me. When I'm through, she and her team will be decimated. But that's in the future. Lots of fun and games to play in the meantime and it's barely starting.

Ah, there she goes. Ms-fix-it Solanki, organising the two young coppers, taking over. She just can't help herself. My fingers squeeze into fists that dig into my palms and I realise that her pretend goody-two-shoes persona irritates me as much as it always has done. I loosen them, but it takes effort as blinding images of all the things I've got planned for her flit through my mind.

There's quite a crowd collecting now and I'm pleased to see some of them have their phones out, recording the amazing vomiting copper. With the pleasant sea breeze and the jovial ambience, it's almost like being at an outdoor cinema watching the inevitable roll-out. Although I don't show it, inside I grin when she casts her eagle eyes over the gathering hordes. Do her eyes linger on me? Probably not. Does she suspect I'm here? More than likely not. Not yet anyway. Why would she? She doesn't know yet what the little gift I've left for her in the bottle kiln is.

I'm particularly happy with my choices in that regard. It muddies the waters just enough to make things interesting and creates a captivating complexity. Not for the victim, of course. No, I wouldn't say 'interesting' was top of his mind at the end. More like pain and fear and, yes, a torrent of rage. Especially when I told him why he'd been chosen for this fate. As I said before, planning and scrupulous research are the mainstays of my decisions. Oh, good one, Jazzy. She's instructed the two numpty coppers to activate their body cams. Standard procedure really, but they're too inexperienced to do that in a crisis. Too flummoxed by what they've seen. Poor sods!

Although I'm convinced she'd never recognise me, I'm leaving nothing to chance – can't let even a single ball fall or my plans might collapse. Reluctantly, I slowly melt away from the bystanders – an old fogey with no other purpose than to wander Portobello in the sunshine.

Chapter 5

Jazzy

Jazzy rolled her eyes, but turned around. Professional courtesy dictated she assist, if at all possible. Hopefully whatever the senior investigating officer wanted to ask her wouldn't take long. 'Yes?'

DI Shanks marched towards her, his intense, almost black gaze raking over her face as she, with less enthusiasm, retraced her steps to meet him halfway. 'Any reason why the victim might be clutching an envelope with your name on it?'

As his words sunk in, a weight crushed her chest like a metal girder. Each booming heartbeat increased the pressure on her lungs. A letter addressed to her found on the body of a dead man in the town where her parents lived changed the game. There was only one person who left her hand-delivered notes and Jazzy had no idea of her current whereabouts. She glanced round, her eyes piercing the crowd, seeking a familiar figure, although deep down she knew it was a futile gesture. If the Bitch was responsible for this, then she'd be too damn clever to be spotted here.

Annoyed with herself for being spooked, she ran her fingers through her hair and tried to control her breathing. Of course, this might not be Mhairi's work. How could she even assume that without seeing the crime scene? If Operation Birchtree – the unit tasked with locating her deviant sister – had the slightest inkling that her sister had returned to the area, then they were duty-bound to inform her – or, if not her directly, then her boss, DCS Afzal. For all the animosity between them, he would have shared that sort of sensitive intel with her. She absolutely wanted to believe that. Although a niggling doubt lingered. Would they keep her in the loop? They were so obsessed with the idea of luring Mhairi back for Simon's funeral that sometimes Jazzy felt like a very low priority on their list – a mere means to an end rather than an integral player in the game.

Whether or not this was the work of her sister, Jazzy had to accept that she couldn't hand over this crime scene. She longed to claim ignorance of why her name could appear on an envelope beside a dead body, but she couldn't. Why had she ever assumed that her coincidental presence at a crime scene in a town with a negligible crime rate would be nothing to do with her?

'Give me a sec.' Heart pounding and her mind filled with muddled thoughts, she pulled her phone out and, hunching her shoulders against the sudden gust of cold wind, she dialled her mum's number. 'Mum, they need my help here. Can't say more than that. So, can you and the kids head home? An officer can take you if you want. Or Dad could collect you.'

Her mum tutted. 'Don't be silly. It's a ten-minute walk and besides, Crumble needs her dog treats.' Her voice took on a sing-song quality as she addressed the dog. 'Isn't that right, Crumble? You'd never forgive me if we didn't get your treats now, would you?' Voice returned to normal, she added, 'Just be home in time for dinner, Jasmine, won't you?'

Although she would have preferred that an officer escort her mum, Jazzy couldn't spare anyone. Every spare body was needed at the crime scene and her mum would be fine in broad daylight in Portobello. 'I'll try my best to be back for dinner.'

With DI Shanks keeping pace with her, Jazzy made her way back towards the kilns, her face expressionless, despite his intense scrutiny. 'So, I assume, DI Shanks, that with this development, you've exited the crime scene until we ascertain how to proceed? I'm sure you're aware, as is the rest of Police Scotland, that anything related to me or the incident before Christmas must be reported higher up. In short, your boss needs to speak to mine, Chief Superintendent Waqas Afzal from Lothian and Borders.' As she uttered the words, Jazzy was conscious of the sweat beading her forehead.

Still studying her, his dark eyes resembling bottomless pools, Shanks smiled. 'Already done. As soon as we saw the envelope, my lot secured the scene, and I pulled out my CSIs. Looks like I'm being replaced by a DI Elliot Balloch. Know him?'

Jazzy's thumping heart slowed a little and the tightness in her chest eased. If Elliot was in charge, then that would make it easier for Lothian and Edinburgh forces to liaise. 'Yes, I know him.'

A smile twitched DI Shanks's mouth. 'But that's all you're saying? Never mind, he'll be here in . . .' He looked at his watch. 'Any time now, really. After all, anything involving Jazzy Solanki is a top priority for Police Scotland, right?'

Unsure whether he was joking or having a dig at her, Jazzy ignored his cocky grin and made to walk past him but he matched her stride, still talking, still grinning. 'Apparently, a pathologist from Lothian and Borders is heading over, along with a forensic team from Livingston, too.'

Jazzy nodded and sped up, trying to create some distance between them, but he increased his pace and matched his footsteps to hers, until finally he lightly touched her arm. 'Whoa, wait a minute, you're too fast for me.'

Obliged to stop, Jazzy slowed and scowled as he stuck out his hand towards her. For a second, she just stared at it, then reluctantly gave it a weak single shake.

'To be honest, DS Solanki, I'm not too fussed about passing

this one over to you and your team. It seems like a hot potato and after everything that's happened to you over the past few months, folk are beginning to think you're jinxed.' He splayed his hands between them, palms up. 'Not me, you understand, but you know the rumour mill?' He winked at her as if to take the sting from his words.

Jazzy's glare served only to widen his grin. 'Oh, come on, Solanki, lighten up. I'm only teasing you. Besides, I'd be happy to risk having a drink with you. If you're up for it, of course?'

For a moment, Jazzy wondered if she'd misheard, but the splayed hands and the pleading, mock-bashful look dispelled that illusion. Her scowl deepened. 'Really? You're at a crime scene and you reckon you can chat me up? Get a bloody life, Shanks.' And with the soft sounds of his laughter following her, she strode away, her cheeks hot with anger. *Bloody arse. Who does he think he is? Jack the sodding lad?*

His voice drifted over the car park. 'My bad, Solanki! Didn't mean to offend. It's just, God knows when I'll see you again. You can't blame me for trying, can you?'

With her stride lengthening, a smile formed on her lips. No man had shown interest in her for years, except for the occasional drunk in the pub on weekends. Her mum reckoned she scared them off with her stern demeanour, a belief shared by Queenie, who frequently told her, 'You need to loosen up if you want a shag, JayZee. What man's going to take a punt on you if he's feart for his life every time you flash that Rottweiler look at him?' This light flirting was a refreshing change for her, and despite the circumstances, her mood had lifted.

'For trying what, exactly?' Elliot's voice was icy enough to freeze a penguin. Jazzy had been so busy in her own wee world, that she hadn't noticed him approach. For a moment she closed her eyes. She hadn't seen Elliot for a while. They'd had a good relationship once, but that had taken a battering when she'd been tasked with ascertaining whether or not he was a bent cop. Of course, she'd always known he wasn't, but he thought that she had entertained the idea that he might be corrupt. Still, it had tainted their friendship and the prospect of possibly having to work with him when he still harboured such resentment wasn't appealing. She understood. If it had been the other way around she'd have been livid too, but now she wished they could get past this obstacle. Especially as their shared work history had been one she'd been proud of.

He'd been the one to rescue her and her siblings when her birth mum, Hansa, had died. It had been his very first day on the job as an eighteen-year-old constable. Over the years since then, he'd earned the traumatised child Jazzy's trust, even when she'd been at her most objectionable. The circumstances of their initial meeting had forged an unbreakable cord between them and, although she wouldn't verbalise it, he was one of the few people she trusted implicitly. He was her best friend – or rather, he had been. Unfortunately, for the past few months their relationship had become distinctly ragged.

As he strode up to her, his overcoat wafting in the breeze, his short hair freshly trimmed and a frown marring his handsome features, his face, as Queenie would say, was tripping him. His tone was sharp and accusatory, which Jazzy attributed to being roped into this new case when he had so much on his plate already. Then she noticed he was glaring at Shanks who had drawn level with them and was grinning like the cat in possession of the proverbial artery-clogging white stuff.

Annoyance replaced Jazzy's earlier momentary amusement, and her smile faded. 'Just trying to strong-arm his way onto the investigation . . .'

Before she could finish the sentence, Elliot glared at the shorter, burlier DI, his blue eyes scouring his frame and face as if the other officer was creating an unpleasant stink. 'Well, *that's not going to happen*, Shanks. Your, no doubt, expert help won't be needed on this occasion.' And without further ado, Elliot swivelled on his heel and marched towards the flapping tape, which indicated that the outer and inner cordons were now securely in place. 'Come on, DS Solanki. Work to do.'

Smarting at his abrupt order, Jazzy had no choice but to follow with a quick glance at Shanks, who unperturbed was grinning as widely as ever at her. 'Got competition I see. Good job I'm irresistible then, isn't it?'

Jazzy bristled at his cockiness, but one of his over-exaggerated winks elicited another grin She waved a dismissive hand as she followed Elliot to the crime scene. 'In your dreams, Shanks. In your dreams.'

Chapter 6

Jazzy

Trailing after Elliot, she scoured the crowd, looking for anything out of the ordinary. Despite the interlude with Shanks, Jazzy couldn't throw off the sensation of being watched. Common sense told her that the killer would be long gone, but then again, sometimes they came back, revelling in seeing the police at work. When Elliot issued directions for an officer to head to Jazzy's house to be with her parents and the Stùrrach kids, Jazzy was pleased. Seemingly, their strained relationship wouldn't affect how he operated as SIO, and she was grateful. She'd already alerted her dad, and he'd immediately set off home. At least if her mother and father were protected, then she could focus on doing her job. Although this eased her tension slightly, the mordant bite of fear pervaded her entire body, making her chest heavy with dread.

Officers trawled the area, looking for CCTV that might show what had happened whilst others had already started door-to-door inquiries. By now they had discovered that two of the most likely cameras had been blocked at around four a.m. that morning. Although they would scrutinise the footage up until then, Jazzy held out little hope of something significant being found. She was convinced that anything useful to their investigation would be discovered here in this confined space, where the as yet unidentified body had been left to taunt her.

It took all her strength to brace herself for what lay ahead, and for once she was glad of the mask concealing her face – at least it offered a modicum of privacy. The metal panel, created to prevent the public from gaining access to the kiln's interior, had been pried from its stone structure. Probably using a crowbar or something similar, and presumably by the killer. As they approached, it was being processed for trace evidence by two CSIs, but Jazzy was convinced that their efforts would prove futile.

Already, with the addressed envelope, this felt like a very deliberately staged crime scene designed for Jazzy's benefit and anyone who'd gone to all that trouble would surely be forensic-savvy and leave little to chance. This wasn't a heat-of-the-moment crime. The location itself was of particular personal relevance to Jazzy. Her regular walk with her mum took her past these bottle kilns. The clincher for Jazzy was the undeniable fact that the nightmare before Christmas all started with her sister infiltrating her space and leaving a letter behind after killing two people, knowing Jazzy would be summoned to the scene. That, combined with the timing of this unidentified body's discovery, made it difficult to believe otherwise.

Although she tried hard not to jump to conclusions, everything about this had her sister's name written all over it. None of that meant that they wouldn't explore alternative possibilities, but it was inevitable that valuable investigative time would be spent ascertaining whether Mhairi was back.

As she struggled into her protective clothing with Elliot doing the same beside her, she was aware of the furtive glances and whispered exchanges of those within the cordon. Her cheeks flushed as she tried to dismiss her negative thoughts. These were her colleagues. People she'd worked with before, people she liked and respected and whom she hoped liked and respected her in return. The urge to yell 'None of this is my fault' was overpowering. An itch at the bridge of her nose heralded a tear gathering in her eyes. Angry with herself, she sniffed and twitched it to prevent more from following. She'd have plenty of time for tears later when she was back in the privacy of her wee house in Bellsquarry.

'You okay?' Elliot's finger touched her sleeve. This was the only sign of concern he'd shown her for weeks, and it set her teeth on edge. Did he really think, after his previous attitude, that he could swoop in and act all solicitous now? Channelling the hurt she'd felt at his absence in her life, she yanked her arm away and stepped towards the red-brick kiln. She was angry with him for his possessive behaviour earlier – actually for his recent conduct for the past while full stop – and wanted to assert her independence and self-reliance. She wasn't a kid. Not anymore and it was time he realised that. 'I'm fine. Let's just do this.'

The entrance was only four feet high and a few feet wide and was angled away from the road on one side and hidden from the flats' occupants on the other. In that respect, it was perfect for the killer to gain entry unobserved, especially under cover of darkness, with the limited camera coverages and few streetlights nearby. With considerable difficulty, they crawled on their hunkers into the cramped area, accompanied by significant huffing and puffing from Elliot, who, although not a lot taller than Jazzy, was far bulkier.

Once she was upright, the fetid stench of the interior forced Jazzy to swallow hard. Heat from the bright CSI lights added to their discomfort and intensified the discordant aromas in the confined space. Already, sweat soaked through Jazzy's clothes. The angled lamps cast moving shadows around the brick walls, lending an even seedier feel to the space. The light caught graffiti tags and slogans, mostly faded, as if aged. Jazzy made a mental note to study images of the 'artwork' in detail later.

What a sordid place to die.

At times like this Jazzy always had Franny Gallagher in her mind; the crime scene manager who'd been drafted over from Lothian whose instructions were to 'stick to the footplates'. Jazzy paused. Instead of angling for a better look at the body, she remained by the kiln entrance. Her routine at a murder was to take her time viewing the scene, absorbing the atmosphere and placing herself in the killer's shoes. She tried to imagine their motivations, each action they'd taken, how and why things had been done in the order they had.

For a moment longer, she avoided looking at the dead man. There was plenty of time for that. For now, she was content to absorb the rest of the space. It seemed a strange place to kill someone, particularly when the murderer had made no effort to cover up their crime. It would have been easy to reseal the entrance and let nature run its course. That way, the body might have gone undiscovered for weeks until the smell was reported to the council. So, what did the killer have to gain from not reattaching the door? They must have known it would invite curiosity, and that was why Jazzy was certain that he'd wanted the victim found quickly. Today? When she was doing her regular walk with her mum? That was a tough one to swallow, especially with the discovery of the addressed envelope. Besides, there was that mysterious anonymous call. Naturally, it could have been someone passing by, but Jazzy didn't believe that.

Behind her mask, Jazzy bit her lip and gave a slight shrug. No matter how hard she tried to avoid making assumptions, she was having trouble clarifying her thoughts. Of course, the letter might be a red herring. Even as she tested the thought out, Jazzy snorted. Who was she kidding?

Then memories of enemies she'd made over her years on the job drifted in. Was it conceivable that some other killer had crawled out of the woodwork and murdered an unidentified male in order to involve Jazzy? It seemed unlikely. She'd put away more than her fair share of violent men in her short time as a detective – that's why she'd earned her sergeant stripes so early. However, she was sure most of the criminals she'd put away were more likely to kill her themselves. That or pay a hit man to do it. She shrugged. The same couldn't be said of those officers she'd beaten to a promotion. Some of them still harboured a grudge, but a set-up like this to get their own back was a step too far. No, they were more likely to gossip about her, make racist and sexist comments behind her back and treat her with disdain. That was one of the reasons she was so happy to be with her own little group of detectives. None of them tolerated that sort of crap and they had each other's backs.

Despite the earthy atmosphere tinged with waste – whether animal or human – and mostly coming from the body itself, the ground was surprisingly free from detritus. Clearly, the metal barrier had worked to keep people out. She glanced back at the makeshift door.

Although the entrance was semi-secluded, who in their right mind would take the chance of someone sauntering past whilst they were in the middle of bundling a dead person into the kiln? Both she and Elliot had struggled to crawl through the low lintel. How much harder would it be to push or yank an uncooperative weight through? Jazzy briefly looked at the victim to assess his height and build. He wasn't big – emaciated, certainly, but he was gangly. It would have been difficult even for a strong person to manipulate him inside.

She frowned. Did that mean he entered the kiln either voluntarily or under duress? If so, why would he do that? Did he trust his killer? Did he know them? Or perhaps he just didn't feel threatened by whoever had ended his life. Jazzy allowed her eyes to drift over the interior again, trying to imagine herself in the killer's mind. What would motivate someone to choose this as a kill spot? Everything, from the unusual location, to the letter, to the dead body, to the lack of care in concealing the crime, yelled exhibitionist. It screamed staged, and it positively reverberated with the words 'look at me'. It was more likely that the killer had either arrived with or planned to meet the victim here. That personalised envelope.

'You thinking the guy was lured here?'

Jazzy anticipated Elliot would reach the same conclusion. 'Yep, looks that way.'

'So . . .?'

Her fingers glided over the contour of the small glass Ganesh statue she carried with her everywhere. The statuette pushed against her crime scene suit from the inside of her jacket pocket and although it usually gave her comfort, today it didn't. She sighed against her mask. The question '*is it all starting up again?*' played on repeat through her mind. Had the nightmare started again? If so, would she have the inner strength to end it once and for all? Right now, though, her priority was this poor murdered man.

'Give me a chance to look at him first.' Her voice was terse, but she couldn't help herself. She needed peace and quiet to think, and her fear that the dead man would have some personal link to her freaked her out. She braced herself and stepped forward, initially focusing on the dirt in front of his feet – she wasn't quite ready for his face yet, not quite ready to see someone she knew lying dead before her. *Come on, Jazzy. You're a bloody Jazz Queen. Stop being squeamish and just damn well do it!*

'So, do you recognise him?' He sounded impatient now. The hood of his protective overalls nipped tightly around his head and although he avoided meeting her gaze, his curt demeanour spoke volumes.

He still hasn't forgiven me. Well, tough, Balloch. I was only doing my job! She ignored his snippy tone and stood statue still. The kiln was claustrophobic and airless, even with only the two of them inside. At least, closer to the centre of the structure, they could stand upright, although the stench of urine and stale booze mingled with the mulchy smell that permeated the enclosed space threatened to knock them flat on their backs. Focused on absorbing every iota of information the interior of the bottle kiln had to give her, she dismissed Elliot, knowing she'd have to confront his behaviour later on. This stalemate between them couldn't be allowed to continue.

The griping of the imaginary barbed wire slicing through her gut continued as she forced herself to look at the slouched figure propped up against the low circular wall. Based on the discarded sleeping bag and the plastic Morrisons bags by the man's feet, their contents – a crumpled fag packet, two pairs of mucky socks and an old jumper – spilled all over the rubble, the guy was down on his luck. An empty vodka bottle nestled by his right thigh. That combined with the BO that joined the other malodorous aromas of stale blood and human waste, indicated that their corpse may well be an unhoused person.

His legs were splayed before him, his feet encased in dirty trainers. The lace on one was loose, trailing in the dampish earth. The other was missing entirely. Beneath his denim trousers, skinny ankles protruded, each wearing socks that looked capable of marching their way to the nearest washing machine unaided. His jeans, although under the dirt, were still bright blue, indicating they were newish. They were stained with an array of blotches that even Queenie would be unable to match. He'd voided both his bladder and bowels and the contents of both seeped out around him like a lake of sewage. This confirmed Jazzy's earlier thoughts that he'd been killed in situ.

She swallowed hard, using mind over matter to ignore the stench before studying his hands, which rested, one on each thigh, both cupped upwards with the letter resting underneath them. His fingernails were ragged and filled with unidentifiable gunk. Hopefully, some of that residue would supply a clue to his killer. They hadn't taken his fingerprints yet, as they wanted to preserve the crime scene as intact as possible for Jazz and

Elliot to view. However, considering the number of people who'd already entered the confined area, Jazzy wasn't sure how 'intact' it would be.

His hoodie and torn jacket followed the same pattern as his lower body clothes. Unwashed and uncared for. His jacket zip was broken. The colour of his sweatshirt was impossible to determine due to the multitude of stains covering it. Plus, most of the alcohol from the bottle beside him seemed to have made its way there.

There was no putting it off any longer. Jazzy jerked her eyes up until they rested on the man's bowed head, looking for identifying markers. Anything that could give her a handle on his identity. Did she recognise him? It was hard to say with his face angled towards the floor and the blood matting his hair. A deposit of coagulating goop meandered down his forehead and over his concave cheeks, streaking them and merging with the residual filth that was layered there. The blood dropped in slow globby drips from his chin and onto his legs. The fact that it wasn't completely solidified indicated that this corpse was fairly recently deceased. But what disturbed Jazzy most were the marks around his eyes. It was as if they'd been pecked by a murder of crows.

At the sight of the damage to the man's eyeballs, Jazzy's mouth filled with bitter saliva and she was glad that this, at least, was one crime scene that Queenie wouldn't have to live with. Queenie's extraordinary photographic memory didn't need to process this ghastly nightmare and then find a way to compartmentalise it all in order to keep herself sane. It was bad enough that this poor bloke's fate would become part of the recurring nightmares *she* struggled to overcome on a daily basis. *What's one more god-awful scene to torture my dreams?*

Jazzy gave herself a mental shake. If this was Mhairi's work, then it was a departure from the norm. Was the mutilation of the eyes rather than their complete removal significant? It could be, but after an unscrupulous journalist had circulated images of the crime scene of a couple murdered before Christmas, nearly everyone on the planet knew that their murderer had removed their eyes post-mortem. The photos had gone viral throughout the dark web and on social media and, despite Police Scotland's attempts to remove them, they persistently popped up again and again.

Normally, that sort of key intelligence would be kept under wraps and used to weed out mock information or the wealth of people claiming to have committed the crimes. However, now that it was out there in the public domain, any wacko with a reason to kill – and even those with none – had been given a way to divert focus from them in the pursuance of murder. The entire sordid story, including the link between Jazzy and the killers, had become journo fodder over the subsequent weeks. Understandably, public interest increased in fervour after her sister had evaded capture, leaving not only a slew of murdered victims in her wake but also injured parties who still struggled to come to terms with their ordeal.

Three incidents of murder involving eye removal had been logged over the intervening months. All three had been swiftly dismissed as copycat murders. The perpetrator had been identified as someone with a personal axe to grind, who thought they could get away with murder by implicating the missing serial killer. Each of them had been apprehended. The frustrating thing was that this wasted valuable time that could have been spent locating the real serial killer.

From Elliot there was an impatient: 'Solanki? You reckon that the eye mutilation along with the letter might be her work?'

Jazzy was slow to respond. 'Why, if this was her work, didn't the Bitch remove them completely?'

'So, you're thinking it might not be her? That some other sick fucker wants to open up communication with you?'

The problem was, Jazzy wasn't sure.

She wanted to yank her hood from her head and drag her fingers through her hair. Her gut contracted and needles of pain shot through it. Eyes shut against the barbaric mutilation and the pitiful figure of the man lying in a pile of his own excrement, his eyes obliterated, Jazzy counted to five – long and slow – till she was calmer. He deserved all her attention. He deserved to be named and his killer deserved to be caught.

So, she pondered the one crucial detail that hadn't been made public about her sister's previous murders – that Mhairi had hidden a different religious icon among the victims' possessions at each of her killings – none of which had been immediately obvious and among the rest of the staged crime scenes had gone unnoticed until Queenie, using her eidetic memory, scrolled through images of each scene searching for links between them. It had been a crucial piece of information linking her sister's various murders going back years and setting the team on track to catch her. Of course, that had gone tits up when she escaped six months earlier, but would her sister change her modus operandi? Jazzy was inclined to believe that, in the interests of maintaining her freedom, Mhairi was perfectly capable of changing things up to play games with them. Killers didn't usually do this, but the only thing Jazzy was certain of was that her sister's return would unleash chaos. Still, a religious icon hidden within their victim's belongings or among the graffiti decorating the walls would be a useful indicator.

In answer to Elliot, she shrugged. 'No idea. We both know what a devious bitch she is. It's not beyond her to have staged this just to mess with us. On the other hand . . .' Again she raised her shoulders.

'What about him? Do you recognise him? I know it's hard, but . . .' Now it was his turn to shrug.

Although her gut told her that she didn't know the dead man, she couldn't be certain. 'Not sure. He's . . .' She wafted a gloved hand, encompassing him and his belongings. 'We need to identify him ASAP. The CSIs can take his prints now that we've seen the body in situ and get them sent off to IDENT1. Let me look at the graffiti before we leave.'

The envelope had been photographed in its current position and now that they'd seen it, the CSIs could bag, seal and expedite it to the nearest lab. Procedure had to be followed. Again, Jazzy pondered the futility of that. The only crucial information would be gained from the envelope's contents. It might just give some insight into what the killer's intentions were.

Before leaving, Jazzy stepped from plate to plate, scrutinising each part of the wall as she went until on her arrival, Franny, the CSI manager, joined her and so only Jazzy could hear said, 'I'll get the team to take extra detailed images of the graffiti, Jazz, and as soon as we've been through his things, I'll get the details sent to you and DI Balloch.'

'Thanks, Franny. Much appreciated.' It wasn't surprising that Franny had intuited what Jazzy was looking for on the walls or among the deceased's possessions, and Jazzy trusted the CSI manager implicitly. However, it thrust home the message that she couldn't be one hundred per cent certain of how well Mhairi's use of artefacts in her crime scenes was known. If that exploded onto the press, then all bets would be off.

The brickwork was filled with tags, slogans, drawings, and etchings. Jazzy had no time to look at them all, so she sighed and turned to leave through the narrow exit, feeling like a surreal Alice in Wonderland. The bottle kiln needed processing and her presence inside was only slowing the CSIs down. She'd seen enough, had done all she could for now. Besides, she wanted to check in with her parents. Her heart sank at the thought. Her mother's earlier entreaties for Jazzy to give up her job weighed down on her shoulders, and that barbed wire in her belly tightened. Yet again, her folks had been dragged into a situation in which they were completely innocent. They didn't deserve this. Not when they'd sacrificed their relationship with Jazzy's grandfather to take her in and bring her up as their own daughter and had provided her with all the love and care that had been absent from her early life. How she wished she could repay them. How she wished she could keep them safe. How she wished she could put an end to all of this for good.

Before she had the chance to pull her hood down or loosen her suit, Elliot was there, his face grim, his manner gruff. 'You know you can't stay on this investigation, Jazzy. This isn't a West Lothian case. I only allowed you onto the scene as a favour to Afzal and because you were already here.'

Not quite believing her ears, Jazzy let out a loud gasp that attracted the attention of nearby officers and CSIs. 'Really? *Really?* You're going to bump me from the case? I don't think so.' She pulled out her phone ready to phone her chief super but Elliot's next words halted her in her tracks.

'It's already decided. Afzal agrees. If this is suspected to be Mhairi's work then it will be shunted off to Operation Birchtree anyway, but in the meantime, Edinburgh MIT will investigate with myself as SIO.'

'Aw, get real, Elliot. You're still pissed because I was asked to work with Dukesy to investigate you a few months ago. I get it. But you can't be pissed off with me forever. I was doing my job. I'm a professional and there is precedence for two MITs liaising. This is all about you and your petty ego. This concerns me. You know it, I know it, the entire damn crime scene knows it, so let me help.'

Elliot's flinty blue eyes flickered, then hardened to ice. 'It's decided.'

Frustration and anger had her fisting her hands as she watched him stride away. Then her heart contracted and she realised that her main emotion wasn't anger. It was something much more profound than that. It was the hollow sense of loss.

Chapter 7

Jazzy

As Jazzy whipped off her crime scene suit and inhaled huge lungfuls of fresh air, a yell from the edge of the inner perimeter attracted her attention. *Queenie.*

'Hey, JayZee, you'll be needing the Jazz Queens with you, will you no'?'

She hadn't realised how tense she was until the sound of her partner's gruff voice reached her ears – backup in the form of one small, rotund, feisty, foul-mouthed woman in her mid-forties and two mismatched blokes in their twenties. Relief surged through her body and the tightness in her gut loosened. The familiarity of her team's dynamics was good for her soul and she laughed out loud at the horrified expressions on the faces of DCs Fenton Heggie and Geordie McBurnie at being publicly outed as the Jazz Queens. Nearby CSIs also snorted behind their masks, probably relieved to have something to break the tension of the horrific crime scene. Everyone knew of the ongoing battle that raged between Queenie and the younger detectives, over her insistence on naming their team the Jazz Queens and right then Queenie's harmless insensitivity was just what she needed. Although, with her friend in bossy mode, she wasn't entirely sure how she was going to tell her that they'd been shunted off the investigation before they'd even started.

Despite her brusque exterior, Queenie was all gooey mush inside and over the months that she'd known her, Jazzy's respect for the woman had deepened. Queenie had lost her twenty-year-old daughter and only child to a supposed drug overdose – which Queenie was convinced was murder. She and her husband Craig hadn't got over it fully, although unless you knew them you probably wouldn't guess at the pain they carried with them daily. When Billi had died, she'd left behind her nine-month-old daughter and with the biological father out of the picture, Queenie and Craig hadn't hesitated to step up and take on Ruby's care. Now a two-and-a-half-year-old, Ruby was the light of their lives. Although Queenie was a grandmother and old enough to be Jazzy's mum, their relationship had blossomed into a rich friendship.

Queenie bustled up to the cordon tape, her face reminiscent of a terrifying tumshie at Halloween as she glared at the younger detectives. 'Aye, you two, get your fingers oot and get yourselves signed in. Then we'll see what his nibs has to tell us. Come on now. Don't hang about like a pair of weasels in the headlights.' As Queenie strode across full of beans and all set to muck in, Jazzy repeated her eye-roll at Fenton and Geordie. 'Someone's had too many red Smarties this morning, I'm guessing.'

Geordie spluttered and winked. 'Aye, you could say that, boss, but she's been worse.'

Jazzy grinned at the understatement. They'd all seen Queenie in an even more abrasive mood, but Fenton was the one who stood up for her. 'Aw, she's not that bad today. She bought us a coffee, didn't she?'

But when Queenie's strident: 'Come on, Haggis, son. What are you doing? Powdering your nose?' crashed through the sea breeze, he grimaced.

'Spoke too soon.'

Their presence lifted the burden from her shoulders a tad. Jazzy tossed her soiled crime suit into the bin provided, and exhaled, wondering how to frame her news.

'Eh, guys. Sorry and all that, but no point in signing in. We've been bounced. We're . . .'

Before she could finish her sentence, a voice from behind her stopped her in her tracks.

'Forgotten something, have you, DS Solanki? Something minor? Maybe the fact that I'm leading on this and *D* team's input won't be necessary. Please sign out and leave.'

Was that a sneer on the 'D'? *Really?* Straightening, Jazzy whirled to face Elliot, her eyes flashing as a stab of anger pierced her heart. How bloody dare he pull rank on her like that in front of her team? She already knew she was being sidelined; still, that was *her* name on that envelope. He didn't have to be such a pillock. At the last moment, a wave of exhaustion rolled over her and, with a single nod, she chose not to rise to his taunting tone. 'How could I possibly forget?'

However, the astonished looks on her team's faces gave her a jolt of adrenalin and, as a red-hot spark sent shock waves through her body, her anger got the better of her. The weariness of just seconds earlier vanished as she continued to walk backwards away from him. 'You best not grip too tightly onto this one either, Elliot. We both know Operation Birchtree will prise this from your mitts as soon as they hear about that envelope with my name on it – especially with the new DCI heading up the operation now. They won't want to make the same mistakes their predecessor did and *we* won't be the only ones left on our arses, will we?'

Satisfied when Elliot's lips tightened, she spun round and marched off with a final: 'Let me know when you have the victim's ID and the contents of that envelope.'

Chapter 8

Ali

I want to scream and rage and throw things about my bedroom. Why don't they get that I can hear them? How can they hurt each other with words and accusations and not see what they're doing to me? That every wound they inflict on each other goes through me first? That they're shredding me to bits?

I swallow and try to distract myself. My ear pods don't drown them out, their strident voices piercing walls to drift upstairs – a caustic sea of hatred washing over me, wiping out every good memory we ever shared. As I glance round my room, my eyes land on my dressing table where the picture of the three of us at Parkhead gala day in West Calder sits in pride of place. I pick it up and study it, before throwing it onto the floor, relishing the sound of the glass breaking. It was a lie. A big fucking ginormous mega lie. Their smiles, all bright for the camera, me with ice cream and raspberry from the Gillespie's van smeared all over my face. How old was I then? Five? Six? God, only ten years ago, and look at the difference. They *hate* each other. Can't stand to be in the same room together and not once have they asked, 'Hey, Ali, you okay?'

It's like they think I'm oblivious. Like I'm still that six-year-old kid, too dumb to realise what's going on right under my bloody nose. Too daft to notice the tension when I come into the room and how they switch their snarls for vacuous smiles and insincere platitudes.

I press my knuckles so hard against my ears that it hurts. Desperate to drown them out, I start singing 'la, la, la, la, la' at the top of my voice. But I can still hear them. It's really doing my head in. I can't concentrate, can't get on with stuff at school and if they found out what I'm thinking of doing on Thursday night, they'd go ballistic. I plonk myself down on the edge of the bed and reach for my teddy bear. I've had it since I was a toddler and it's the same one I'm clutching in the ice cream photo. I bury my face in his fur and let the tears flow. Their voices rise, followed by the door slamming as my dad storms off to work. No doubt to get some peace and quiet and forget all about us. Forget about me. I scrub my cheeks dry, pent-up rage driving me as I grab my phone and send off a text.

Ali: Hey babe, still on for Thurs? I'm defo in. I'll sneak out. My ma and da won't even notice 😂

I look at the screen, half hoping Jan has changed her mind. That she's got someone better to go out with. I mean, why would January, Jan for short, Carmichael be bothered with someone like me? But when her reply comes in, I take a deep breath. I don't know what to think or feel.

Jan: (👍But don't let me down, hen. Will let you know where and when tomoz. Get ready to party

Shite, it's all too real now. I've never done anything like this before. Never rebelled. Never had to. But seeing my da coming out of the spare room this morning with a wheelie case has rocked me. *Is he planning on leaving us?* He'd smiled at me, but it was that tight forced smile he uses when he's blocking me out and my pulse started racing like a bloody woodpecker in my chest and I could hardly catch a breath. *Crap, why is this happening to me?* I thought I was going to have a heart attack and keel over on the carpet in front of him. That would have bloody taught him. At the back of my mind, though, I wondered if that would solve all their problems. No need for them to stay together if I was dead. I doubt they'd even miss me.

I'd googled the pounding heart and weird breathy thing. Apparently, it's not uncommon for kids to have some undiagnosed cardiac issue. Teenagers did occasionally just collapse and cop it for no real reason. For a while, that really freaked me out. A heart condition! Shite, that was scary and on cue my heart began its thudding again and I really thought it was going to stop.

When my breathing calmed and the hammering stopped, I continued googling. And came up with an alternative diagnosis – thanks Dr Google – which seemed more likely. The thought that stress and anxiety could bring on these panic attack thingy doodahs was a bit reassuring. Mainly because it wasn't life-threatening. I read all the articles about mindfulness and meditation and realised it wasn't that much different from the exercises my therapist had had me doing. Maybe I should start them up again.

I should have told them about it, but after the self-harm thing last year, when they found me cutting my leg and then found my stash of razors and shite under my bed, I didn't want to. That had been awful – all that counselling and talking and feeling their eyes follow me wherever I went. It was bad. I'd no privacy, and it took ages for me to convince them I wouldn't do it again. Thank God they're too preoccupied with themselves to bother with me right now. I shove my hand under the hem of my shorty pyjamas and run my fingers over the scars on the tops of my thighs. They are fading now. I didn't have many because I'd made sure they weren't deep and besides, they'd caught me and booked me in. A cry for help, according to the psycho – oops, I mean psychiatrist. Still, the desire to slice my skin and release the tension was pecking away at my head. I'm not going to do that. I refuse to take that route again. Not for them, but for me.

Today, when Jan had come to me at school, I'd been lethargic. Like my limbs were encased in concrete or something. At dinner-time, not wanting to talk about everything, I'd avoided my best mate Isla and sneaked outside to the playground. Despite the drizzle, I snagged one of the outdoor tables near the football pitch. Who cared if I got wet? Who cared if it was pneumonia that killed me and not my bloody thudding heart? When Jan slouched over and grabbed one of my crisps, my heart sank. Being in close proximity to Jan Carmichael was never a good thing. I wished I'd stayed indoors with my pals – safety in numbers and all that. Now, she had me on her own, who knew what she would do? She was a right bitch, was Jan and if she had her pals with her, she'd taunt me for being a goody two shoes – and the rest. I wasn't *terrified* of her, but I *was* scared. She'd been in a few fights before and was pretty close to being excluded permanently, so hopefully she'd bear that in mind.

I was used to her bullying – all my friends were. And mostly we tried to ignore it, but then again, usually we were together. Today I was on my own, but when I glanced round, she was by herself too. She slid into the seat opposite me. Despite the school make-up ban, her bright, shiny scarlet lips curved into a smile that I wasn't quite sure what to make of. 'Fancy doing something wi' me on Thursday?'

Her words hung between us. What the hell was she playing at? I cast another glance around, certain her motley crew would be sniggering nearby, phones at the ready to record whatever diss Jan was about to deliver. Only a couple of younger boys were there, kicking a ball around, their anoraks flying out behind them while running.

'What?'

Her signature eye-roll told me that Jan hadn't been abducted by aliens and replaced by this strange girl sitting opposite, asking me a question with a degree of civility she'd never shown me or my group before. Her tapered nails were sharp enough to have my eye out as she tapped them on the bench. Then avoiding my eyes, she shrugged. 'My mate's let me down. I'm going to the pub in Bathgate on Thursday. Wondered if you want to come with.'

'Me?' I pointed at my chest and snorted. 'Yeah right. What's wi' the big wind-up, Jan? There's no way you'd be seen dead wi' me outside of school. So what's really going on?'

She repeated her pretend nonchalant shrug then rested her elbows on the table. She leaned close, her breath soft against my ear, and minty with a touch of fag, and said, in a taunting tone, 'You scared, Ali? Too scared to upset your ma and da, eh? Won't they let you out on a *school* night? Is that it?' She dragged her summer coat around her and folded her arms under her chest, her overly made-up face all attitude and scorn. 'Don't know why I thought you'd be up for some fun. Should've known you'd be too chicken.'

She marched away, then when she was a few feet away, she spun around and strode back towards me. I just looked at her all glaikit like, wondering what she was up to now. But the next minute, she'd grabbed my phone, which was unlocked, and jabbed her number into the contacts, before tossing it onto the table. 'You change your mind and decide you're not a wimp, then text me. We can have a right laugh, you and me. I'll show you what a good time's like without your stuffy mates around putting a dampener on things.'

Then she'd whirled away, her untidy bun flopping as she bounced along.

I'd sat there for ages, analysing what had happened. Who the hell was this new Jan? The one who wasn't being a bitch to me? The one who'd asked me to go to the pub with her? As the bell rang to signal the end of dinnertime, I stuffed my phone in my pocket as I wandered back inside for the afternoon's lessons and forgot all about it.

Now, I sit, hugging Ted to my chest and try to slow my breathing. It'll be all right. I've committed myself and it'll be all right. Then a thought occurs. This was likely just one of Jan and her minging mates' big wind-ups. By tomorrow, she'll have circulated my message round the school and be slagging me off left, right and centre. No way would the school's bad girl Jan Carmichael be seen dead out with me, so actually I've nothing to worry about. I stand up and move towards my wardrobe. On the off chance that I'm wrong and Jan's invitation was genuine, I better sort out something to wear. I grin, something that my parents wouldn't approve of, but that would be skimpy enough to fit in with Jan's dress sense.

I laugh at myself. Who am I kidding? There's no way I could wear the sort of clothes Jan does, so she'll have to put up with it.

Chapter 9

Jan

Jan tapped her phone on her lips. It had been so easy in the end. She had been a bit worried when the dozy bitch hadn't bitten at dinnertime. She'd given it her best shot, but when Ali wouldn't commit, she'd thought she might have to wave bye bye to the dosh she'd been promised. Mind you, it wasn't in her nature to give up without a fight. No bloody way. The Carmichaels were renowned for being scrappers. Her dad was in the nick for plastering some poor sod who'd got in his face at the pub one night. Still, if the stupid cow hadn't been in touch tonight, she would have tried again the morra.

With a shudder, Jan pondered the embarrassment factor. Surely that alone would be worth a few extra notes? She'd bet on her new iPad that Ali didn't own a lick of make-up and as for her clothes? OMG, she'd probably turn up in a frock for Christ's sake. Rapidly beginning to regret that the lure of easy cash had reeled her in, Jan pursed her lips. She was to take her to the Tartan Sporran in Bathgate. Those were her instructions, though it was beyond her what anybody would want with that wee loser. But it was Jan's local. She had a wee cleaning job there before school every morning. Last thing she needed was that wee cow turning up dressed like a goody two shoes and making Jan a laughing stock. The upshot was that there was no way she could allow Ali to dress herself. The only solution was to bring the cow here to her house. Get her tanked up a wee bit. Put her in a boob tube and a mini skirt and whap some slap on her pus. Problem solved.

Of course, she could still change her mind at the last minute. That wouldn't surprise her. Chances were, she'd be too scared to lie to her ma and da. Scrolling through her phone, Jan thought about that. Then it came to her. The likes of that party pooper needed to be treated mean. If Jan made it easy for her to back out, then she would. On the other hand, if she made it harder for her, quids in the stupid wee fanny would go through with it. It was all about tactics, delicate handling and subtle manipulation, and if there was one thing Jan was good at, it was manipulation. Her strategy would be to play it cool and let Ali think she'd found somebody better to go out with. Somebody trendier. Then, last minute, she'd contact her and tell her she'd meet her near school. By then, Ali would be so relieved that she hadn't been supplanted that she'd be gagging for it.

Satisfied with her plan, Jan stretched her bare legs out and studied her painted toenails with a critical eye. Nah, the turquoise was naff. She wouldn't be seen deid going out with that on. Mind you, it would do for Ali. She sighed. Shite, she'd have to give her a pair of high heels too. She clicked her fingers as an idea struck. Those ones her sister had in the back of her wardrobe would do. She'd never miss them, anyway.

With her plans made, Jan rummaged about in the bottom of her bright pink Primark bag and eventually found what she was looking for. Taking out the burner phone he'd given her, she flipped it open. There was only one number in there and he'd warned her not to use it for anything else. *Like I'd be seen dead using that in public, anyway!*

Jan: Deed done. All sorted for Thurs.

Moments later, the reply came in.

Good work. Cash as arranged on arrival at the venue.

Venue? Fucking *venue?* Like it was the O2 arena and not the sodding Tartan Sporran? Pillock needs to get wi' the game! She hurled the phone back into the innards of her voluminous bag and threw herself back on the bed pissing herself laughing. *What an arse!*

Chapter 10

Jazzy

Jazzy, desperate to check that her parents and the kids were okay, was glad of Queenie's lift. Of course, her mum was in her element when she'd arrived with the Jazz Queens, supplying drinks and homemade baking all round. Crumble, off duty now, was happy to snag attention and pats from the guests, whilst Jazzy tried to smile and act like she wasn't concerned by the unexpected turn of events. Her dad was a carpenter and had a large order to fulfil, so once reassured that his wife was safe, he'd returned to work. Jazzy remained in the kitchen for a bit and then left her mum with Queenie, Fenton and Geordie.

Aware of Benjy's heavy silence and the way he randomly flicked from channel to channel, seemingly unable to engage with anything, Jazzy joined the teenagers in the front room. Benjy barely acknowledged her when she squeezed onto the couch between them and continued his relentless channel hopping. Ivor was drawing on a massive pad, which she rested on her crossed knees, her strokes fast and firm. Jazzy watched her create a group of dancing women, some wearing saris. Ivor, fascinated by the colours and texture of the fabrics, never grew tired of sifting through Lillie's sari wardrobe and often incorporated the designs in her own artwork. However, in recent weeks, Ivor had taken to replacing their legs with multi-coloured whirlwind symbols, which imbued their dance moves with vitality and energy. These women were ferocious! On closer inspection, their eyes, which might typically be languid, were piercing and sharp with sparks of fire erupting into the surroundings like a cacophony of power.

The symbolism wasn't lost on Jazzy. Ivor was creating dynamic females, fortified with strength and the power to protect themselves, and this therapy appeared to be working for the girl.

Benjy, on the other hand, slouched beside her, the TV controls discarded on the coffee table. He had clenched his fists and placed them over his ears, making Jazzy wonder, not for the first time, just what he was trying to drown out.

They sat in silence for a few moments and then Benjy half turned, his eyes accusing, his hands now writhing in his lap. 'It's her, isn't it? She's back.'

Jazzy would have given anything to deny it, but she didn't see how lying to these two would be a good idea. Over the years, in her job, she'd learned that being truthful in times of distress was important. On her other side, Ivor's hand stilled and her gaze shifted towards Jazzy, both awaiting her answer. There was a lot at stake here. Exhaling, she shook her head. 'Honestly, we just don't know yet . . .'

Benjy snorted and made to jump up from the couch, but Jazzy grabbed his arm and continued, 'However, we can't exclude that possibility. Not yet. Now, none of what I'm about to tell you can leave this room. Do you understand?'

Both teens nodded, although Benjy couldn't quite meet her eyes. *Oh, Benjy!*

Choosing her words carefully, Jazzy kept her tone as matter-of-fact as possible. 'There has been a murder, and the killer left behind a letter addressed to me. We're awaiting an ID on the victim and forensic analysis before we can see what's inside. We're taking no chances and I've called Uncle Pedro to take you home. He's on his way. But for now, you're safe here.'

The teenager's uncle Pedro had become a firm friend of Jazzy's over the months and with his history as an army doctor and veteran and the contacts he'd amassed in those roles, Jazzy had unofficially used his network in the past. More recently, Pedro had enlisted some of his army mates to secure the perimeter of Stùrrach in case the teens were targeted again, and as long as they stayed in the village, at school or with Jazzy, they would be safe.

Arms flailing, Benjy jumped up, his skinniness more apparent than ever as he hugged his oversized hoodie around him and yelled, 'This is your fault, Jazzy. It's because of that fucking funeral. That's why she's back. You should let him rot in hell. He doesn't deserve a funeral. Doesn't deserve anything, and neither does she. She's a monster. A fucking monster!'

Stunned, Jazzy blinked up at the distraught boy. There was so much truth in his words that she didn't know how to respond. However, Ivor did. 'Come on, Benjy. You're not being fair. The only reason Jazzy's going ahead with this is because they reckon they can lure the Bitch back.'

Eyes sparking, Benjy turned to Jazzy. 'You should have killed her. You *need* to kill her. That's the only way we'll be safe. She has to die.' And then his hands were at his ears again as he shook his head, moaning, before falling back onto the couch, tears streaming down his cheeks.

Ivor wrapped her hands round her cousin and whispered soothing words; then, eyes meeting Jazzy's, she gestured towards the kitchen. 'Go on, we'll be fine, Jazz. You do what you have to. Go speak to your mum and the team.'

It was true, she did need to speak to her. No doubt Benji's outburst wouldn't have gone unnoticed and despite her attempt at being the genial hostess, Jazzy hadn't missed the shadow in her mum's eyes. Yet again, she'd brought this to their door, and she hated herself for it. Maybe she should do as her mum said and change jobs, but that option wasn't open to her. Not till she was sure they would all be safe. Until Mhairi was locked up for good.

Determined to reassure her mum, Jazzy was happy to drink coffee, eat cake, and allow her colleagues to entertain her, whilst Ivor soothed her troubled cousin in the living room. Gradually, the tension drained from Lillie's shoulders. Her laugh tinkled through the kitchen at some outrageous story of Queenie's. *Why can't it always be like this?*

Finally, Jazzy shuffled in her chair and raised an eyebrow at her partner. The smile fell from her mum's lips as she correctly interpreted her daughter's movement. 'Back in work mode already, Jasmine?' The slight bitterness in her mum's tone was softened by her quivering lip. 'Don't worry, I'll leave you so you can update your team but . . .' She inclined her head towards first Queenie, then Geordie and Fenton in turn. 'The four of you should put an end to this. I told Jasmine this earlier and now I'm telling you. Don't let me down. One way or another, you need to finish it. For everyone's sake.'

Her words, an echo of those Benjy had uttered not ten minutes ago, sent a chill through Jazzy. They were both right. This really had to end soon.

She clicked her fingers and Crumble moved to her side. Lillie, regal as a duchess, stood, palm resting on the table and her voice quiet but unwavering, said, 'Above all, care for one another.'

For a moment nobody spoke, then Fenton jumped up and wrapping his arms round Jazzy's mum, he squeezed before saying in a determined tone, 'That's our plan, Lillie. We'll put an end to all of this.' His eyes flicked between his colleagues as he repeated her words. 'One way or another.'

Lillie patted him on the arm and extricated herself from his grip. 'That's all I needed to hear.' And, Crumble by her side, she left the kitchen, closing the door behind her. Moments later, the sound of a gardening programme drifted through the closed door.

'Thanks, Fe . . .'

But Jazzy was interrupted by Queenie's brasher tones. 'Aye, Haggis. You did good there, sonny. For once. Well done.'

Jazzy shook her head and winked at her young colleague.

Geordie, trying to manoeuvre his long legs under the table without kicking anyone, cleared his throat and in a fair imitation of Queenie, said, 'So when the hell are you going to share the info, JayZee? You know, update your team? Give us all a front-row seat to what went on in that bottle kiln, eh?'

The accuracy of his tone elicited a smile from Queenie as Jazzy leaned forward, undrunk coffee before her. She filled them in on the scene inside the kiln, her thoughts and her doubts.

Fenton's brow was furrowed as he tried to navigate his way through the wealth of information Jazzy had shared. 'So . . . it could be her?'

Queenie tutted and reached for another of Lillie's famous currant rock buns. 'Keep up, Haggis. That's what she said. We're none the wiser.'

She took a huge bite and, crumbs spattering from her mouth continued, 'So, there's no point in us getting our breeks in the proverbial fankle till we have all the facts, is there? Me? I'm happy to hang out here and provide protection for Jazzy's mum. You lot can head back to Livingston, if you like.' She turned to Jazzy. 'Any idea what's for dinner? I could fair go a plate of your ma's palak paneer curry right about now, and does she have some of that Dhokra in the fridge? Love that with lashings of that cucumber raita she makes. Nothing better, eh?'

Before any of them could reply, Jazzy's phone rang. *Elliot!* His name on the screen had her stomach clenching again, and she regretted devouring the piece of carrot cake her mum had insisted she eat. Whilst she wanted to find out the victim's ID and his link to her, she was nervous about the contents of the envelope. She stood and began pacing round the table as she answered: 'Elliot.'

'You'd better get back here, Solanki. The victim's ID has come through.'

Jazzy's heart thundered like a runaway train and in a mirror image of her mum's earlier anxious action, her fingers fluttered to her mouth as she stumbled over her words. 'Who? . . . Is it anyone I—'

But Elliot spoke over her. 'And bring your team with you.'

Throat dry, she grabbed her cold coffee and, ignoring their expectant faces, she took a slurp. This time, she was in control of herself, and her voice had an edge to it. 'I *asked* if it was someone I know?'

Opposite, Fenton grimaced and shrunk back as if waiting for a bomb to detonate. Queenie, face screwed up like a duck's backside, nodded furiously, her arms folded under her chest and a scowl scrawled across her forehead. Only Geordie was grinning. He loved a bit of drama, that boy.

'Jesus, Jazzy.' Elliot's words exploded down the line, frustration coating every one. 'I'm at the crime scene and the bloody vultures are here. I'm not about to bandy information around like Santa Claus doling out presents. You'll be updated when you arrive. Now just get yourselves over here.'

When he hung up, Jazzy slammed her palm onto the table top, then rolled her eyes at her team. 'Shite. He's almost as much of a dick as the dickless wonder at the minute.'

'All not well in Balloch and Solanki land, hen?' Queenie's tone was studied indifference, but Jazzy knew her partner was desperate to find out more details about the abrupt rupture of Jazzy and Elliot's long-standing friendship.

Brushing her colleague off, Jazzy grabbed her coat and strode from the kitchen. 'Come on then, you heard what the boss said: chop chop.'

Chapter 11

Benjy

As the door slammed behind Jazzy, Benjy folded over on himself and crossed his arms over his head, covering his ears, trying to block out the stupid persistent song that played on and on in his skull. Now that Jazzy had gone, it was louder. *'Girls and boys come out to play'*.

With Ivor's arms round him, her familiar fresh vanilla scent telling him that she was here – that she was alive – the usual tormenting images of blood draining onto a frosty ground from his cousin's motionless body were superimposed by a different figure. Jazzy! *'The moon doth shine as bright as day'*.

He began rocking a low moan, working from his chest and out of his mouth as Ivor clung to him, whispering reassurances that they both knew were lies. *'Leave your supper and leave your sleep'*.

Then Ivor's tone changed. Her words were laced with fear as she dragged his fists away, allowing the song to amplify. *'And come with your playfellows into the street'*.

'Look at me, Benjy! Just fucking look at me!'

He shook his head, petrified to open his eyes, worried the

blood was real, worried he couldn't erase it from his mind. In case *this* was a dream and Ivor was already dead. But she persisted, gripping his hands in hers, her fingers digging into his palms, the pain calming him somehow until his breath eased and the tinkling, jarring tune faded. He looked into her eyes, hating the fear he saw there. Hating himself for causing more anguish, especially when Ivor had been through so much. He yanked one hand free and rubbed his sleeve across his eyes, soaking up the salty tears that had dribbled down to his mouth. 'I'm scared, Ivor. I'm scared for you and I'm scared for her. I can't forget what happened. It haunts me day and night. I can't unsee the blood, unhear the noise.'

'I know, Benjy. I understand.' Ivor pulled him to her and they stayed in that position for a long time until she broke the silence. 'We'll take care of Jazzy, Benjy. We'll look out for her like we've been doing. The Bitch won't get near her, not on our watch. I promise.'

Benjy nodded. 'Yes, we'll keep her safe.' But as he spoke, his mind was a quagmire of anger and the thirst for revenge tied his stomach in knots. When would this ever end? What could he do to get past this?

Then, as Uncle Pedro arrived to take them home, his booming voice echoing through from the hallway, Benjy leaned closer to his cousin, his fingers clasping hers, and spoke so only she could hear. 'And . . . after the Bitch is gone, I'll get help, Ivor. I promise.'

Chapter 12

Jazzy

On their arrival back at the bottle kilns, Jazzy jumped from Queenie's car and made a beeline for Elliot, who stood behind the crime scene tape. A bunch of journalists were being bundled to the opposite side of the road, their moaning protestations catching on the breeze and, thankfully, landing short of Jazzy's ears. They weren't her favourite professionals, and she was glad they'd been relegated well away from the scene.

Elliot was on his mobile, his body angled towards the kilns and, judging by the way he ran his hands through his short hair and tapped his foot on the pavement, he wasn't enjoying the conversation. As Jazzy neared, she caught a few snippets. 'Course I'm sure. IDENT1 doesn't get stuff like that wrong.'

Elliot held the phone away from his ear and rolled his head in an attempt to release some tension from his neck, which allowed a tinny female voice to drift into the space between them. 'Well, if *that's* who your victim is, I suspect this is nothing to do with Operation Birchtree and everything to do with that rape case Solanki fucked up in Edinburgh, don't you? Particularly with all the intel we have on him, plus that logged police report of a fight from a few days ago. You can keep the case for now, but let's see what the note addressed to Solanki says and keep me updated.'

Fucked up? Jazzy's cheeks flushed. She hadn't fucked up. No, that had been her boss. Whoever was on the other end of that call should know that.

As Elliot hung up, Queenie, her breathing laboured, lumbered up. He bowed his head for a moment and exhaled, then thrust the device back into his pocket. When he turned to face Jazzy and her colleagues, he'd schooled his face into a neutral expression. Ignoring Jazzy's scrutiny, his gaze drifted over each of the other three in turn, and his expression soured. 'We got the ID on our friend in there.'

Still irritated that he hadn't simply revealed the victim's name over the phone when he'd clearly told whoever he'd just been speaking to, Jazzy, chin lifted pugnaciously, glared at him. 'Well? Who is it? Who were you talking to then and what's all this about a fight?' Jazzy circled her finger towards the pocket where his mobile now resided.

Aware that she was being unreasonable, she hesitated. No one in their right mind would accuse Elliot of melodrama. No, that was more Queenie's style. Why was she provoking him? Especially when their friendship wasn't exactly amicable at the moment.

She paused and tried to recalibrate. Elliot looked as exhausted as she felt, and *he* wasn't the enemy. 'I'm sorry, I'm being a bitch. It's just . . .' She did the same finger-rolly thing, but this time in the direction of the bottle kiln. 'It's a lot.'

'Aye, I get that. It is a lot.' He gestured for the four of them to approach and as they huddled together, after checking no one else was in earshot, he lowered his voice and filled them in. 'That was the new DCI who's heading up Operation Birchtree – DCI Niamh Connolly. She's happy to delegate this to me, and when I tell you who the dead man is, you'll understand why.'

Queenie snorted, but somehow still managed to whisper her

indignation. 'Och, come away with you, laddie. Just spit it bloody out. Who's the deid guy?'

Eyes on Jazzy, Elliot shrugged. 'It's Lewis Fletcher, Jazz.'

The name hit Jazzy like a sledgehammer.

'*No* . . . It can't be.' She stumbled a little and Geordie grabbed her arm, helping her right herself. Blinking furiously as if that simple motion could bat the images into touch, she groaned, deep in her throat as the wider implications of this murder hit home.

She hadn't thought about Fletcher in a long time. Not since before Christmas, when she considered the possibility that *he* might be her stalker. That seemed a lifetime ago. Remembered images and snippets of police interviews with him when he'd been accused of raping Lucy Taggart flicked through her mind. Memories from that time he assaulted her, making her flinch as the reality of her failure to see him convicted sank in. She'd kept them locked up for so long and now, realising that the corpse she'd looked at and not recognised mere hours before was him, they were released.

With her team exchanging puzzled glances, it was left to Queenie to ask the inevitable question. 'Who the bloody hell is Lewis Fletcher when he's at home?'

Jazzy exchanged a glance with Elliot, who shrugged and looked away. A few months ago, Elliot would have stepped in and, in order to protect her, would have explained the situation. He'd have spared her this, but Jazzy had to accept that the days of Elliot being her saviour were long gone. She exhaled. 'He was a rapist I arrested maybe five years ago. Although he got off on a technicality, he did it. There's no doubt whatsoever of that.'

She backed away from her team. 'Look, Elliot will explain. He knows all about it . . . but I can't . . . I just can't. I need a minute.' She stumbled backwards until she found a quiet spot behind a police van. As she leaned against it, she cast her mind back to the Fletcher case. It still haunted her. It was one among the handful that she hadn't been able to come to terms with. In her mind's eye she could vividly visualise Lucy Taggart, bruised and bleeding and fighting for her life on a filthy pavement in Leith. Barely sixteen, the girl had been attacked and brutalised by Lewis Fletcher as she made her way home from school after choir. The extent of her injuries required an emergency hysterectomy to save her.

Over the course of the investigation, Jazzy had become very close to Lucy and her family and when, because of her senior officer's incompetence, Lewis Fletcher had walked from court a free man, they had been beside themselves with grief and rage. And most of it had been directed towards Jazzy. Lucy's brother, Dwayne, had blamed her and had begun a campaign of low-level harassment against her, which had necessitated in her relocating to Lothian and Borders police. Had Dwayne Taggart finally taken matters into his own hands after five years? If true, why would he leave a written message for Jazzy with his victim? Dwayne might not have been as academically clever as his sister, but he wasn't stupid either. Surely, he'd realise the simple act of leaving a note for her would place him firmly in their crosshairs.

She was missing something, but the only way to figure out exactly what was to work the investigation. Head bowed, she counted to five, schooling her breathing back to normality as she prepared to rejoin the others. With a final sigh, she straightened, rubbed her hands down her clothes, tightened her ponytail and went back.

They turned as one to greet her, their expressions serious, their eyes filled with worry . . . and that simple act gave her the strength to reciprocate with a slight smile. She angled her body to include Elliot, although her gaze never veered from the faces of those in her immediate team. 'Obviously the victim's ID means we have to pursue other motivations; however, although Operation Birchtree and the new DCI appear to have dismissed any connection between Fletcher's murder and the Bitch, I can't be quite as cavalier. I . . .'

Elliot's tut, followed by an elongated exhalation, brought a flush of colour to Jazzy's cheeks. She paused and clenched her jaw. 'You got something to add, DI Balloch?'

Elliot's insincere smile soured the air. 'That's not what DCI Connolly said, though. Her actual words were "until we have exhausted all other avenues and explored all other possibilities around the murder", Operation Birchtree trusts me to investigate. If we uncover unquestionable evidence linking Lewis Fletcher's murder to Operation Birchtree, they will naturally take charge.' He turned to Jazzy, his patronising tone enough to turn her flush beetroot red. 'It's all about maximising the use of resources, Detective. I'm sure you understand. With that in mind, and at Afzal's request, D team is back on the case. I'd like you to attend the post-mortem. Fletcher's body is already at the mortuary.'

Queenie, with a quick glance at Jazzy, stepped forward and placed a hand on her arm. 'Yes, I'm sure we all get it, DI Balloch. Yet again, the powers that be in Police Scotland are so far up their own arses, they can barely see the light when they open their mouths. Based on Jazzy's account, there are too many similarities in there . . .' she jerked her thumb towards the bottle kilns '. . . with other crime scenes we know are the Bitch's work, for it to be dismissed out of hand. We need some joined-up thinking, some cooperation, some cohesive strategy development. You get mah drift?'

Queenie was right. The eyes, the mutilation, even the envelope addressed to her all spoke of Mhairi, but one look at Elliot's face told her he wasn't about to embark on a discussion about it. A heavy sadness landed on her shoulders. How had they allowed this to happen? Why hadn't she forced him to listen to her explanations earlier? Made him understand that she had never doubted him, that she'd agreed to her boss's request because she trusted no one else to work as hard to prove his innocence as she would. Now it felt that all they'd been through together, everything they'd shared, had disintegrated into a pile of ash and been blown away on the wind. Now she wondered if she and Elliot would ever be able to rebuild their lost relationship – their lost trust.

Chapter 13

Mhairi

Watching a plan unfold is incredibly satisfying. I toss my phone on the sofa, satisfied that my other little arrangement with the mercenary wee cow, Jan, is in hand and concentrate on the here and now.

The backdrop of the bottle kilns, with all those tiny worker bees buzzing about around them, drifting in and out, all at one with their world of death, blood and gore, is somewhat soothing. I've brought them all here. I orchestrated this and although they don't know it, they are just puppets dancing to my tune. I laugh out loud. There's the pukey PC, still on the job. Good lad, didn't think you had it in you to stick it out. And there's the enigmatic Elliot Balloch. God, he looks haggard, and he's not enjoying that phone conversation, is he?

As I watch, I try to define how I'm feeling. It's something one of my childhood therapists recommended – Mr Smelly, I called him. He was one of the ones I didn't kill! I grin at that thought, then force myself to remember his words. *'Imagine a situation, Mhairi. Imagine your responses to that situation. How it makes you feel inside. Now, wrap your arms round the emotion, Mhairi, and hold it in place. Let it breathe and fill you from your feet right up through your stomach and chest and into your head. Think about your heartbeat. Is it fast or slow? Think about your body. Think about your muscles and your skin. How do they feel? How do they react to whatever emotion you're hugging tight? Now, put a label on it – joy, fear, anger, happiness, love . . . It's your feeling, Mhairi. Your emotion so you can label it however you want. Just allow yourself to become acquainted with it and embrace it like a long-lost friend. Welcome it into your body and allow your body to direct you. Doesn't that feel good?'*

I tried my best. I really did, but despite my efforts, my mind continuously returned to my initial kill. The rush of something indefinable. Joy? Exhilaration? Adrenalin, maybe? But that wasn't one I could share. How could I? The only other emotion that roused me from the flatness of my feelings was the one that surged through me when I was ripped away from Jasmine and Simon, and that was fury. Sheer unadulterated rage. In the end, I decided Mr Smelly was talking shite, because there were really only three emotions – rage and exhilaration and emptiness and sometimes there wasn't a lot to differentiate between the first two.

Today, most people would experience pride at what I've orchestrated. Self-satisfaction at a plan gone well, so that's what I choose to label my non-existent emotion. There's something almost sensual about witnessing first-hand the results of your machinations. Not quite as sensual as the actual killing itself, but not a bad second.

I drift through to the spare bedroom. The one I'm using as my office, and cast a cursory glance at my laptop to check my camera feed. Yes, everything is A okay over there in Glasgow. Nothing to worry about. Nothing's been disturbed. No movement. I laugh, still buzzing from being down there within spitting distance of the scene. I wander back through to my observation point. So much better than going to the pictures.

Ah, interesting, she's returned! I wondered how long these clowns would take to ID the body and process the envelope so they could examine the contents. I must say, I've been anticipating Jazzy's reaction to my little staged set-up for weeks now, but I didn't expect to have a front-row seat for it. Well, okay, 'front row' is an exaggeration, but I'm close enough. Although you can't see the entrance to the kilns from my top-floor flat, I've got a bird's-eye view of most of the cordoned-off area and with the binoculars; it's almost like she's directly before me.

That Queenie cow's face is tripping her because she's been made to abandon her Land Rover. The two lads – the gangly bouncy one, DC Geordie McBurnie, and the wee shy one, DC Fenton Heggie – get out the rear seat and follow their boss. I laugh as the wee one tries to keep up with the other two whilst grabbing his wayward tie as it flaps over his shoulder. Maybe he's scared it'll strangle him. What a shame that you've only got wee pitter-patter feet, son. The bigger one has his eye on the ball, though. He's striding shoulder to shoulder with Jazzy straight for DI Elliot Balloch. How touching to witness his loyalty to my sister. Wonder how he'll feel when the bitch betrays him like she did us.

I exhale to release the negative-energy memories of Jasmine's duplicity and paste a smile on my lips. Another trick of Mr Smelly's. Apparently, it's a way to deceive your brain into believing you're happy and unstressed. Never worked for me, but at least, I blend in when I employ that tactic in daily life. My smile widens into a grin as Jazzy swoops in on her prey, her chin lifted aggressively. She waits on the other side of the police tape while he's on the phone. Bad luck, Jazzy. Your high dudgeon will have to simmer for a few moments more.

I take the opportunity to zoom in on her as she stands, arms folded under her practically non-existent boobs, glaring around the area as if scoping out her enemies. She'd do better to look upwards. On a whim, I wave. Nobody will see me. I'm invisible up here with my binoculars in hand and my tripod and mobile recording everything direct to my laptop so I can watch the entertainment again and again and again. I scan her features, one by one. Jazzy's darker skin has always intrigued me. Simon and mine is lighter. Our hair fairer, our eyes green. That's why Jazzy was always the brunt of the schoolyard racism. As a kid, I'd envied her brown skin and those huge chestnut eyes. Even her hair – when our ma hadn't shaved it off, that is – was beautiful to me. All silky and soft.

The memory of the night when our mum died comes to mind. That was one of the nights Mummy dear sheared off Jazzy's gorgeous hair because she had head lice. In retrospect, over the years, I've often wondered if even then, when Jazzy was a child, our mum sensed her disloyalty – her perfidy. Perhaps that's why she treated her so harshly. Maybe that's why she hated her, but loved us. Perhaps, even then, Jazzy was marked by treachery and deceit.

Today, her black hair's tied up in a long ponytail that slithers down her spine like a poisonous snake. How apt, for that's what she is – a viper on a mission to poison and betray everything she touches. My fingers itch to grab a pair of scissors and run down there. I laugh as I imagine me bursting through the crime scene tape, roaring at the top of my lungs, a pair of gardening shears in hand. *When I reach her, I grab the slithering viperous hair and in one snip, it's in my hands. I raise it aloft like a vanquishing hero returning home. A fanfare of pipers play and everyone – the CSIs the police officers, her team even Elliot Balloch and that obnoxious gnome, Queenie – begins a rapturous applause. Whilst Jazzy Solanki collapses in a heap in the middle, loud booing and hoots of derision fill the air.*

I blink and shake my head. I've zoned out again. How long for this time?

The isolation in that cold cottage messed with my mind. The visual disturbances are occurring more regularly. Mostly,

I enjoy them because they help me focus on my end goal, but occasionally, they come when I'm out and about and I have to be ultra-vigilant then. This one can't have lasted long, because Balloch is still on the phone and Jazzy is still pissed off.

As the trumpet strains fade, I peer through the binoculars again. She's frowning, biting her lips, and not for the first time judging by the state of them – they're all cracked and bloody-looking. Her eyes look haunted with grey bruises under them. I hope she's having those nightmares again, but if she's not, then she soon will be.

I thrust a handful of Hula Hoops into my mouth and begin munching. This is so exciting. Being back in the game feels amazing, and the knowledge of what's coming adds to the excitement.

This part isn't exactly crucial – I mean everything else will still play out as planned, but it is important. If I've pulled this off, then she'll land all the harder when she finally falls – and believe me, Jazzy Solanki, fall you most certainly will. My misdirections will put her off the scent. The more missteps they take now, the better, because when everything falls into place, she'll never be able to forgive herself for her stupidity. She will be broken, completely OBLITERATED!

I yell the word at the window and it bounces back at me, sweet-smelling and filled with promise, filled with certainty – a gift for the future, one that will satisfy me, whether in this world or the next.

He's off the phone now, so I settle myself in my comfy chair and savour the play as it unfolds. Maybe when it all becomes clear to the cow, she'll realise that I've done her a favour. Clearing up the scum that she left on the streets, rounding up her enemies and making them pay, because she was too damn cowardly to do it.

Chapter 14

Jazzy

This post-mortem was more personal than usual for Jazzy. Normally, in such circumstances, her sympathy was firmly with the deceased. Everyone faces mortality in the end, but its inevitability always gave her pause. Made her hope that the person on the pathologist's slab had lived their life well. That they'd be missed and that, regardless of any mistakes or bad deeds they may have committed in life, death would provide closure and perhaps peace.

Despite Lucy's testimony, Lewis Fletcher had been released 'on a technicality' because her idiot boss had cut corners, which resulted in key pieces of evidence being thrown out as inadmissible. God, those words made her want to scream. She'd ranted and raved at Elliot about the injustice of a system that allowed a monster like him to go free. She'd wished him dead countless times, and this was the first time Jazzy just could not empathise with the victim.

Jazzy had been there when Lucy Taggart was found. Her body was battered and Jazzy was the one to pace the hospital corridors with the girl's family as they waited for news of her condition. She had offered support and a sounding board for the family, and she'd been Lucy's confidante when the girl couldn't burden her family with the darkness of her thoughts and details of her recurring nightmares. She'd mopped up her tears and cried with her when Lucy grieved for the children she'd never have.

It was she who had convinced Lucy Taggart to testify against her attacker when none of his other victims could summon the strength to do so. When the massive cock-up in court had occurred, Lucy had slapped Jazzy, almost dislocating her jaw. The girl's regime of training at her local gym had made her stronger, both mentally and physically, and Jazzy had accepted her punishment unflinchingly. It was the very least she deserved. And after that she had refused to report the incidents of human and animal excrement that were posted through her door, the slashed tyres, the graffitied bodywork on her car, the broken windows, or the anonymous calls. She'd endured all of it in silence, because she'd let Lucy Taggart down. She'd bought into a system of justice that sometimes wasn't fit for purpose and, as a result, the Taggart family suffered whilst Lucy's rapist – their tormentor – got off scot-free.

Of course, she'd known that Dwayne, Lucy's brother, was to blame for the campaign against her. He'd made that clear enough. Regardless of Elliot's constant nagging, believing herself culpable for the family's trauma, she'd refused to retaliate by making a formal complaint. As it turned out, the only persecution Dwayne wasn't responsible for was the cards sent by Mhairi. When Jazzy had finally looked ready to break, Elliot had spotted an opening in Livingston and convinced her to transfer, and she'd welcomed the opportunity for some respite.

Viewing Lewis Fletcher, laid bare on a stainless-steel slab, evoked a plethora of emotions. Over the years she'd periodically checked to see that he was keeping his nose clean and had known that after the court case, despite escaping prosecution, he'd lost everything – his family, his job, his home. Regardless of his case being thrown out, he hadn't been found innocent. Muck sticks! The Taggart family made sure of that. The one thing he hadn't lost, though, was his freedom, and that stuck in Jazzy's craw because she'd promised Lucy that they had him – and they had. The forensic evidence had been airtight.

As they'd waited for the PM to start, she read through the document on Fletcher forwarded by Fenton. Although he'd never served time for Lucy Taggart's rape, his previously cushy lifestyle had taken a hit and he'd become involved in criminal activity that had led to a couple of short stints in HMP Addiewell where he'd succumbed to the temptation of drugs and alcohol. As happens with so many criminals, his addictions soon resulted in a descent into a downward spiral of hopelessness.

When she first saw his emaciated body in the bottle kiln, she'd made assumptions about his lifestyle that evoked feelings of sympathy. Now, aware of his identity and with Fenton's report confirming her earlier conjectures about his lifestyle, her compassion had drained away. Some may think he got his just deserts and, for the first time, Jazzy agreed. For her, it was all about Lucy and that courtroom. It was about Lucy being denied the right to take back control of her life. It was about her being unable to move on because her rapist had evaded punishment. It was about Lucy being aware that he walked the same Scottish streets that she did and that at any moment she might bump into him again. So, no, Jazzy couldn't find it in her to feel sorry that he was dead.

That didn't mean she wouldn't fight tooth and nail to put his killer behind bars, though, and therein lay another quandary. Jazzy suspected that when forensics had fully processed the envelope with her name on it and they'd gained access to its contents, the evidence may well lead to Dwayne Taggart's door and at the very least, they'd be duty-bound to visit the Taggarts, and those scars didn't need opening again.

Fenton had also supplied a recent background report on the Taggart family. Mr Taggart – a brusque, no-nonsense railway worker who had wept like a baby when he saw what his daughter had suffered – was now a widower. Mrs Taggart had died of cancer three months previously and Lucy lived in the family home with her dad. Dwayne, her older brother, had set up his own plumbing business and was still living at home. He also attended regular AA meetings to keep on top of his own addiction. Nobody had escaped unscathed from Lewis Fletcher's actions, and it bothered Jazzy that even more grief may be about to land on the Taggart family's doorstep.

Pulling herself into the present, she spoke through the intercom. 'Hey, Doc, can you give us a summary?'

'Ah, Jasmine, you're always too keen to cut to the chase, as they say in those appalling American TV shows. I do all the detailed intricate handiwork and all you want are the edited highlights. Shame on you.' Behind his mask, Dr Lamond Johnston's eyes twinkled, taking the sting from his words. 'But you'll have to wait as I'm only just beginning to unravel the forensic mysteries of Mr Lewis Fletcher's final hours on this earth.'

It had been too much to hope that she'd get easy answers, so, with Geordie next to her, she settled behind the screen to watch. Observing Dr Johnston at work was like watching an artist reveal the secrets behind their best creative pieces. His every movement was measured, respectful, fluid and exact, leaving little room for Jazzy's instinctive queasiness to surface. Beside her, Geordie did a grand job of also hiding his discomfort.

Dr Johnston's voice wafted through the tinny speakers, which allowed communication between the two areas as he examined the external body prior to weighing and cataloguing data about the internal organs. 'Caucasian male, aged between thirty and thirty-five. Severely malnourished, with a multitude of old scars all over his body.'

His gloved fingers pointed to an area south of the man's right kidney where a ragged ropey scar indicated a previous stab wound and then drifted to another on the left side, but slightly higher. This one was shorter, but would still have required stitches. 'I've witnessed similar injuries on convicts and gang members' bodies. Additionally, observe the knuckles that have been broken and left to heal untreated.'

He lifted the victim's right hand and showed distorted digits with HATE – a letter to each finger – tattooed above the knuckles. Jazzy frowned. Many who'd spent time in the nick or in prison gangs had similar tattoos, yet the sight of these on the man lying on the slab beneath irked her, probably because she knew him. Knew the hatred he'd spread, the misery he'd left behind him. 'Cause of death?' Her words came out sharper than she'd intended – snippier and accusatory.

Dr Johnston's hands stilled, and his eyes found Jazzy's, a puzzled frown pulling his brows together, but his voice was mild as he replied. 'We'll come to that, Jasmine. You know I have procedures and processes to follow.'

Jazzy had the grace to look contrite. 'Sorry, Doc. My connection to Lewis Fletcher, combined with the eye mutilation, has me on edge. However, that's no excuse for snapping at you. I really appreciate you expediting this PM.'

'No matter, Jasmine. It's only natural that this will have an effect on you. You wouldn't be human if it didn't.'

Although he was masked up, Jazzy recognised the smile in his eyes as he studied her through the window. With a slight shoulder shrug, he turned away and concentrated on the body. Shaking his head morosely, he rested his hand, almost soothingly, on the deceased's shoulder. 'Unfortunately, man's inhumanity to man has reared its ugly head again, Jasmine. Alas, I do understand the significance of this death and the modus operandi that concerns you.'

In a rare display of anger, he glanced up, his wise old eyes sparking, his voice tight as a drum. 'You have to finish this, Jasmine. You and your team need to end this. It's too much, you understand? This is too much, even for me. I'm finding it harder to find peace with each of these bodies. I prayed for it to end, but I realise now that was a pointless endeavour. Even with faith, evil has to be sought out, overcome and eradicated without mercy.'

The bitterness of his words stunned Jazzy. She'd never heard the doctor speak like this and the implication that his belief – one he held so firmly close to his heart and lived his entire life by – couldn't offer him the solace he needed to cope, was like a bucket of ice-cold water being flung over her. She studied the older man, noticing how his scrubs sagged loosely from his shoulders, how his shoulders slumped, the persistent frown lines scarring his forehead and her chest contracted at his pain. Beside her, Geordie shuffled his feet, his gangly frame clumsy and uncomfortable in the confined space. How many more times would Jazzy hear those words before it all ended? She was in no doubt that, like Benjy and her mother, Dr Johnston was referring to Mhairi.

Jazzy cleared her throat and her words, lighter than air, floated through the silence, and hung there between them, weightier than a cannon ball and filled with a mix of barbed emotions – anger, fear, terror, hatred, acceptance. 'So, you think she might be responsible?'

'Ah, Jasmine, I can't confirm that. Yes, there are similarities to her previous MO, yet there are also disparities. She's a clever woman and we are well aware that she manipulates the vulnerable. This *could* be her work. Equally, it could be that of a sycophant or even a copycat. The only certainty is that this is directed towards you and *that's* why you need to end this. Until she is caught, the questions and uncertainties will persist. I suspect that's what makes her tick.'

He cleared his throat. 'And any enemy of yours with their finger to the pulse will capitalise on this, Jasmine. You've got your work cut out. None of this doubt and uncertainty will stop until she's apprehended.'

'Catching her is my priority, Doc. But I can't be blinded by the ghost of her presence either. We have to consider her influence in this, but likewise, there are other possibilities.'

As if satisfied of her sincerity, Dr Johnston lifted his hand from the dead man's shoulder and, using both hands, turned Fletcher's face towards her.

Jazzy's palm involuntarily rose to cover her mouth and leaned forward. Her mind scattered and the urge to vomit was strong. She swallowed hard, willing herself to calmness as beads of sweat popped on her brow. In this clinical room, amidst bright lights and disinfectant, she saw the man who had vowed to end her life. Her eyes never leaving his emaciated frame, she jumped up and stared at what he'd been reduced to. Before, all she could think about was the Taggart family's suffering. Now, she wondered if Dwayne Taggart had, as he'd promised all those years ago, taken the law into his own hands.

'Are you okay, Jasmine? Shall I continue? I could wait . . .'

'No, Doc. Go on. We need every piece of information that can be gained from this PM if we're to get to the bottom of this.'

Geordie joined her by the glass and squeezed her arm in a silent show of support. 'I've got this, Jazzy. You go and sit in the doc's office. Catch up on whatever Fenton and Queenie are doing.'

She hesitated. This was her responsibility. She should be there, but then her phone rang and Dr Johnston waved a hand in her direction. 'Go. Do your job. I'll finish up here and then Geordie and I will join you in my office for one of my speciality coffees and I'll report my findings directly to you then. How does that sound?'

Despite her stubborn desire to 'do her duty', Jazzy was swayed. Her phone continued to ring and with an abrupt nod, Jazzy strode from the room, mobile already held to her ear as she spoke with Uncle Pedro, who had arrived in Portobello to take Ivor and Benjy home.

'Thanks, Pedro. We can't be certain it's her. Not yet. I'll keep you in the loop, but in the meantime, look out for those two, especially Benjy, will you? He's fragile.'

'Aye, Jazzy, I will. I'll keep my eyes peeled too.'

As she hung up, the weight on Jazzy's shoulders felt a little lighter. Talking to Uncle Pedro always had that effect on her.

Chapter 15

Mhairi

Some of my enjoyment departed with Jazzy and her band of officers. I'm drained and exhausted and I know I must've had one of my out-of-body experiences because I've lost some time. Not long, minutes maybe, but I hate losing control. When I was a kid, it happened sometimes too and my mum – the skank that adopted me, not the dead one – told me not to tell anyone about it. It's possible she was scared they'd blame her, or worse still, that they'd take me away from her. It didn't bother me so much in those days. It was just something that had happened to me after that cow broke her promise to us and we all got split up.

Skank Adoptive Mum asked me to describe it to her, like knowing what was going on would make it stop. I told her it was like being in the pictures watching myself on the big screen doing weird things. Things I knew were wrong. Except, even though I could see this actor version of myself do those things, I knew it was really me.

I knew it was me stabbing my dolls and chopping off their hair. Swearing out the window at passers-by. Hitting and kicking and spitting at the Skank, threatening her with a knife, biting her, locking her in her room, stealing matches and threatening to set fire to the house.

Every time when I broke free from the fuzz, I pissed myself and my skinny body convulsed with violent trembling spasms. My limbs shook and my heart thudded, and all I could do was cry myself to sleep. When I woke up, I could relive it all again when I saw my dolls, or the bruises and bite marks on Skank Mum.

The blackouts stopped when me and Si found each other again. When it was me and him against the world, the zone-outs died away. But now? Well, they come more and more often.

I've no idea when Jazzy left the scene outside, but I'm shivering in the middle of the kitchen, a knife in my hand, wet trousers on and the stink of piss in my nostrils. There's nothing I can do other than lie down before I collapse, so I yank off my soiled clothes, grab the duvet from the bedroom and wrap myself in its warmth. Then I fall onto the couch and succumb. When I wake, my head aches and my body shakes. I'm dehydrated with that familiar tangy metallic taste in my mouth and my limbs are heavy and achy. Recently the recovery time has become longer, but considering the long months and intense days, it's understandable. I want to doze more, but sleep won't come and instead I find my thoughts drifting to a long-ago memory.

Even although I was only twelve, I remember it like it happened only yesterday, the day I met my step-great-papa McCullough. I didn't want to make the trip. I hadn't wanted to meet some boring old man. Especially someone I'd never heard of before, and who I wasn't related to. An old geezer my adoptive mum hadn't kept in touch with for a long time. Mind you, I was at that 'difficult' stage – so she, the Skank Mum, told anyone who'd listen. That amused me because I couldn't remember ever not being at a difficult stage. Still, she did try to get used to me and I was supposed to try to get used to her. Course, I wasn't making any effort whatsoever. It was so much more enjoyable watching her struggle to help me 'adjust'. She was like a dog with a non-stop wagging tail and drooling mouth, desperate to please, desperate for a smile, a pat on the head, a scratch of the ears. As for me, I was like an angry Rottweiler, all hackles and bared fangs. She didn't stand a chance, poor cow.

Maybe the trip was her last hope to connect with me. Maybe she remembered her auld step-papa with affection. Reckoned that if anyone could break down my barriers, smooth my hackles and round off my fangs, it would be him. Or maybe she had a last-minute burst of guilt. We were his only living relatives and despite him not being my blood relative, he'd made a lasting impression on her – okay not a strong enough one to make her keep in touch bar the odd Christmas card or to lift a phone or indeed to check on his welfare by making the trip to see him. It wasn't far, really. Three hours along the A87 and over the Skye Bridge from Kyle of Lochalsh to Kyleakin and you're there.

I wanted to drive further south and ride the ferry. I'd never been on one and was desperate to try it. No doubt had I asked, she'd have agreed. Anything to take the truculent look off my face and make her feel like she was breaking down my barriers, and that is precisely why I kept my mouth closed. Since the big betrayal, I had schooled myself not to rely on anyone else, not to open myself – not even a crack because when you do you're basically presenting your belly, handing the person a knife and saying: 'here, gut me alive, why don't you?'

The memory fades, the jitters pass, and by the time that's happened it's quieter outside the flats. With the duvet wrapped round me like a Mr Blobby–sized toga, I haul myself to the window. When I look out most of the police and CSIs have gone and I feel blindsided. As if I've missed all the fun of the fair and now I can only listen to it on the news, which is what I do.

Chapter 16

Jazzy

Jazzy sauntered into the pathologist's office and made herself at home on the chair opposite his desk. She'd been here on numerous occasions. The lingering musky scent of his aftershave mingling with tobacco smoke never failed to calm her. It gave her the illusion of being a child wrapped in a blanket cuddled into a grandfather's lap and being enthralled by an exciting tale of heroes and villains.

Of course, Jazzy had never experienced anything like that. Her grandfather refused to be involved with her in any way. Yet, as a child, she had yearned to be showered with that sort of unconditional love. That's likely why she spent so much time cuddling with her siblings and sharing stories of fairies whisking them to a palace where they would be doted on. It wasn't until she was taken in by her biological mum's brother and his wife that she felt secure.

Everything in Lamond Johnston's office reflected his commitment to his family. Photos of his wife, children and grandchildren entertained visitors with tales of adventures by the beach, at fun parks, in ruined castles. As well as his family's importance in his life, his devotion to God was apparent in the personal adornments that peppered his work space – the haunting painting of Christ on the cross, head bowed, droplets of blood flowing from his wounds on one wall; the small statue of a crucifix, nestled on a shelf between his textbooks and a well-thumbed copy of the Bible; and the intricately carved fish with the word JESUS filling the body that stood beside his computer.

Religious symbols! Jazzy bit her lip and thought of the crime scene. Although certain things pointed towards this being linked to the Taggart verdict going so disastrously awry, Jazzy had been wrong-footed too many times by her sister not to want to fully investigate the other option. Of course, Elliot would prioritise locating Dwayne Taggart and the rest of the extended Taggart family. The entire community had been equally angry at the outcome of Fletcher's trial. Some of the more vocal members of women's groups and the online trolls who'd issued threats would need to be considered too. But uneasiness niggled Jazzy. She'd ensure that the crime scene photographs, and any evidence retrieved from the kiln were scrutinised for evidence of religious symbols. In her previous killings, her sister had planted a variety of spiritual items, from different faiths at the crime scenes she'd created. Unfortunately, because they differed in type and could easily have belonged to the victim, it hadn't been till Queenie was on the case that those murders had been linked back to the mutilation of Jazzy's birth mum's dead body.

When Dr Johnston bustled in, he brought with him the sharp scent of antiseptic, which strangely enough didn't detract from the illusion of warmth and tranquillity. 'I might not be as handsome as George Clooney, Jasmine, but I'm well able to provide you with a Nespresso.'

Jazzy grinned. 'Oh, I'm sure you could give Clooney a run for his money in the looks department, Lamond.'

With a gleeful chortle, the doc sorted out their drinks,

humming some obscure, yet familiar hymn under his breath before plonking himself behind his desk and smiling over his cup. 'Well, I'll give you the highlights for now, and I'll get the official report over to the team when I've typed it up – cutbacks, you know, so no assistant today.'

Jazzy took out her phone, ready to take notes, whilst the pathologist blew on his coffee and collected his thoughts. 'I won't bore you with all the details about height, weight, age and suchlike as you already know that, I believe. There's no doubt that Mr Fletcher was murdered in the bottle kiln. However, I'll leave it for you to figure out the logistics of how his killer lured him there.' He took a sip of his drink. 'The toxicity report will tell us whether he was just inebriated or if there were any other drugs in his system.'

He quirked an eyebrow at Jazzy. 'I'm assuming the contents of the vodka bottle analysis haven't come back?'

'Not yet.'

'Okay, well the bruises all over his body indicate he'd suffered a severe beating, but most of them are older. Geordie told me he'd been involved in an altercation with Dwayne Taggert a few nights ago? That would account for most of them. The bruising makes it hard to distinguish any newer bruises. Cause of death was an upward thrust of a non-serrated, long-bladed weapon through the top of the gut and into the heart. It might have been a kitchen knife, but it's not certain.'

'Good to have an idea of the type of weapon we're looking for, though.'

Dr Johnston exhaled before continuing, 'Now, let's discuss the mutilation of the eyes after death. I'm assuming you're keen to get my take on that?'

'Yes, definitely. What can you share about that?'

'Of course, I compared the wounds to those carried out by Mhairi and I'm sorry, Jasmine, but it's inconclusive. There were hesitation marks, but then . . .'

'She's smart enough to be able to feign hesitancy to put us off the scent . . .'

'Exactly. Plus, there's the rather large discrepancy in that Lewis Fletcher's eyes were left *in* the eyeball, whilst with her previous victims, she moved and displayed them. Mhairi is skilled at misdirection and subversion, but we might be searching for non-existent threats. Perhaps we're looking for bogeymen where there aren't any.' He frowned and gave his head a slight shake, clearly remembering that there was one very murderous bogeyman at large. Reaching over, he placed his hand on the ichthys carving, as if to take solace from it. 'This murder, tragic though it is, might prove to be the result of the most basic of human instincts. Revenge. I'm sorry I couldn't be of more help, Jasmine. I truly am.'

Jazzy smiled and stood. 'I just wanted to convince myself that it couldn't have been her, but . . .'

He steepled his fingers before his lips. 'The evidence is inconclusive?'

'Let's just say, I've always been sceptical of ninety-five per cent certainty, but we've got other investigative strands to follow, so that's what we'll do.'

She moved over to the door, but before she could open it, Dr Johnston cleared his throat. Jazzy turned. 'Something else?'

A flush had gathered in the doctor's cheeks and his rapid blinking brought a frown to Jazzy's brow. 'You okay, Lamond?'

'Oh, yes, yes, of course I am. It's . . .' He cleared his throat again. 'I don't want to overstep the mark, but – and you can tell me to butt out should you feel I'm doing just that – I heard you had taken on responsibility for your brother's funeral. And . . .' His next words came out in a rush of uncertainty. 'I understand how difficult it must be for you, in the circumstances, so I wanted to offer my services.'

Jazzy's frown deepened. Mention of her brother had brought an immediate tightening of the clamp in her gut. Everyone believed she was crazy to consider complying with his final requests, but Jazzy hadn't expected Lamond to be one of them. 'I'm not sure what . . .'

'Och, I've not made myself clear, have I? I'm offering to speak a few words at the funeral, in lieu of a religious leader. If it's inappropriate, feel free to refuse. The last thing I want is . . .'

But Jazzy had strode back across the office and round Lamond's desk. In an action she'd never done before, she hugged the older man tight. 'You're the only one who hasn't tried to dissuade me, Doc.' Then, because tears threatened to spill down her cheeks, she released him and was out the door in a flash, leaving only a mumbled 'I'll think about it' in her wake.

Chapter 17

Jazzy

Her coffee break with Dr Johnston meant Jazzy was running late for the briefing Elliot had scheduled, and by the time she'd parked her Mini and run through the corridors and up the stairs, she was hot, sweaty and a little breathless. She dreaded having him as SIO, yet knew it was for the best since he was based in Edinburgh and only the envelope addressed to her and her connection to the victim had warranted it being diverted to Livingston. The thought of being sniped at, talked down to, or worse still, subjected to stony silences – all of which he'd resorted to over the past few months – left her cold. The only thing that could make the situation even more unbearable would be if DCI Dick was also present, and knowing her luck . . .

Taking a deep breath and channelling the theme tune she and Queenie used to bolster them to face difficult situations, Jazzy thrust the incident room door open with '*JayZee Queen. Top-notch, cool and mean. Hot stuff with a killer gleam. This girl's gonna whoop your arse*' playing on repeat in her head.

Unfortunately, the door clattered against the wall, startling everyone. A sea of faces – her team, uniformed officers, the civilian analysts – now faced her and Jazzy wished she'd channelled a bit less of the JayZee Queen and a lot more of the invisible Queen. Her cheeks flushed, and she knew they'd be that awful beetroot red that made her frown lines stand out like Belisha beacons. She hated being stared at, but there was nothing else for her to do but to brazen it out, so she raised her chin and strode down to the seat Queenie had saved for her near the front. Thankfully, her nemesis, DCI Dick, was nowhere in sight. Elliot, arms folded across his chest, his shirt sleeves rolled up and his tie discarded beside his jacket, which lay in an untidy bundle on the chair behind him, was inscrutable as his eyes tracked her progress.

As she slid into her chair and everyone turned back towards Elliot, she said, 'Sorry I'm late. Got held up with Dr Johnston at the PM.'

This was not the complete truth as Geordie had also been at the PM, yet been on time for the briefing. She tensed, waiting for Elliot to take issue with it. Instead, with a shrug, he dismissed her apology, cleared his throat and stepped forward. 'Before we begin the updates on this investigation, I have some news to share.'

A wave of sideways glances and low-level fidgeting accompanied this statement. Jazzy's tension increased. Did it involve Mhairi or something else? Judging by Elliot's expression, whatever the big announcement was about, it was serious. She leaned forward, her stare fixed on his face, her heart thrumming and Dr Lamond's posh coffee lurching around in her gut.

'Superintendent Afzal wanted to share this news, but he's been called away. So, I'll do it instead. Due to DCI Dick being seconded elsewhere, the Major Incident Teams currently lack a DCI. With budgets being slashed it has been decided that the existing DIs in A and B teams will step up on a temporary basis to cover some of the DCIs roles . . .' He looked round the room, his gaze lingering for a fraction of a second on Jazzy. 'So, although DS Solanki has been nominally in charge of D team since Christmas, the team requires a DI to be in overall charge.'

Jazzy's eyes narrowed, but it was Queenie who spoke. 'Nominally, eh? *Nominally*. So *nominally* means *actually* leading D team to solve the whole gang warfare subterfuge, when neither Edinburgh nor Glesca divisions could, eh? It means *actually* being seconded to a high-profile secret investigation to root out corruption in Police Scotland, am I right? Or wait a wee minute . . .' She clicked her fingers and grinned. 'I get it, nominally means *actually* being headhunted to handle an undercover officer? Yes, I think it's clear now . . . *nominally* means *successfully* doing all the serious stuff oor Jazz did just a couple of months ago. Is that no' right?'

Whilst Jazzy rather wished her friend hadn't raked up the whole 'handling an undercover officer' and 'corruption' angle, she appreciated that she'd jumped to Jazzy's defence. And with her dander up, Queenie kept going. 'I suppose, though, that the high heid yins don't agree with that definition though? Nae chance. No, we're bound tae land up with some "up his own arse" DI with BO and an attitude problem from bloody Timbuktu or worse, Edinburgh . . .'

Elliot held Queenie's gaze, a slow smile spreading across his lips as he waited for her to catch on. Under her breath, Jazzy groaned as realisation dawned on Queenie. '*You?*' She couldn't have injected any more scepticism into the single word if she'd tried. '*You?*' she repeated as if hoping for a different outcome.

'Some top-notch detecting there, Queenie.' Elliot's tone was light, each word layered with amusement. 'Yep, I'm the "up his own arse" DI *without* BO and an attitude problem from Edinburgh, because Timbuktu is just too far to commute. Sorry to disappoint.'

While everyone else in the room grinned, Queenie gracefully gave a half-hearted apology. 'Aye well, I suppose as DIs go, you're not too bad and at least we know all your bad habits, because we've worked with you before.'

Assaulted by conflicting thoughts about this development, Jazzy swallowed and then pasted on a smile. 'Well congratulations, sir. That's good news. I'm happy to revert to my sergeant duties.'

As if awaiting a signal from Jazzy, Fenton and Geordie offered their congratulations and after a few moments, Elliot called the room back to order. 'In the incident room or in private work conversations, it's Elliot. Only use my rank when we're in public or with the bosses, okay? Right. Now that's dealt with, let's get cracking. I don't know about you lot, but I want to get home soonish. It's been a long day. So, first things first. The lab have processed the envelope and not surprisingly, apart from the deceased's DNA and random smudged fingerprints thought to belong to those processing the envelope at various stages in the production line, and none of which belonged to Lewis Fletcher, they got no hits.'

Come on, come on, come on, get to the point, Elliot! Jazzy had expected those results, and what she really wanted to know – what they all wanted to know – was the contents of the letter. It took forever for Elliot to scan the report, but at last he got there. 'No useful forensic evidence found in the interior of the envelope, but the complete report is available if you want to read it.'

He met Jazzy's eye for the first time since she'd arrived and continued. 'Inside was a single, generic sheet of paper with only five words typed in capitals on it.'

He pressed a button on the keyboard and an image of the note appeared on the screen.

HE GOT HIS JUST DESERTS.

For a second, the room was silent. Like her, everyone had expected something more personal to Jazzy. She let out a breath she hadn't realised she was holding. 'That's it?'

She scowled at Elliot as if blaming him for the lack of information on the note. 'That's all? For God's sake, if we'd realised that was it, we . . .' She paused and corrected herself. '*I* would have been less inclined to factor my sister into things.' She shook her head. 'If it had been Mhairi who wrote that note, she'd not have been able to prevent herself from taunting me, or making some sort of threat. This reads like a factual statement because Lewis Fletcher *got* his just deserts, didn't he? He was a violent rapist who escaped punishment for it, leaving his victims devastated.'

'Aye.' Queenie rubbed her palm across her nose and sniffed. 'I think you've got a point there, hen. That note is from someone desperate to right a wrong, not a psycho killer like your sister, determined to torment you any and every way she can.' As Queenie exhaled, a waft of cheese and onion crisps drifted through the air. 'My money's on that wee lassie Lucy's big brother, Dwayne, but . . .' She straightened. 'That doesn't mean we let our guard down. That bitch will not stay away forever, especially when we've got that other wacko bastard to bury, if you get my drift. No, she'll be back before too long, causing mayhem and murder.'

Although she might not have expressed it quite like that, Jazzy agreed with her colleague's sentiments. The focus for now – as Dr Lamond's verbal report showed – had to be on locating Dwayne Taggart as their most likely suspect until proven otherwise. 'I have to say that Dr Lamond seems to agree with Queenie's assessment, too. He will upload his PM report shortly, but he told me he found nothing to indicate Mhairi's involvement in Lewis Fletcher's murder, except for the partial mutilation of the eyes. Time of death is estimated at between three and five a.m. Hesitation marks were present around the eye mutilation and a single forceful upwards knife wound from the lower abdomen, which caught the heart, is cause of death.'

But caution and her previous doubts made her continue. 'There are a few things that worry me. I mean, I can believe that Dwayne Taggart might want to direct that message to me. He hates me and he conducted a campaign of terror on me after Lucy's case was thrown out, so I can accept that he would want to taunt me – to tell me that he succeeded where I failed. I get that. But . . .'

She wished she could swallow her niggle of doubt and leave her concerns unsaid, but that wasn't Jazzy's style. Having experienced a great deal, she knew the extremes her sister would go to, to create havoc. They thrived on it. It was their life's blood and Jazzy would never forgive herself if she ignored the five per cent of doubt that pawed at her brain and sent shivers up her spine. She met Elliot's gaze head on. 'But why would he choose to kill Lewis Fletcher in Portobello, inside a sealed bottle kiln and specifically on the day my mum and me always stroll that way?'

Fenton, whose eyes hadn't left Jazzy's face as she spoke, nodded. 'I wondered that myself. What about that anonymous tip-off that led to the discovery of Fletcher's body at around the time you and your mum were there . . . That's well dodgy.'

Extracting his long legs from where he'd hooked his feet around the chair leg, Geordie took up the baton. 'Would Dwayne Taggart really go to such lengths to seek revenge, especially after six years? He could have murdered him any time. I mean, we know he and Fletcher had a violent altercation a few nights ago. Why not—'

Queenie interrupted. 'Ah but, maybe the fight brought it all back for Taggart again. Maybe a chance encounter in the pub, after a few bevvies, reignited his anger. You know dredged up auld wounds? Spewed up a shedload of animosity that had been simmering like a cesspit for the past six years.' She paused for breath, her hands flapping in front of her. 'I mean, that meeting must have highlighted his failure to protect his wee sister from her rapist, or to get justice when the bastard got off. *That* to me seems more like it, do you no' think? Christ, judging by the bruises you say were all over Fletcher's body, Taggart damn near killed him the other night anyway and he would have if the pub landlord hadn't dragged him off. Makes sense that he'd want to finish the job off.'

Case rested, Queenie slouched back onto the chair and slapped her hand on her thigh in a weird cowboy 'eee ha' motion.

Jazzy understood where Queenie was coming from. She was burying her head in the sand because facing the alternative would take her back to a hell she'd rather forget. Though her expression suggested otherwise, Queenie was fully aware of Mhairi's deviousness. Which was why Jazzy kept her response calm. 'We proceed with Taggart as our main suspect, but there's no harm in considering other options. That's all we're doing. Preparing for the worst doesn't mean we'll conjure her up, Queenie, but we need to be realistic. We can't underestimate her and until Operation Birchtree gets its finger out and finds her, we're lumbered with scrutinising everything that impacts one of our team members to within an inch of its life. It's called self-preservation, okay?'

Despite her sulky strop, Queenie nodded. 'Aye, s'ppose so.'

'Right, glad we've settled that,' said Elliot, rubbing his hands together, his light tone recalibrating the atmosphere in the room. 'Let's move on. Fenton, what's on the CCTV footage?'

'Short answer is zilch. Some cameras were broken. I'm assuming on purpose as they're the ones facing from the flats and the main road towards the kilns. We're sweeping businesses in the vicinity for their video footage. Hopefully, we'll get a hit and, of course, uniforms are doing door-to-doors in the surrounding area.'

Elliot addressed the sergeant from Portobello, who had joined for the meeting. 'Updates from officers on the ground?'

Jerome, the burly officer, shrugged. 'Regrettably, just more of the same. Nobody's seen anything, but I've assigned three constables to continue in the morning and the night shift will keep an eye out there. Forensics have finished with the crime scene, although we've left the tape in place for now. We've also secured the bottle kiln and I've authorised regular walk-bys overnight. I'll be in touch again tomorrow. Maybe we can FaceTime rather than me driving over?'

'Suits me, Jerome. Okay, Geordie, what have you got? Any luck on locating Dwayne Taggart?'

'Not yet. His dad says he's not seen him for a few days and his friends say the same. We've taken a few statements and, to date, all the relatives we've been able to locate have alibis. So far nothing pops and it's sensitive.'

Unable to stop herself, Jazzy jumped in. 'What about Lucy? Has anyone talked with her?'

Geordie glanced at Elliot, then looked down. It was his turn to blush. 'Thing is, Jazz, she won't talk to anyone but you. Refused point-blank and although we initially suggested you should steer clear of the Taggart family, it looks like we have no alternative. She wants to speak to you and considering the circumstances, we don't have a lot of choice, do we?'

Jazzy closed her eyes as images of Lucy Taggart hit her like bullets from a Gatling gun. Lucy, in her hospital bed, broken and unrecognisable. Lucy crying, ripping tissues one after the other in her lap. Lucy summoning up a tremulous smile. Lucy squaring her shoulders as she prepared to give evidence in court. Lucy, unadulterated hatred twisting her features, glaring at Jazzy as her rapist walked free.

Jazzy shook her head, not sure if she was trying to dislodge the memories or if she was refusing to visit Lucy Taggart. Then she caught Elliot's eye and everything changed. He nodded, only once, but that single action told her as clear as if he'd yelled it from the top of Arthur's seat that he had faith in her. Jazzy shrugged. 'Right, that's decided then. Tomorrow, first thing, I'll see what Lucy Taggart has to say.'

Chapter 18

Jazzy

Jazzy, with her cat, Winky, trailing behind her, checked her locks for the third time that night. No matter what Queenie believed, Jazzy couldn't shake the feeling that they were missing the big picture and that something different was at play. There were too many coincidences stacking up. Simon's suicide, along with the murder of a rapist she had failed to convict, didn't take into consideration the fact that he was killed in the town where her parents lived and the body was discovered after an anonymous call, while she was in the vicinity.

Then there was Benjy to consider. She'd spoken to Uncle Pedro earlier and he'd told her Benjy regularly hassled Ivor to hang out outside Jazzy's home because he was so worried that Mhairi would attack Jazzy. The thought of the boy's anguish made her drag her fingers through her hair. She'd texted Benjy to check in on him, but as usual he replied with a smiling emoji and a thumbs up. Then, when she'd texted Ivor, she'd said Benjy was acting weird – as if he there was something going on in his head. Jazzy really had to make the time to check in on the two kids in person, but when?

All of these thoughts burled round in her head, making her brain ache. Both she and Uncle Pedro had forbidden Ivor to leave Stùrrach with Benjy without telling them, but she knew what teens were like. She rubbed Winky's tummy and then gently ejected him from her lap. The only light illuminating her front room was the yellow glow from the hallway as she went over to the window and peered out, stretching her neck to see both ways. Letting the blinds close she sighed and closed her eyes for a moment to ground herself.

She didn't look forward to going to bed tonight. The day had been filled with an overwhelming number of triggers for her, and sleep would be a battle of the nightmares. Each one vying for dominance of her nocturnal mind and leaving Jazzy sweating and anguished as she tried to force them away and grab some kip. Most nights, she'd fought sleep and although her therapist had prescribed sleeping pills, she hated the lethargic way they made her feel in the mornings. Besides, until she caught Mhairi, she needed to remain alert at all times. So, not even gritty eyes and a pounding headache would allow her to knock herself out.

The proposed meeting with Lucy Taggart the following day preyed on her mind. She'd no idea why Lucy had demanded she visit her, but she wasn't looking forward to it. She couldn't imagine how all of this had impacted Lucy. Yes, she'd be glad that Fletcher was dead, but how would she feel about them pursuing her brother? Jazzy hadn't seen her since that day outside the court and, respecting Lucy's privacy, she'd opted not to use her powers as a serving police officer to check up on her. Of course, she'd kept tabs on Dwayne – she wasn't stupid and he had posed a threat to her, but since she'd transferred to Livingston, the threats had stopped and, until the past few months, Dwayne Taggart hadn't been on her radar.

She needed a distraction, so she flung herself on the couch and pulled the folder she'd been avoiding looking at towards her. She needed to make decisions she had neglected for too long.

Simon's funeral was looming and the funeral directors were champing at her heels to finalise the arrangements. Organising the funeral had been made harder because no one thought she should pander to the outlandish demands he'd written in his will, which meant she had no one to discuss it with. No one to help her sort her way through her mixed emotions and fine-tune the organisation.

Of course, Operation Birchtree was eager for it to happen. That's why it was on Friday. With few other leads to pursue, they hoped it might entice Mhairi back. Jazzy partly agreed with them. Mhairi would return to pay her last respects to her twin, but then Jazzy kept second-guessing herself. The bottom line was that unlike Simon who'd been all grandiose show, Mhairi – although partial to a bit of flamboyance herself – also possessed a keen sense of self-preservation, which meant that she was ruthlessly selfish and could control her sentimentality if indulging in it would put herself at risk. She had warned the previous Operation Birchtree head, but they ignored her. Now, the new DCI was spamming her inbox, pushing the point. Jazzy was too tired to respond.

The actual organisation and timings were being taken care of by Operation Birchtree with attention to security details. She gathered that officers would be brought in from nearby forces to flood the area. Surveillance teams would monitor the funeral parlour and the route to the cemetery and, at some point, they would arrange a meeting to review all of that. However, Jazzy felt they hadn't considered the psychology of her sister. She was devious and methodical and able to second-guess and circumvent any plans her pursuers could make.

Jazzy opened the folder and looked at the funeral requests handwritten by Simon. As her fingers traced over them, her throat clogged up. *Oh, Simon, what did you become?* What a stupid question. She knew what her brother had turned into. He and his twin had grown into the monsters that were most feared throughout Scotland. Scotland's only familial serial killer duo.

Their only close challengers were Burke and Hare, who strangely enough also cast their killing net as far as West Lothian. Jazzy's siblings joined the ranks of Scottish killers, alongside notorious figures such as the unidentified killer Bible John, Peter Tobin, and Peter Manuel, who faced execution on the Barlinnie gallows in 1958. Of course, there were other notorious killers of Scottish origin, but her siblings were the ones who tortured Jazzy, like a persistent itch that made her want to claw her skin down to the very bone.

Journalists and podcasters had published screeds about them – most of it fictional. She'd lost count of the number of times journalists wanting to pay for her story had approached her, but all they wanted to do was to inflame fear, and that would play right into Mhairi's hands. Besides which, Jazzy had a hard enough time balancing her own emotions.

Simon, despite his 'devotion' to Hinduism and his belief in reincarnation, had insisted on being buried. He'd even paid for his plot in a local cemetery, a stone's throw from Jazzy's Bellsquarry home. Cynically, Jazzy wondered if that was designed to taunt *her*, but in black and white, he'd written his delusional reasons down: *I've chosen this site, so that the warriors to follow in my revolutionary footsteps will have a place to visit in pilgrimage.*

It was a toss-up whether that was his deluded mind or his cold-blooded, manipulative one talking. Jazzy slightly came down on the side of the latter. Of course, he was mentally ill, but that didn't prevent him from being manipulative.

Jazzy was prepared to organise a funeral for Simon, but was not going to follow his wishes to create a pilgrimage site at his grave. Her brother's grave would remain unmarked. No headstone or nameplate. Just a grave with a flat sandstone to signify where his head rested.

What she couldn't get her head round was the 'service' element of the funeral. How could she, in good conscience, celebrate the life of a killer who had inflicted such widespread suffering? Of course, when she remembered him as a child, her heart broke all over again.

Exhaling, Jazzy picked up her mobile and dialled a number she'd never used for personal reasons before, and certainly not this late at night.

'Hallo?'

Jasmine couldn't speak. The tears that had threatened earlier fell silently down her cheeks and all she could do was wipe them away. As if understanding the purpose of her call, Dr Johnston, his voice reassuring and calm, said, 'It's okay, Jasmine. I know this is hard for you. Do you want me to come over? We can work out the best way to lay your brother to rest.'

With a muffled gulp, her voice thick, all Jazzy could manage was: 'Yes please,' before mumbling her address and hanging up.

She hadn't known where Dr Johnston lived, but it turned out to be nearby in Kirknewton. She barely had time to wipe her tears and fix a few cushions before he arrived at her door. However, it was long enough for embarrassment to set in and as she led him through to the living room, her words were stilted, her movements jerky. 'Have a seat. Tea? Coffee?'

But Dr Lamond's eyes were on the small hand-carved mandir Jazzy's dad had crafted. After Ivor, Benjy and Queenie had noticed it hidden on the topmost shelf, she'd realised she was hiding it for no reason and that the mandir stood as a symbol of her dad's love for her. She'd placed her collection of elephants around the mandir and her Ganesh statues inside, along with some divas and an incense holder. Nowadays, when she listened to her meditation recordings, she lit the divas and the incense or agarbatti, as it was called in Gujarati – and faced the mandir. The love with which it was created bolstered her mood.

'Oh, this is beautiful, Jasmine. Truly exquisite.' He turned, his smile wide. 'But to be frank, I didn't have you down as a practising Hindu.'

His obvious delight in her dad's creation swept all her unease away. It was just like Lamond to manage a tense situation with a light touch and dispel her earlier embarrassment.

Jazzy moved over and ran her fingers over the lacquered wood with its intricate turrets and arched front. 'My dad's a carpenter. He made it for me and my mum has furnished it with all these Lord Ganesh statues. He's the remover of obstacles.' She shrugged. 'It makes my mum happy to have them here. She blesses them every time she comes, and it reassures her to feel that, even in her absence, she has offered me some protection. She's very religious. Me, though? Well, I'm pragmatic about it. I enjoy its beauty and I love elephants. I don't practise Hinduism. Not like my parents, but I meditate in front of it.'

His gaze drifted round the room, soaking up her paintings of traditional Indian women in various classical stylised poses, the one of Jazzy herself, captured by Ivory in pride of place in the middle. Jazzy allowed him time to absorb her home, wondering why she wasn't on edge. Maybe the onslaught of new friends who'd visited her home over recent months had inured her to that prickliness she used to feel when her space was invaded.

He turned, his eyes alight, and the same musky smell that she'd experienced earlier in his office encompassed her – after-shave mingled with pipe smoke. He walked over to the couch and plonked himself down. 'I'd love a coffee, and then you can tell me all about your brother.'

Jazzy swallowed, a frown playing across her brow. 'Why would you do this, Lamond? I mean, you, of all people, have seen what he and my sister are capable of. You did the post-mortem on their recent victims. You know he's a monster and yet you've offered to speak for him at his funeral.'

Lamond nodded. 'Yes, I saw what those two did, and I abhorred the pain they caused. However, he was God's creature. I know you don't follow any faith, Jasmine, but that isn't necessary. You hold in your heart such love for the child he was, and that's the life we will celebrate. We'll do it regardless of faith or belief

in a great power. We'll do it because it is the right thing to do.'
He smiled. 'I'll take two sugars and a drop of milk with mine.'

Still pondering his words, Jazzy turned towards the kitchen.
'Jasmine?'

She turned to face her friend. 'That's what distinguishes us from them, you know. Our ability to look beneath the monster and try to find a shred of good.'

Jazzy wasn't sure she was at *that* stage yet, or whether she could ever look further than the destruction her siblings had caused, but maybe it was a good philosophy to follow.

Chapter 19

Mhairi

Once the hustle and bustle of the crime scene ended, it felt somewhat anticlimactic. I hadn't been able to settle. The news reports were just regurgitating the same old crap about the murder and though I had tried to focus on washing my pissy clothes and tidying up the flat, my heart wasn't in it. That's why I'm here in Bellsquarry at midnight, despite having somewhere else to be. I'm not the only one here, spying on my sister dearest either, though.

I stay well back, hidden by the bushes, and observe the clapped-out old car that's parked in shadows well down the street. I wouldn't have noticed it if a slight movement of the shadows inside the car hadn't caught my eye. Well, well, well, if it isn't those two wee bairns from before Christmas. I didn't manage to kill the girl then, but I could do it right now, if I wanted to. I'm tempted, I must say. The thought of Jazzy's face if she found them, throats cut, lying there tomorrow morning, is almost too delicious to resist. But I've got other things to do tonight, so I rein myself in.

I thought Jasmine dearest would have been a tad more observant after today's little enactment, but she's let that slip. Tut, tut,

tut, Jazzy. Not good enough. Seems all my pains to disguise myself tonight might have been unnecessary. It's best to be sure of these things. She won't recognise me even if she decides to go for a late-night stroll. I'm not stupid enough to use the same disguise from earlier when I was walking about Porty. Can't be too careful. She's an observant one is Sister Dearest and although she barely glanced at me, who knows what connections our subconscious brains make? Tonight, I'm wearing shoes with inserts that give me an extra three inches in height, a short brown wig with a tartan flat cap on top, and I've bound my chest to create a more masculine appearance. Besides, it's dark and there's no way she'll notice me at this time of night.

I've learned from last time too. When I scope her out, I park my motorbike off road and jog down from the back roads that lead up to the Lang Whang. With Simon gone, I get a strange comfort from being near her. I know she's paranoid – I've seen the falderal she goes through before going indoors. Sometimes she peers through the dark, her eyes scanning the neighbouring gardens, and I wonder if she senses me nearby. It's risky and I don't do it often, but today's the start of the countdown and I just couldn't stop myself.

Her shadow is illuminated against the curtains as she potters around and I wonder what she's thinking. Has she put things together? Is she aware I'm back? Or has she followed my misdirection and assumed the bottle kiln experience was all her failure to prosecute Lucy Taggart's rapist? Oh, I hope so. I really do, because that will make it so much more enjoyable when she begins to suss out that she's completely off the mark.

That stupid task force they've got going has no chance of finding me because they don't understand me. Jazzy does though. She's their only hope, yet they're keeping her in the dark. Well that suits me.

I put my binoculars in my backpack and begin a slow amble to the back roads, but then headlights fill up the street and I shirk back into the shadows. Has our Jazzy got herself a male companion? About time the stupid cow got laid. Might loosen her up. My sister's far too tense for her own good.

The car – an old model Lada – creaks to a halt in front of Jazzy's Mini and I take my cap off as a branch from the neighbour's tree threatens to tug it off. When it catches me on my face, I wrench it from the trunk and toss the branch aside, clean up the blood with the beret before thrusting it into my pocket. My attention's distracted by the prospect of discovering what old loser drives such a car. Not anyone on her team, because I know all of their cars. An old geezer gets out, yanking himself upright using the car door for support – Christ if that's Jazzy's love interest, she's set her sights low and the age high – he must be thirty years older than her at least. He turns to lock the car – with a manual key, would you believe? For God's sake, Jazzy, talk about the bottom of the barrel, hen. For a moment his head of white hair is illuminated in the streetlight and I grin. Well, well, well, if it isn't the old pathologist – Dr Lamond Johnston – well that's a turn-up. Wonder what auld holier than thou's doing on Jazzy's doorstep at this time of night.

Not for the first time I wish I was a fly on the wall inside my sister's house. I've not been able to gain access because she's so paranoid, but I'd love to know what she gets up to in there. Judging by the bags I've seen under her eyes, she doesn't sleep much. Wonder if she has nightmares? Course she does. Jazzy was always too fucking sensitive. No point in hanging about and, besides, I've got other stuff to fry tonight, so I tip my flat bunnet at her window and skedaddle. No rest for the wicked and boy, does Jazzy have a big surprise coming her way. Wish I could be a fly on the wall for that one too.

But for now, I've got things to be getting on with. So, I depart with a last lingering glance in the direction of her poxy wee house and wave a theatrical hand at the two teens who, unknown to them, have been given a reprieve . . . For now.

Chapter 20

Benjy

He hadn't meant to drag Ivor out again. He really hadn't, but something compelled him. He'd spent most of the day thinking, trying to work out a way to be proactive. That's what Ivor said helped her, being proactive. She had her art, but what did Benjy have? Nothing – just a sense of uselessness, a desperation born of feeling he had no control over his life. Everyone else made the decisions about what was good for him. His mum force-fed him food, which he then purged down the toilet, Ivor told him he needed therapy, Uncle Pedro paid ex-soldiers to look after him and Jazzy colluded with him. It didn't matter that he knew it was because they cared about him. That didn't calm the fear, or dull the stomach-curdling anger that roiled in his gut. It didn't stop that fucking song doing his head in, taunting him. *'Girls and boys come out to play'*.

He'd tried to block it out by forcing himself to think about what he could do. How he could snatch back some control. How he, stupid, weak, falling-to-pieces Benjy could make a difference, and as the final strains of the sodding nursery rhyme faded to an irritating but manageable background tune – *'And come with your playfellows into the street'* – the beginnings of an idea took hold, then another followed shortly after and that constant griping in his belly eased just a little. Ivor was right. Being proactive was the first step to recovery. The big question was would he be brave enough to carry his plans out? It was like a test of his willpower. A symbolic chance for him to regain some of the Benjy he'd lost.

He'd been too wired to stay within the confines of Stùrrach after that and so, although he wouldn't confide in his cousin, he convinced her to take one of their drives, which inevitably ended at Jazzy's house. Before he could implement any of his plans, he had to be sure she was okay. Then, maybe, he'd be able to settle for the night.

They took up their usual parking spot in the shadows and settled in for a few hours of listening to Ivor's playlist and scoffing the bags of crisps she always brought with her.

He recognised the old doctor when he pulled up and the knowledge that Jazzy wasn't alone, that she had friends, made him less guilty about the words he'd said to her earlier. He loved her. He really did and she wanted the best for him and Ivor; deep down he knew that. But that didn't stop him directing his anger at her. Next time he saw her he'd apologise. She'd be okay with that. Jazzy always was.

Something caught his eye from the side mirror. Was that a figure in the shadows? He blinked and pulled the rear-view mirror round so he could double-check, but there was nothing there. Maybe he was just seeing monsters where there were none.

He smiled at that and Ivor said. 'You're smiling, Benj.'

He nodded. 'Yes, just happy Jazzy's got other friends. Makes me feel she's not alone.'

Ivor gripped his arm and squeezed. 'So, can we head off home then? I'm freezing.' And without waiting for an answer, she pulled away and they headed back to Stùrrach, the nursery rhyme faded but still present, keeping him company as she drove. *'Girls and boys come out to play'.*

Chapter 21

Wednesday

Ali

Can't bloody believe it? They're still at it. Went to bed last night, and they were at it. Yelling at each other, slamming doors, stomping about like a couple of wildebeest on the rampage. Woke up this morning and they're still at it. All whispered snarls in the kitchen and rattled plates and dishes. When will it all stop? It's got to bloody end soon or I'm going to lose it big time. The tightness is there again – it's like it lurks there waiting to bloom into a full-on panic attack and I'm petrified. Terrified that the next time I won't be able to catch my breath and I'll die up here all alone with them downstairs, casting frosty glances at each other and point-scoring.

I saw *him* when I arrived from school yesterday. The other man. I have biology club on a Wednesday, but I pleaded period pains and skived off. He was just leaving – the boyfriend – his car pulling away when I turned the corner. He didn't see me. At least I don't think he did. I hope not, because the last thing I need is for her to find out I know. If I did, it wouldn't be a secret anymore. It would be out there in the open and everything would blow up.

The thought of getting up and joining them in the kitchen sends my heart skittering all over the shop and the tightness in my chest presses harder. Fuck! I need to sort this, or they'll suspect something's up. I don't want to pull a sickie because they'll hover over me and then my plans for later will be scuppered. I slide my hand under the mattress and pull it out. My bag of antibacterial wipes, and my razor blades. For a long moment I stare at it, trying to talk myself out of it, knowing I'll feel like crap if I do and that I'll still feel like crap if I don't. At least if I resist, I won't have the guilt or the sense of being a failure to contend with. I swallow hard, and shove it back underneath, pushing my arm in as far as I can so there's no way she'll find it if she decides on one of her 'spot checks for Ali's self-destruction kit'.

As tears sting my eyes, I drag myself from the bed and head along the corridor to the bathroom. I have been sharing it with Dad since he got relegated to the spare room. Their voices, all snarky and mean and twisted, drift upstairs like poisonous gas threatening to take over the entire frigging house. Sometimes I hate them. Sometimes I wish I was dead and then I wouldn't have to listen to this crap and wonder what the hell's going to happen to us. I lean on the sink and stare at myself in the mirror. My eyes look enormous and battered – like I'm mental or something. How can they not see it? Why can't they see what they're doing to me? How can they not see *me*?

After my shower – God it was bliss with the water pounding on my head because at least I couldn't hear them – I get dressed, unplug my phone from the charger, and fire off a text to Isla.

Ali: Got a favour to ask, Isl ☺

Isla: kay. What?

Ali: Speak in school, yeah? Meet me at the bench before school?

Isla: 🔥 *but why the big mystery?*

Ali: Tell you then, but you got to promise not to go all ballistic on me

Isla: As if. 😄 *See you later.*

113

I feel better now I've arranged to meet Isla. She won't be pleased about it, but at the very least, she'll cover for me. I know she will. As I leave my room, I hear the kitchen door open and Dad's voice. 'You can be a real fucking bitch sometimes, you know that?'

Then he's striding down the corridor, and from the top of the stairs I see him, rolling a suitcase along. He bumps it down the steps and onto the drive before slamming the door shut behind him. The sound reverberates through the house, shaking it to its very core, and for a second, I wish the whole thing would just fucking collapse and bury me. But no such luck. I creep back to my room and give it five minutes before retracing my steps. It's hard, but I force myself to skip downstairs and head straight for the door, yelling in as normal a voice as I can: 'Running late, Mum. See you later.'

I'm halfway down the drive when she appears at the door and yells after me. 'Ali, catch.' She lobs a cereal bar at me and waves me goodbye. And in that second, I love her. I catch the bar and open my mouth to tell her, but she's already turning back inside, phone to her ear, and I've missed my chance.

Chapter 22

Queenie

Queenie yawned and scratched her oxter. She was in early to view the CCTV footage of the fight between Lewis Fletcher and Dwayne Taggart prior to her meeting with the bouncer and manager of the Black Swan pub in Murrayfield. She'd also hoped to convince Jazzy that she should accompany her to meet with Lucy Taggart, but her colleague had refused. That was the thing with Jazzy. She liked a bit of self-flagellation. The stupid wee lassie thought it helped to assuage her guilt. Thought it was her duty, her responsibility, or some such daft notion. She wasn't to blame for the fiasco with that rape trial, but the woman wouldn't be told. *I made a promise to Lucy Taggart, Queenie, and it all went wrong. I owe her this.* Queenie repeated the words in a whiny tone that had no resemblance whatsoever to how Jazzy had uttered them.

'Talking to yourself, Queenie? You know what they say? It's a slippery slope and all that.' Geordie slipped into the chair next to hers, his legs stretching under the table so she could see his toes sticking out the other side. *Bloody lanky git!*

She made a show of looking at her watch. Her lips pursed as

if she was about to deposit a kiss on some unsuspecting passer-by. Geordie edged away from her just in case. 'You said half seven and . . .' he too made a great show of looking at his watch '. . . what have we here? Oh yes, seven twenty-five. So, not late.'

'Aye, but you didn't fetch the coffees, did you? Mega fail, Geordie, mega fail. You know it's the last person to arrive's job to bring the drinks . . . and if they're a cheeky long-legged bugger like you, maybe even a bacon piece too.'

'How does that even make any sense? I mean, how could I know I was the last to arrive until I got here . . .?'

'Aye well, that's where a bit of forward thinking wouldn't go amiss. You should've brought the drinks on the off chance I was already here. Besides . . .' Queenie prodded a thumb into her chest '. . . I bought them yesterday for you and that wee numpty, Haggis.'

Grinning, Geordie got up and walked to a desk near the door, where two coffees in takeaway cups and two wrapped rolls sat. 'God job I thought ahead then. Now, can you get the footage up whilst I unwrap the rolls and for God's sake tuck a napkin in your front. I'm not interviewing a witness with you looking like a kid's party gone wrong.'

Queenie huffed, but did as he said. Craig had pressed this shirt for her that morning and she was hoping to get two days' wear out of it. He'd got a bit moany about being her dogsbody and never having an iron out of his hand. Not like it was her fault she sploshed Choc-o-pops down the first one he'd ironed this morning, was it? Accidents happen, don't they?

In silence, they watched the CCTV footage of the scuffle a few times as they ate their rolls. The relevant part only lasted about ninety seconds, so she rewound an extra minute and they watched it again. First at normal speed and then slowed down so they could absorb the detail.

Dwayne Taggart's van drove past the CCTV and then parked in a space that only allowed the camera to record the front end of the vehicle. His headlights went out, and moments later Taggart walked in front of his van, head down, absorbed in something on his phone screen as he strolled towards the pub entrance.

Queenie paused the recording. 'Completely oblivious to his surroundings, isn't he? Like a bloke heading into the pub for a business meeting, like he said in his statement, eh?'

'Aye, that's how it looks. In that case, why can't we trace the number of the guy who arranged the meeting and why hasn't he come forward? Local news channels have broadcast loads of appeals for information on the brawl and any subsequent sightings of Taggart.'

'Are you suggesting that Fletcher lured him there and not the other way around, like we initially thought?'

Geordie shrugged. 'Could be. Let it play again.'

As Taggart slowed, and laughed, still engrossed on his phone, another figure – Lewis Fletcher – unsteady on his feet, weaved towards him. He'd clearly had a skinful and was zig-zagging all over the joint. However, his chin was tilted upwards and his entire posture emitted waves of determined aggression. Meanwhile, Taggart glanced up, saw the drunk guy, appeared to dismiss him as non-threatening and, speeding up a little, looked back at his screen. Then, it looked as if Fletcher had said something because Taggart stopped and spun round on his heel.

Queenie paused the recording again and zoomed in on his face. 'Look?'

Geordie leaned in and clicked his teeth. 'He looks surprised, confused.'

'Aye, that's what I'm seeing.'

She pressed play and Fletcher lurched forward, his fists balled by his sides. Taggart took a backward step, hands splayed before him, shaking his head. Fletcher raised his arm, pulled his fist back and sort of dived towards Taggart. Taggart retreated and Fletcher's fist grazed his chin as he fell forward and landed on his face, bursting his nose open. Not deterred – or maybe anaesthetised by the amount of alcohol in his bloodstream – Fletcher batted away Taggart's outstretched arm and heaved himself up. No sooner was he upright than his fist was back and barrelling into Taggart's face. Taggart reeled backwards and hesitated, blinking a few times, before ramming his knuckles into Fletcher and landing a kick to his balls for good measure.

Two men rushed over from the pub entrance. One dressed in black with a white shirt and tie – either an undertaker or the bouncer. He grabbed Taggart's arm and forcefully pulled him away, phone out to report the incident to the police as was logged on the system. Another person – the manager – knelt beside Fletcher, prone on the ground and yelled up at Taggart. Taggart stood, wide-eyed, staring at the unmoving man lying on the pavement. His face had paled and his shoulders slumped.

Queenie stopped the recording again. 'So . . .?'

'No shite! I'd put money on Taggart not recognising Fletcher till that point. Look at him. He's shaking. He looks ready to keel over. If that guy's not in shock, then my granny's a banana.'

Tapping the screen, Queenie exhaled. 'So, if he didn't recognise Fletcher and he was oblivious to his surroundings, he hadn't set up the meeting, had he? Fletcher was the one who seemed to expect Taggart to be there. What the fuck is that all about? Why would Fletcher want to have it out with Taggart?'

'Maybe he blames Taggart for losing his job and his home . . .' But Geordie's tone was sceptical. 'Six years have passed. Why now? There's something here we're not seeing. This isn't as straightforward as we first thought, is it?'

'Aye, something's definitely rotten in the state of Edinburgh.'

Geordie grinned. 'Didn't have you down as a Shakespeare lover.'

'Eh?'

'You know, the something's rotten quote you paraphrased just then.'

Queenie ran her fingers through her hair. 'Shakespeare? Fuck's sake, laddie, get yourself an education. That was Burns, no' bloody Shakespeare. Did they no' teach you anything at school?'

And with Geordie shaking his head in disbelief as he trailed after her, she marched out, grabbing her jacket and announcing to the empty room. 'Shakespeare? Bloody Shakespeare? The laddie's a damn Philistine!'

Chapter 23

Jazzy

Jazzy had woken feeling like a steamroller had rolled over her body, breaking every bone. Her head throbbed, her eyes were gritty and her throat was raw with all the tears she'd shed with Lamond Johnston last night. He'd listened to her talk about her conflicting emotions about her brother and hadn't judged or criticised or made her feel bad for still caring about him even after everything she'd done. It had been cathartic to express her deepest, most horrible thoughts without fear of being found wanting. During the evening, they'd decided that after the funeral directors lowered the coffin into the grave, Lamond would say a few words about Simon as a child and offer the hope that his final resting place would bring him peace. It was enough and an immense weight was lifted from Jazzy's shoulders by finalising her brother's funeral. It was a dignified plan. It wasn't flashy, which would mock the harm he caused – but it was heartfelt. Jazzy was comfortable with it, which Lamond had told her was the most important thing.

After the pathologist left, she slumped in her bed and cried.

For hours the tears had flowed as memory after memory engulfed her and, instead of shutting them down, she'd allowed them free rein. Her guilt, grief, and anger poured out of her, like a bloodletting. Finally, she fell into an exhausted sleep, devoid of dreams, for the first time in months. That it was so short-lived was her only regret.

As she drew up in front of the Taggart family's familiar house opposite Leith Links, she wished she was better prepared. During the drive, she'd considered why Lucy Taggart might want to meet her. She could think of only one possibility: to lambast her once more for failing to bring her rapist to justice. Now, Jazzy had given Lucy additional cause to hate her because if things had gone to plan six years ago, they would have locked Lewis Fletcher up in prison. Instead, he was languishing in a mortuary, and Lucy's brother Dwayne was on the run from the police. She studied the house, wishing everything could have been different. She'd spent countless hours there with Lucy in the past, but the passing of time had brought a shabbiness to the once cheerful home. The small square of lawn had become overgrown and filled with weeds, the windows appeared grimy, and a greyish aura of despair surrounded the building. It seemed like it had given up when Lucy's rapist went unpunished. The curtains twitched in the front room, alerting Jazzy to the fact that her arrival had been noticed. No point in dilly-dallying.

She walked up the small path, but before she rang the bell the door opened and Lucy was there in front of her. For a moment, the two women stared at each other. Jazzy drunk in the healthy sheen on Lucy's face. Her hair, once dull and listless, was transformed into a sleek bob that framed her face. Her cheeks were no longer sunken and her eyes shone with life. Lucy met her gaze with inscrutable silence but stood back and motioned for her to enter. Jazzy wondered what the other woman saw when she looked at her – the police officer who had once been her friend and offered her support? Or did she see a liar? An unfeeling bitch?

Lucy, straight-backed and silent, walked through to the living room and after only a moment's hesitation, Jazzy followed her through. 'Coffee?'

Unable to find her voice, Jazzy nodded.

'Sit down then, Jazzy. I'll only be a minute.'

Jazzy's feverish eyes devoured the changes to the once familiar room. The suite was different and the absence of knitting bundled in a basket next to the armchair by the fire reminded Jazzy that Lucy's mum had recently passed away. Pictures on the wall – Lucy's graduation photo, brought a smile to Jazzy's lips. Lucy had been an A student, and it filled Jazzy's heart to see that, despite the trauma she'd suffered, the girl had completed her degree. Her parents would have been so proud of her. The only child in their family to achieve such a thing.

Lucy returned with two mugs, one of which she deposited on a small occasional table beside the couch, before retreating to the chair by the fire. 'Sit.'

Jazzy perched on the edge of the sofa and waited. This was Lucy's show, not hers.

Intent dark eyes studied her for what seemed like forever, but Jazzy resisted the temptation to fidget. Finally, Lucy spoke. 'You look like shite, DS Solanki. Mind you, I'm not surprised. Especially considering all that stuff with your siblings.' A smile flickered for a second on her lips and then was gone. 'Siblings, eh?'

Assuming it was a rhetorical question, Jazzy nodded, but didn't reply.

'You'll be wondering why I requested this visit?'

Jazzy's voice was hoarse, but she managed a simple 'Yes'.

'Well, I'm not gonna lie. I'm glad that bastard's dead, but no matter what you lot think, and regardless of that stupid fight the other night, Dwayne didn't kill him. Dwayne's not a killer. Someone set him up. Some bloke arranged to meet him in that pub for a business deal. He's got a wee plumbing business has Dwayne. Done well for himself. Let go of some of his rage. He wouldn't risk all of that. Not for a piece of shite like Fletcher.' She pursed her lips and inhaled. 'Look, it's quite clear. Instead of the fella he was expecting, Fletcher turned up in the car park and attacked him. Dwayne saw red and he shouldn't have, but he *didn't* go out of his way to find him. He's moved on from that angry lad he was. We've all moved on.'

Jazzy took a sip from her coffee. 'So where is he then, Lucy? If he didn't do it, he should come forward so we can eliminate him from our inquiries.'

Lucy frowned. 'That's why you're here, Jazzy. I've no idea where my brother is and he wouldn't leave me worried like this. I've checked out everywhere he might have been. His mates, girlfriend, ex-girlfriend, ex-employers – everybody I can think of and nobody's seen him.' She leaned forward, her intent gaze compelling Jazzy to hear her out. 'After all we've been through as a family, he wouldn't disappear without letting Dad and me know he's okay. Aye, he had his rough times. Barely held it together if I'm honest, but he pulled through and he's been holding it together for a while now. He'd not fuck it all up over Fletcher.'

She snorted. 'Sometimes, I think that bastard lost more when he escaped legal justice than he would have if he'd done his few years in the nick. He lost everything that day. And seeing him descend into the bottom feeder he was made us happy, made it easier to come to terms with it all. You didn't keep your word, but the bastard suffered, and that was enough for us.'

'So, what are you saying? We're all square?' Even as she uttered the words, Jazzy knew that no matter how Lucy replied, she would never forgive herself.

Chin raised, Lucy stared, eyes cold as ice, right into Jazzy's. '*No chance!* No, you let us down. We deserved to see him go down *publicly* for what he did, and that didn't happen. You don't get off so easy, DS Solanki. No, what I'm saying is *you* owe *me* big time.'

As Lucy allowed her message to settle, Jazzy's stomach contracted – and there it was again – the clamp, gripping her gut and squeezing it like there was no tomorrow. With Fletcher dead, Jazzy could only think of one thing that Lucy might expect from her, and that was a promise she couldn't make. Surely, Lucy understood that?

Eyes narrowing, Lucy smiled a humourless smile, as if sensing Jazzy's disquiet. She wasn't letting Jazzy off the hook and, as the words fell from her lips, Jazzy began shaking her head. 'I want you to find Dwayne and prove he's innocent.'

'You know I can't . . .'

Lucy snorted, her eyes flashing, her lips curled. Every part of the younger woman's body seemed to radiate venom and every ounce was directed at Jazzy. She took a step closer to her prey. 'Don't you dare, Jazzy Solanki. Don't you fucking dare say you can't promise me. You were all too quick to promise last time, weren't you? *This* is on *you*. This entire fucking thing is on you. So, you better find my brother and make things right.'

For a moment, their eyes locked, then Jazzy's shoulders slumped. Despite all that the woman had endured, Jazzy would have to let her down again. How could she promise something she couldn't guarantee? Despite her misgivings, Dwayne was still officially the main suspect and she couldn't let Lucy down again by giving her false hope. From somewhere, she found the courage to stand her ground. 'The only promise I can make is that I'll do my job, Lucy. You know that. I'll do my utmost to find out who killed Lewis Fletcher, but if it was Dwayne, then there's nothing I can do about that.'

Lucy snorted. 'Grow a fucking backbone, Solanki. You're nothing but a coward. My brother didn't kill anyone. You better prove that. Now get the fuck out of my house.'

Chest tight and aware that she could have handled that situation better, Jazzy strode back down the narrow hallway and burst out onto the path, glad to escape into the fresh air. Guilt hung round her like a cloak. She'd let not just Lucy, but the entire Taggart family, down again. A haunting cry echoed from the living room as the door slammed shut behind her. Jazzy closed her eyes and hesitated before continuing back to her car, knowing that Lucy's heart-wrenching sob would echo in her heart for a long time.

Chapter 24

Ali

Isla had met me as promised at the bench, but she hadn't been at all keen to cover for me.

'Come on, Ali, you're really going to go out with Jan Carmichael? On a school night? Really?'

After each of her questions I'd nodded, my certainty of my friend alibiing me fading with each nod. Isla's face screwed up as she looked at me, her head shaking from side to side.

'Come on, Isla. Please. I just want . . .'

'Want what, Ali? To get rat-arsed with someone you hardly know? To get grounded for the rest of your life? To . . .'

'Yeah, yeah, I get it Isl, but can't you just . . .?'

Isla jumped up, yanking her schoolbag onto her shoulder and exhaled. 'You can say you're at mine, but if your mum and dad ask, I'm not gonna lie for you.'

I nodded. At least, in spite of her reservations, Isla wasn't going to dob me in. That was probably the most I could hope for. Now that I'd sorted a story out with Isla I felt happier about seeing Jan later on.

The day dragged on, washing like background music right over my head. I'm desperate to see Jan, to finalise our plans but the cow's not even turned up for school. Not after I've made plans with her. Maybe she'll come in for the afternoon session and look for me here again. Who am I kidding though? It's more than likely all been a huge wind-up. Why would Jan Carmichael want to hang out with me, anyway? I should have known that the queen of the school bitches wouldn't choose to spend time with me. Why would she, when she's got all her cronies around? Bitch probably got a better offer.

I'm torn between relief and annoyance that my plans for tomorrow evening have fallen through. Mostly relief if I'm honest. I've never done anything like this before and I've never been in a pub without Mum and Dad either and definitely not one like the Tartan Sporran. I've heard it's a right dive. It pisses me off that I'm not good enough for a skank like Jan Carmichael. Not good enough to keep my parents together and not good enough to go to the diviest pub in Bathgate with the school bad girl, either. I know it shouldn't hurt, but it does. It *really* does. Nobody likes rejection after all.

After Biology, Isla makes a beeline for me, probably wants to try to talk me out of it again, but I'm determined. Besides, she's with Benjy and Ivor and I can't be doing with them today. Ivor's okay, but that Benjy's getting weirder by the day. I've seen him walking round the football pitch talking to himself. I know they went through some crap last year, but I've got my own crap to deal with. So, I pretend I don't see them and dodge outside like I did yesterday. The very last thing I want is Isla asking why I won't be going to her place for revision tonight instead of going ahead with my plans. I just need some space. Some time on my own. Don't think Isla has ever broken one of her parents' rules. Why would she? She doesn't need to escape a toxic environment, does she? No need for her to rebel.

It's not that I want to fall out with her. It's just that she wouldn't get it. *Her* ma and da are normal. You know, no blazing rows, no stony silences, no nervous tension all the time? *They* talk nicely to each other and Isla would just assume I'm exaggerating. She'd be all, 'I'm sure it'll pass, Ali. They'll sort it out. Promise they will.' Then she'd want to show me something on her spanking new iPad as if I was all sorted and everything was okay because *she* proclaimed that it would be and everything's always okay in Isla world.

I know that's unfair. Isla's a good mate. She'd listen to me and she'd try her best to understand *and* she'd try to cheer me up, too. It's just . . . I don't think they *will* sort it out. Not this time, because I know something my dad doesn't know and keeping it secret's making me sick. I know about the fucking boyfriend.

'Ali, Ali.'

Crap, even her voice is so reasonable. So full of concern, maybe even a bit of hurt creeping in. I'm acting like a real cow, but I can't stand to be with her right now. I need someone different. Someone to force me from my comfort zone and make me feel something other than this incessant dread.

I scurry on, pushing other kids out of the way, and in my haste to escape I ignore their pissed-off yells. I need to be outside. Away from the busy school corridors. Away from the voices and laughter that are giving me a headache. It's like they're magnifying in my ears, taking over my body. Disjointed voices yapping at me – 'she's going mad'; 'she's losing it big time'; 'look at her, running away like a frightened rabbit. With a daughter like her, it's no wonder her parents don't want to stay together.'

My bag bounces against my side as I raise my hands to my head and try to block out the sounds. That pounding thing's happening again in my chest and, as I burst through the doors, raking in big gulps of air that slice my throat before choking me, I run. My soles slap against the concrete in time with my heartbeat. I need to get away. I need to get to the bench. The voices fade as I focus on moving forward, my eyes on the empty wooden seat, my throat aching with the effort of drawing air into my lungs.

When I reach the table, I fall onto the chair, thrusting my schoolbag on top and trying to get a grip. I'm sweating now too and as I sit, head bowed, fighting to inhale, my fingers creep towards my bag buckle and rest there, taunting me, almost begging me to do it. To take it and slam the metal prong through my palm. From nowhere, the belief that this is the only way I'll gain control fills me. It's the only way I'll survive today. Tears well in my eyes and still I struggle to draw in air. I wonder if I'm going to faint, and that makes the banging in my chest worse. *Shite, shite, shite, shite, shite! Get a grip, Ali.* Just get a fucking grip before one of the tossers with the ball notices. Bad enough that Jan and her pals are probably having a laugh at my expense without a bunch of boys telling their mates that I'm a weirdo who cries on her own in the playground at dinnertime.

My finger finds the sharp end of the metal spiky bit of buckle and it's like a strange calm descends. It's yellow in colour – like the sun – all warm and fuzzy and calming. Not like the scarlet cloud that hangs over our house. On automatic pilot, I tug my sleeve up and with my left hand holding the spike steady, I drag it right over my arm – not too hard – just hard enough. Enough to release the blood and, as I watch the maroon globules gather along the two-inch line, I am embraced by a golden cushion. My chest loosens, and the air flows unfettered into my lungs. This must be why they call it mellow yellow. The thought makes me smile, but it also brings me to my senses. I shouldn't have done this and especially not here. Not in public. A furtive sideways glance tells me I've been lucky. No one's bothered about the weird loner on the bench furthest away from the school building. I rummage in one of the many side pockets in my backpack and extract my antibacterial wipes. I should have cleaned the buckle before I used it, but this will have to do. The bleeding has already stopped. It wasn't a deep cut. Not this time. I mop it, use another wipe, then pull my cuff back down, promising myself this will be the last time.

My phone pings and when I flip it over and see Jan's name on the screen, my heart skips a beat – but in a good way this time.

Jan: You still okay to paaaartaaay on Thursday? 😍 😎 😷

I can hardly believe it. We're still on.

Ali: Yeah, where and when?

Jan: After school. Meet you at Costa, then mine. CU then. Don't forget, though, it's our secret.

I clasp my phone to my chest and am grinning from ear to ear when Isla sits down opposite me. Thank fuck, she's ditched the other two. 'Didn't you hear me calling you, Ali?'

She looks at me with her big reproachful eyes, her tone all 'what's got into you' and that takes a bit of the shine off Jan's message. But not too much. I shrug and grin. 'No, must have been daydreaming.'

She casts me one of her sideways glances – the one that says, *Aye right!* 'What are you so happy about?'

I shrug and answer, 'Why wouldn't I be happy? The sun's shining, isn't it?'

Chapter 25

Jan

It was like the bastard was watching her because no sooner had Jan finished texting the dozy cow on her real phone than the one at the bottom of her bag vibrated. She was waiting at Livvy bus station to catch the one home. Her sister, the bitch, had discovered she'd nicked her shoes, so she'd had to resort to Plan B. A bit of shoplifting from the Primark in the Almondvale Shopping Centre. Shame she couldn't check out the Bathgate one as it was closer to home, but the bastards were on to her there, so Almondvale it was. At least it was busy, and she managed to snag what she wanted. Alongside her make-up, she'd shoved in the nicked shoes, skimpy top and skirt. No way was she going to fork out for clothes for that girl to wear tonight. No bloody chance and if she had to shoplift, then she might as well make it worth her while. She'd give the bitch *her* old clothes to wear tonight and she could wear the nice new ones she'd swiped.

Hearing the phone made her feel uneasy. Vulnerable like, and she glanced round, checking to see if anyone was watching her. Apart from a crowd of kids waiting for their bus and an auld granny with one of them tartan trollies and a pisshead murmuring to himself in the corner, there was nobody about. Maybe she was being paranoid. It's not like she'd been followed, was it? She cast another glance round, then shrugged and delved deep to find the burner phone. This might be a public place, but it wasn't like any bastard was paying her any attention, was it? Still, she didn't want to keep the cash cow waiting, so she pulled the phone to the top of her bag and, keeping it semi-hidden under the clothes she'd nicked, she glanced at the text . . .

Trust everything's in order for Thursday?

Fuck's sake! Jan rolled her eyes and repeated the phrase under her breath, making her voice all posh and stuck-up. '*Trust everything's in order for Thursday?*' Stupid posh bastard, but posh bastard or not, Jan wasn't going to keep him waiting. Her fingers flew over the screen as she composed her reply, chortling like an alky who'd found a fiver and a bottle of whisky.

Jan: Oh yes. Thanking you for your felicitations. Everything is tickety-boo for Thursday. And yourself? Are you well?

Her grin widened as she reread her sarcastic reply and her finger hovered over the send button. Did she dare? Nah, no point in pissing anybody off. Not when there was dosh at stake. As her bus pulled into the stand, she deleted her words and instead inserted a thumbs up, before thrusting it back in her bag and hopping onto the waiting bus.

Chapter 26

Queenie

Queenie parked in the Black Swan car park and peered through the windscreen at the pub. It was situated on the Murrayfield Stadium side of the Glasgow to Edinburgh (via Falkirk) railway line, a stone's throw from the rugby stadium. It was a quiet residential area where fighting was anathema. She frowned and tapped her fingers on the steering wheel.

Things weren't adding up. Statements from Lewis Fletcher's fellow rough sleepers, his ex-wife, former friends and colleagues, made it clear that this wasn't the sort of establishment that he'd have frequented – not anymore. Not since his descent into homelessness and addiction. 'Well, we're here, Geordie boy. Get yer arse oot of my car – we've work to do.'

Geordie, who'd endured Queenie's singing all the way from Livingston to Murrayfield, looked relieved as he stepped from the car into the warm summer breeze. Queenie hefted herself out and joined him by the Land Rover. Hands deep in her pockets, she scowled around the area as if expecting a plague of rampaging zombies to appear from the adjoining streets. 'Something's not right, Geordie. What do you reckon?'

The other detective looked around, taking in the rows of detached houses that backed onto the car park at one end and the row of shops that did the same at the other. 'This is far from the spit and sawdust pubs Lewis Fletcher would frequent. It's all a mystery.'

'Aye, one we'll need to unravel before we leave here.' Queenie tutted and took note of the few vehicles parked in the car park. All were upmarket models boasting newish number plates. Although the manager would be waiting for them inside, she wanted to see the lay of the land for herself IRL, as that wee waste of space Haggis was always saying. Bloody pillock! In real life? Shite, kids these days needed to get their heids out of their computers and run around playing a wee game of peevers or chap door run. That'd sort them out!

She trailed behind Geordie, who sped over to a space further along, eyeing the positioning of the security camera in relation to the parking spot. 'I think Taggart parked here, Queenie.'

Queenie joined him. He was right. The angle of the camera would render most of Taggart's vehicle out of shot, leaving only the front of the van and the number plate visible. She walked to where she thought his car door would be and waited, hand extended, as if ready to slam the door shut. Her face was a balloon of pure joy. There was nothing she liked more than a scene re-enactment. It made her feel all Columbo. 'Well, what are you waiting for, son? Get ye're skinny arse over there. You're going to be Fletcher and I'll be Taggart. We'll act out the scene, complete with the appropriate expressions and suchlike. I'm not expecting an Oscar or anything, son, but we should gie it our best shot.'

Geordie groaned. 'Do we have to? Really?'

'Don't be such a misery guts. It'll be informative. We can assess where that wee nyaff Fletcher was before he came into view. There's a lot resting on this, so keep your wits about you.'

Unable to disagree with Queenie's logic, Geordie shambled over to the approximate area from which Fletcher had come. Around him were a few shadowy car spaces with no CCTV coverage backing onto gardens with high fences. If Fletcher had been loitering here, he'd have been almost unnoticeable, especially with the car park fuller than it was today. This area was well away from the footpath leading to the parking area. Assuming he hadn't jacked a car and driven in or been dropped off, in order to have approached Taggart from this direction, Fletcher would already have been there.

Queenie surveyed the spot Geordie had chosen with critical eyes. Had Fletcher been waiting in the shadows? For Taggart specifically, or just any random punter? If he was waiting for Taggart, it threw up all sorts of additional questions. Like, why and *how* the hell had he known the other man would be there at that time? Why would he lure Taggart here to an area he must have been unfamiliar with? And why now? The incident report stated that Taggart claimed to have arranged the meeting in the Black Swan only an hour earlier. Had it been Fletcher on the phone? That seemed unlikely because he'd been rat-arsed when the incident happened only an hour later. Coincidence? Could Fletcher have been hanging around ready to pick a fight with anyone? Queenie tutted as, like an ear worm, Jazzy's 'there's no such thing as coincidence' squirmed in her ear accompanied by an image of her friend, arms crossed and expression earnest as she drummed that principle into Fenton and Geordie. Jazzy took the training of the two inexperienced detectives in her charge very seriously.

Shoulders hunched and casting wee sideways glances about him, Geordie waited for Queenie to begin her walk, phone in hand, towards the pub entrance. He wasn't an actor for Christ's sake – at least not unless he was in drag. As Misty Thistle, he could ham it up with the best of them, but as Detective Geordie McBurnie, he found this sort of thing excruciating.

'Come on, Geordie, son. Are you ready? Remember, you're off your face, so act like it, eh?'

She started to walk, and Geordie tried to estimate the necessary pace to make sure he arrived at the correct position at the correct time. This was hell for him and it wasn't helped by her loud running commentary.

'Gie it some laldy, Geordie. You're no' oot for a walk in the park, yer supposed to be pissed ass the proverbial fart. Bring your acting skills into play. Make it realistic, otherwise there's no point in doing it, is there?'

Geordie's scowl deepened as he chuntered under his breath. 'I'll bloody kill you, Queenie. Why, for once, can't you be like everyone else?'

'What's that?'

'Nothing.' His head jerked up, panicking that she'd heard his whispered moans, but she was too busy channelling Taggart, absorbed in some hilarious reel or something on his phone. He stopped. Frowned, then . . . 'Queenie . . .'

'I'm not Queenie. I told you we need to channel . . .'

He raised an arm and pointed beyond her to the building backing onto the car park behind her. She turned, took a moment to register what he was pointing at and then spun back to him, grinning. 'Ye belter, son. Ye absolute bloody fandabidozi belter. Fingers crossed it's operational, eh? Now, let's have a wee look at where the actual fight took place. Then you can hotfoot it round there and grab that camera footage before they delete it.'

There was nothing to indicate that a bloody fight had taken place a few yards from the entrance to the Black Swan. Any blood had been cleaned away, but that wasn't what Queenie was interested in. She wanted to ascertain how much of the incident would have been visible to the pub patrons. Most had claimed not to see anything, but in light of her disquiet about the 'chance' meeting between two men who had managed to avoid each other for six years and who both had motive to hate each other, she wanted to re-interview any witnesses who hadn't come forward. She took out her scraggy wee notebook and a pen, which promptly leaked all over her fingers, prompting Geordie to offer his. 'So, are we agreed those three window tables to the right there, and the two to the left, plus the smokers' shelter, would all offer a prime view of the incident?'

'At a push, maybe the third table to the left, but I think only the person sitting at this side would be able to see here because of that bush.'

'Aye, I'll add that seat to my list. Hopefully their internal security cameras will help us ascertain who was sitting in those seats, for it always takes yonks for them to go through their till receipts and payments and knowing our luck they'd insist on a bloody warrant.'

Queenie closed her notebook and began marching purposefully towards the entrance where a man – presumably the manager – was watching them. Over her shoulder in a voice that carried through the car park and which the manager would certainly have heard she said, 'I'm away in to see what his nibs the mediocre manager, and beefcake the brainless bouncer, have to say.'

Geordie flinched and, with an apologetic shrug to the flushed-faced manager, he headed off to collect the footage as Queenie descended on the pub all business and no arguments. 'So, I've seen the CCTV from this camera, son, and I've read your statement, but I'm a wee bit puzzled.'

She strode past the man, who, wrong-footed, took a moment to catch up as she marched over to the table where another man – the bouncer from the CCTV footage, sat. Smiling from one to the other, she plonked herself down. Neither man seemed completely comfortable with Queenie's amiable look, but as the manager slid onto the seat next to his employee, he said, 'We're here to help in any way we can.'

Queenie beat the rhythm from the *EastEnders'* theme tune on the table top, her grin widening. 'Well, that's what I like to hear. Witnesses prepared to do their civic duty, you know? Give a wee bit back to society? Contribute to law and order. That's all pure dead brilliant. So . . .' Her grin faded, and she inched forward to the edge of the seat, her arms resting on the table top as she sent a severe glance first to the manager and then to the bouncer. 'What made you two decide that Dwayne Taggart was the aggressor in this particular instance?'

Mediocre Manager blinked a few times, as if this was the last question he expected to be asked, whilst Brainless the Bouncer looked as if he didn't fully understand the question. This fact was substantiated when he screwed up his face and elicited a single sound. 'Eh?'

Queenie leaned over and patted his arm. 'Aw, there, there, son, dinnae fash yerself. I know that was a hard one.'

The bouncer's confused look intensified, but Mediocre Manager stepped into the breach, all bluster and sarcasm. 'Well, it was obvious, really. The homeless guy was on the ground, his nose bust and the big guy was looming over him, ready to lamp him again. He'd have killed him if we hadn't dragged him off.'

Brainless nodded, but Queenie persisted. 'Aye, but did you *actually* see the big guy lamp the wee one?' As the two looked at each other with blank expressions, Queenie huffed as if they'd caused her a great inconvenience and took her phone from her pocket. 'See, if you look here – this is the footage from your camera. What do you see?'

She played the minute or so before the bouncer, followed by the manager, appeared on scene. Both watched until the end before Mediocre leaned back and exhaled. 'Shite . . . the wee one whammed the bigger one and was so pissed he landed on his face.'

'Aye, that's about the sum of it, right enough. Puts a wee bit of a different complexion on your official statement, does it no'?'

The two men looked agape at Queenie, who shook her head in a 'well my hands are tied' sort of way. 'I mean, that's like false evidence, if you get my drift.'

'But we didn't mean to. That's what we thought happened. I mean, two guys brawling in the car park and one on the ground with his nose bashed in, what were we meant to think?'

The bouncer's words came out on a high squeak and an avalanche of halitosis that had Queenie edging backwards.

'Aye well . . .' She paused, tapped her chubby finger on her lip and then clicked it. 'I know, you get me your till receipts for all the punters in these . . .' she indicated the tables that she and Geordie had identified as having possible eyewitnesses to the fight '. . . and the footage from that camera over the bar that includes these tables, and we'll say no more about it, eh. How does that sound?'

For a second it looked like Mediocre Manager might object, but then, true to his name, he acquiesced and got up to get the information Queenie had requested. 'Won't be long.'

'Aye, a wee soda water and lime, since I'm on duty, would be nice, thanks. And a bag of Nobby's nuts too.'

The manager rolled his eyes and, shoulders hunched, sidled towards the office with a: 'Sean, get the officer her drink.'

In her element, Queenie picked up her phone and was halfway through a game of Candy Crush when Geordie hustled back in. 'You'll never believe it, Queenie.'

'Shite. I've nearly beaten my highest score. Can it no' wait?'

The bouncer pushed her drink towards her and flung the nuts on the table, before glancing at Geordie. His chin lifted in an 'I suppose you want one too' kind of way. Geordie shook his head and plonked down beside Queenie, waiting till the bouncer had departed before grabbing Queenie's phone from her hand and turning his towards her instead. 'Look at this.'

With an exaggerated sigh and an eye-roll to underline her displeasure, Queenie took his phone and pressed play on the CCTV footage and watched in silence. When she'd observed the clip, she hit play again, and then a third time for luck. 'Well, Geordie, are you no' the wee spanker?

'Eh, no.' Geordie glanced round, hoping the bouncer was still out of earshot, but Queenie's voice was loud and judging by the guy's grin, her words had carried over to the bar.

'Dinnae be modest now, son. You're a wee spanker all right. You're my wee spanker, aren't ye?'

'Again, *no*.' Geordie's tone was forceful, but rather than argue the point with Queenie, he'd lost such arguments too many times to want to lengthen this one, he diverted her attention back to the clip. 'You saw it too?'

Queenie grabbed her glass, downed a few mouthfuls of her drink and rammed her mouth full of nuts before responding and, of course, when she did, Geordie was showered with chilli-flavoured crumbs. 'Aye.' She lowered her tone. 'That wee scrotum Fletcher wasn't on his own in those shadows. Blink and you might have missed it, but no. Definitely someone there. We need to get this enhanced. See if we can get an ID.'

Mediocre Manager returned, a USB of the bar footage in one hand, and a print out of the transactions from the relevant tables in the other.

'You're a wee belter, son. We'll not forget your cooperation.' And grabbing the stuff, she and Geordie went back to her car. 'We'll get one of those civilian analysts to go through these receipt printouts and then get a uniform or two to follow up with the punters. Who knows what this lot might have seen? We need to direct their attention to that part of the car park.' As she swung from the entrance, she gripped Geordie's knee and squeezed. 'Good work, son. I know there's a reason I brought you with me and not that wee useless Haggis.'

Geordie smirked. 'You know as well as I do that Fenton would have got the footage just as I've done.'

Queenie laughed. 'Aye, but don't tell him that, will you? It'd just spoil my fun.'

Chapter 27

Jazzy

Still shaken from her meeting with Lucy, Jazzy was desperate for a reported sighting of Dwayne Taggart, but when she got back to Livingston, there was still none. Lucy's conviction that her brother wouldn't go AWOL like this made her nervous. What were they missing?

The briefing had already started when she walked in, but it soon became clear that where she hadn't progressed the investigation, Queenie and Geordie had.

With a nod in her direction to acknowledge her arrival, Elliot turned to Queenie. 'So, let me get this right, Queenie. You're telling us that someone else was in a shadowy part of the car park with Fletcher just prior to the fight between him and Taggart?'

Frowning, Jazzy perched on the edge of a table at the front of the room. This wasn't what she'd expected Queenie and Geordie to come back with, but she was pleased with their attention to detail and so proud of them. *D team rock!*

'Aye.' Queenie bounced on her toes. 'We'll show you in a minute, although we've sent it off to the techie squad to get it enhanced. Geordie will get his copy up on the big screen and you'll be able to see it for yourselves. But that's not all.' Her grinning face was flushed and full of pride. 'Me and Geordie watched and rewatched the initial car park footage and it's clear that not only did *Fletcher* start the fight, but that Taggart, initially at least, had no idea who he was. No' surprising really considering how minging he was. It's all well dodgy.'

Elliot nodded. 'You can say that again. So, let's view it. Geordie?'

Geordie stepped up and with the blinds shut to avoid the glare Jazzy, Fenton, Elliot, Geordie and Queenie watched the clip with the shadowy figure in the depths of the car park.

'It's not very clear. Hard to make out features or even the gender of the person.' Jazzy, leaning forward, narrowed her eyes, then sank back into her seat, unsure if she felt relief that they couldn't identify Fletcher's companion or if the heavy weight of worry intensified. Everything Queenie and Geordie had brought back threw the previous day's assumptions into doubt. Of course, Jazzy's thoughts inevitably went to the Bitch. What if all of this was just a massive, elaborate manoeuvre designed to freak her out? It wouldn't be the first time Mhairi had behaved erratically. Modifying her tone to cover her exasperation, she shrugged. 'Let's hope they can clear it up a bit, otherwise all we know is that Fletcher was with a shadowy figure moments before he attacked Taggart, but that's not to say this person had anything to do with it.'

Elliot nodded. 'That's true, but the incidences of coincidence are increasing. First, we have proof that Taggart didn't start the fight, and now this. I don't know yet what it means, but I don't like it. Not one bit.'

He turned to Jazzy, his eyes lingering over her face as if to determine what her thoughts were. When his brow furrowed, Jazzy guessed that he'd noticed how strained her face was. She pulled her slumped shoulders back and wished he'd focus on someone else. She was well aware that if he'd been able to avoid her meeting Lucy Taggart, then he would have done so, but there had been no choice. Their priority was locating Taggart sooner rather than later and a little bit of discomfort for Jazzy was a small price to pay. Unfortunately, that meeting had produced nothing concrete and Jazzy was convinced that Lucy would have told her if she had the slightest inkling of her brother's whereabouts.

Elliot raised an eyebrow. 'How did you get on with Lucy Taggart? Any clues where her brother might be?'

Puffing her cheeks out, Jazzy exhaled. 'No. She's insistent that he wouldn't have killed Fletcher. That he's calmed down and that he's got his life together and wouldn't risk it on account of him.' Biting her lip, she paused, her eyes drifting between her team members.

'JayZee?' Queenie stepped close to her and rested her hand on Jazzy's arm. 'Did something happen?'

Jazzy exhaled and, avoiding meeting anyone's gaze said, 'She wants me to find him.'

'Aye well, that's what we're all working towards, isn't it?'

Jazzy's smile was tight. 'She wanted me to promise to prove his innocence . . .'

Her words hung in the air until Queenie broke the silence. 'Fuck me.'

With a strangled half-laugh, Jazzy nodded. 'That's what I thought.' She met Elliot's gaze before he could speak. 'Don't even ask, Elliot. Of course, I said that wouldn't be possible, that I couldn't promise that, but . . . it made me wonder if we've got this completely wrong. Then there's what you and Geordie found out . . .' Lucy's parting shot – that she was a coward, that she had no backbone – taunted her, but that was something she wouldn't share with her team. Yet another piece of evidence of her failure to bundle away out of sight, till it popped out to taunt her when she was alone. She was used to that, wasn't she? So, what was one more guilt trip to Jazzy?

143

Elliot studied her for a moment and that piercing look told Jazzy that he knew she was keeping something back. He'd always been able to tell, but he wouldn't question her further – not then. Not in front of everyone else. His mobile rang, and Jazzy was glad when his attention shifted. Elliot's laser eyes saw too much. But no sooner did that thought cross her mind than she saw his shoulders slump and his eyes widen. Her stomach contracted and her heart skipped a beat. *What now?*

At last, when Jazzy thought she couldn't stomach the uncertainty for a moment longer, he hung up and exhaled in one long, low breath. 'We've located Dwayne Taggart and . . .'

'He's dead.' The words shot from Jazzy's lips like two bullets through a silent night.

Elliot inhaled sharply. 'Yes. I'll get Doc Johnston there ASAP and a team of CSIs is already en route. The paramedics pronounced death at the site, but flagged it as suspicious.'

'Where?' Queenie was already grabbing her jacket.

'Cobbinshaw Loch. Close to the Cobbinshaw Loch cottages. I'll ping you the exact location.'

Jazzy groaned. Of course, being out in the sticks, the likelihood of eyewitnesses or CCTV was minuscule. 'Murder? Suicide? Misadventure?' Each word was clipped as she shrugged and followed Queenie from the room. How the fuck was she going to tell Lucy Taggart this?

Chapter 28

Jazzy

It felt like barely two minutes since Jazzy had attended a crime scene in this area. Only a couple of months ago, outside a village called Tarbrax, not a stone's throw away from Cobbinshaw Loch, her team had been called to another major incident. Now, with Dwayne Taggart being identified in situ, there were so many unanswered questions to consider, not least, what the hell was he doing in Cobbinshaw? Taggart had no reason to be in this area. He was a Leith man, with his business interests focused around Edinburgh, and although Cobbinshaw Loch wasn't far from Edinburgh, it seemed an unlikely place for Taggart to frequent. That, combined with the strange choice of deposition site for Lewis Fletcher, had alarms exploding in her head. If Taggart had killed Fletcher in such an extravagant way, it didn't seem likely that he'd be so filled with remorse afterwards that he'd kill himself.

It wasn't long before they approached the road near the refurbished loch cottages and took a left onto a single-track road. After bumping over potholes for five minutes, a line of vehicles – some police, some CSI – came into view, parked as close to the roadside as possible. Thank God there had been no rain for a while. Queenie parked behind a police car and she and Jazzy exited as Fenton and Geordie pulled up behind them. Further along the track, Jazzy could see a bustle of activity and the white-suited figures of everyone on site. She was reassured to see that the CSIs were already there and had erected a crime scene tent, which would protect the body. So far, there was no press presence, but who knew how long that would last?

'You know what I'm thinking, JayZee? I'm thinking that this is a very remote spot for a body to be stumbled upon.'

'Dog walker, I've heard.' The gruff reply came from a cadaverous constable in a high-vis tabard who carried the scene sign-in forms. He scratched his nose with the end of his pen. 'Not that they hung about or anything. Very irresponsible, if you ask me. Nah, the bugger just phoned it in saying he'd been walking his dog and found a body, then he hopped it, not even leaving a name. Totally unacceptable. You know, in my day, you wouldn't get that sort of behaviour. Folks looked out for each other, but nowadays. Hmph! Rush, rush, rush . . .'

'Aye well that's as may be, but we need to get onto the scene so if you could just let us sign in we'll get suited up and be out your hair.' Queenie scrunched up her nose. 'I'm sure you've got lots to do.'

But PC Jacobs hadn't finished sharing his observations. 'Poor sod, drove up and left his van at the end of the track. That's how we managed to ID him so quickly.' He rolled back and forth on his heels, beaming like he'd invented gravity. 'Name's there see? On the side of the van: *Dwayne Taggart Plumber.*' His skeletal frame paused its movement as a less than perfect smile took over his face. 'Put two and two together like. I'd seen the BOLO earlier and . . .' he tapped the side of his head with two fingers '. . . once seen, never forgotten. Bet neither of you two can claim that, eh?'

As Queenie's face reddened and she stepped forward, ready to challenge the officer, Jazzy stepped in. 'Thanks, PC Jacobs, have the CSIs processed the van?'

'CSIs are on it, ma'am.'

'Right, in that case, my team and I will head down to the inner cordon and you can continue staffing the outer cordon. Nobody else is to get in except the pathologist if . . .'

'He's already here. Tall bloke with grey hair.' He studied the sign-in log. 'Dr Johnston, it says here.'

With Queenie's pointed, 'Nobody likes a know-it-all, son,' hitting its mark the constable blushed. Shaking her head at her partner's pettiness, Jazzy signed in, followed by the rest of the team and after ducking under the tape, they grabbed their crime scene overalls. After suiting up, they approached the tape, Geordie and Fenton tagging along behind. Jazzy scowled at Taggart's van. Surely if he'd been driving that, an ANPR camera somewhere would have caught it over the past couple of days. But if not, then she wanted to know why not. Had he parked it in a garage somewhere? Maybe he'd holed up there too and then only driven it to this remote spot in the dead of night.

Her eyes drifted to the signage on the side of the vehicle: *Dwayne Taggart Plumber*. As she noticed the painted eyes that filled both the 'G's in Taggart, she shifted on her feet. The eyes were eerie – as if they were zeroing in on her, specifically taunting her. But not only were they creepy, they were incongruous. Why would a plumber select eyes rather than a toilet or a pipe or a tap as part of his logo? She stepped closer to the van and studied the logo. The incongruity of the logo irked her. She turned to the nearest CSI. 'Can you spend some extra time processing the logo, particularly the eyes inside the 'G's?'

The hooded CSI got up from his crouched position and approached the van, observing the area Jazzy indicated. 'You think there's something dodgy there?'

Jazzy shrugged. 'Just a feeling, but . . .'

The CSI peered at the eyes and blinked a couple of times. 'Hmm, well spotted. I'm not sure these were part of the original logo, but when we take the van in I'll get them to specifically check that area.'

She might be seeing clues where there were none, but Jazzy was relieved that it would be followed up. She stood for a few more seconds pondering the significance of eyes and trying to work out if she was over-reacting to a simple anomaly. Fletcher's eyes had been mutilated, but not removed. It might signify something.

'Okay to have a look inside?'

'Aye, we've done a preliminary sweep – they'll do a more detailed one at the garage. Just don't touch anything unnecessarily.' Whilst Jazzy opened the driver's side, Queenie opened the passenger side and Fenton and Geordie took the rear. The interior of the cab was littered with empty Costa coffee cups, rolled up Greggs takeaway bags, a couple of Subway wrappers and a faintly unpleasant but unidentifiable stink. Queenie sifted through the detritus on the floor as Jazzy turned to talk to the CSI who'd processed the van. 'Did you find anything of note?'

'Well, there's a lot of prints and a lot of crap inside to process. No suicide note, though. We did what we could in situ, but Franny's requested it's taken in so we can process it at our leisure. Says it's linked to a murder, so we're dotting all the I's on this one.'

She slammed the door closed and sauntered round to where Fenton and Geordie peered into the storage area. 'Anything?'

'Nah.' Fenton jumped down. 'Just your usual plumbing stuff, from what I can see.'

Geordie lowered his voice. 'Did I hear the CSI say they haven't found a note?'

'Not yet.' Jazzy turned around and examined the markers the CSIs had dotted around, signifying possible evidence that would be photographed in situ, collected and processed. Her gaze followed the trail Dwayne Taggart must have taken – his final steps? And she tried to imagine what was going through his mind.

Why now? Why would he break now? Had the incident with Fletcher at the pub reignited his anger? Her eyes went down to the mud track and as she slowly walked towards the crime scene tent, she scanned the trail from side to side. Nearly at the tent, she paused and moved over to the side of the trail where grass and nettles fought for dominance. Was that area there squashed? 'Queenie, what do you make of this?'

Queenie huffed over and bent over from the waist, her butt stuck in the air like a target. 'Tell yer auntie Queenie what you see, hen.'

Despite her focus, Jazzy smiled. Queenie was irrepressible and at times like this you needed someone like her to lighten the mood. 'Look, do you think this grassy patch and these nettles look like they've been squashed?'

Queenie sniffed. 'Aye, I think you're right, JayZee, but I'm no' really sure it's relevant. I mean, so what if Taggart squashed a bit of greenery on his way to the loch? He's a big cumbersome bloke, so I'm only surprised there's no' more patches like this.'

'Aye, but Queenie, what about this mark, here?'

As Queenie bent further forward, at risk of toppling onto her face as her body weight veered off centre, Jazzy steadied her.

'Hmm. I think you've got something right enough. That's a tyre mark or a wheel.' With her entire weight on Jazzy, Queenie pulled herself upright and shrugged. 'No telling when that was made though, is there?'

That was true, but still it needed to be logged, so Jazzy gestured to a CSI to photograph and mark it as evidence. 'See if you can spot this type of mark elsewhere. Were there any marks like these near the body?'

'Not that I'm aware, but I'll double-check. They look fresh to me. I'll see if we can take a cast – maybe get a tread mark.'

Satisfied, Jazzy nudged Queenie. 'Come on, let's see what Dr Johnston's got to say about it. You two, head back and organise door-to-doors on those cottages up the road and, Fenton, see if you can locate any cameras that might help us establish some sort of timeline.'

Approaching the crime scene tent, Jazzy considered the information they had at hand. It seemed that after lying low for a day, Dwayne Taggart had driven his van out here, parked it and then walked a further one hundred yards down the road and what . . . killed himself, drunk himself to death, died of exposure? None of it added up. Lucy had been adamant that her brother wouldn't go AWOL and not contact her or her dad, and that held a ring of authenticity. Taggart was fiercely protective of his family, so it seemed unlikely he would leave them to worry if he could avoid it. Of course, until the van had been fully processed, they didn't even know if he'd been alone when he arrived here. 'Too many unknown factors, Queenie.'

'Aye, you're not wrong there, hen. Something feels off about this.'

Reaching the tent, Jazzy pulled the flap open and poked her head in. Already the heat from the forensic lights had increased the temperature, but Jazzy knew that Dr Johnston would account for that when establishing the time of death. 'Can we come in?'

Dr Johnston, from his kneeling position next to Dwayne Taggart, twisted round. 'Come away in. I'm not happy with this, Jasmine. Not happy at all.'

Walking forward, sticking to the floor plates, Jazzy exchanged a glance with Queenie, who loitered a little behind, as if Jazzy's body would protect her from the worst of the scene. Queenie focused on the pathologist, because although she was getting better at compartmentalising it, Queenie didn't do blood and gore. As they drew level, Jazzy's nostrils twitched. 'Alcohol? Whisky?'

'Hmm.' The elongated sound carried a hidden meaning, and Dr Johnston raised an eyebrow. 'Overkill if you ask me, Jasmine.'

'Oh?'

Dr Johnston got to his feet, shaking his head. 'It's all been staged. Perhaps someone wanted us to believe that Dwayne

150

Taggart got drunk and slit his wrists. But this is not a suicide and wherever Dwayne Taggart's wrists were slashed, it wasn't here. The absence of blood tells us that. Apart from anything, he's been dead for at least two days, probably longer, which means, of course that he didn't kill Mr Fletcher.'

Wow! Jazzy didn't know what to say as she looked down at Taggart's body. He lay, head resting on a rucksack, his sliced arms splayed to either side of him and his face angled to the right, a razor and an empty bottle lay to his left. His shoes and socks had been removed.

'So, what you're saying is, he didnae top himself, then? Didnae use the self-service checkout? Hit the highway of no return . . .?'

'Queenie! For God's sake.'

Queenie huffed and rolled her eyes. 'I'm just saying . . .'

Dr Johnston broke in. 'No, someone moved him here from somewhere else. Hypostasis, or livor mortis, here on the soles of his feet, indicates he was left in a sitting position until after livor mortis set in. I'm wondering if the person who moved him also murdered him. Someone's playing with us, Jazzy. Too many silly mistakes for it not to be deliberate taunting, and that worries me. It worries me a great deal.'

It worried Jazzy too. If Dwayne Taggart was dead before Fletcher, then had Fletcher murdered him and not the other way around as they'd first thought? If so then, who had murdered Fletcher? Lucy's name jumped into Jazzy's mind, swiftly followed by another name – Mhairi. She pulled the hood away from her face, the elastic making her feel claustrophobic. She looked at Queenie. 'What are you thinking, Queenie?'

'Me? I'm thinking this is fucked up.'

Dr Johnston, although he wasn't a swearer, nodded his agreement with Queenie's analysis. 'Quite.' He gestured to one of the CSIs. 'You can take him now.' Then he turned back to Jazzy. 'I'll expedite the PM, Jasmine. I'll give you a time once I've juggled things around.'

Together, the three of them left the tent and retraced their steps back to the crime scene tape. Jazzy was removing her suit when a disturbance further along the road attracted her attention.

'You bitch. You absolute fucking bitch, Jazzy Solanki. You let him die. You let *me* down six years ago and now you've done it again.' Fenton and Geordie appeared from nowhere and grabbed Lucy Taggart's arms, gently trying to pull her backwards away from the scene as the mortuary staff moved in with their trolley, an empty body bag on top. Her face was bright red, her hair awry and her eyes flashing with hatred at Jazzy. 'I'll fucking kill you, Solanki. I'll kill you.'

In the distance, Jazzy recognised three journalists approaching. Smelling blood – or more likely alerted to the drama kicking off, they broke into a jog, cameras bashing at their sides as they tried to break past the phalanx of officers who stepped in their way. *Pity they hadn't been more on the ball when Lucy Taggart gained entry!*

Two uniformed officers stepped in and between the four of them they guided Lucy back towards the Nissan, which she'd abandoned, blocking the track. Jazzy raised a shaking hand to her forehead and wiped globules of sweat away as she watched the skinny figure struggle and rail against the officers. *I should have done better.* Lucy Taggart deserved no more grief in her life. Jazzy wouldn't forgive herself for it.

'No!' Queenie gripped her arm, her fingers digging right into Jazzy's flesh. 'Don't you dare go there, hen. Don't you dare. This isn't your fault. She's just angry, that's all. You can't take this on yourself.' Queenie, blinking rapidly, looked up at Jazzy and lowered her voice. 'I'm worried you're going to break, JayZee. I'm worried you'll take one thing too much onto your shoulders and it'll obliterate you. You *need* to let it go.'

Jazzy couldn't speak, so instead she nodded and forced a smile that was more of a grimace onto her lips and, brushing past the journalists, ignoring their loaded questions, she marched back to Queenie's Land Rover and slammed the door on the squawking vultures outside. How could she not take it on? She'd let that girl down and now her brother was dead too. How much more death and destruction would she have to take responsibility for?

Chapter 29

Mhairi

Things are hotting up again now and that knowledge has given me the energy boost I need. It's hard living like this – pretending to be someone else all the time. So many balls to juggle in the air – remember to be in character, make sure every disguise I use is perfect.

Of course, it was risky to scope out her house, but I couldn't resist and it gave me the adrenalin to carry out the rest of last night's activities and, let's face it, the work was physically exhausting.

I turn Radio Lothian up for the news, and there it is.

'*Reports are coming in of a body discovered on a well-traversed track near Cobbinshaw Loch. A spokesperson from Police Scotland confirmed that a fatality has occurred and say a statement will be issued after the family has been contacted. Now in other news, a primary school in Pumpherston is holding a sponsored three-legged race in aid of . . .*'

So, he's been discovered. I rub my hands and throw myself down on the couch. The TV's on STV and I'm just going to spend the rest of the day relaxing and seeing things unfold in the media. Who knows, maybe I'll be lucky enough to catch a glimpse of her at the scene – that's if the bloody papers get there in time. After all my hard work last night, a bit of 'me' time is the least I deserve. It's not easy manoeuvring a dead bloke onto plastic sheeting, making sure it's taped up, and then hefting him into a wheelbarrow to transport him to the back of his van, only to have to repeat the entire carry-on at the dump site. I mean it's not as if I can ask anyone for help, is it? Imagine . . . 'Excuse me, do you think you could spare a moment to help me lug this very dead person around?'

'Nae problem, I'll take the legs and you take the shoulders, like.'

'Oh, thanks ever so much. Not sure I could manage such a dead weight on my own.'

'Aye, any time, son, any time.'

I spend a full five minutes laughing at the incongruity of the image. It's good to laugh after all. But when I sober up, my thoughts drift to her. I wonder what she's thinking. I mean, she'll be there at the scene, following the breadcrumbs I've dotted around the place. How quickly will they fit in the PM and establish time of death? I reckon they'll prioritise it. Course they will and any investigator worth their salt will work out pretty much straight off that it's a staged suicide. And, let's face it, Jazzy is one of the bright ones. She'll be all over the place trying to slot the pieces together, desperate to work out who killed Lewis Fletcher if Dwayne Taggart was already dead.

I wonder how quickly her thoughts will drift to me. I reckon I'm never far from her mind. They've no idea where I am and no idea where I've been and, in that moment, a flutter of something – not love – but maybe as near to that emotion as I can get, flickers in my chest as I think of great-papa McCullough and the refuge he provided me with. It's soothing – calming, and just like that I pull the duvet up to my chin and my mind drifts back to when I first met him – the man who saw what I was and still protected me, even in his death.

The last signpost I saw before we jolted our way along a narrow lane road that took us further and further away from civilisation was for a place I'd never heard of: Aird. Blink twice and you'd miss it. My heart sank as the road became bumpier and the sky darker and filled with grey roiling clouds until finally Skank Mum edged the car through a gate that hung off its hinges and was wedged in its half-open state by years of weeds and brown grass. Through the windscreen a stone single-storey building stood amid a yard of discarded car parts, household junk and moss-covered debris. Its roof was thatched, but even to my inexpert eye I could tell it needed repair and the smoke spiralling from the chimney made me wonder how the entire ramshackle abode didn't just burst into flames and die.

As soon as I stepped from the car, a gust of wind bringing with it pellets of sleet froze my cheeks and a shuddering shiver rattled my bones as I wrapped my coat around me and waited for her to take the lead. Hesitantly, she glanced my way, and I schooled my expression into one of indifference. Her slight shrug amused me. Who was she kidding? Did she really think her nonchalance looked anything other than false as she set off, her boots sludging through puddles of mucky water? I trudged after her over the slush-covered muddy ground and as we approached the front door of the bleakest-looking building in the bleakest-looking place I'd ever been, a glimmer of interest fluttered in my chest. If nothing else, this wasn't the boring old family reunion I'd anticipated, and that intrigued me. Perhaps Mother wasn't as boring as she seemed, after all.

Skank Mum bent over and plunged her hand into a pile of sleet and grappled around, before pulling a key out from under a tonne of pebbles flattened by years of inclement weather. Her hand was muddy and wet, yet she smiled as if she'd found the largest Easter egg ever. 'Soon be inside, sweetie, and then you'll be able to warm up.'

I had my doubts about that. The barren landscape and the falling darkness promised no warmth, and I had no hopes that the indoors would be any more hospitable. Once inside, the not unpleasant smell of real wood burning combined with a stale fustiness assailed my nostrils. When she flicked a switch, the amber yellow light barely lit up the cramped hallway. Undeterred, she edged along the corridor aiming for the only door that remained closed – the one at the end.

She raised her voice, her tone the same cajoling sing-song lilt that she used on me. 'We're here, Papa McCullough. It's me and my daughter. Can't wait for you to meet her.'

Now secure in my warm soft nest, the radio on low. Adele singing about her impossible aim of setting fire to rain and the flickering images dancing across the TV, I'm content. My limbs are languid, my muscles relaxed, but then I see her on the screen, striding away, that long hair of hers wafting from side to side as she walks, her hand up, palms out, denying the journalists any comment. And at once my peace is gone. Replaced by fiery hatred. Jazzy Solanki, sister dearest, you better watch out, because *this* is only the beginning. Tomorrow I really begin to pull your strings. You'll be my little puppet, dancing about and running in circles, not knowing what will happen next. Tomorrow will be a nightmare for you because I'm going to make you pay, Jazzy.

A surge of anger balloons in my chest and I go light-headed for a moment. If she was there in front of me, I'd pummel her stupid face till every feature is obliterated.

'YOU WILL PAY!' I yell it as loud as I can, enjoying feeling it bounce back and hit me in the face.

Chapter 30

Jazzy

The hours since she'd attended the crime scene near Cobbinshaw had passed in a blur, but even as she performed all the various tasks required of her, Jazzy's mind kept returning to Lucy Taggart and the look she'd given her. It hadn't been the venom and hatred in her eyes that affected her so much. It was the despair that lurked there, too. Everything from the slump of her shoulders to the roughness of her lips and the frown lines fanning out from her mouth showed that Lucy was a woman at the end of her rope. Jazzy hoped that this wouldn't be the final straw. The one that broke Lucy Taggart beyond repair.

It was a relief that Dr Johnston had moved things around to prioritise Dwayne Taggart's post-mortem and after a hurried meeting with Elliot to bring him up to speed and for him, as SIO, to make sure that Queenie was on top of co-ordinating the forensic evidence as it came in, they'd headed to St John's mortuary to attend the post-mortem. Meanwhile, Fenton and Geordie remained at the scene to co-ordinate interviews.

On the way over, Elliot had attempted to engage in conversation. 'Been a while since you and I attended a PM together, Jazzy.'

But, preoccupied with the deluge of thoughts that she couldn't quite sort out, Jazzy just nodded, not really focusing on him or his vacuous observations. She wasn't in the mood for small talk with Elliot and hadn't fully forgiven him for his attitude in Portobello, anyway. He'd taken the hint, and they'd entered the mortuary in silence, Jazzy for one glad to see that Dr Johnston was ready to start. In the clinical observation suite, she could focus on whatever he was about to tell them and hopefully that would provide some much-needed clarity. Right now, all she had going on in her head was a sludge of confusion that Elliot's presence did nothing to clear. If she'd been with Queenie, they might have chatted and voiced their thoughts out loud as Lamond shared his ongoing findings. Instead, Jazzy rested her forehead on the glass, watching and listening in silence, whilst Elliot stood, hands in pockets and laser-eyed, observing the clinical process with the detached look Jazzy had seen him use many times before. He wasn't a fan of post-mortems. But had felt as SIO it was his duty to attend this one. Lamond's initial observations at the crime scene had made it clear that this might be pivotal to making some sort of sense of the deaths of these two men.

Two hours later, feeling a little shell-shocked and in need of a caffeine hit, they made their way back to the station. Elliot was on the phone rounding up the troops for a briefing to share any data that had been collected in their absence.

As Jazzy parked in the car park outside the station, Elliot cleared his throat and glanced at her. She turned towards him, assuming he was about to make some sort of observation on the PM findings, but he touched her arm and lowered his voice. 'Are you okay? I know what happened with Lucy at the scene and I know what you're like. You need to stop putting other people before yourself.'

Jazzy blinked away the sting of tears that nipped behind her eyes and, not trusting herself to speak, shook her head. *Not now, please, not now!* But she couldn't get the words out over the lump in her throat. She didn't want to do this. Not with Elliot. But he didn't pick up on her cue and continued. 'This has got nothing to do with you, Jazzy. You're not to blame for Dwayne Taggart's death. Nor for Lewis Fletcher getting off in the first place. It was that wee scrotum of a DCI who was to blame, not you. You have to stop giving in to this saviour complex of yours.'

Until the 'saviour complex' phrase, Jazzy had been willing to give him the benefit of the doubt and just brush off his concerns, but his choice of words got right under her skin. A wrecking ball slammed into her from nowhere, knocking her earlier resolve to be civil to Elliot into the wind, along with all her inhibitions. She struggled out of the car, slammed the door and waited till he got out too. Glaring at him over the roof of her Mini, every muscle and tendon in her body tensed so taut they almost vibrated. Her head thumped with pulsating rage and she slammed her palm on the roof of her car with such force that she left a dent on her pride and joy. But she didn't care, so angry was she.

For months Jazzy had been containing her emotions, bundling them up inside a ball of barbed wire and keeping them inside her and gradually, day after day, the ball had strained against the barbs, and now, with Elliot's unthinking words, they were about to explode from her with no thought to the consequences. The intensity of the situation overwhelmed her, making it impossible to follow her therapist's advice and open up to Queenie, Fenton, or Geordie.

From the pit of her diaphragm, the words erupted as loud and forcefully as the tears that streamed unheeded down her cheeks. They resonated round the car park, causing people – even those in the distance – to look askance at the two detectives. 'What a fucking hypocrite you are, Elliot Balloch. Such a damn piece of work. Saviour complex? *Saviour complex?* Who are you to land me with that title? You're the one with the bloody *saviour*

160

complex. You're the one who's spent your entire career trying to save little Jazzy Solanki from the hell in which you found me.' She stopped to gulp in a lungful of air and choked. Elliot made to move round the car towards her, but she raised her hand, palm out towards him and this time when she spoke, each icy word landed between them like a mallet to their friendship – quiet and deadly and clipped. 'Don't. You. Dare. Come. Near. Me.'

'But . . . you're . . .'

'Aaaaaaagh.' Jazzy clamped her nails into her scalp, shaking it from side to side with fervour as if she could dislodge his voice from her head. 'You don't listen. You don't listen to what I'm telling you and somewhere along the line, you think that because *you* rescued me then, when I was a child, that you have to do it *still*.'

Fighting for breath, tears dripping from her chin onto the roof of the Mini, she shook her head. This time when she spoke her tone was quiet, regretful. 'I never wanted you as my hero, Elliot. I wanted you as a friend. But look what you and *your* saviour complex have ended up doing. You've ruined any chance of friendship we ever had because all you want to do is fix me. You can't get it into your head that it's not your job to do that. It's not up to you to sort me out. I'm not a child. I don't need your protection. I'm a colleague. No more, no less. That's all I am.'

She swept her hand across her eyes and sniffed. 'I'm a professional and if you can't treat me as such, then I wish you'd just fuck right off back to Edinburgh.' And with Elliot's gaping mouth and dark frown imprinted on her retinas, she marched away. 'I'll be at the briefing in five.'

Even as she strode away from him, her anger dissipated, leaving in its wake a dull throb of emptiness. *What have I done?* She couldn't explain it to herself, yet she understood that her momentary loss of control had cost her dearly. With their already fractured relationship, there was no way their differences could ever be healed now. Head down, she barged past people, intent

161

on finding sanctuary away from prying eyes. Thankfully, the lift was empty when she got in and soon she was upstairs, finding her familiar refuge in the rarely used loos at the end of the corridor. Once inside, she collapsed with her back against the door and then, hearing the shuffle of feet and murmur of voices outside, she turned the lock. Eyes closed, she let the last of her tears trickle down her cheeks and tried to ignore the persistent voice in her head.

There you go again, Jazzy. Letting someone else down. Who will it be next? Queenie? Fenton? Geordie? Which of them will you discard from your life like a dog turd on your shoe? Just like you discarded me and Mhairi. Everything you touch crumbles and dies, Jazzy. You destroy everything you touch. You are to blame. You are to blame for all of it.

She pressed the heels of her hands against her ears and burrowed in on herself, her chin almost touching her chest. If she opened her eyes now, she knew who she'd see: Simon. Not the grown-up adult one, but the little boy looking up at her. The trust in his eyes turning to hurt, fear, disappointment and then finally acceptance as she turned her back on him. It was that last expression that tore her apart, that made her berate herself. She'd just let Elliot down, like she had her siblings when she left them to falter in the foster system. When she'd failed to stop them transforming not into the caterpillars they should have, but into rotting squirming maggots, eating through every good thing they could find.

She shook her head to dislodge the unwelcome images. It was her mind playing tricks on her. Her guilt conjuring up more ways to self-flagellate, and she knew she had to stop it. Stop it before she ruined every relationship in her life. She swallowed hard, walked over to the sink, and leaned against the icy surface. Tap on, she scooped handfuls of water into her mouth to soothe the glass shards down her throat until she was calmer. Her hair was a mess, so she undid her ponytail and combed her fingers through the strands, dislodging huge clumps of it. According to her therapist, another symptom of her stress. Her hair, once glossy and voluminous, was matte and listless. Spots had erupted across her forehead and chin as if she was a teenager again.

Yet it was what she saw when she looked deep into her eyes that distressed her the most – dark fathomless pools of despair – emptiness, a void. How could she face everyone like this? How could she face Elliot? She'd have to apologise and perhaps, if they worked at it, they could resurrect some semblance of a working relationship. But she doubted that. She'd crossed a line that even Elliot couldn't forgive. The saviour complex stung – in part, she realised because of the kernel of truth in it, but he too had that self-same complex. Maybe its pull is what had kept them connected all these years. But they couldn't go on like this.

Throwing the long strands of greasy hair into the bin, she washed her hands and then splashed more water on her face. There was only one solution to this problem. She'd told him he should run back to Edinburgh, but that wasn't feasible. He was an inspector and she a sergeant. A sergeant still on probation too. No, there was only one way forward. She would have to apply for a transfer.

The realisation thumped her in the gut like a sledgehammer. She'd be giving up her team – the three people she'd grown close to over the past few months. People she trusted to have her back. She visualised Fenton's puzzled frown and Geordie's disbelieving glare and shuddered. Yet more people she would be letting down. As for Queenie? Well, she just couldn't go there. Not now. Not when she felt so vulnerable. Queenie would feel her betrayal the worst and Jazzy already felt the weight of that on her shoulders.

Then there was her home. Her beautiful little bungalow in Bellsquarry. The place she'd put down roots. She shook her head. No, she couldn't do it. She couldn't transfer out of Livingston. Maybe just a move to one of the other teams. Maybe A team. That would be enough. She wouldn't be under Elliot's command

and she'd still be able to see her friends. She'd have to make it work, for she realised now that there was no way she could give her friends up. No way she could destroy the haven of peace she'd created at home. No, she and Elliot would just have to swallow their anger for each other and be professional at work. For now, though, she had a briefing to attend and her priority had to be working through the morass of contradictory evidence concerning Dwayne Taggart's and Lewis Fletcher's murders.

Chapter 31

Jazzy

If she'd hoped to slide into the room unnoticed, she was wrong. No sooner had she stepped inside than Queenie had turned, hands on hips, and her eagle eyes raked her face. 'For God's sake. What's happened to you? Would you *look* at the state of you? The cat sicked you up and dragged you in, did it? Pulled you through a hedge backwards, eh? Got mangled by a steamroller? Christ, you're a right ticket. Lipton's orphan, that's what you are.' As Jazzy sidled into a seat, Queenie yanked her thumb in Elliot's direction. 'As for his nibs, phew, the way his pus is out of sorts, anybody would think he'd landed face first in the cadaver at that PM.' She paused, her nose turned up as her mind ticked over. 'Aye, flat into a cow pat or, worse still, like a skelped arse . . .'

'Queenie . . .' Elliot's tone brooked no argument. 'If you could join us at the table, I'd like to limit the briefing to just the team for now.'

Risking a glance at him, Jazzy flinched when his gaze skated over her, his face dark and inscrutable except for the tell-tale flush on his cheeks. He'd discarded his jacket and rolled his shirt sleeves up, ready for a long briefing. She pulled her chair close to the table and, avoiding the well-meaning enquiring looks from her team, focused on her tablet in front of her, her phone next to it. This was going to be a long and extremely tense meeting.

Elliot took a chair between Geordie and Fenton, but angled it so she wasn't in his direct line of vison. That suited Jazzy, because she was having enough trouble ignoring Queenie's pointed looks and frequent sighs when she didn't respond to her mumbled questions about her wellbeing, without having to contend with angry looks from Elliot, too.

'Right, so it's looking increasingly like our previous line of inquiry might be defunct. I'll update you about Dwayne Taggart's post-mortem, which DS Solanki and I attended.' He paused to gather his thoughts. 'Firstly, the most important finding from the post-mortem is Dr Johnston's confirmation that Dwayne Taggart probably died in the early hours of Monday morning – a full day before Lewis Fletcher's approximate time of death, which investigators have determined to be sometime in the early hours of Tuesday morning. Ergo . . .'

Fenton, sitting back upright, chair pulled as far under the table as possible, couldn't contain his excitement. '. . . Taggart didn't commit suicide.' He beamed round the room, his smile fading when the only response was from Geordie, who mumbled something uncomplimentary about 'a teacher's pet'.

'Yes, that's right, Fenton. Taggart was already dead, which raises the question of . . .'

Again, Fenton opened his mouth to interject, but seemingly realising that Elliot was in no mood for interruptions, clicked it shut again.

'Bloody wee swot, Haggis. You after a promotion or something?'

Elliot sighed and closed his eyes for a second, then; 'Queenie, just shut the hell up, and you too, Fenton. Ordinarily I'm all for a bit of banter and a bit of interaction, but . . .' He glanced at Jazzy, his lips tightening. 'Not today, eh?'

For once, Queenie, seeming to pick up on the seriousness of his mood, backed down and slumped into her chair, arms folded in front of her, a single nod indicating that she'd shut up.

'As I was saying, that raises the question of who would kill him. But before we consider that, let me finish sharing the other findings from the PM. Firstly, hypostasis indicates that Taggart, as we'd expect, had remained in one position long enough for lividity to set in. Basically he was moved from a sitting position, where his backside and feet were all in contact with a hard surface – a hard chair and the floor – is the doc's best guess. You can check that out from the images in the PM report.'

Jazzy didn't bother to look at those images. It had been bad enough seeing the mottled dark red skin in real life without reliving it. Queenie, too, declined to look; however, Fenton and Geordie flicked each one. Fenton sporting an eager expression zoomed in, lingering over various aspects of the photos. Geordie, on the other hand, grimaced and groaned his way through them at speed before thrusting his tablet away from him.

'Faint restraint marks – most likely cable ties – were visible on the wrists and ankles, but lividity and cause of death indicate that someone removed the restraints at some point. Dwayne Taggart's wrists were slit vertically down the veins on either arm, and he bled out. The preliminary tox report shows the presence of phenobarbital – which was also found in Lewis Fletcher's tox screen and is often used to incapacitate victims. You can read the full report at your leisure.'

For a moment nobody spoke.

Consulting his tablet, Elliot looked up. 'Queenie and Geordie's work at the Black Swan, where the two men had their fight last week threw up a few interesting facts. Firstly, that Fletcher had been the aggressor and secondly that unaccessed CCTV from an adjoining premises confirmed Fletcher had been loitering in the shadows with an as yet unidentified person prior to the attack. Any joy in having the image enhanced, Geordie?'

Leaning back and stretching his lanky frame, Geordie shook his head. 'They've enhanced it as much as they can, but to be frank, unless we come up with a suspect, and can match height and build, the footage will not help with an ID. Still, it does perhaps indicate Fletcher was acting with someone else when he challenged Taggart.' He paused, scratched his chest through a gap in his shirt. 'Unless, of course, it was just an unrelated meeting – maybe a drug deal or something.'

'Anything else from that line of inquiry? What about the punters in the pub? Did they see anything?'

'Thanks to the analysts' quick turnaround on the till receipts, we were able to identify all but two of the parties in the pub and uniform have spoken to all of them, plus the people they were with. None of them noticed the two men until after the fight had started and the bouncer and manager had intervened. Dead end there, I'm afraid. I've got a team of uniformed officers scrawling CCTV to see if they can catch our mysterious stranger on any of the cameras around the pub. Long shot, but' – he shrugged – 'I'm thinking we might get lucky.'

'Okay, good work, you two. Now, any word from the Taggart crime scene? Has forensics come up with anything?'

'Well . . .' Fenton flicked his screen and took a deep breath before responding. 'Nothing from door-to-doors. Two of the cottages nearby were empty and the occupants of the other two saw nothing. It's the middle of nowhere, so there's no CCTV we can use. Having said that, I've got a couple of not so willing bodies to trawl through the CCTV from the main roads that lead to the loch to see if we can locate Taggart's van and do a backward trace on it. Who knows, we might be lucky, although I noticed the number plate was covered so ANPR won't be any use. It's a matter of going through hours of footage in the hope it'll pay off.'

Queenie shuffled in her seat, frowning at her tablet as if it was an alien entity. 'Some forensics have come in. A bit of blood in the back of the van matched to the deceased – nothing unexpected in that. They did their techie type wonders with that weird singular tyre mark Jazzy noticed at the scene. They found a few fainter marks at intervals between the van and the deposition site. I'm guessing it's no' a unicycle, so we're no' looking for a guy with a red nose and an orange wig.' She scrolled down a bit and sniffed. 'Aye, here it is. The forensics bods suggest it could be a wheelbarrow, although the marks were so faint they got no useful markers for make and model on that.' She turned to Jazzy, shaking her head. 'How the hell you noticed that first track, JayZee, I still don't know. It was very near invisible.'

Jazzy shrugged. 'Pays to spend a wee bit of time looking at the scene as a whole. If it hadn't been for the crumpled plants, I wouldn't have spotted it.'

'Eh, so? What are we saying? That the killer used the wheelbarrow to transport the body?' Geordie's tone held a degree of awe, which he covered up, but added, 'I wondered how he manged to lug a dead weight that distance. I mean, Taggart's a hefty lad, isn't he? And it was a good couple of hundred yards. Not an easy carry by any means.'

'What I'm wondering, though,' said Fenton, 'Is how the killer got away from the scene, pushing a wheelbarrow. I mean, that's something that would stick in folks' minds.'

Queenie tutted. 'Oh, Haggis, Haggis, Haggis, you need to cultivate your knowledge of the world of gardening.' She grinned at Geordie. 'See what I did there, Geordie my man. Cultivation, gardening . . .'

'Queenie.' Elliot barely breathed her name, but it was enough of a warning for Queenie to gather herself. 'Aye well, my Craig's a bit of a gardener, you know, and he raves about his collapsible lightweight wheelbarrow. A brilliant purchase, if you ask me – definitely an inspired invention. Not that I'm putting my Craig on the damn suspect list – no way. He has enough bother hefting a wee bag of mulch onto the thing – besides, he was with me last night.' She wiggled her eyebrows. 'I can vouch for that, all right. We made a right night of it.'

Despite her tension, Jazzy's lips twitched. She remembered how much Queenie had moaned about Craig buying the wheelbarrow, but to hear her now you'd think it had been her idea. 'So, the killer transported the body in a collapsible wheelbarrow and left the van behind. They must have hoofed it back to where they left their actual getaway vehicle. Worth putting out a call for any sightings of abandoned vehicles in, say, a five-mile radius.'

'Five miles? Really? You think five miles, JayZee. What sort of superhuman do you reckon this killer is? The six-million-dollar man, or maybe he's Batman and flew back to his bat mobile, or Spider-Man, eh? Nah, my reckoning is that he might have hoofed it to the loch and took a boat to one of the wee jetties?' She prodded the unfortunate Fenton who sat right next to her, on the arm. 'Get that actioned, wee man.'

Rubbing his arm, Fenton added it to the actions for the day.

The meeting trundled on for another half hour and Jazzy felt herself getting more and more anxious by the second until she couldn't contain her thoughts anymore. Avoiding Elliot's gaze, she waited for a lull in the discussion before saying in a measured tone that didn't betray her anguish, 'Are we just going to ignore the possibility that the Bitch has something to do with this?'

For the first time since the meeting started, Elliot met her gaze whilst the others, sensing the tension that radiated between the two, exchanged surreptitious glances and feigned interest in the various reports on their tablets. Nostrils flaring, he placed both palms on the table as if he was about to jump to his feet. His tone could have sliced wood. 'Operation Birchtree is up to date with our investigation and any potential links to *your* sister are being investigated as part of *their* ongoing process. Your sister is *not* your concern, Sergeant Solanki. Your *only* concern is the investigation into the deaths of Dwayne Taggart and Lewis Fletcher. Do I make myself clear?'

Beside her, Queenie drew a sharp intake of breath whilst Jazzy's cheeks burned. *How dare he talk to her like this?* Injecting every iota of anger and disbelief she could muster, she maintained eye contact with him and spat a single word across the table: 'Crystal!'

It hung for a moment in the middle of the group, threatening to smash onto the surface and shower them with jagged glass. But before anyone could say anything, Jazzy stood up and left the room. *So much for a professional relationship between us.*

She could have slammed the door, but she wouldn't dignify Elliot's behaviour with that sort of display of anger. However, as soon as the door closed behind her, her legs shook and she only just made it a few yards down the corridor before she had to lean on the wall for support. Heaving in deep breaths, she ignored the well-meaning enquiries after her health of a PA who, judging by the pile of files he carried, was en route to a meeting. She wanted to move. To put some distance between herself and that damn room, but she wasn't sure her legs would carry her to the lift, so she waited, hoping that no one would exit the room and see her in this state.

She forced her legs to comply as she pushed herself away from the wall and down the corridor. She might not be able to stand being in the same room as Elliot at the moment, but that didn't mean she couldn't pore over the information they'd gathered already. There must be something between the Portobello crime scene and the Cobbinshaw Loch one that they were missing. If Mhairi had a hand in these two deaths, she wouldn't be able to resist leaving her mark at the scenes. The image of the logo on the side of Taggart's van flashed into her mind. What was it about that logo that had her hackles rising? Jazzy slammed her way into the office where D team was situated and threw herself into a chair in front of her computer.

As she waited for the damn thing to warm up and allow her access to the reports from both crime scenes, her head thumped, but that wouldn't deter her. She rolled her head, trying to loosen up the tension in her neck when it hit her. All along, they'd been saying how smart Mhairi was, so it wasn't beyond the realm of possibility that she'd deliberately altered her MO – not completely, but just enough to cast doubt on things. Whereas before Christmas and with her earlier crimes, she and Simon had exhibited flamboyance and over-the-top crime-scene-setting at every scene, maybe she'd decided to work under the radar.

Jazzy bit her lip for a second, then her fingers rattled across the computer keys, accessing the photos taken at each scene. If this was Mhairi, she would want to manipulate them, to toy with them, and part of that manipulation could be a deliberate change in her style. As Queenie, Geordie and Fenton sidled in and took up position at their own computers, Jazzy felt their eyes on her. She sighed. Now wasn't the time for lengthy explanations about what had just kicked off in the briefing, but nor could she act like it hadn't happened. Instead she opted for honesty. 'I know you all want to know what just happened, but, for my sake can we just let it go for now? It's too fresh for me to talk about.'

'Aw, but hen . . . we're your mates, your team, your confidantes. Surely you can . . .'

Before Queenie could finish, Geordie nudged her, cleared his throat and spoke over her. 'Aye, that's fine, Jazzy. What do you want us to do?'

Relieved that Geordie had intervened, Jazzy pushed her chair back and smiled at her team. 'Crime scene photos, guys. Fenton, you and Queenie go through the bottle kiln ones and Geordie and I will take the Cobbinshaw ones.'

'And we're looking for . . .?' Fenton asked.

'Oh, for fuck's sake, dae you need spoon-feeding every step of the way, Haggis?' Then Queenie stopped, scrunched up her face, and lowered her tone. 'Eh, what exactly are we looking for, JayZee?'

'You two are reviewing the images of the graffiti on the bottle kiln walls – keeping an eye out for any signs that may link to

Mhairi. I got Franny to catalogue close-ups of the entire wall. I want you to use your extraordinary mind, Queenie. I'm certain there's something there. The Bitch is smart enough to tone it down in the interests of anonymity, but she wouldn't be able to resist taunting us. We just need to find whatever she's left behind that links her to these murders. Geordie, you and I are on the same job, but we have a less closed-in environment. You already went over the van, so this time you scrutinise images of the deposition site and surrounding area, go over the evidence lists forensics have logged. Think as laterally as you can and focus on anything that might, however thinly, link to the Bitch, or anything odd. Anything that seems out of place. Nothing is too weird to be considered at this stage because we've got damn all else to go on. I'm going to go over the images of that van, internal and external. She left something. I'm sure of it. For her it's like a battle of wills – a challenge to best me and she won't make it easy for us this time.'

Chapter 32

Ali

I can't get the image of my dad dragging that stupid suitcase out of my mind. I know I'm being daft, but I keep thinking that it's not just Mum he's leaving, it's me too. Mr Bruce yelled at me for being late in English and Isla kept looking at me like she didn't know me. I've never felt so alone in my life. So utterly and desperately alone. Nobody understands how I feel and how can I explain it to them when I don't understand it myself? Yeah, the constant bickering with the parents is hard to live with, but it's more than that. Deeper than that. It's insidious – that's what it is – this thing that takes control of my mind, that completely envelops me and suffocates me – it's relentless when it strikes and when it's at bay, the threat of it descending makes my chest tight and my heart skip random beats.

Meeting Isla this morning was a complete disaster. She was in a right mood with me. And still not keen on covering for me. She tried guilt tripping me about how much it would upset my folks, but I'd had enough and all of a sudden, that bloody insidious wave of despair was there, bearing down on me and, as

I struggled to keep my head above the water level, the sensation of drowning swept me away. I hardly noticed myself scratching my arms, raking my nails over my forearms again and again, until Isla grabbed them and made me stop. She wrapped her arms round me and patted my back as I wept. 'Oh, Ali, what's wrong? None of this is like you. Tell me what I can do to help.'

But there was nothing she could do, except cover for me, but her face told me she wouldn't. I shook my head and summoned up a smile from somewhere. She didn't look convinced, but the bell rang so she let it go and together, arm in arm, we'd walked into school. Now, here I am at what I consider 'my bench', on my own, wondering why if he loved me, my dad would leave me without a word.

The boys are there again, three of them, yelling and kicking their football, their faces alive and filled with sheer enjoyment of the moment. And that weirdo Benjy, cowering near the fence, with his cousin Ivor beside him. He's so lame. I tuck my arms inside my opposite sleeve, and pick at the scabs my frenzied scratching had caused earlier. My gaze moves over to the group of first-year girls on their phones. Their laughs and giggles ring out across the playground. I frown. When was the last time I felt so carefree? It had been a while since I last laughed with Isla and my other mates like that. When was the last time I felt happy?

I try to conjure up a memory of me laughing with Isla, but all I remember is snapshots of them giggling over a daft romcom, or stupid reels on Insta and me there smiling, but not connected. Not part of the joy – somehow separate from it – alone and desperate to feel part of their happiness, but instead my chest tightened, and I had to struggle not to lose it. I close my eyes, but still a tear seeps through my lashes.

Maybe the reason I agreed to go out with Jan Carmichael was to jolt my system. Dad counts his macros to kick-start his metabolism. Maybe a similar thing will work with my head. Maybe surrendering to the moment will shake me back to reality.

Maybe if I take a risk, do something unconventional, something that goes against everyone's expectations, all the jumbled thoughts in my head will finally fit together, and I'll be happy. At the very least, maybe it would grab their attention. Maybe for once the parents would see me. See me and realise I'm self-destructive, that I'm wavering on the edge and that if I can't set myself straight, I might jump.

I grab my phone and text.

Ali: Dad, where are you? Why did you leave without saying goodbye? Why did you take a suitcase?

My fingers tremble as I read what I've written. I need to know. I can't get through the day without knowing. I press send and then wait. We've got a rule. No matter what we're doing, no matter where we are, we respond, even if it's just a holding text. That way, we know we're okay. I snort. Okay? Like a stupid text tells the recipient that you're okay. It's just words. All just words. Not real. Not probing beneath the surface, not acknowledging the chaos inside.

Dad: Hey Ali. Busy at work, so just packed a few bits and pieces to tide me over. You okay? Sorry for not saying bye. Was in a rush. Love you xx

I read it. Just what I was thinking earlier. Words tell us nothing. They distract from what's really going on. Lies, that's what they are. Lies because he can't handle telling me the truth and neither can my mum, and it's doing my head in. I look down at my hands. My fingernails are caked in blood and now I notice my sleeves are sticking to my arms. I grab my antibacterial gel and slowly peel my sleeves back, and I see that they're stained with blood and the scabs on my arms have reopened, and even more scratches are there. How could I not have felt myself doing this? I wad up some tissues and set about cleaning up my wounds. If only my life would be so easy to clean up. That niggling thought – the one that's coming more and more frequently these days sidles in, like a demon on my shoulder, tempting me. Maybe life would be easier for me if I wasn't in it.

My breathing speeds up and I feel like I'm suffocating, but I swallow the thought down and stand up, trying to regulate my breathing. I'll go out with Jan Carmichael. I'll do things I've never done before. I'll take risks, I'll disobey my parents, I'll try to recalibrate this faulty brain of mine . . . And if that doesn't work? Well then, I'll have to think of something else.

Chapter 33

Jazzy

'Ye wee beaut! Absolute bloody belter! Magic, pure dead magic! Did you think ye'd escape me? Aye well, let me tell you, ye serial-killing bitch, *I'm* the smart one around here. The brains of this operation, the Jazz Queen wi' the super power.' Queenie jumped up did a shoogly, uncoordinated wee choo-choo train circle round her desk before high-fiving her three colleagues.

Excitement thrummed through Jazzy like an electric shock. They'd been at it for hours and everyone else had gone home, but still the four of them, fortified by cups of coffee and occasional screen breaks, kept their eyes on the prize. 'What you got, Queenie?'

'Come on then, Haggis, son. Just enlarge that image there onto the big screen, eh?'

Fenton jumped to it and within seconds, one of Franny's graffiti images from Lewis Fletcher's crime scene in Portobello was there. As if the projected image wasn't big enough, everyone, except Queenie who was slumped in her chair, eyes closed, and massaging her temples, had jumped to their feet and started scouring the psychedelic pictures. The images comprised overlapping swirls, smaller images merging into larger ones, and some escaping half formed from a larger pattern.

Jazzy squeezed the bridge of her nose and blinked a few times, trying to dislodge the gritty feeling that had been building beneath her eyelids for the last few hours. She could barely distinguish one part of the landscape from the others. To her, it appeared as if numerous artists had added to and covered a mishmash of colour and shapes. If only they could peel the layers back one at a time. She looked at the other two, Fenton with his lips pursed up, head pushed forward, moving in small increments as he scanned the image inch by inch. From nowhere, Geordie brought a magnifying glass that he was using to try to see what Queenie had spotted, his eyes scrunched up in concentration. 'We can't see it, Queenie. You'll have to tell us.'

'Aye, granted, the artists are nae Banksys. A bloody nightmare of colour – that's what they've created. It's like a Hieronymus Bosch withoot any of his tortured talent, a splodge painting of crap, the product of a meth-induced mind. Christ, mah wee Ruby could do better than that.'

Geordie tossed his magnifier on the desk and stepped back. 'Your grand wean might be the next Banksy but what the hell are we supposed to be looking at?'

'I'll gie ye a clue, shall I?' Full of self-importance, Queenie got up and, rocking back and forth on her heels, tapped her lips with her index finger. 'I've got it. It's all in the mind's eye.'

Jazzy wanted to reach out and strangle her. They were all knackered, and Queenie's shenanigans were pissing her off big time. She opened her mouth to berate her grinning colleague when Geordie snapped his fingers, his words coming out hesitantly. 'Is it that? The scales?'

'Gie yersel' a brownie point, Geordie. Well done.'

Jazzy and Fenton stepped in closer, trying to see what Geordie saw. 'Nah, still can't see it,' was Fenton's verdict, followed almost immediately by an 'Ooooh, yes, there it is.'

Jazzy pinpointed the small square area that Fenton pointed to and exhaled slowly. How Queenie had seen it, she'd no idea, but this was it. The tingling in her bones told her it was.

'Can you enlarge just that wee section, Fenton?'

When the area was enlarged, the four of them stood in silence for a moment, looking at the dark scales. They saw that the left-hand side of one of the balances was only partially visible – the side containing the eyeball from which blood dripped – while the other cup, which was more visible, held a tooth.

'An eye for an eye, and a tooth for a tooth.' Jazzy shook her head. 'It's her. It's got to be.'

Fenton was on his computer. 'It's a phrase dotted all over the Bible. Deuteronomy, Exodus, Leviticus . . . certainly covers the religious aspect and maybe because she had to dial back her MO, she replaced the eye removal with a bit of mutilation and this.'

Geordie had picked up his magnifier again and nodded. 'It even looks like it's fresher than the surrounding graffiti.'

The snap of Jazzy's fingers clicking together startled the team and, as she started frantically scrolling through the images she'd been viewing, they gathered behind her. Finally, she stopped and leaned back, a satisfied smile on her lips. 'There, look. This has been preying on my mind since I saw it earlier. I even got forensics to get the garage to expedite tests on it.'

She pointed at the logo on the side of Dwayne Taggart's van. The one with the two eyes in the middle of the 'G's. It's her, I'm sure it's her. He wouldn't be so crass, would he? He's a plumber for God's sake not an optician. He'd use U-bends in his logo not bloody eyes.'

The others peered at it and nodded. But as sudden exhaustion swept over Jazzy, she rested her elbows on the desk and groaned. 'It's not enough, though. They'll never go for it. Not in a million years. They'll say we're stretching – looking for links that aren't there.' She looked round at her team. 'Maybe they'd be right.'

All three of them shook their heads, but it was Queenie who spoke. 'No, JayZee, they're not right. We know her. We've studied her. This is her. This is definitely a link between the two crime scenes and although it might not be conclusive evidence yet that it's the Bitch's work, it's very strong circumstantial evidence. Now we just need to prove it and corroborate the link. I'll get on the phone to Franny and pull in a favour – maybe she'll go back and process that bit of the wall for us – maybe lift some prints or get some indication of when it was painted or what it was painted with. But for now, we're all knackered, and it looks like you've found nothing at the Taggart scene, so we'll give it a rest tonight and tomorrow *I'll* go over those images, too. It's easier for me. Then when we find something there to link the two scenes and with whatever forensic backup Franny comes up with, we'll go to that new DCS at Operation Birchtree and insist she take heed.'

Jazzy stretched, her entire body crying out for rest, but there was one more thing to explore. She looked at each of her team members because she knew she couldn't be the one to do it. All of them were knackered – completely and utterly spent, but she needed this doing tonight. It was too important to wait. 'Fenton, I know you're desperate to get home, but I need you to head over to the Taggart place in Leith and ask Lucy about the signage on Dwayne's van. See if she has any photos of it. I want proof positive that those eyes are a recent addition and . . .' She shrugged. 'I don't think I can be the one to go.'

Fenton summoned up a smile and nodded. 'No probs. I'll go.' And as he gathered his stuff together, Geordie sidled over to his friend. 'You want some company? I could do with a drive.'

Queenie glanced at Jazzy and grinned, her hands pressed to her chest. 'Oh, does it no' dae you proud to see the two weans looking out for each other?'

Chapter 34

Thursday

Benjy

Ivor had insisted that he seek help for the post-traumatic stress she was sure he suffered from. She was getting help for hers, but Benjy was scared that if he revealed how much was going on in his mind, they would lock him up. Lock him up in that place they had Jazzy's brother – and everyone knew what had happened to *him*. Not that the bastard didn't deserve to die. Not that Benjy wasn't glad he was gone. Only one more demon still out there threatening him and everyone he loved. If only the Bitch would die too, everything would be all right. But what if she got to his loved ones first? That's what Benjy was terrified of. So, he came to a decision. In order to protect Ivor, he couldn't enlist her in his crazy shenanigans anymore. Despite the persistent musical accompaniment, Benjy took a second to congratulate himself on making another decision. Wow wee, big sodding deal. So, you made a decision, Benjy. Aren't you the big man?

'*And come with your playfellows into the street*'. The word 'playfellows' taunted him. Apart from Ivor and possibly Jazzy, if she was still speaking to him after his outburst the other day, he had no one. No one his own age. Everyone at school thought he was weird and he had to give it to them – he was weird, specially after seeing Ivor with all that . . . He groaned out loud and was rewarded by the damn rhyme nearly bursting his eardrums. *'THE MOON DOTH SHINE AS BRIGHT AS DAY'.*

His desire to protect Ivor was the reason he was on his own, his actions fuelled by nervous energy and fear. It had taken him over three hours to walk all the way from Stùrrach to Jazzy's house, but he'd been compelled to come. The memory of the shadowy figure he'd thought he'd seen outside her house the other night kept intruding and the idea that maybe if he went back there he'd find out if it had been real or a figment of his imagination wouldn't let go. Besides, he was trying to be proactive like Ivor said. Something wasn't right, and the persistent chimes in his head reinforced his anxiety. *'Girls and boys come out to play'* was the rhythm of his march. Yet, for once, he welcomed it, as it had stoked his anger as he walked. *'The moon doth shine as bright as day'.* Every step had been purposeful. He *had* to get to Jazzy. He had to see for himself that she was okay, for the gnawing in his belly made him doubt her safety. He had to make sure that shadowy figure wasn't real. He'd never forgive himself if something happened to Jazzy. *'Leave your supper and leave your sleep'.*

He skipped past the Brucefield estate and took the shortcut to Jazzy's street. *'And come with your playfellows into the street'.* Sweat dripped from him and as he'd walked, his head filled with the stupid nursery rhyme. He'd watched the colours of the sky change as dawn slowly descended. Although he knew he should appreciate the beauty of it – Ivor would have revelled in the pink and purple hues streaking the sky – he felt nothing. Inside, he was numb – as if someone had ripped every emotion except fear and anger from him. Everything he did was like watching himself in a film. Like an out-of-body experience. Sometimes he wondered if he was in fact dead and his ghost was lingering on earth. Maybe he was like that girl in *The Lovely Bones*. He and Ivor had loved that book. But deep down he knew he was alive because his terror was too all-consuming to be anything other than real. It engulfed him, sapped his energy, made him jittery and kept his heart pounding like a drum. Sometimes he wondered what would happen if the drum skin burst. Sometimes he wished it would.

It was just after six in the morning now so after scanning the area, looking for unfamiliar vehicles, sudden movements, or anything suspicious and finding none, Benjy settled himself behind Jazzy's neighbour's hedge where he could monitor her house. He'd done this before, although he hadn't confided this fact to Ivor, and the spot where he had burrowed inside the hedge was like a nest to him. A little protective cocoon where nobody could see him. He didn't expect any activity until after seven, so when her door burst open early and Jazzy, still tying up her long hair in a bobble, flew down the steps towards her Mini, Benjy knew something was up. Her movements were spiky, her face tense.

'Girls and boys come out to play'. The refrain hammered like a million woodpeckers in his head, ferocious and taunting and painful. As Jazzy pulled away from the kerb, he extricated himself from the hollow and watched her. A sensation of such dread overtook him. His eyes searched the area, laser-like and piercing, looking for anything strange – a bogeyman in waiting, a car slipping out to follow Jazzy. But there was nothing. He walked over to where he and Ivor had parked the previous night and crouched, as if sitting in the passenger seat, and once more scoured the area, trying to locate the spot where he'd seen that weird shadowy figure that almost looked like it had been waving at them. It looked quite different and less threatening in the daylight, but still the niggle of fear stuck.

He got up and mooched slowly along the road, stopping periodically to glare at the ground or study the gardens for a hiding place. He'd almost given up when he saw it. A cap tossed by the grass verge under a tree in a garden a few doors down from where they'd parked. Was it evidence that someone was there watching Jazzy? He peered more closely at the verge and his heart sped up as he noticed the grass was trampled on. No way could someone trample it unless they were hiding there in the shadows. He bent over and picked the hat up, his heart hammering against his chest, the infernal rhyme speeding up and louder again now in his ears – a cacophony of dread! It was – a cap, a tweed one like he'd seen old men wear. His spine tingled in warning and his eyes darted round looking for someone, anyone who could be a threat. He should have got out of the car the other night. He should have checked! If anything had happened to Jazzy, it would have been his fault. Whoever this hat belonged to, he was sure they were spying on Jazzy.

Then he realised something else. His actions had brought Ivor here too. His actions had put her at risk.

He fell to his knees, consumed by dread, and curled into a ball on the grass, covering his head with his arms as that damn tune banged on inside his skull. *'The moon doth shine as bright as day'.*

When he eventually calmed down and the nursery rhyme quietened enough to allow him to concentrate, he took out his phone and dialled. 'Ivor, I need you.'

Within half an hour, she arrived. Pale-faced and anxious, she listened to what he said, looked at the cap and the branch clutched in Benjy's fingers and sighed. 'We need to get this to Jazzy.' but Benjy grabbed her hand. 'She's not there. She left earlier in a real rush.'

Ivor hesitated, then: 'We'll go home and tell Uncle Pedro everything. He'll get these things to Jazzy.'

Despite the tears pouring down his face, Benjy was calmer. Ivor's presence soothed him, so he readily acquiesced as she bundled him into her car and drove them home. Once there she snuck him into her bedroom and left him there to sleep whilst she headed off to speak to Uncle Pedro. 'Don't move till I get back, Benjy. Just stay there and try to rest. You look knackered.'

Benjy nodded, but as soon as he heard the front door close, he got up and sat on the edge of the bed. Whilst she'd been driving, his commitment to his plan of action had solidified in his mind. He had to make this infernal song stop, and he had to take action and he had to get better. He waited a while to make sure she wasn't coming back and then crept out of the house as silently as he'd snuck in. He had a mission in mind, but first he needed to grab some tools and other things from his dad's shed.

Chapter 35

Jazzy

By the time she parked skew-whiff outside the police station just after six thirty, Jazzy had no memory of the frantic drive to get there in record time. She peered round the half-empty car park expecting to see Queenie's Land Rover, but it wasn't there and neither were Geordie nor Fenton's vehicles. Instead of her usual strong morning coffee, nervous energy fuelled her as she thrust the car door open and after slamming it behind her, stormed into the building, barely acknowledging Sergeant Hobson on the front desk as she made for the elevators and the chief super's office. Afzal had called her at six a.m. – waking her from sleep – and without any greeting had told her to come in urgently.

As the lift creaked its way upwards, Jazzy took a deep breath and tried to order her thoughts. It was worrying that Afzal had called her here rather than direct her to whatever crime scene had come in, and that made her breath hitch in her chest. Fractured memories of the previous night's nightmares weaved their insidious way into her conscious mind and, as she tried to thrust them away, she couldn't help gripping her Ganesh statue tightly and praying to a

God that she didn't believe in, that the bloody broken bodies of her friends and family wouldn't turn out to be a reality. She was surer than ever that Mhairi was responsible for the Fletcher and Taggart murders. Lucy had confirmed to Fenton and Geordie that the eyes on Taggart's van weren't part of the original design and when she'd seen the van the previous week, she was sure the eyes hadn't been there. Together with Queenie's find it meant Mhairi was orchestrating it all. And now the order to come in urgently.

Thoughts of another murder barrelled their way to the front of her mind and she wondered who her sister's latest victim was. As soon as the lift doors opened, she barged through and marched to the chief super's office, where with a peremptory rap on the door she flung it open and strode in. The sight that greeted her made her pause, her mouth open, her desperate pleas for information dying on her lips. She frowned as Afzal continued to roll up the sleeping bag that lay on the small couch in the corner of his room, before thrusting it in the bottom of a cupboard and turning to face his daughter with a self-conscious smile that didn't quite meet his eyes. 'Long night, so grabbed a few winks here.'

The faint smell of sweat and his crumpled shirt, half untucked from his trousers, testified to that. A knot of concern tightened in Jazzy's stomach as she observed her estranged dad's sleeping arrangements. Just as quickly, she thrust it away. She was more concerned with why she'd been dragged in so early and so abruptly. Seemingly picking up on her mood, Afzal tucked his shirt in, poured them both a coffee and gestured to a chair beside the coffee table on which two items lay. For a moment, Jazzy studied the older man. Despite his sunken cheeks and thin lines meandering across his forehead, his expression did not indicate the type of bad news she had anticipated.

Grateful for the coffee, she slipped into the chair and cupped the drink in her hands, allowing its warmth and aromatic fragrance to calm her bit by bit as she focused on slowing her heartbeat whilst he settled opposite her.

He picked up one of the two evidence bags, opened it and extracted the contents. 'These arrived overnight in a single package addressed to you. Some drunk guy dropped it off and could offer little sense other than that he had been given a bottle of whisky to make the delivery. He's in the cells for now and we're hoping he'll be sober enough to offer some sort of description later on today. Although we can't count on that.'

Jazzy nodded and, as her eyes zoned in on the burner phone in his hand, a chill ran through her. For the past seven months, all of Jazzy's electronics had been monitored on a regular basis and any packages arriving at the station addressed to her or any of her team had been forensically assessed before arriving at her desk. Apart from the note at the Fletcher crime scene, nothing ominous had arrived for her either at home or at her place of work. Until today.

Jazzy knew of only one person who would send a burner phone to her. Her sister. She shivered and her skin crawled as if Mhairi's eyes were on her right there in Afzal's office. Amidst the weight of responsibility pressing heavily on her shoulders, she could sense her closeness like never before.

Afzal handed the burner phone to Jazzy. 'The techie bods have swept it for any crap that she may have put on it, but they didn't find a sodding thing. As far as they could tell, and believe me, they put this burner through its paces, there's nothing on it that could be used to trace you, record you or hurt you. Not even a saved number.'

Jazzy snorted. 'Wouldn't have expected one. That's not Mhairi's style. She wouldn't want to give me any control by letting me decide when to speak to her. No, she'll be enjoying this. She knows we're so desperate for any clue to her whereabouts that I'll carry the damn thing with me wherever I go.'

His eyes bored into hers. 'You're right. Even though it's possible that someone else is observing you, we should assume it's her.'

'Aye, I know. No going off on my own. An escort to and from the station, regular sweeps of my vehicle and home. Yep. I know the drill.' She paused. 'But I want the same precautions for all of them. You know how twisted she is. She'll stop at nothing to get at me.'

'Already sorted. We'll talk more about that later. We won't take our eye off the ball on this, Jazzy. You have my word.'

Shoving the phone in her pocket, Jazzy gestured to the remaining bag, which contained the envelope the phone had arrived in. 'Please tell me you found something on this?'

'There was nothing traceable on the envelope except, as you'd expect, a whole load of random prints and so forth that will take forever to sort through. The forensic team is prioritising it. There's nothing about the padded envelope that makes pinpointing where it was bought simple. It is highly likely that she wore gloves when handling it, and the address label is typed. The only telling thing is the postmark. It's an Edinburgh one. Of course, we know she enjoys mucking around with us, so that doesn't necessarily mean she's in the area.'

He paused and exhaled before opening the laptop that was on the coffee table. 'Of course, I've had to forward this information to Operation Birchtree. DCI Connolly – the new task force leader – would like to speak to you. Have you met her?'

Jazzy shook her head. Having been excluded from all but the most trivial reports from Operation Birchtree after she'd refused to keep visiting her brother, Simon, she hadn't been privy to any of the reshuffle politics. Now, it appeared that the arrival of this phone may have opened up channels of communication.

'She's waiting for our call.' Afzal hesitated. 'She's ambitious, Jazzy. Just caw canny around her; that's all I'm saying.'

Jazzy thought that was interesting. Couldn't she spare the time to walk down from the top floor to discuss this? Before Jazzy could respond, he activated the call and, with Jazzy still pondering his words, a well-preserved woman in her fifties, wearing a navy power suit and with a riot of curly red hair, appeared on the screen. Uneasy with meeting new people, Jazzy leaned forward and attempted a smile, which was met with barely a twitch of the older woman's lipsticked lips. Not into social niceties then. Jazzy's hand slid into her pocket as she waited for one of the two senior officers to speak.

'So, we meet at last, DS Solanki. I've been updating myself on your contribution to Operation Birchtree . . .' she paused and glanced off screen as if someone else was in the room with her '. . . such as it was.'

Jazzy frowned. Such as it was? *Really?*

Beside her, Afzal shifted in his seat, but his tone was mild. 'Jazzy's team uncovered two previously unidentified Scottish serial killers. That's quite an achievement. Plus, she spent many months attempting to extract information from her brother regarding his twin sister, who is still at large.'

'Yes, until she decided to go rogue and scupper that avenue of investigation.'

Jazzy's cheeks flushed with the slap of blame issued by this senior officer, whom she'd only just met. Hackles rising, she barely restrained the impulsive reflex to get up and leave the meeting. She'd done nothing wrong and Connolly had no right to make her feel guilty. She managed that all on her own every single damn day. But this was too important so, remaining silent, she gritted her teeth and focused somewhere to the right of the woman's shoulder.

Afzal frowned. 'I think Jazzy's cooperation regarding the ongoing funeral arrangements of her brother and the operation around capturing Mhairi, should she appear there, prove her commitment to locating Mhairi.'

Shuffling some paperwork on her desk, Connolly continued, 'Yes, that is ongoing and we appreciate your cooperation, Detective. However, although it is significant that the phone arrived the day before the planned funeral date, there is no solid

191

proof it was sent by your sister and our current intel suggests she is *not* in the area. However, to be certain we'll clearly need you to carry that phone, and my people have taken measures to monitor any calls to and from it in real time. From our point of view, that level of monitoring should suffice at this stage.'

Jazzy leaned forward, her eyes flashing, a deep frown furrowing her brow. 'What about the Taggart and Fletcher murders? Aren't they too coincidental not to be linked to Mhairi?'

'I don't see why, Detective. My team has analysed the reports and concluded that there is not enough evidence to link these deaths to Mhairi. Although both victims are linked to you, I think it's safe to say that these cases are entirely separate from Operation Birchtree and you are on the cusp of closing them, I believe.'

'But don't you see? This is exactly the sort of twisted ploy Mhairi would use,' she said. 'She's devious and likes to play games. Besides . . .' She swallowed and, aware that she should have given him a heads up on Queenie's discovery, she cast a glance at DCS Afzal. 'Yesterday, my team discovered Mhairi's calling card among the graffiti on the walls of the bottle kiln where Lewis Fletcher was found.'

The slight tensing of Afzal's shoulders was the only sign that Jazzy's words had surprised him and, with Connolly's laser eyes burning into her, it was unlikely she registered that fact. 'You what?' Her gentle Irish lilt hardened and her lips tightened.

'We only discovered it last night.'

After Jazzy had explained what they'd discovered and sent the relevant close-ups, the DCI took a moment, then: 'I still think this is tenuous. Someone could have added this artwork at any time, and we have no concrete proof that your sister did it. However . . .' she spoke over Jazzy's 'but' with a wave of the hand '. . . considering heightened tensions around the upcoming funeral, the phone and this possible, but unlikely scenario that somehow your sister was involved in these two deaths, I suggest you and your team exercise extreme caution in the coming days.

DS Solanki, make yourself available later on today to my strategic ops manager, who will update you on the final arrangements for your brother's funeral. Now, if you have nothing more for me, I'll let you get on with your day.' And before either Jazzy or Afzal could respond, the screen went blank.

For a moment, all Jazzy could do was blink in disbelief at the dark monitor. *Is that woman for real?*

Afzal exhaled. 'She's not an easy woman to get on with, is she?'

Jazzy shook her head, then risked a glance at him. The stubble on his chin and his sallow complexion tightened her heart – just for a moment – a nanosecond, really. 'I'm sorry, I should . . .'

'No apology needed, Jazzy. Your team did what they always do and pulled a rabbit out of the hat, and I realise that you've had no time to update either Elliot or myself yet.' He paused. 'I'm still on the fence about this. However, Jazzy, I trust your gut instincts, so we'll take additional steps to ensure the protection of you and your team. You have to get me more concrete evidence though, and damn quickly. Now, let's get Elliot over here and together we can discuss strategy.'

Discussing strategy with Elliot was the last thing she wanted to do, but it was a necessary evil and, regardless of the deterioration in their personal relationship, Jazzy trusted Elliot's professional instincts implicitly.

Chapter 36

Jazzy

By lunchtime, the rest of the team had gathered in CS Afzal's office. Seeing Jazzy and Elliot already there, their bemused expressions soon became puzzled frowns as they registered the two evidence bags containing the phone and the envelope it had been delivered in. Whether it was the serious expressions on their faces or the inevitability of something like this happening, Queenie straight away understood the implications of that phone.

'Aw, Christ, JayZee.' Queenie dragged her fingers through her already awry hair and, glowering at the offending items as if she expected them to jump up and grab her by the throat, stepped away. 'When the buggering hell did those arrive? You no' think of giving your partner a wee heads up, eh? You know, keeping me in the loop, like? Extending the common courtesy of being a team player, eh? Did you no' think of doing any of those things?'

Jazzy shrugged, but offered no platitudes. How could she? She'd wanted to bring the team in earlier, but Elliot and Afzal had vetoed that by insisting on getting their strategy together first and she had to admit to herself they'd been right.

'Eh?' Fenton, nose scrunched up like a startled dormouse, edged closer and looked at it. 'Not sure I'm getting why you're all aeriated, Queenie.'

'Aw, for Fanny Tootsie's sake, can you no' get on the same page as the rest of us, Haggis? You know, keep up with the grown-ups? Use those brain ce—'

'Queenie.' The warning tone in Chief Super Waqas Afzal's voice elicited a tut and an exaggerated eye-roll from Queenie, but she shut up, and thrust her hands into her jeans pockets, her chin raised to express her annoyance.

Afzal exhaled. 'It was addressed to Jazzy and delivered here overnight, and alongside another disturbing coincidence, myself, Elliot and Jazzy have spent the morning strategising.'

Jazzy rolled her eyes. There it was, that damn word again. Strategising. If she never heard it again in her life, she'd be *happy*.

The glare Queenie sent her partner was razor-sharp. 'What other disturbing coincidence?'

Hesitating only briefly, Jazzy dived in explaining what Benjy had discovered that morning outside her house and his feeling that someone had been observing her on Tuesday night. 'Pedro dropped the cap off earlier and it's being processed as we speak and a forensic team are already processing the grassy area. But, as you can imagine, with the arrival of the phone, which we have to consider might be from Mhairi, if Mhairi has – as Benjy believes – been watching me, then it is an escalation in the threat level against us.'

For a moment they all remained silent as they processed the implications of these revelations. Then: 'Boss, have you checked it over?' Geordie asked, his eyes fixed on the bags as if he expected them to explode. 'Not just for forensics, but in case it's booby-trapped, or got a tracking device or some sort of destructive software on it.'

'Not my first rodeo, son.' Afzal's warning tone became clipped and impatient.

Jazzy inhaled. Her team, much as she respected their individual abilities, were not presenting themselves in their best light to the chief super today. 'We're all over the place, sir. With the funeral coming up and that painting we found at the Fletcher scene yesterday, we're all just a little . . .' Unsure how to describe her team's state of mind, she rolled her hand in the air and grimaced.

However, Queenie came to her rescue. 'Aye, we're a wee bit frazzled, sir. You ken cream-crackered, knackered and puggled as crap.'

Afzal's features softened. 'I understand that. So D team get a pass for now. Let me tell you what we know about it, eh?'

After he'd finished, the room remained silent until Fenton exhaled and said, 'What I don't get, is why hasn't she just used an encrypted phone to call you on your exiting number?'

Jazzy snorted. 'It's all a game play. She wants to be in control and the idea of me hanging on the end of a phone waiting for her call plays into her narcissism. It's about denying me any control. Because we're so desperate for any clue to her whereabouts, she knows I'll carry the damn thing with me wherever I go.'

'You told Operation Birchtree about this?' Although Queenie's eyes were on Jazzy, it was the super who answered. 'Em, well, they're not as convinced as we are that Mhairi is nearby. They are focused on the funeral arrangements and are reluctant to accept the possibility of her being responsible for the Fletcher and Taggart murders.'

Geordie glared at him. 'But you told them about what Queenie found.'

This time Elliot went in to bat. 'It seems we need more concrete evidence before they'll accept what we all know in our hearts.' He risked a glance at Jazzy. 'They're at the disadvantage of never having the dubious pleasure of being in her presence. Of seeing first-hand how she operates and what she's capable of.'

Geordie glowered. 'She's such a devious cow. The sooner she's banged up, the better. Why the hell is Operation Birchtree not making any headway?'

'Yeah, we all want to know that.' Queenie glared at Afzal. She had little respect for the man after discovering he was, in fact, Jazzy's biological father and had deserted her, leaving her with an irrational and alcoholic mother as a child.

Afzal cleared his throat. 'DCI Connolly has agreed to use Operation Birchtree's resources to monitor any calls to Jazzy on that mobile.'

'Aw, big wow-wee. Monitoring calls? They'd be as well flying a rocket to the moon. Can they no' be a bit more proactive?' Queenie jumped to her feet. 'Besides, there's no way she's keeping that. No way this side of haggis hunting season is JayZee keeping that. Not over Geordie's deid body, not over my deid body and – much as I'm not that fussed about him – not over Haggis's deid body either. We're unanimous on that, so . . .'

'She's keeping it.' Afzal directed a laser gaze to Queenie, which made her jaw slacken and leave her last words unspoken. For a moment, he closed his eyes and exhaled then looked upwards as if to ward off any further arguments. He said, 'It's not ideal . . .'

Queenie had her tongue back. 'You're no' kidding.'

'. . . but we're out of options. This, although *you* might not like it, DC McQueen, and although Operation Birchtree might not agree, may be a huge step forward. It's a chance to make contact. If we caw canny, maybe we can reel her in.'

Queenie, her face scrunched up like a troll's, shook her head from side to side. 'It's no' up to you though, is it? It's no' your choice, it's . . .'

Jazzy sighed. 'Aye, Queenie, that's right. It's not the boss's choice, it's mine and I've already agreed to it.'

Queenie, open-mouthed, turned to Jazzy, a worried frown pulling her brows together. 'Aw, no, hen. No. You don't need to do it. You don't need to put yourself in the fir—'

But again, Jazzy interrupted. 'I'm already in the firing line.

197

You know that. Whether or not I carry this phone, whether or not I answer it when she rings, whether or not I want any part of this, I've no choice. I'm already walking about with a target on my back and we all know how many murders she's already responsible for. More than we've discovered, I suspect. So, no. I'm not happy about it, but as far as I can see, this is one way of enticing her out of hiding. She'll love thinking she's got one up on me. Plus, she's got more than one score to settle with me now – she'll hold me responsible for what happened to Simon.'

Chuntering under her breath, Queenie wandered to a seat as far away from Jazzy as she could and plonked herself down as if too weary to stand for a second longer. Jazzy hated to see her friend like this. Queenie was only looking out for her and she loved her for that, but there was no alternative. None whatsoever. She dragged a chair over beside her friend and sat, waiting for Fenton and Geordie to join them. The Jazz Queens united, reluctantly perhaps, but united nonetheless, before asking the question they were all dying to ask. 'Soooo.' Queenie slumped in her chair. 'The bottom line is we're on our own.'

'No, that's not what we're saying, Queenie. Of course not.' Afzal looked at her. 'We've spent the morning working out a strategy to keep you all safe.'

There it was again. That damn word. Jazzy tensed, preparing for the inevitable backlash that would follow when the 'strategy' was revealed.

All red-faced bluster, Queenie bristled. 'Och, I know your security plans. No going off on oor own. An escort to and from the station, regular sweeps of oor vehicles and home. Yep. We know the drill.'

'Queenie, just listen to him for a second.'

An abrupt nod told Jazzy that Afzal appreciated her intervention. He dragged his chair closer to his desk and sat, arms crossed on the shiny surface, whilst Elliot stood behind him like a bodyguard. The thought amused Jazzy, for she knew that by the end

198

of this briefing her dad may well need one. In the silence, Jazzy studied him. In recent months, she'd avoided contact with him and this had been the closest she'd been to her birth father for ages. His dark hair had always been speckled with grey, but now there was even less black. His shoulders were more rounded and his suit hung from them like a scarecrow wilting in the summer's heat. He was, she supposed, tenuously linked to Mhairi. He was her father and she was Mhairi's half-sister. In another world he could have been Mhairi's stepdad. But he'd left. And their awful biological mother had given birth to twins by another man. Maybe he never thought of himself as linked to Mhairi. Maybe it was Jazzy trying not to feel alone in her link with the serial killer.

Something fluttered in Jazzy's chest, but before it had the chance to flower into something more solid, she tightened her lips and willed it away. This man had left her in danger. He'd left her to the whim of a violent mother. She owed him no allegiance, no pity and whatever was troubling him – whether it was this ongoing hunt for her sister or some other troubles – was no business of hers.

'Because resources are tight – budget cuts, you know how it is? We're having to be creative to keep everyone safe and because I'm taking this threat seriously, I'm hoping that you'll all agree to my proposals – extreme though they may seem – because to be honest, it's the only solution I've been able to come up with at such short notice.'

Geordie and Fenton, eyes wide, blinked. With his gangly legs stuck out straight in front of him, Geordie's fingers tapped a tattoo against his thigh. Fenton's crossed legs jammered up and down, and Queenie offered nothing more than a loud snort.

'I'll start with you, Queenie. I'm concerned about Craig and Ruby, so we've arranged a wee holiday for them with Craig's aunt Gladys in Cornwall for the summer. It's remote and it won't interfere with his lecturing as it's the holidays and . . .'

Queenie was on her feet. 'What the hell? How do you know

anything about Craig's aunt Gladys? And besides, what gives you the right to make plans for my husband and granddaughter without consulting us?'

Jazzy cleared her throat. 'Eh . . .'

Queenie whirled round, eyes sparking. '*You? You* suggested this? *Et tu, Brute.* What sort of friend are you?'

'Quee . . .'

'Aye well, I'm no' impressed. No' impressed at all. Besides, Craig will never go for it.'

Stomach churning, Jazzy stood and reached out to her friend. 'Ah, Queenie, Craig's already agreed. It makes sense, doesn't it? You want to keep Ruby safe and that's one way to guarantee it. The next few days could be make or break and the last thing we want is for that bitch to target your loved ones. My parents and Crumble are going to Bradford to my mum's brother's for the duration. Anything to keep them safe and you know how hard it is for my mum with a guide dog – learning new routes, navigating strange territory . . . we're all making sacrifices here.'

Queenie shrugged off Jazzy's hand, her teeth biting her lower lip so hard, Jazzy was sure it would bleed. But at least she sat down, legs extended before her and crossed at the heels. Still, she avoided Jazzy's gaze and Jazzy wondered how many more of her friends would be scowling at her before Afzal had finished outlining his plans. The chief super took a beat before clearing his throat. 'Right, well, let's crack on.' He smiled at Fenton. 'Fortunately, you're quite easy to sort out, DC Heggie. Your fiancée – congratulations by the way – is already on an extended work placement in Birmingham, so . . .'

Fenton nodded. 'But what about my parents? They can't just up and move. My mum's a dentist and my dad's been diagnosed with early onset Alzheimer's. That's just not possible.'

'Yes, we agree, so we're issuing them with regular police drive-bys and will add additional security measures such as panic alarms and so forth in their home. They'll be as safe as they can be.'

Fenton clearly wasn't happy. Had he even considered the idea that his parents could be at risk until this meeting? Jazzy thought not.

Afzal turned to Geordie next. 'Our primary concern with you, Geordie, is your boyfriend, Guy. So, we've taken steps to protect him too, but I'll get to that in a moment.'

'Of course, we've got the kids over in Stùrrach to consider. Jazzy thinks that because Ivor escaped her sister last year and because she's developed a close friendship with the two, we consider both teenagers high-risk targets. So, we've enlisted Uncle Pedro's help. He's brought the Stùrrachers up to speed and is enlisting some friends, whom I know nothing about. I'm just glad they'll be there, as backup.'

He glanced at Jazzy. 'Do you want to continue?'

Jazzy's lip turned up. How dare he? How dare he try to palm this last and most annoying aspect of their plan on her? 'You get paid the big bucks. *You* do it.' Her tone bordered on insolence, but after Queenie's angry words and the general heightened atmosphere, nobody appeared to be adhering too much to protocol.

'Em, excuse me.' Geordie's face was red, almost matching his hair, his eyes flashing. 'You haven't told me how you're protecting Guy. If you're protecting everyone else's loved ones and families, then you better be protecting Guy too.'

'Of course, our plans include protecting Guy. If you'd just let me finish.'

Geordie, legs pulled back, skinny elbows resting on them, glared at Afzal as if calculating how many steps he'd need to reach him if his plans to protect Guy were inadequate.

'As previously mentioned, resources are tight and well, the truth is, we can't afford to offer you individual protection when you're off duty, so . . .' the end of the sentence came out in a rush as if Afzal hoped that way, no one would quite get the implications of it '. . . we're asking you to move into a safe house for the duration.'

Jazzy's team exchanged glances whilst she kept her head down. Jazzy had doubts about how the team would react to this new development. She herself hated the idea. Much as she cared for them, the thought of being in close proximity to them twenty-four-seven freaked her out. What if they heard her torment during her nightly nightmares? That would be unbearable. How could she lead them if they saw her at her weakest? It was unthinkable.

Eyes on Queenie, almost matching scowls on their brows, Fenton and Geordie, their tone full of horror, responded in synchronicity. 'Together?'

Then, a beat later, Geordie backed up their question with a 'Nah, you can't mean together. I mean, not with . . .'

When his voice trailed off, Fenton took up the baton. 'You mean me and Geordie together, right? And Queenie and Jazzy together . . . but separate from us, aye?' As he spoke, he shrugged and grimaced in apology to Jazzy for hoping she'd have the sole responsibility of living with Queenie.

Meanwhile, Queenie was grinning. Her wrinkled face lit up like a guy on top of the bonfire on Guy Fawkes Night. 'Aw, come on, kids. It'll be a laugh. The Jazz Queens living together and working together. It'll be great. Like being at Malory Towers, or St Clare's or Hogwarts. I used to dream of that when I was a kid.' Queenie took on a wistful tone as she sighed. Jazzy knew why Queenie's childhood dreams had been of boarding schools filled with camaraderie, decent food, and mischievous pranks. It wasn't hard to work out that with her upbringing in Glasgow that would be her escapism.

'Being a wizard?' Fenton pursed his lips up shaking his head. 'But . . .'

'Don't be so bloody dippet, Haggis. Of course, not a bloody wizard, you numpty. I mean, being part of a big gang of friends. Living together, making plans together, getting up to all sorts of high jinks. Aw, it'll be grand. We'll have a ball, us four.'

'Six.' Afzal tapped his desk top. 'There'll be six of you. That's what I was trying to tell you, Geordie. Guy will join you at the safe house. He works from home as a website designer, so it's not an issue for him.'

A flush rose in Geordie's cheeks as he stood. 'What do you mean, not an issue for him? How the hell do you know? How do you know he wants to shack up with a bunch of' – he wafted his hand in the air to engulf his team – 'bloody misfits and . . .'

Jazzy caught his eye. 'It was me, Geordie. I spoke to Guy this morning before the meeting. Explained the danger we were all in, and he agreed.'

Eyes flashing, Geordie's lips curled into a snarl. 'Just like that, eh? Just at the drop of a hat, Guy agreed to this? To living with you lot for the foreseeable future? Don't bloody think so.'

Jazzy exhaled. She hadn't wanted to approach Guy behind Geordie's back, but she was glad that she had. Unknown to Geordie, Guy had been worried about his partner's mental well-being – his mood swings, his weight loss – and he, as much as the rest of them, wanted Mhairi caught and the threat she presented eliminated once and for all. With a glance at the others, she lowered her voice and, ignoring everyone else, spoke to Geordie. 'He's worried about you. Guy viewed this temporary arrangement as a means to an end, not an inconvenience. The only way we can ensure everyone's safety till she's caught, and he recognised that lumping us together, although inconvenient, was a way to focus resources where they'd do most good . . .'

Fenton, a frown pulling his brows together, counted on his fingers. 'Me, Jazzy, Queenie, Geordie and Guy. That's just the five of us. Who . . .'

Jazzy groaned and her eyes flicked to Elliot, who had sat in silence, his face like a thunderstorm ready to kick off. This was both her worst nightmare and the least palatable part of the plan. Of course, she wanted Elliot to be safe, but to live with him? No, that wasn't on her radar. How uncomfortable would having Mr Grumpy in close proximity be? To be fair, he was as unenthusiastic as she was about the idea. He cleared his throat. 'I'm the sixth, folks.'

With everyone's attention focused on trying to gauge *her* reaction, Jazzy's cheeks burned as Elliot continued, his tone laden with sarcasm. 'That won't be a problem, will it? We are all on the same side, right? Unless, of course, anyone still has lingering doubts about my *loyalty*.'

The burn in Jazzy's cheeks intensified, and a red-hot poker of tension scratched up her spine as her lips tightened. 'No doubts on my part, Elliot. There never was.'

But he'd already jumped to his feet and headed from the room. 'I'll see you there later on. Fenton, you're sharing with me, so no bloody snoring.'

For long seconds, the five remaining in DCI Afzal's office sat in silence, avoiding meeting each other's gazes as they tried to get their heads round the disruption to their lives. Jazzy bore the weight of having taken decisions that affected her team without consulting them on the matter. Given more time, Jazzy would have handled this situation differently. However, time was of the essence and with Simon's funeral imminent and with all the risk factors that entailed, she'd chosen to act, telling herself that her team's safety trumped democracy any day of the week. That didn't stop her from being aware of the reproachful glances being sent her way. Only Queenie's cheerful humming as she, no doubt, planned midnight feasts with lashings of ginger beer and chocolate made her feel better. She cricked her neck, wishing the tension would magically disappear, but knowing that was an unlikely scenario.

'So, JayZee, where is this safe house . . .?'

Jazzy cringed, but luck was on her side for once, as she was saved by the ringing of DCS Afzal's phone. Glad of the reprieve, yet knowing she was only putting off the inevitable, Jazzy paused as he glanced at the screen. 'Waqas Afzal speaking, what can I do for you, Niamh?'

Jazzy got up and approached him, never breaking eye contact, as he responded with a series of affirmatives. When he hung up, he nodded to Jazzy and pointed at Queenie. 'DCI Connolly has requested both of you to attend a crime scene in Pollokshaws.'

Jazzy's mouth fell open. The hot flush drained from her cheeks as she exhaled a slow breath. Connolly, only that morning, had told Jazzy her involvement with Operation Birchtree was limited and had demanded concrete evidence that Mhairi was back and now, here she was requesting their presence at a crime scene. There could only be one reason for their presence being requested by the task force. The Bitch had struck again! For a moment, she didn't know how to feel or what to do. However, Queenie addressed the latter question by grabbing her elbow, dragging her into the lift, and jabbing the button repeatedly as if that alone would speed up its descent.

Under her breath, she said, 'You okay for this, JayZee? Don't forget. You're a Jazz Queen . . .'

From somewhere, Jazzy summoned a smile and concluded Queenie's sentence to the tune of Queen's 'Killer Queen' lyrics. '*Top-notch, cool and mean. Hot stuff with a killer gleam. This girl's gonna whoop your arse.*' Saying the words elicited a flicker of resolve inside Jazzy. But would it be enough?

Chapter 37

Jazzy

Jazzy had never attended a crime scene in this part of Pollokshaws. The area was in Glasgow and not part of Lothian and Borders. That Connolly had demanded their presence here was telling, particularly after her attitude that morning. The tension in the air as they entered the crime scene corresponded with the tightness spreading across Jazzy's shoulders with every step she took towards what, judging by the sombre faces, promised to be a gruesome and traumatic sight. And all the time, the weight of that damn phone in her pocket burdened her. It was like a bomb waiting to go off and knowing that her sister could detonate it at any time exacerbated Jazzy's anxiety. Not knowing what her sister had planned was almost unbearable, but what was worse was not knowing how close she was. As she walked from the car to the crime scene, she felt that she and Queenie had giant targets on their backs.

The property was a normal three-bedroom ex-council house with an extension and a garage downstairs and an additional room on top. The garden was basic but well tended; the windows were clean. In short, there was nothing on the outside, bar the closed curtains, to indicate the horrors that awaited inside. The uncertainty of their role at the scene concerned Jazzy. DCI Connolly's only words as she'd chivvied them through the formalities of signing in had been 'You'll see.' Of course, the inference had to be that somehow or another, they suspected the Bitch was responsible for this murder and therefore, they wanted Jazzy and Queenie to confirm their suspicions, but it really irked that, in her infinite wisdom Connolly had provided no information on the victim, including his or her ID, the scene, or even the cause of death.

Queenie, on edge at the prospect of another scene, chuntered under her breath. She would have to process and then find a place to store it, so it wasn't at the front of her mind every time she spoke with her husband or cuddled her grandchild. 'Bloody heads up would be nice. A wee wink and an "it's not one to get your knickers in a fankle about" or a "brace yourself, girls, it's a blood-soaked whammy", or a "get your sick bag handy because projectile vomiting won't be out of the question on this one". Not much to ask, is it? A wee word of warning so you know what to expect. So, you can brace yourself and get your game face on. So we can . . .'

She wasn't wrong, either. Common decency should dictate that they didn't have to visit the scene cold. Jazzy placed a gloved hand on Queenie's sleeve and squeezed. 'You've got this. You know you have. Just close your eyes for a second, then concentrate on the ceiling. From there, move your head inch by inch, processing each thing as you go. You don't have to see everything at once.'

'Aye, I know we've practised this technique of yours, JayZee, but who the hell knows if it works in practice, eh?' She shuffled closer and lowered her voice. 'No way I want to puke my load in front of all these Weegies. Fuck no. I've got my reputation to consider.'

The front door was open and despite the through-flow of

air, the metallic smell of blood hung heavy in the breeze. An early sign that the scene would not be a clean one. Already the CSI team's yellow markers were dotted about the hallway and upstairs. Floor plates marked the way to a room on the right where Jazzy could hear professionals processing the scene. With Queenie behind her, Jazzy, adrenalin surging through her body to prepare for what was to come, took a last deep breath of the fresh outdoor air, pulled her mask up and stepped through the doorway onto the first plate.

The first step was always the worst, and the prospect of bearing witness to murder always cast an extra layer of sadness. Unfortunately, Jazzy Solanki was all too familiar with troubled passings – it went with her job – but one potentially caused by her sister who remained at large after so long, was worse. The pitying melancholy in the CSIs' averted gazes intensified Jazzy's own discomfort. It cast an ominous cloak over everything and the promise of more to come when she saw whatever she'd been summoned to view. She'd once asked Franny Gallagher, the crime scene manager she worked with most, how she coped with a ceaseless parade of death.

Franny's response had been revealing. 'I take a moment to respect the victim, to lament their loss. A sort of silent pause, an offer of condolence, a nod to the expiration of a human life. And when I've done that I focus on helping the victim in the only way I can. I concentrate on the job at hand, organising my team, and together we collect as much physical and forensic evidence as possible. That way we can learn the truth about the deceased's final moments on this earth. That's what helps me cope and keeps me going.'

She edged down the hallway, noting the absence of photos or paintings on the wall. The carpet beneath the treads was of good quality and the walls appeared to have been recently painted. It had the feel of a bachelor's home – not overly sentimental, but well cared for. Not that she was qualified to make that assumption.

The only bachelor she knew was Elliot and his flat was crammed with photos, ornaments, and paintings.

At last, with the blood smell stronger now, she turned into the living room. In that moment, before she set foot over the threshold, Jazzy's instinct was to throw up her hands and say, 'You know what? I can't do this. You're on your own. I absolve myself of all guilt and feelings or responsibility for my sister's actions. So, here, take this fucking phone, catch the Bitch yourselves and let me know when you have. I'm outta here.'

Instead, she ignored the urge to flee, forcing herself into the zone. Still sticking to the plates, she walked over to the lifeless body and sighed. There was always something grotesque about being confronted by the hard-fought, violent death of a person, but when it was a younger person with their entire life spread out before them, it affected Jazzy more – although a child's death by violence was the hardest to bear. A young victim or a vulnerable one intensified the sadness, amplifying it like a DJ mixing an unpleasantly mocking soundtrack and forcing people to listen. A soundtrack filled with anger, rage and sheer frustration at the futility of it all, at the pointlessness of cutting a living being's life short.

Suited and booted, Jazzy and Queenie studied the man lying in a pool of vomit in the corner of the room, a tourniquet tied tight round one arm and a syringe hanging from his vein. Although the curtains remained closed, the crime scene lamps illuminated the area, and their heat intensified the sour vomit smell. When Queenie placed a gloved hand over her masked mouth and gipped, Jazzy gripped her arm forcefully. 'Look away, Queenie. Stare at the ceiling, but whatever you do, don't you bloody dare chuck your load. Just swallow it.'

Although she didn't remove her hand from over her mask, Queenie, as irrepressible as ever, said, 'There are a few things I could say to that, JayZee, – like "said the vicar to the nun", or "said the actress to the bishop" or . . .'

Conscious that, despite being invited to attend the scene, their presence was barely tolerated, Jazzy lowered her tone to a sibilant whisper. 'I'm warning you. Don't you fuck this up for us. We've only just got our feet in the door and I don't want your Doc Martens landing us with our arses kicked to the kerb.' Sensing that Queenie was about to respond, but also thankful that their brief interlude appeared to have distracted her from her nausea, Jazzy pinched her colleague's arm. 'Don't make me wish I'd left you back in Livingston. Just do your thing, because the only access we'll get to this crime scene will be through your memory. Once the high heid one has taken whatever she needs from us, we'll be sent back home like Bo Peeps with no sheep.'

Reassured by Queenie's single nod, Jazzy left Queenie to memorise the scene whilst she concentrated on interpreting it. The presence of the tourniquet and syringe could have had this death dismissed as a self-inflicted overdose. However, it was evident that this was no ordinary drug-related death, considering the brutal beating that the victim, a young man in his twenties, had endured. Although with the blood and bruising, it was hard to ascertain the precise cause of death. That was a job for the pathologist.

Although found alone in his empty house, Jazzy was convinced that the staged overdose scenario indicated another presence at the scene. However, Jazzy could not immediately see anything that indicated that this was the work of the Bitch. So, why did Operation Birchtree take over the scene? And why did they divert Jazzy and Queenie here? Jazzy couldn't work with her hands tied behind her back and she had no intention of doing that now. If Niamh Connolly wanted her help, then she could share, instead of leaving them working blind. If this murder could be connected to the elusive Bitch, Jazzy needed to know.

Neither Queenie nor Jazzy were impressed by the sideways glances the officers in their crime scene suits cast their way. Of course, some of that palpable animosity might be to do with the fact that Livingston CID – Jazzy and Queenie specifically – had closed the raging turf wars that neither Edinburgh nor Glasgow Major Incident Teams had been able to. But that was another story.

Jazzy, accustomed now to the acrid stench of excreted bodily fluids, looked round the room. Like the hallway and garden, the living room was nicely decorated, if somewhat lacking in personality. A huge TV dominated the wall space opposite a two-seater couch, and two matching armchairs completed the quartet of seats around that focal point. A coffee table with a *Men's Health* mag, an empty beer can, a half-drunk scummy coffee mug and a weird walkie-talkie-type phone stood in front of the two-seater. However, the victim lay sprawled in a corner of the compact room, away from the seating arrangement, with an upturned dining-room chair beside him. Jazzy frowned. She moved closer, inspecting the man's wrists. As expected, she could see bruising and a ridge around both wrists where someone had tied him. Her eyes roamed around the area, then she asked the nearest CSI, 'Were any cable ties found here?'

Looking momentarily startled, the man exhaled, then shook his head. 'Not to my knowledge.'

Okaaaay! The marks on the victim's wrists clearly indicated that someone had tied him to something at some point, and the upturned chair seemed to be the likely candidate. 'Can you swab the chair for DNA? I want to know if he was tied to it at any time.'

The CSI nodded and extracted the necessary equipment from his tool box. If the cable ties were missing, then it stood to reason that the killer had removed them and taken them away when they left. 'Was that chair brought in here from the kitchen?'

The CSI paused mid-swab and looked up from his hunkers at Jazzy. 'I believe so. There is a small dining table and two matching chairs in the kitchen.'

'Two?' Jazzy frowned. 'Not three?'

The CSI nodded and then busied himself with the task in

hand. Jazzy turned her head and saw that DCI Niamh Connolly stood behind her. Had she indicated to the CSI that he shouldn't share information with Jazzy? If so, that was petty. They'd been invited here, but Jazzy would bide her time. She had her secret weapon, after all. Talking of which, she glanced round and saw Queenie near the door, eyes wide, but her gaze was systematically going over the crime scene in small incremental stages. A rush of pride blossomed in Jazzy's chest. Queenie was doing it. She was studying the crime scene, and she wasn't puking her load. Keen for answers, Jazzy turned and squared up to the DCI. 'I was just trying to ascertain whether this chair had been brought in from the kitchen, which it appears that it has. So, my next question is, where is the fourth chair? Do you know?'

Something flickered in the older woman's eyes, but then she deflected. 'I take it you noticed the restraint markings?'

Jazzy nodded. 'Not difficult to miss. You've ID'd the victim? Care to share that ID with myself and my colleague?'

DCI Connolly sighed and glanced round the room. Buying time? That knowledge sent a stab of annoyance through Jazzy. She and Queenie had their own investigation to deal with, and if DCI Connolly wasn't prepared to play ball, then Jazzy would tactfully withdraw and leave them to it. They hadn't wangled an invitation, after all. Her mind buzzed with questions, eager for answers. After months of fumbling about in the dark with little progress and a stalled investigation, where a high-profile serial killer remained at large, they'd appointed Niamh Connolly as the new senior investigating officer, and Jazzy had yet to get the measure of her. Although it did bode well that she had requested Jazzy and Queenie's presence at the crime scene, her attitude now they were here was confusing.

Her own boss, DCS Afzal, informed her that, for the sake of continuity in processing the deceased, they had also requested the pathologist, Dr Lamond Johnston, to conduct the PMs. Which was yet another sign that DCI Connolly suspected that this murder was the work of Mhairi. So far, Jazzy had seen no indication of that, and that further puzzled her. Since their attempt to use Jazzy to elicit information from Simon to find Mhairi had fallen flat, Jazzy had been sidelined from the investigation by Operation Birchtree.

Now, DCI Niamh Connolly studied the pair, but behind her face mask, her expression was impenetrable. 'So, DS Solanki.' A nod to Queenie. 'And of course you too, DC McQueen. What do you make of this? Do you recognise this poor soul?'

Jazzy cast a sideways glance at her, wondering if her question was a trap of some sort. A test to see if she would share what clearly was already known intel. To see if she would cooperate with the investigation moving forward. Test or not, though, Jazzy redirected her gaze to the dead man's face. She had been too busy processing the scene to focus on his identity, but now she frowned. He was indeed familiar to her, although she couldn't place him. Had she arrested him, perhaps? Regardless of her inability to match a name to the tortured features of the victim, she had no hesitation in acknowledging that she recognised him. Why would she? Despite her misgivings about the efficacy of the previous leadership of the task force, Jazzy's commitment to the progression of that investigation had never wavered. She would happily give DCI Niamh Connolly her full support and she could only hope that she was effective as the chief super had promised. Still, she kept her response short. 'Yes, but no idea where from.'

Connolly inclined her head and waited, presumably expecting Jazzy to elaborate, but it was Queenie who spoke. 'I don't recognise him, which means I've never seen him before because believe me, if I had, I'd know it.' She splayed her hands palms up before her. 'Look, we wouldn't be here if *you* hadn't already identified the deceased, now would we?' Short and round, her hood weirdly positioned so its cinched edge cut diagonally down the side of her nose, almost obscuring her right eye and giving her a piratical air, Queenie gave a huff, which she accompanied with an eye-roll in

Jazzy's direction, and raised her chin pugnaciously. 'If you want our input, then you shouldn't really mess about. There's no side to us, you know? We're straight-as-dies sort of folk. If we can help, we will. That no' right, JayZee?'

Thankful for the mask that hid her smile, Jazzy nodded. 'Look, DCI Connolly . . .'

'Niamh, please – when it's just us. I'm not one for insisting on formalities.'

Using the other woman's first name felt wrong at such a recent acquaintance, and again Jazzy was besieged by the thought that this entire situation – inviting her and Queenie to the crime scene, the DCI's familiarity, her laid-back attitude – might be some sort of ploy. Jazzy hesitated, her therapist's words at their last session drifted into her head: 'Jazzy you need to learn to trust more. Go on, I dare you. Take the plunge this week and trust someone, for once.'

Her gaze flitted back over the body as she ignored the DCI's interruption and continued her sentence. 'I'm not sure why we've been invited here, but we're happy to help move this investigation forward. He . . .' she gestured to the dead body slumped beside the upturned chair as if he'd slipped from it in the throes of a convulsion '. . . is familiar to me, but you're going to have to help me out. I can't pinpoint when our paths crossed, but clearly you think his death is connected to my sister, so wouldn't everything progress a lot more smoothly if you just told us who he is?'

The DCI inclined her head and clicked her tongue against her teeth before replying. 'You're right. This unfortunate man was one of your half-brother's nurses from his time in Clydebank psychiatric hospital prior to his transfer to Carstairs.' She looked at Jazzy who gave a nod of acknowledgement. Yes, now she had the context she did recognise the man and could visualise him in his nurse's gear.

'His name is David Paltrow, and we dragged you over to Pollokshaws because clearly someone tortured and murdered him, and we think it's linked to our ongoing investigation into the whereabouts of your elusive half-sister.'

All the pieces fell into alignment. Connolly wanted to see if Queenie and Jazzy could discern any markers that might link this man's murder with those committed by her sister previously. Jazzy turned. Her gaze landed on the long-range two-way radio on the coffee table. 'You think he was in communication with my half-sister using the walkie-talkie?'

'Seems likely.'

'Hmm, but although they're untraceable, surely they have limited coverage, which proves she's based nearby – or certainly within a couple of hours' drive of here. Unless you have something more specific than that?'

Frowning, DCS Connolly sighed. 'To be frank, we're no further forward in locating your sister, but the death of someone linked to your half-brother – no matter how fleetingly – is too much of a coincidence for us to ignore. Particularly in view of Simon's death, his upcoming funeral and the two murders in Portobello and West Lothian. It's logical to increase vigilance and so we have markers on as many of Simon's – and yours, for that matter – known associates. Even those that he had limited contact with. Hence . . .' She wafted her hand in the air to encompass the crime scene.

Drawn once more to David Paltrow's body, Jazzy could only nod. Whilst detaching her victims' eyeballs was one of her sister's preferred post-mortem activities, there was no evidence of that here. That aside though, Mhairi was intelligent enough to enjoy taunting them by changing her MO if she thought it would benefit her in some way.

As she looked at Paltrow's bulk, she wondered how the Bitch, without Simon's help, could have subdued and tortured such a large and fit young man. If this was her work, did this mean that she'd somehow procured some help? What sort of person would be perverse enough to go along willingly with her sister's

215

brutal tendencies? Or, if not willing, then how had they been coerced? Whatever the answer to her questions, it was with a sinking realisation that Jazzy accepted that her sister was back in the area and actively cleaning up shop – or maybe she was getting her revenge on those she thought had slighted her brother. When all was said and done, who really knew what her sister's deranged, chaotic mind was up to? That depressing thought was enough to send a chill through her that lodged itself in her gut. She'd always know this day was coming, but that didn't make the possibility any more palatable.

DCS Connolly touched her arm. 'I wanted you to see the body in situ and – after dismissing your concerns regarding Taggart and Fletcher, this seemed like a coincidence too far. DCS Afzal agreed. But that's not all. Come.' And without another word, Connolly made her way from the room leaving Jazzy and Queenie staring open-mouthed at each other. What now?

Chapter 38

Benjy

If Uncle Pedro thought he was invisible, then he was severely deluded. For the past hour, Benjy had been aware of his constant shadow as he trailed aimlessly around the nooks and crannies of Stùrrach carrying the hammer. He knew who to blame. Bloody Jazzy! He hadn't meant to upset her, but he was so worried about everything all the time. That was why he staked out her house and rarely left Ivor's side. Constant anxiety drove every sodding thing he did.

Right now, he was on a quest and he didn't need a witness – and there, right on cue, it started up again, that fucking nursery rhyme pounding in his head, sneering at him, creeping him out. *Girls and boys come out to play* . . . He shook his head, trying to dislodge the refrain – but it persisted – *The moon doth shine as bright as day* . . . all tinny and echoey. He wanted to bang it against the nearest brick wall. A high-pitched giggle escaped his lips. He clasped his hands over his mouth. *Christ, what if I did? What if I ran full throttle, head first, into that wall over there?* Like a jittery old homemade black-and-white video, the sequence rolled out inside Benjy's head.

Running, running, building up speed, faster and faster. Head down, ready for impact. Keep going, don't lose your nerve.

In Benjy's imagination it ended with him in a heap, blood pouring from his skull, and Uncle Pedro trying to staunch the flow. He blinked. He could pinpoint the exact point of impact on the wall, see an indent where his head connected with the brick, the blood rolling down pooling on the pavement. Fuck, this was bad. They'd probably send him to Carstairs! He shuddered. The very thought sent panic surging through him, catching in his chest. That wasn't funny. Not funny at all, so why did he want to laugh? Why, when he was struggling for air, was the urge to roll about the floor in hysterics so strong? Another falsetto giggle escaped through his fingers, louder this time. God, wouldn't that be rich? Him locked up in the state hospital with the ghost of fucking Simon Says. Jazzy could visit them both at the same time. *We could have a fucking tea party!*

Tears rolled down his cheeks and that damn ice-cream van tune kept on playing – *Leave your supper and leave your sleep* – on repeat. Benjy fell to his knees – curled into a ball and wrapped his arms round his head – *And come with your playfellows into the street . . .*

Strong arms engulfed him, pulling him upright. 'Come on, son. I've got you.'

Uncle Pedro's familiar woody smoke smell wrapped round him like a duvet on a winter's morning. Benjy fell against his solid bulk and allowed the tears to stream down his cheeks and the shudders to rack his skinny body. For so long, he'd held it all in, trying not to worry anyone, trying to deny that he was haunted by dreams of that dark afternoon, trying to move on like everyone else had. But he couldn't. Not till the Bitch was caught. The tinkling, taunting tune began to fade – *Girls and boys come out to . . .*

'There, there, son. You're all right. I've got you. You're safe. Nobody can get you. Nobody can get any of you. I won't let them.'

Arms clutching his uncle, Benjy gulped. 'I'm on a quest.'

Uncle Pedro nodded, allowing Benjy to step away from him. 'Need a hand with that, like? I've got nothing else to do and there's nothing like a quest to start the day.'

'It might be illegal, though.'

'Aye, that right? Well, maybe tell me what's on your mind and we'll see just how illegal it is. How does that suit?' Uncle Pedro tapped one finger on the side of his nose and winked.

Benjy began walking with Uncle Pedro beside him. He'd never told anyone about the dreams and that sodding nursery rhyme, but now that he'd come up with the quest, maybe it was time to tell someone. 'I'm going to kill that fucking music in Sam Steel's auld ice-cream van.'

Uncle Pedro blinked a couple of times and cast a sideways glance at the boy. 'The music, eh? In Sam's ice-cream van?'

'Aye.'

'Any reason for that, son?'

Here it was. His chance to share it. Uncle Pedro's huge hand squeezed Benjy's shoulder, just once, to tell him he wasn't alone. 'I fucking hate it! It gets in my head and then . . .' He stopped, bit his lip.

'And then . . .?'

Benjy stopped, exhaled and turned to face Pedro. 'And then I'm back there. Back at that farmhouse, back with Ivor all bloody and dying, back with Jazzy on that bike and those two bastards laughing and getting off on all the pain . . .'

They stood facing each other – two figures in the freezing wind, unaware of anything else around them. Benjy held his breath, waiting for his uncle's response.

'Aye, well, we better get a move on if we're going to kill that damn wireless before Sam gets back from Almondvale.'

The obstruction in Benjy's chest eased. He grinned and a tiny flicker of hope blossomed as they walked towards Sam Steel's van, hammer at the ready. When he'd done this, he could move on to planning for stage two of his plan.

Chapter 39

Jazzy

Connolly dodged the busy CSIs and marched out of the room, retracing her steps along the hallway before proceeding upstairs. Casting puzzled glances at each other, Jazzy and Queenie followed. Once at the top, the smell of rotten meat was almost overpowering, and the intensified metallic blood smell again caught in Jazzy's throat.

Queenie gipped and covered her face with her hand. 'Aw, fuck. It's giving me the boak.'

Jazzy grabbed her arm and pinched hard. 'Hold it together, Queenie. I'm warning you. You're *not* going to boak. You're just *not*, okay?'

The air held a meatier quality than downstairs. Connolly directed them to the closed door of the spare bedroom, behind which the answer to one of Jazzy's earlier queries presented itself. There, in the middle of the room, was an upturned chair identical to the one in the living room. The difference was that, although copious amounts of blood were smudged around the carpet, there was no body.

Beside her, Queenie gipped again and took a backward step. Her partner's cheeks bulged with the effort of not vomiting. 'Have a quick look and then go back downstairs, Queenie. I've got this.'

Pinching her nose, her eyes watering, Queenie forced herself to cast her gaze around the room, logging every single detail as she did so. Then, with a nod at Jazzy and the DCI, she backed along the corridor and then dived downstairs as if the hounds of hell were after her.

With Queenie gone, Jazzy's eyes narrowed as she considered the implications of this scene. This amount of blood loss was inconsistent with David Paltrow's wounds and this quantity indicated severe and death-inducing blood loss. So where was the body?

Her eyes drifted towards the four cable ties, tossed on top of the coagulating blood. Throat clogged in protest at the combined assault on her senses, Jazzy exhaled through her nose, her brain working overtime, her mind making jumps and connections at breakneck speed.

Standing in the doorway, Connolly spoke. 'We reckon whoever was held captive here . . .'

'. . . had his wrists slit.' Wide-eyed, her gut clenching and unclenching, Jazzy swallowed hard, forcing the words out. 'We've just discovered Dwayne Taggart's murder site.'

Connolly nodded. 'Yes, his van was kept in the garage downstairs. We've matched the oil leakage from there to the oil your CSIs sampled at Cobbinshaw. Plus . . .' She pointed to track marks in the blood.

'Wheelbarrow marks that will match those found yesterday,' said Jazzy.

Fuck, fuck, fuck! Her chest tightened as the implications crashed down on her. She should have stuck to her guns when they found Fletcher in Portobello. Why had she allowed them to dissuade her? She should have been more insistent and now . . . Then it dawned on her. They knew that by the time they'd discovered

Lewis Fletcher's body, Dwayne Taggart was already dead, but what about David Paltrow? 'You have an approximate time of death for Paltrow?'

'Provisionally, your Dr Johnston believes it to be sometime during the early hours of this morning. We're assuming he was killed when the killer, presumably your sister, collected Dwayne Taggart's body to dump at the loch.'

Jazzy bowed her head as a low burning ball of anger grew inside her. The desire to smash up the room was so strong she almost thought she wouldn't be able to prevent herself. For months she'd been living on her nerves, her body on high alert and now that all her fears had been realised, she wasn't sure how to process her anger, her despair. As if sensing how close Jazzy was to losing it, Connolly moved over and placed a hand on the younger woman's arm. 'Come on, DS Solanki, let's find somewhere quiet where we can talk and let the CSIs get on with their job.'

Again, without waiting for Jazzy's response, Niamh Connolly, back erect, nose in the air, strode out of the sordid bedroom, through the hallway, down the stairs and outside into the bright sunshine. Once there, she pulled her hood down and inhaled deeply, her hair catching the sun as she moved her head from side to side as if loosening tension in her shoulders. Still without a backward glance, she ducked under the crime scene tape and removed the rest of her kit before thrusting it unceremoniously into the waiting bin. She waited, her hands on her hips as Jazzy and Queenie, who still looked pale but more composed than her partner, joined her.

Chapter 40

Mhairi

'In breaking news, police have been called to a house in the Pollokshaws area of Glasgow. An unnamed source confirms that the reports of a body being found on the premises are true. Over to Bryce Coburn, our reporter on the scene.'

'Thanks, Kirsty. As you can see, police and crime scene investigators are on the scene and a police cordon has been established outside the residence. Representatives from Police Scotland have offered a no-comment response to queries about the incident. Oh wait . . . the arrival of the police pathologist seems to confirm reports of a body being discovered. More updates as events unfold. This is Bryce Coburn signing off for STV. Over to you back at the studio . . .'

I can barely contain myself. There's something so very special, almost sexy, about seeing your work acknowledged on national TV. It lends it gravitas, stresses the importance of what my plans have resulted in. I'd changed things up a little this time – no point in making it too easy for them. Where would be the sport

223

in that? So instead of just leaving an anonymous tip-off with the police, like I'd done previously, I used an intermediary to be the bearer of the bad news. When you have as many contacts as me, it's easy to choose the most fragile of his co-workers to do a 'welfare check' on poor Davy Paltrow. Poor bastard got more than he bargained for.

As that rather dishy reporter spoke, I scanned the worker ants in their white crime scene suits, hoping to see Jazzy, or even that ugly dumpy cow Queenie, but there was no one remotely resembling that distinctive Little and Large team. I had to content myself with an image of Paltrow's colleague looking a bit green round the gills, standing in the background with a hot drink in her hand watching the comings and goings. Another life touched by my evil hand. Still, the buzz lingers. They'll be piecing things together by now – for fuck's sake, I hope so, anyway. I've left the dozy bastards enough clues, after all.

I sip my orange juice and flick through the channels. I'm a bit on edge – lethargic and slightly out of it. I can't settle and I don't want to lose it again, not when tonight's my big night – the beginning of the end, whatever that might be and however that might unfold. Maybe a bit of *Escape to the Country* or something, but when I flick to BBC Scotland, it's the tail end of *Politics Scotland* and I can't be arsed with that. Load of crowing bastards in Holyrood giving it all yackity, fuckity, yak, yak, yak, like they know what the hell they're on about. Instead, I opt for the Disney channel and flick down the film options . . . *Shrek*, *Spider-Man*, *Dune*, then there it is: *The Lion King*. My heart skips a beat and I hesitate, my finger hovering over the play button on the control. Should I? Do I really want to make that wee trip down memory lane?

My mind floods with memories so vivid, I almost recoil from the richness of them. It's like I'm back there in time – a wee bairn again with all my life in front of me and, for a moment, I'm caught up in the romance of it all. Could things have been different for that wee lassie with the brown hair, green eyes and huge smile? Honesty tells me 'no', but that doesn't stop the waves of nostalgia flowing over me, taking me back there, to that time, before I became a killer. To the time before I learned just how happy being a deviant made me.

Our ma lies in a puddle of her own puke, blootered, worse than I've ever seen her before. The stink of the booze makes our eyes sting and while I stand hand in hand with Simon, my other thumb stuck in my gob, Jazzy's in our ma's purse. She keeps looking at her, checking to make sure she won't catch her, for we all know what'll happen if she does. Jazzy's backside will be tanned again and we'll be lucky to get beans for our dinner.

'Jazzy, don't. She'll catch you, won't she, Mhairi? and then you'll be in big bother.' Simon's voice wobbles, but I can't speak. The thumping in my chest is a mixture of excitement and fear, but Jazzy's determined. She takes out some pound coins, shoves them in her pocket, then grabs our hands and drags us along the lobby, down the stairs and out of the house. Soon as we're free, we start to laugh – the three of us a wee trio with money to spend for a change.

'Come on, it's the school jumble sale day and we can go now.' Jazzy grabs our hands and pulls us towards the school. Everybody's been talking about this for days. We've seen other kids bringing bags full of their old clothes and toys and everything's been piled up in the hall. We didn't even bother to show Ma the note asking for donations of baked goods. Why would we? She can barely remember to open a tin of soup for us most nights; why would we think she'd be able to make rock buns or anything else? We get there and Mr Wilkinson, who tells us all sorts of things about adders and mice and stuff, takes pity on us and lets us in without paying for a ticket. Jazzy's eyes are so bright, her smile so wide – she's so beautiful and I don't care what the other meanie kids say – she's the most beautiful thing I've ever seen.

Jazzy drags us over to the cake stall and buys us a piece of the tablet Mrs Russell, our teacher, had made. It was so sweet it made our teeth hurt, but Simon and I loved it so much we thought we'd died and gone to heaven. We rarely got treats like this. With sticky hands and mouths, we strolled round the hall, our eyes eating up all the beautiful toys and games piled high on the tables. I tug Jazzy's hand. 'Why did they give these things away, Jazzy? If I had even one of these things, I'd never, ever give it away.'

A frown dimmed Jazzy's smile, and I hated myself for taking some of the pleasure from her day. Jazzy always looked after us, always made sure we were okay and now I'd upset her. But then she hugged me. 'They're just lucky, Mhairi, but you know what? We're luckier than they are. Do you know why?'

Simon and I shook our heads, and she grinned – her mouth opened so wide, her teeth glinting in the hall lights, the sheen on her hair making it all silky and smooth-looking. I love her sooooo much. 'Because we've got each other, that's why.'

Her confidence filled my heart with love as she dragged us towards the video stall. 'Come on, you two – we can't stay much longer in case she wakes up, but let's see if we can afford a final treat before we go.' When we got to the stall, she held her hand out with the remaining money on it and asked Mrs MacDonald what we could choose. Mrs MacDonald was Jazzy's teacher, and she often brought her guitar into school and played songs for the class. Jazzy loves her.

'Oh, Jasmine, I think you've got just enough there to buy your brother and sister a video each and one for yourself.'

Simon chooses *Toy Story* because he wants to be an astronaut like Buzz Lightyear, but I choose *Lion King* because I like the picture on the front. Instead of a video for herself, Jazzy asks if she can afford the tiny Lion King toy and the Buzz Lightyear one and my heart's never been fuller than when Mrs MacDonald handed the videos to Jazzy and the toys, one each to me and Simon.

I come back into the moment and realise my cheeks are wet and Simba's face is frozen on the screen. What the fuck? Why am I crying? But I know why. Of course, we'd had to wait till Mum went out or was comatose in her bedroom before we could watch our videos and Jazzy made us hide our toys. She knew that if Ma caught sight of them, she'd throw them away or break them, just to hurt us. It was a real treat and Jazzy did that for us.

Watching *Lion King*, cooried in with Jazzy between us, holding hands so tightly and our hearts filled with such love for each other, the film all about the love between families, the taste of tablet on our lips, I'd felt an indestructible bond between us and, in that moment, I knew we'd be together forever. It wasn't long after that when we made our blood promise.

I scrub my knuckles over my face. Why did everything have to change? Why did all the bad stuff that followed have to happen? I hadn't thought about that day for years, and now my head's all heavy with memories.

Despite, my mixed feelings, I press play and as the credits roll and the familiar music fills the room, I can almost feel Jazzy sitting next to me, her hand holding mine tightly, and imagine that Simon isn't dead – that he's sitting on her other side, moaning because we're watching this first, then *Toy Story*.

Why did she have to spoil it all? Why did she have to betray us? Now it's only me and her left . . . but not for much longer.

Chapter 41

Jazzy

They walked out of Greenbank Close and along to a grassy area where they found a series of benches facing the busy Auldhouse Road. David Paltrow's house was in a cul-de-sac on the boundary between Pollokshaws and Auldhouse. Jazzy, relieved to be out of her cloying crime scene suit, followed DCI Connolly to a bench. While she elected to sit on the bench beside the DCI, Queenie stood, hands thrust deep into her trouser pockets, making fist-like bumps either side of her crotch. A sure sign she was barely containing her annoyance.

From experience, Jazzy suspected she wouldn't be able to do that for long, so she slipped on her sunglasses and angled her head so she could see the DCS. 'So, what's the score? You didn't drag us over here on a whim, did you? And you already knew the deceased's ID and the link to the Taggart and Fletcher investigation we're working on. So why are we here? Previously, a concrete link like this would have had our investigation whipped from under our noses before we could say tam-o'-shanter, so what's changed?'

Niamh Connolly closed her eyes and thrust her short legs out, crossing them at the ankles as if the only thing on her mind was soaking up some of the rare Scottish sunshine. The seconds lengthened as Queenie and Jazzy waited for her reply. Irritation sliced through Jazzy's chest, but she gave Queenie a swift head-shake and bided her time. This was an interview tactic Jazzy had used herself to maximum effect on many occasions and although it pissed her off to have it used against her by a senior officer, she was determined not to respond churlishly. Instead, she adopted an interview tactic of her own and mimicked Connolly's stance, allowing the silence to linger.

When the DCS finally opened her eyes and glanced at Jazzy, her lips tightened before, with a shrug, they slackened into a reluctant smile. 'Why do *you* think you're here?'

Jazzy shook her head before speaking. 'Oh no. With respect, neither Queenie nor I have time for guessing games. This is your show. You ordered us here. The ball's in your court.'

Connolly clicked her tongue then rolled her head. The resultant crackle was audible as she did so. 'Okay, DS Solanki. Let's cut to the chase, shall we? I've taken over this investigation because it stalled under its previous leadership and I have requested DCI Dick to be my deputy.'

Jazzy's heart stuttered in her chest. All of them, especially those in D team, had breathed a collective sigh of relief when they were informed that DCI Dick was on 'sabbatical'. Never in her wildest dreams had Jazzy imagined he'd been transferred to a key position in the Operation Birchtree task force. Her hands clenched into fists as the ramifications of the Dickless Wonder's involvement in such a crucial investigation sunk in. However, although she was gutted by the news, there was little she could do, so she opted for silence.

Queenie, on the other hand, showed no such restraint. With her cheeks a mottled beetroot, she kicked the bench leg. 'Dick? You mean DCI Dick. Our Dick? Nah, you can't be . . .' Jazzy nudged her with her foot, but Queenie was in no mood to take a hint. '. . . serious. For crying out loud, he took the initial investigation off in a completely wrong direction, costing us hours of valuable time.'

No matter why they'd been dragged here, Jazzy didn't want Queenie's righteous indignation to land her in bother, so she jumped up and glared at her. 'Queenie, be quiet!'

Eyes narrowed, DCI Connolly's gaze switched from Queenie to Jazzy, the deliberate way she moved her body so Queenie was no longer in her line of vision was the equivalent of a slap in the face and, although her expression was neutral, the steel in her tone left no doubt of her underlying anger. 'I make it a habit *not* to tolerate insubordination, and I don't respond well to histrionics from demoted detectives. I don't need to explain the critical decisions I make to you or . . .' with her lips curled into a sneer, she flicked a glance at Queenie '. . . your sidekick. However, it is fair to say that under the previous leadership, progress was slow and I don't want this investigation to stall under my lead, which is why I'm calling in every resource at my disposal in order to move this forward. DCI Dick, a valuable and trusted colleague of mine with a proven track record, is one such resource. I will not have him maligned. Is that clear?'

She turned her stony gaze on Queenie, who shuffled her feet before offering a mumbled 'Aye, okay.'

'It better be.' Connolly's gaze bored into Queenie, causing the colour to rise in her face, before, seemingly satisfied that her point had been made, she looked at Jazzy. 'You and DC McQueen, and to a lesser extent your team, have valuable insights into your sister, her motivations, and perhaps even her mindset. Personally, having looked at the files and spoken to my colleagues on the task force, I believe it was a mistake to sideline you after you broke contact with your brother earlier in the year. It was, I might add, in my opinion, unconscionable that you did so without first consulting the task force leadership. If, and I repeat *if*, I allow you any input moving forward, I will not tolerate that sort of defiant behaviour. You should remember that your rein-statement to sergeant is on a probationary basis. It wouldn't do to jeopardise that now, would it?'

There were many ways in which Jazzy could respond to this and, as she took a deep calming breath, a few of them flitted through her mind. Of course, Jazzy – and Queenie – wanted to be part of the investigation in whatever small way they could. Although, between them, they had many valuable insights into how Mhairi worked, Jazzy accepted that, despite the Bitch's mach-inations, her own involvement could only be on the periphery of the action. Gut clenching, Jazzy allowed her displeasure to flare in her eyes. She was no pushover after all. 'No indeed, ma'am.'

Connolly smiled and shook her head from side to side. 'Now, now, now, Jazzy. It's Niamh when we're alone. Surely, you've not forgotten already, have you?'

Jazzy, teeth clenched, ignored Queenie's *Psycho* shower scene stabbing actions and managed a 'No . . . Niamh.'

Connolly crossed her arms over her middle and raised her face towards the sun again. 'That's more like it. We should start as we mean to go on. Now, if, as I believe, this crime scene is indeed the work of your sister, I want you both on board the investigation, albeit in a strictly limited capacity. Shall we call it a consultative role?' Connolly scrunched up her face and made that same tongue-clicky sound as earlier. 'And, let's be clear here, I *do* mean a severely restricted and wholly supervised capacity. I acknowledge that you and DC McQueen . . .' she inclined her head in Queenie's direction '. . . are used to conducting more gung-ho investigations, but be warned, such behaviour will not be tolerated. Not on my watch.'

A dull throb by her temple, and the tightness in her chest told Jazzy she was near to losing it. Her hand went to her pocket and as her fingers moved over the familiar contours of her Ganesh amulet, she willed herself to relax her shoulders.

Connolly, oblivious to Jazzy's internal struggle, continued. 'Having said that, there are still *huge* questions that cause me concern. For example, the ease with which your sister evaded capture and how she has managed to remain at large all this time.'

Connolly paused, shifted her head to catch Jazzy's eye, and accompanied her glacial smile with an insouciant shrug that belied the tightness of her mouth. 'I'm sure you'll agree that identifying those who have helped her evade justice – *whoever* they are – is a priority for the team.'

Jazzy's brow furrowed as she attempted to decipher the meaning behind Connolly's words. Surely the DCS wasn't implying that Jazzy or someone on her team had helped Mhairi to escape? Jazzy's fist clenched around Ganesh, the sharp edges digging into her palm, but she didn't care. A flame of red-hot anger sliced through Jazzy. She'd heard enough and had kept her cool for too long. She straightened, towering over the shorter woman who remained sitting on the bench, a slight smile hovering on her lips. 'I hope you are not inferring that either myself or any of my team has helped Mhairi? That would be ridiculous. *All* of my team are dedicated officers whose scrutiny of the investigations of the murders, previously not linked to her, was instrumental in identifying her as the killer and linking it to the murder of the Clarks and the psychiatrist in Armadale.'

A hand placed on Jazzy's forearm, covering her tense muscles, accompanied Connolly's girlish and insincere laugh. Jazzy pulled away, but maintained eye contact as the senior officer spoke. 'Sit down, Detective Solanki. You're making a scene.'

Breathing heavily, Jazzy counted to five before retaking her seat on the bench. Queenie, who had drifted a few feet away, came and stood behind Jazzy's shoulder like a miniature turnip-shaped avenging angel from an alternative universe, ready to swoop down in Jazzy's defence should the need arise.

'Someone leaked information to your sister and facilitated communications between her and your brother, and now we have another victim with links to Simon. We now believe your sister is back and attempting to call the shots. My primary consideration is catching her before she claims any more victims and I assume, DS Solanki, that this is also your desire?' Head tilted to one side, Connolly waited till Jazzy gave an abrupt nod, before continuing. 'You will *not* have access to all the files, but will be called upon to offer insights as and when required. You will *not* actively pursue leads or angles independently. Every action in the furtherance of locating Mhairi Smith will be done strictly by official task team members and *solely* under my direction. Is that clear?'

Jazzy's cheeks were hot and her lips tight with barely suppressed rage. She'd thought the dickless wonder was bad, but maybe she'd been wrong, for Connolly was worse, but at least she wasn't banishing Jazzy from the investigation completely. It was that thought alone that allowed her to inhale a deep breath and respond calmly. 'Crystal clear. Myself and my team will cooperate in whatever capacity you deem best.'

'Good.' The DCI's smile widened. 'You will liaise with DCI Dick at his request and you will be under his direct supervision.'

Connolly's grin as she jumped to her feet and walked away throwing a 'He'll be in touch in due course,' was the final nail in the coffin.

Chapter 42

Queenie

Struggling to keep up with Jazzy, who strode ahead, Queenie gave a pretty damn accurate imitation of Niamh Connolly. 'You *will* liaise with DCI Dick at *his* request and you *will* be under *his* direct supervision.'

She got why Jazzy was furious. She was furious, too. How dare that jumped-up bloody woman drag – no, *order* – them over to Pollokshaws and then treat them like the hired help. The entire team was invested in catching Jazzy's half-sister, but none more so than Jazzy herself. To imply that she suspected the leak had come from within their team was gutting and insulting. 'How bloody dare she, JayZee? How bloody, buggering, bollocksing dare she? Who does she think she is? The boss of us? Crime investigation's answer to bloody Yoda? The bloody Dalai Lama of policing?'

Jazzy ground to an abrupt stop by the passenger's side door and swivelled round, giving Queenie some much-needed time to catch up and to control her laboured breathing. Jazzy's face mottled, her lips turned white, and her entire demeanour reminded Queenie of a volatile volcano ready to erupt at any moment. Queenie couldn't blame her. She'd seen first-hand what Jazzy had been through over the past few months, and she'd witnessed the toll it took on her. So, she braced herself for the eruption, ready to intervene only when her friend's anger was spent. But Jazzy surprised her.

Instead of venting and ranting, Jazzy's shoulders slumped and she released a long slow breath, pulled the door open and, without another word, flung herself onto the seat. Approaching the driver's side with caution, Queenie wondered how to proceed. Had Niamh Connolly's aspersions been a straw too far?

Queenie raked her fingers through her short, wiry hair. She eased herself into the seat and waited. If she'd been expecting Jazzy to comment on Connolly's inferences, she was disappointed, for when Jazzy finally spoke to her, it was in a calm and reasonable tone, with none of the venom or anger that she must have felt – and that worried Queenie. There was only so much anguish and torment you could bottle up inside and still function without killing yourself.

'So, Queenie, what did you take from the crime scene? Copycat or sister dearest herself?' Jazzy's unemotional, flat tone as she observed the passing cars through the side window was eerily absent of a connection with the world. It was as if she'd shut herself down and was functioning robotically. If her monotone hadn't been accompanied by an agitated, tap, tap, tapping of her fingers on her thigh and the joogling of her leg, Queenie would have been more worried. As it was, a wave of relief washed over her as she realised that Jazzy was just trying to cope, using any strategy available. For now, that seemed to divert her attention away from the fly in the turd, also known as Niamh Connolly, and focus it on analysing the crime scenes they'd left less than an hour previously.

Reorienting herself, Queenie placed her hands on the steering wheel and dredged up the perfect memory she had already stored in the file in her brain, marked: *the Bitch's crime scenes*. She rubbed her eyes, her stubby little fingers pressing hard into the sockets as if she could obliterate the crime scene she'd just witnessed. It took her only a moment to respond as the images drifted like a video reel through her mind. 'No eyes! Torture, yes, but the eyes remained intact. Same with Fletcher's body at the bottle kiln. The Bitch is evolving. The connections are too specific to be a random copycat.' She used her fingers to count off the connections. 'One, you have links to Fletcher and Taggart; two, it seems likely that Taggart was tortured and killed at this crime scene; and three, there is a connection between Simon and David Paltrow. Even with the absence of the removal of body parts, it's got to be her. We should have listened to your instincts at Portobello, JayZee. We've been thinking it for days now and here's irrefutable proof.'

Jazzy nodded and pulled her seat belt on. 'Yep, she's back. I hate to say it but, the Bitch is well and truly back. And she's being smart. She's not compelled to mutilate in particular ways as other serial killers do – it's all a game for her and she adapts and changes her modus operandi to mess with our heads.' Folding her arms over her chest, Jazzy scowled out the window. 'All of this makes it even *more* important for us to be involved in this, no matter what crap Connolly throws at us. We both know why she's come back now, don't we? For the damn funeral!'

Queenie turned the ignition. 'Aye, we do that. But, Jazzy, did you notice . . .?'

Jaw tensed, Jazzy slapped her hand on the dashboard. 'The satellite phone on the coffee table? Yes, I bloody did. That's how she's communicating. That's why nobody has made a link between any of those in contact with Simon and her.'

Queenie joined the flow of traffic. 'Do you reckon they've cottoned on?'

Jazzy snorted. 'Well, if it was left to the dickless wonder, I'd have my doubts, but for all her snide jibes, I reckon DCI Niamh Connolly is as sharp as a thistle. She'll be on it. I just wonder when exactly she's going to call on us for our expert opinions.'

Jazzy's leg stilled, and she swivelled round to face Queenie.

236

'She's playing us and, worse than that, she's calling all the shots. She wants to use Simon's funeral to lure Mhairi in, which is fine, but we both know she's too smart to be caught that way. Three people are dead, and despite Operation Birchtree's hypothesis that Simon's death will bring her home, we're only *now* making a concrete link to the Bitch. It's not good enough. She could be anywhere and we're trailing along behind her as usual.'

Queenie screwed her face up, then shook her head. 'Anywhere? You really think so?'

'You don't?'

'Nah, I think your sister's directing this whole drama from somewhere nearby. She's close enough to feel involved in it all. No way would she be able to distance herself from this. It's too personal for her. *You're* the umbilical cord keeping her close at hand. You're the key to this – you're the enema that will have her exploding into the limelight like a sackful of shite when she deems it's the right time.'

Jazzy bit her lip as her friend's words settled and Queenie would have given anything to be able to ease the pain that had her friend's fingers massaging her temples. It killed Queenie to see her like this and to feel so helpless about it all.

But Jazzy exhaled and braced her shoulders. 'So, Queenie, what's she going to do next?'

Queenie shrugged and turned the key in the ignition. 'She's going to keep on playing her games. She's going to keep on taunting you and those close to you and she's going to try to pull something off at Simon's funeral.' As she edged into the flow of traffic, she paused, then: 'Which again is why you should distance yourself from that entire fiasco. A fucking funeral? Who does he think he is to demand a funeral? And more to the point, to demand that you organise it?'

Jazzy sighed and wafted her hand in the air. 'Give it a break, Queenie. This is hard enough for me. You know that. I'm not doing the entire bloody headstone business and all the other crap he wanted. I couldn't stomach that, but nor could I stomach not putting him to rest either. Besides, like you mentioned earlier, this funeral might just be what flushes Mhairi out. It's too good an opportunity to miss and I'm sure the very efficient and ambitious Niamh Connolly will have the entire area covered. She sees this as her chance to catch Mhairi – she won't leave anything to chance. If the Bitch turns up, she'll be caught.'

Queenie snorted. She didn't have Jazzy's faith in Connolly or the task force and she suspected Mhairi could run rings round them. Queenie wanted to make sure that Mhairi Smith was apprehended before Simon's funeral, which meant they had hours to catch her. 'Do you think Operation Birchtree has any usable intel on the Bitch's current whereabouts?'

Jazzy shrugged. 'No idea and by the sounds of it, this trading information is a one-way street with us giving them our intel and them keeping a stony silence about anything they've found out.' Jazzy paused as Queenie pulled onto the motorway. 'You know, Queenie, I think we need to go back to the start and analyse every piece of intel we have since her suspected return. WE need to go through the Portobello investigation with a fine-toothed comb and . . .'

'Aye, and . . . do it all without that bloody wee upstart Connolly getting wind of it – or Dick, for that matter.' She glanced at Jazzy, wondering if now was a good time to bring up the blazing row Jazzy and Elliot had had just before they were diverted to Glasgow. 'You reckon Elliot will play ball with us? You know, be up for a bit of underhand dealings? A wee bit of fudging the boundaries, going off-piste, like?'

Jazzy shook her head and fell silent.

Queenie exhaled. Boy, was it going to be tricky to investigate without Dick or Connolly getting wind of it and particularly when the relationship between Elliot and Jazzy was so fraught. Hopefully, those useless wee turds Haggis and Geordie had copied their files before Operation Birchtree snatched them all. Queenie could only hope that in the aftermath of the task force taking over all their current investigations, D team wouldn't be sent to a mega big case elsewhere. They could conduct their illicit investigation more easily if they were assigned busywork.

She risked a glance at Jazzy. If only Jazzy wasn't on such bad terms with both the DI *and* the super. *Really, the girl could take lessons from me on tact and diplomacy.* She shrugged. Who knew? Maybe they would invite them to the hallowed headquarters on the top floor and they'd be able to gather some useful intel. Hell, Queenie was even prepared to bat her eyelashes at the smarmy old dickless wonder if it got them a head start on locating the Bitch.

Chapter 43

Ali

Jan's house is as manky and disordered as I had expected. The heavy stink of cigarette smoke hung in the air, providing a backdrop to the scent of Jan's too sweet perfume. It's nothing like mine and, strangely, it feels good to be here. The chaos resonates with how I feel. Maybe it's just part of my rebellion, but it puts my mum's obsessive cleanliness into perspective. Jan's gaff shows that there's a happy medium where everything doesn't have to be so precise. Well, maybe that's pushing it a bit because this isn't so much a happy medium as complete chaos and so different from the oppressive crap at home. It makes me feel rebellious and different somehow. Just what I need!

Jan's bedroom is so small, we can only fit in together if one of us scrunches up on the bed. Piles of clothes, some with their tags still on, some clearly worn and in need of a good wash, cover every surface. Half-used eye shadows and lip glosses clutter a rickety sideboard with a mucky mirror where someone, presumably Jan, cleared a circle, to put her make-up on. The new Ali thrusts the *why not just clean the whole thing?* thought away. *Come on, Ali, this is your rebellion night. This is your chance to show them you're not just their pristine, obedient little daughter who doesn't get a say in anything.* I'd finally convinced Isla to cover for me, but she still isn't happy about it. Still, she is my bestie, and that's what friends do, isn't it?

As I lean against the wall, studying the tattered posters Blu-Tacked to Jan's peeling wallpaper – Zayn Malik, Lizzo and Jason Derulo – I force myself not to scratch my arms. Jan glares at me as if she senses I'm about to back out. She grabs a used glass from the table next to the bed, sniffs it, nods, and then from nowhere produces a bottle of cheap vodka. She tips some into the glass – gestures to an open can of Pepsi Max and says, 'Help yourself,' as she thrusts the glass towards me.

I've never had voddy before and don't want it now. Shite, my folks would have a hairy canary if they thought for a minute I was underage drinking and doing something haram. That thought stiffens my spine. After all, isn't my mum doing something haram when she screws her boyfriend? I grab the glass and as she prepares a drink for herself, I add the flat Pepsi right up to the brim and sip it. It is foul. Jan grins and lifts her own filled glass, with only a trace of Pepsi to colour the clear liquid and says, 'Cheers, Ali. Here's to an unforgettable night.'

I don't like the look that flickers in her eyes for a second, and I wonder if she's setting me up. If this is some Jan Carmichael pissing-about prank. Then I straighten my spine and take another sip. I can't help shuddering as the alcohol nips my throat but Jan just laughs. Then, placing her glass on the table, she grabs a bunch of clothes from her bag. 'Here, try these on.'

They still have their tags on. I'm gobsmacked. She'd gone out and bought me clothes for tonight. Doubts traipse through my mind, trampling on my earlier defiant confidence. Is this because she thinks I look too geeky? Because she thinks I'll let her down otherwise? I look down at my jeans and the long-sleeved top I'd chosen and compare them to Jan's skimpy shimmery crop top with the scooped neckline that leaves nothing to the imagination. Her nipples are visible through the flimsy fabric and I realise she's gone braless. I feel like a fucking frump with my virgin white bra. I can imagine my mum's disapproving frown if she saw Jan, and all at once I want nothing more than to whip off my respectable, goody-two-shoes bra and let it all hang loose just like Jan. But I'm not Jan. I'm too self-conscious to let my nipples poke against my T-shirt and show my belly. Apart from anything, some of my scars would be visible.

She's over by the scummy mirror now, straightening her hair, the thrum of music from her phone getting into my head. Why does it have to be so loud? But her head is bobbing along and there's no way I'll ask her to lower the volume. No way.

I pick up the tight cropped turquoise leggings she'd thrown in my lap. 'How much do I owe you for these, Jan?'

She meets my eyes in the mirror and laughs. 'Chill, Ali. Didn't fucking pay for them, did I? Lifted them from Primani.'

It takes a moment for her words to sink in and when they do, my heart sinks. Underage drinking, shoplifting . . . what other illegal things would my night out with Jan entail? I take a deep breath and smile. This is make-or-break time. Either I give in and go with the flow, or I get up, grab my stuff and scuttle home with my tail between my legs and face whatever crap Jan and her friends would deal out at school. There's no real choice. I've come this far, so gritting my teeth, I yank my long-sleeved T-shirt over my head, toss it onto the floor beside Jan's discarded clothes and, before she can see the scabs and scars on my arms, slip the shoplifted top over my head.

Thankfully, the sleeves are long and cover the marks – but the rest of the garment offers no such modesty. Scooped at the front and back, it's cropped to sit just above the waistline of the jeans.

'Thatta girl. Go, Ali!' Jan's approval fortifies me and I struggle out of my jeans, replacing them with the turquoise leggings that feel just a little too tight. She pouts in the mirror and layers her face with an undercoat of foundation as if desperate to conceal her near perfect skin. I don't get it, but I suspect that I'll have to go with the flow and add some gunge to my own face. I shimmy over the bed and stand behind Jan, trying to see my reflection in the cloudy mirror. Jan edges sideways so I can get a better view and I have to admit, I look good. I've never worn anything like this before and it feels good to pretend to be someone else for a while. Let's face it, being me isn't a bundle of joy at the minute.

'I'll straighten your hair for you, if you like?' Jan sprays perfume over me, making me cough, then stands up and gestures to the seat. I meet her eyes and detect a challenge there, so I nod and sit down, taking a swig of voddy and flat Pepsi from my glass before watching in fascination as she divides my hair into strands and begins transforming me into a dark-haired Barbie. Right there and then, I decide to let her apply my make-up too. In for a penny, in for a pound. Besides, I can always scrub it off at Isla's before I go home. *Fuck, I'm such a rebel!*

Chapter 44

Jazzy

'You look like shite, Jazzy.' Geordie, all gangly limbs and frowning concern, had jumped up as soon as Jazzy and Queenie walked into the food court at McArthur Glen Designer Outlet. Without another word, he pushed Queenie aside, swept Jazzy up and ushered her over to his seat as if she was a doddery centenarian rather than a healthy woman in her late twenties. If she hadn't been knackered, she would have struggled against his ministrations, but she had nothing left in the tank and besides, the concerned expressions on both his and Fenton's faces were almost her undoing as they shoved a portion of fish and chips across the table and took up sentry position on either side of her.

On the way back from Pollokshaws, Uncle Pedro had phoned her and told her about Benjy's meltdown, worried her. *Never rains, but it sodding pours.* What worried her more, however, was Uncle Pedro's medical assessment that Benjy's recovery would be aided by being present at Simon's funeral. She understood all about closure – that was what she hoped to gain for herself with the funeral – but she wasn't sure she'd be able to sell that idea to Niamh Connolly. Besides which, even with Uncle Pedro's vanguard of bodyguards around, it still felt too risky.

She sighed. For so long she'd been on her own, in her own little private bubble of 'coping' and it took some getting used to to realise that she had a team around her – and not just any old team but the Jazz Queen team – who would do anything for her and friends who she cared about too. She'd grown closer to these three people than to anyone, except for her parents and Elliot – although that closeness was in doubt for now – yet their loyalty and concern took her by surprise every single time.

'What the hell? Like I've not had a trauma to deal with? That crime scene wasn't a bloody Monet painting, you know? No scented, perfectly formed lilies with bridges overlooking them in Pollokshaws, you know? Not a bit of relaxing Glasgow foliage in sight, no restful gently lapping waves on the banks of the Clyde. No. It was a bloodbath and, in case yous two have forgotten, *I'm* . . .' she punctuated the last word with a thumb prod to her own chest '. . . the one with the photographic memory. I'm the one that can't superimpose a bloody lily pond over the dead guy. It's me who'll be trying to ram every bloody iota of that scene into a bloody closet in my heid.' She transferred the thumb prod to her temple. 'Then you lot will say, "oh, Queenie, can you confirm if the blood spatter went up the walls?" or "oh, Queenie, can we just check that the dead guy's head was resting in a pool of vomit?" or "oh, Queenie, is it right that there were weird trails through the blood?"'

Queenie delivered each hypothetical question in a high-pitched voice, which unfortunately caught the attention of a family at the neighbouring table and a young couple sitting opposite. Whilst the parents of the family glared at Queenie, the toddlers seemed to think her imitations were the funniest thing since Peppa Pig. The teenagers edged closer as if desperate for more gory details, but Fenton sprung up, glared at the two youths, who immediately retreated backwards, and relinquished his position beside Jazzy.

With all the magnanimity of the queen, she slipped into the vacated seat and glared round the table. 'Well, for once, Haggis isn't his usual useless self.'

Rubbing the back of her hand over her brow, Jazzy shook her head. She needed to eat, but the vinegary smell of the chips made her nauseous and although appreciative of her team's support, she wanted to be alone. Just her and Winky snuggled up under a duvet, curtains closed, security on and no interruptions. Except with the 'safe house' arrangements in play that would not happen any time soon. For now, though, they had to work out their plan of action and to do that, she had to rein her irrepressible partner in. 'Stop being such a drama queen, Queenie. I've had enough of that for one day. Let's just work out where we are, what we know and what we're going to—'

Geordie interrupted her, clearing his throat and, when she glanced up, Fenton's face was bright red and his eyes darted everywhere, except at her. Then a deep, familiar voice said, 'Do you mind if I join you?'

All the sounds of the food court receded to background noise – the laughter, the rumbling conversations, the sounds of rustling paper and trays clattering on tables occupied a space behind her. The colour drained from Jazzy's face. And she glared at Geordie who mouthed, 'I'm sorry.'

So, he bloody well should be. What was he thinking to invite Elliot here, to their clandestine meeting, especially after he'd witnessed their bust-up earlier?

She turned her glare to Fenton, who continued to avoid her eye. And then before she could formulate a response to Elliot's question, Queenie stepped into the breach. 'Well, that depends, doesn't it, son? Are you going to have a go at Jazzy again or are you going to swallow your pride and apologise to the lassie? Can you no' see she's done in? Bloody cream-crackered, had it up to the gills with senior officers crapping in her porridge like some narcissistic, vengeful fucking seagulls.'

246

Christ, if Queenie didn't watch out, her arse would be well and truly kicked off the force, especially if Elliot was still in the mood he'd been in earlier. Jazz, head bowed, wafted her hand at a vacant chair at a neighbouring table and replied. 'Help yourself. It's a free country and we're just having a late . . .' she glanced at her watch and grimaced when she saw how late it was, and in response her stomach elicited a loud and very long rumble '. . . lunch.'

To stave off a repeat of the embarrassing sound, she grabbed a handful of cooling chips and shoved them in her mouth, gagging a little as the grease clogged up her throat. What was wrong with her? She needed to eat, so why was every mouthful such a chore recently? Of course, her continually churned-up gut didn't help.

'You should be thankful that I'm not here in my capacity as your senior officer, Queenie.' Elliot's tone was mild, yet firm as he dragged the chair over and settled himself opposite Jazzy. 'Just so you know, I'll give you a pass on the "son" comment and on the disrespectful insinuation that I'm on the same level as DCI Dick and his new bosom buddy DCS Connolly. I'm not, as well you know.'

Queenie huffed and puffed under her breath, but remained silent. His gaze burned into the top of Jazzy's head as she finally swallowed the food. She grabbed an Irn-Bru can, relieved that it wasn't one of the daft Raspberry Ripple or Mango and Papaya flavours that seemed to be all the rage, and took a long sip.

'I owe you an apology, Jazzy. I behaved unprofessionally, and I think we both know that I'm still processing the fact that you suspected me of being a bent copper.'

Jazzy's head jerked up, her mouth open to reply, but three other voices got there first.

'Don't be a . . . well, what I mean to say is, don't be daft – oor JayZee's never thought you were a bent copper . . .' was Queenie's contribution.

'She only did it so she could prove you *weren't* on the take,' said Fenton, his face a blossoming rouge of discomfort as he avoided looking at Elliot.

'Nah. You got it all wrong, boss. Jazz was only making sure nobody else stitched you up.'

Elliot smiled and looked at Jazzy. 'That true, Jazzy?'

With her heart filled with emotion that her team had stood up for her, she could only nod. If she tried to speak, she thought she might burst into tears, but Elliot's nod seemed to loosen the vice in her gut a smidgen and that felt good.

'I know why you're meeting here. You're not happy that you're being given only limited access to Birchtree and you've lost confidence in their ability to catch Mhairi and I have to say, I'm with you. I'm not one for blurring the lines on the job, but . . .' he raked his fingers through his hair, making it stand up in erratic spikes not dissimilar to Queenie's hairstyle '. . . in this instance, I'm motivated by two things. One, I'm pissed that we didn't follow Jazzy's instincts about Lewis Fletcher's murder and two, it incenses me that DCI Dick has become Niamh Connolly's right-hand man. That's a fucking recipe for disaster from the start. So, we're left with no options. We need to keep digging into the Fletcher and Taggart murders, as well as these ones over in Pollokshaws, and we need to inveigle as much information from the task force as we can regarding their intel – or I suspect, lack of, on Mhairi's current whereabouts and of course, anything that crops up on the David Paltrow murder. You agree?'

Jazzy leaned her elbows on the table. 'I've been thinking about that. We need to start in Portobello. She chose Porty because of my connection to the place. She'd have been there. She's bound to have been and if we're thorough enough, we might just pick up her trail.'

'I'm on that. I'll get two analysts to scrutinise the footage and I'll re-interview any of the people in neighbouring flats who got flagged by the constables and I'll catch up on the few that were missed.'

'I've been thinking too, Jazzy.' Fenton ignored Queenie's slow clap and her 'Gaun yersel' wee man'. 'I want to go back over Mhairi's past relationships. She was adopted and her adoptive mother raised her for several years. That's the longest relationship she's ever had, other than Simon. Stands to reason that – ignoring the fact that Mhairi killed her in the end – there's a lot of history there. I'm not sure we've given that enough consideration. I'd like to focus on that, if that's okay?'

It made sense. 'I need to spend some time ironing out the final security arrangements for the funeral on Monday with Connolly. But that can wait till tomorrow. It's logical to assume that the Bitch, despite our precautions, will know exactly when it is and will plan something around that time. We need to catch her before then. So, it seems like we've got a plan. Queenie and I will try to find out what we can from the task force and Elliot will . . .' For the first time, she looked at Elliot. His searing blue eyes seemed to see right into her soul, but Jazzy shook off that infantile reaction. He'd been a pig and her ire would not be abated by a soulful look and a half apology.

He grinned at them and, pushing his chair back from the table, got to his feet. 'My job is keeping them all off your backs and covering your tracks.' He had the audacity to wink at Jazzy as he walked backwards, away from the table. 'You can thank me later, folks.'

If it hadn't been for the fact that she realised just how much Elliot was risking by involving himself in this, Jazzy would have been as irritated by his attitude as Queenie. But whilst she swallowed the sharp retort, Queenie's tact clearly didn't stretch that far, although she mumbled her thoughts behind her hand in a comment only the three remaining at the table could hear. 'Cheeky wee bampot.'

Elliot's grin widened, and he clicked his fingers. 'Nearly forgot, Connolly and Dick want you two upstairs in the new task force offices first thing tomorrow. But in the meantime, the super says you're to all head to the safe house and get settled in. Before heading back into the station.'

All eyes turned to Jazzy. In all the excitement the team hadn't pressed her for details on their new living premises and although Jazzy knew she'd have to come clean soon, she had hoped for some space to collect her thoughts before dropping that bombshell. Elliot's words had put the kybosh on that. With every one of her muscles aching because she'd been holding herself so rigidly, she downed the rest of her can, playing for time. She should have told Queenie earlier. That would have made this revelation a little easier, but they had been consumed by the implications of that god-awful crime scene. Yanking her ponytail tight, she inhaled and braced herself for the avalanche of shit that was about to descend on her. 'Well, em, I had hoped that . . .'

'Never mind soft-soaping us, JayZee. Just spit it oot, hen. Where's this safe house? Is it some place wi' a jacuzzi? Have they commandeered one of the better hotels for us? That would be rare.'

Jazzy held Queenie's gaze. 'Not exactly, Queenie. Somewhere closer to home. In fact, it's your . . .'

She didn't even need to finish the sentence before Queenie was in her face, fists clenched at her sides. 'You got to Craig, didn't you? You sidestepped me and went for the weakest link. You sweet-talked my hubby behind my back. Appealed to his conscience. That's what you did, didn't you? Come on now, admit it. You used our friendship to . . .'

'I don't get it. What are you two on about? Where's our safe house?'

Geordie yanked at Fenton's sleeve and, shaking his head in warning, nodded to Queenie. 'That's where our safe house is.'

Fenton's expression was so intense that it would have been comical if not for the fierce tension in the air. 'Crap? Really?'

Geordie grinned. 'Aw, think of the positives, Fenton. Craig will have left a freezer full of food. It'll be great.'

'Look, I didn't intend to go behind your back, Queenie. It was the only house that was big enough to accommodate all six of us comfortably and Craig wanted you to be safe. That was the bottom line. He wants you to be safe and if we're together, then the chances of keeping us all safe are higher.'

Queenie, her face tripping her, slouched in her seat. 'Aye, well, that doesnae mean I'm happy with it, but at least I'll get to sleep in my own bed, so that's a bonus.'

Jazzy grimaced. 'Eh, well, Craig's allocated the rooms, Queenie . . .'

'Aw for shite in a snowball's sake, the bastard's giving up our king-sized bed with the en suite to that lang streak o' misery and Guy, hasn't he? I'm divorcing him. That's it. I've decided. First thing the morra, I'll be filing papers.'

Fenton raised a tentative finger in the air and cleared his throat. 'So, where . . .'

Queenie turned on him, her glare ferocious. 'You just wait and see, Haggis. I'll put you in Ruby's play hoose in the garden, if you gie me any more of your cheek.'

Chapter 45

Mhairi

No time for this little detour of mine. I've got packing to do and this evening to plan for, after all, but I'm curious. The auld drunk delivered the phone first thing, so they've had all day to check it all out and plan their next moves. Wonder what Jazzy's thinking. Wonder how much of a panic my wee gift will have induced. The thought of her being at my beck and call energises me. She'll hate it. I know she will, but she'll have to carry the mobile with her at all times, just in case, and it's that uncertainty I'm going to capitalise on. It'll be like having me sitting on her shoulder, a not-to-be-ignored part of her life. A shudder hurtles through me and I grin. It's such a good feeling to have the great Jazzy Solanki hanging on the end of a line. As I wait, that Blondie song 'Hanging on the Telephone' keeps me company and before long I'm tapping my foot in time with the beat in my head.

Then there's all the Pollokshaws scene. Bloody love that! It's in the news and everything and still they have no actual proof it's me. No DNA – nothing forensically to lay the blame at my door. My mind jumps to Jazzy's team *and* that ineffective task force they've got hunting me down. Bunch of incompetents. I'm curious about how much of a threat they view this as. My fingers itch to dial the number and speak to her. To hear her voice and to put the fear of God into her. Where would be the fun in that? The pleasure is all in having her dangling, not knowing when I'll strike, not knowing when that phone will ring. Besides, that's not on my list for today's activities. Neither is hanging around in the green space around the police station, dressed like an octogenarian, but I can't resist. You see, we've got this invisible link, have Jazzy and me. And now with Simon dead, it's like that bond has got stronger.

I see her leave in her wee Mini and soon realise she's part of a three-car convoy. Her, that Queenie cow and an unmarked polis car. Singing a wee tune to myself, I take a wee daunder round the grass, before heading back towards the shopping centre where I've parked my latest car. I know where they're heading, so there's no need to rush.

By the time I park a few streets away in Bellsquarry and walk towards her house, she's already coming out carrying a cat travel basket and a wheelie case. So, Afzal has realised just how much of a threat I am. The thought fizzes through my veins as I watch her climb into the passenger seat beside the wee fat cow and drive off, followed by the unmarked car.

With the rest of my busy day ahead, I've no time to follow them, so I take a moment to recalibrate. I'm not sure how I feel about this. I'd got used to her being here in Bellsquarry. But what the hell, wherever she is, it makes no difference to me, for when the time comes I know exactly where she'll be. Just where I need her.

Chapter 46

Queenie

As soon as she stepped through her front door, Queenie felt the gap normally filled by her husband and granddaughter. Not in the way she always experienced the absence of her daughter. Not in a heart cut out, devastated way, but more in an untethered sort of way. It felt like someone had removed her ballast, and she was floating aimlessly without any support. Craig and Ruby's absence had shifted her universe, unsettling her and leaving her off centre. They were her anchors. The rocks that supported her and kept her grounded. Her constant companions and not having them nearby was torture.

She took a deep breath, inhaling the lingering scent of Craig's aftershave, and that familiarity grounded her a little. Although she was pissed off with JayZee, a conversation with Craig, who was still on the train to Cornwall with Ruby, made her see the sense in the arrangements. Keeping this little troupe of Jazz Queens safe was the priority, and that was easier if they were all occupying the same house. True, she'd have preferred an anonymous lodge, but she'd just have to put up with it.

Fenton staggered through the door behind her, his suitcase bashing her on the legs. 'For fuck's sake, Haggis, you trying to knee-cap me?'

Flushing, he deposited his case by the door and tried to avoid her gaze.

'Aw for God's sake, get that bloody monstrosity of a case and come wi' me. According to the instructions given by my soon-to-be ex-husband, you're in Ruby's room with Elliot.'

She thrust open a door, revealing a vision in vibrant techni-colour with My Little Ponies, teddies and giraffes lined up, glaring at them from a corner by the window.

Fenton popped his head in and groaned as a grin the size of a melon appeared on Queenie's face. 'Aye, that's right, son. You'll be on the Lilo on the floor beside the cuddly toys.'

'But that's no . . .'

'Rank, son. Rank. When *you're* the DI, you can have the single bed with the My Little Pony duvet.' And chortling to herself, she left him to unpack. Maybe this sharing malarkey would be fun after all.

'Right, Geordie and Guy, you're in here.' She ushered them into a double room with a king-size water bed. Striding over, she rummaged through the bedside cabinet, grabbing an armful of sex toys before leaving. 'I've left the nipple lick. It's nearly done, but feel free to use it if you want.'

Guy's deep, sonorous guffaw made Queenie grin. *A lad who gets my sense of humour can't be all bad*, Queenie thought. She walked back to Jazzy, who lingered by the front door, Winky's cat basket by her feet. 'I'll just sleep on the couch, Queenie. You can have the bedroom for yourself. It's only fair. After all, it is your house, and it's my fault we've all invaded it.'

'Och, don't be daft, JayZee. The spare rooms got two single beds. You and me'll be fine in it.'

'No, honestly, Queenie, I'll give you some sp . . .'

'Truth is, JayZee, it used to be Billi's room and although Craig cleans it, I don't go in there. Brings back too many memories. I'd appreciate the company. If you don't mind, that is.' She tried out a tremulous grin. 'Besides, it'll be like having a sleepover. Never had one as a kid.'

What she didn't stipulate was her determination to be there with Jazzy when that phone rang.

Jazzy walked over and wrapped her arms round Queenie, refusing to let her wriggle away. 'You're brilliant, you know that, Queenie. I'm up for a sleepover with my bestie. We can even do face masks and watch whatever you want on TV. But, I have one condition . . .'

'Oh, aye, what's that?'

'No bloody farting. Fart once and I'm on that couch. Understood?'

Queenie laughed and raised her hand for a fist bump. 'Understood, boss.'

Chapter 47

Ali

My heart sinks as I take in my surroundings. The place is a total dive. I should've known it would be. I feel awkward in these clothes, and not just because Jan stole them, either. They're too revealing. Too skimpy. They're everything I'm not and I realise I don't want to be this new Ali. This is the last place I should be. The parents would go pure dead mental on me if they knew I was in Bathgate and not at Isla's house, like I told them. They like Isla. Think she's a good influence on me. I'm not so sure they'd like Jan, though.

I snort and avert my gaze from the weird figure in the corner, fiddling on their phone with their hood up like some gangster in a rap. Who the hell am I kidding? Of course, they wouldn't like Jan – why would they? I'm not even sure I like her. She'd be their worst nightmare for a friend of mine, but what the heck, so what? It's not like they *really* care, is it? If they did, they'd be honest with me and they wouldn't ignore my feelings. It's about keeping me under their thumbs and panicking about what the neighbours think and all that crap.

They're too busy arguing and discussing every single gripe they've had against each other. It's worse when they move on to the whole 'how to bring up their daughter' – that would be me – theme. They're supposed to be the adults, right? Yet they can't see what they're doing to me – maybe they just don't care. They can't see how bad things are – what I'm doing to myself. My fingers rub over the plaster on my palm. If they knew what I'd done on purpose to myself with the buckle, they'd go spare. Maybe I should tell them. Maybe that way, they'd stay together. I rip off the plaster and scrape at the scab. If they stayed together, it might be worse, though. They'd probably kill each other and instead of having two bedrooms and the chance to play them off against one and other, I'd be on my lonesome.

Sometimes I reckon they think I'm just a bloody stookie or something, for all the attention they pay me. Don't they get that I know what's going on? It's not like I'm a wee lassie anymore. I've got fucking eyes, don't I? But they don't get it. They're too wrapped up in their own selfish misery to give a second's thought to mine. I mean, don't they understand that this is a big deal for *me*? That I should be part of their furtive wee discussions. After all, their hissing voices make a mockery of them being civilised to each other.

I down another half mouthful of the voddy and Coke Jan bought me and almost retch. I'm not a drinker. Don't like the stuff, but I'm committed to my night of being rebellious. Acting out. Deep down I get that this is self-destructive behaviour – I'm not a thicko, am I? It's just another way I've found to hurt myself. To punish myself for all the things I must have done to feel like this. As my eyes flit around the half-empty bar for the umpteenth time – the Tartan fucking Sporran, I mean, *really*? – my heart sinks. What the hell am I doing here? It's a bloody dive. I take in the sad fading tartan carpet and the has-been photos on the mustard-coloured walls and grimace. My dad wouldn't step foot in here even if he was paid to. That thought cheers me up, for tonight, as I keep reminding myself, is all about pissing off the parents.

So much for a night on the toon. That's what Jan promised after all. A good night, oot with plenty of fit guys falling over themselves to buy us drinks. I'd thought we might hit one of the nightclubs. They're bound to be better than this sad wee hovel filled with smelly foul bastards. I shudder as I spot the weirdo in the corner staring at us. Gives me the creeps. Then there's the uninterested barmaid who's only got eyes for the gallus wee dark-haired bloke by the bar.

Soon as we walked through the door Jan spotted him and back went her shoulders, out went her tits and bat went her eyelashes. Soooo bloody predictable! What a bloody disgrace to feminism she is! I doubt Jan Carmichael's ever heard the word, never mind knows what it means. Her 'whisper' is loud – meant to drift over to the bar. Delivered with what she no doubt thought was a heavy seductive tone, she intended the fit bloke to hear her. 'Widnae mind a go wi' him, Ali. What do you think?'

What is she thinking? She's got nothing on the barmaid who casts her a look that says: 'Aye right, hen, gie it yer best shot'. The guy doesn't glance away from the red-haired girl. Why the hell would he? She's gorgeous.

But Jan's not deterred. So, boobs out and nipples poking against her tight T-shirt, she marches over to him and leans her arm on his shoulder, like she's bloody Beyoncé or something. I almost pished myself laughing when he turned around and looked her up and down, his lips curling in distaste before he brushes her arm away with a, 'Aye, in yer dreams, hen.' He winks at the redhead, who scowls at Jan as if ready to gouge her eyes out.

But Jan, not bothered by this rejection, shrugs and leans on the sticky bar, waiting for the lassie to come over and serve us, which was when a tall, half pished gangly red-headed guy sidled up and wrapped an arm round her shoulders, his left palm resting on her boob like he'd done that before. I want to boak. James fucking Bond, he's not, but she simpers like a cat with the cream. I want to thrust my fingers down my throat and spew my load. He's disgusting! Not only is he rat-arsed, but he stinks of BO with overtones of Lynx Africa and stale fag smoke.

'Come on, Jan, hen, you and me, eh? Never mind that Shuggie, he's spoken for, but me . . .' he prodded his mucky T-shirt with his thumb and wiggled his shoulders '. . . on the other hand, I'm young, free, single and desirable.'

I almost choke on his last words, but Jan's all simpering smiles and not so subtle lingering hand strokes down his filthy chest. *God, Jan, get a bloody grip, eh?*

Waving his other hand at Shuggie's girlfriend, behind the bar, the guy says, 'Voddy and Cokes for these two smashers and my usual, Jeanie, my sweet darling.'

Jan links her arm through mine and drags me over to a booth in the corner with a sticky circular table and after pushing me in, she slides in after me, her bright red lips pouting in what she no doubt thinks is a seductive come-hither look. She sits erect – boobs still struggling for containment under her skimpy top – and simpers as the butt-ugly guy struts over and, eyes all over Jan, like the look alone would remove her clothing, slides a drink across the table to me. He hands Jan hers, his fingers caressing her hand as he does so – *boak alert, boak alert* – and then slides in beside her.

The first sip of vodka makes my eyes water. Must be a double, for it's strong as fuck. I contemplate returning to the bar to get more Coke, but the ginger-haired lassie's simpering up to her boyfriend and I can't be arsed interrupting them. Whether I go to the bar or stay here, I'm still a fucking gooseberry. I get out my phone and scroll through my messages. There're tonnes from my mum. Looks like she's sussed out I'm not with Isla. *Fuck!* Not being with Isla's only the half of it though. My mum would have a fit if she saw me drinking alcohol. She'd go all 'we don't drink, it's haram' on me. Like I've not seen them downing a bottle of red on a weekend. As for my dad? Shite, he'd have an even bigger paddy if he saw what I was wearing. Then there's the fucking death traps she calls shoes. Five inches higher than my usual footwear and they're nipping my toes like crap and my heels feel like a pound of mince.

What the hell am I going to do? So much for my massive, big rebellion. So much for excitement and living on the wild side. All I see looming in front of me is years of being grounded, a lifetime of dark looks and pointed silences from my mum, and a ballistic meltdown from old Popsy dearest. What a bloody mess I've made of this. With only the prospect of a rollicking at home, I resign myself to putting up with the abysmal evening a wee bit longer – but not too long. I need time to plan my 'return to overprotective parents' strategy.

Jan's all right over in the corner with that manky bloke. He's over her like a rash, necking her and slipping his hand under her T-shirt. It's gross. Maybe I should drag her away, even if she goes ballistic on me. I mean, what the actual hell does she think she's playing at? The bloke's an arse – a complete and utter bawbag, but Jan's pissed after that half-bottle of voddy she downed in the taxi on the way over and the bottle she guzzled at her house. There's no way she'll listen to me. Besides, he's twenty, and she thinks that makes her all that.

What the heck possessed me to come out with Jan Carmichael, anyway? Isla was right. I barely know her. We don't speak, interact, or have classes together at school. What the hell was the big draw? I scowl and risk another sip of voddy. No way would Jan Carmichael study the sciences, not when she can barely spell her damn name and only scraped three Nat 5s last year. I shouldn't have been so naïve. I should've realised that she only invited me as a last resort, anyway. I thought she'd make me pay for the drinks but she bought the first round and that waster bloke bought the second. But still . . . I'm not one of the cool kids, and Jan definitely is. She's the alpha queen. The one all the wasters look up to. What the hell was I thinking? There's no way she'd ask me out if any of her proper mates were free.

Instead of trying to prove something to myself and piss my mum and dad off, I should have gone to Isla's house like we'd planned and finished my biology homework. Can't believe how grateful I was for Jan's invite. Got myself all psyched up to be Jan Carmichael's chosen mate for the night. Talk about stupid.

My heart picks up a beat as I realise how foolish I've been. Last month, before all the whispered conversations and arguments started, I wouldn't have dreamed of hooking up with any of Jan's crew. Me and my real mates, like Isla, spent hours slagging them off behind their backs. Talking about how they'd amount to nothing, but secretly wishing we were a bit more like them and less like the nerdy kids. Here we were, the academics, the brainy kids – all en route to one of the best unis Scotland, or the UK, had to offer, but I hadn't broken a rule in my life. I was all set to sail high and achieve loads, but what about living? For all Jan and her mates' faults, at least they had fun!

My only solution is to cut my losses and leave now. Maybe if I'm honest and tell Popsy dearest and Mum that I just wanted to hurt them, that I knew they were splitting up and that it frightened the hell out of me, maybe they'd understand. Maybe they'd see I'd behaved out of character and learned my lesson. Last thing I want is for them to cancel the school France trip next year. Yes, that was the best solution. Maybe I could swing by Isla's and change out of these trashy clothes before they saw me. At least that would be one less thing they could hold over me. That decided, I lean over. 'Hey Jan, I'm gonna split. You coming?'

'Aw, no, Ali. Not yet, it's still early. It's not even half nine yet. Don't be such a wuss. Thought you wanted to experience a bit of life on the wild side.' She snorted, her smudged lipsticked lips all mean and angry-looking. 'Maybe you're just a big daddy's girl after all. Come on, just ten minutes more, eh?'

Even though I know she's pushing my buttons, her words

get my gander up because she has a point. I only came with her tonight to stick two fingers up at my folks. Now look at me. A few angry texts and I'm all for throwing in the towel and sloping off home all red-faced and ashamed with apologies on my lips. Maybe she's right. Maybe I am just a wuss. My one attempt to flaunt my dad's too-strict rules and my mum's over-fussiness and within a couple of hours I'm regretting it big time. Then I look at Jan, with her tongue down some arsehole's throat, wearing cheap crap from Primani and not a care in the world as long as he buys her a drink or two, and I realise that *I'm* the arse. I was foolish to believe that going to a seedy pub in Bathgate would be the answer. That it would make them stop arguing and stay together.

I sigh and plonk myself down, handbag clutched in my lap, and glare at the bloke with the ginger hair and the hard-on that's pushing against his trackie bottoms. *Fuck's sake, subtle eh?* 'Five minutes, Jan, and then I'm going, with or without you.'

'Chillax, girl.' *Hard-on's got a voice then.* 'I'll see you get home all right. Look, I'm good for the taxi fare.' He rummages in his pockets, which makes his hard-on bounce revoltingly as he drags a handful of notes and dumps them on the table. He winks at me. 'Me and Jan here are gelling, you get it? Getting to know each other. You don't want to be a spare part – is that it? Take the money and get a taxi at the road's end. Cross my heart and hope to die. I'll get Cinderella here home before midnight.'

A lazy smile crosses his face and he peers at me through booze-addled eyes, struggling to focus. 'Do yourself a favour, hen, and stop spoiling our fun. Off you go. I can't say fairer than that now, can I?'

Jan seems to think this is hilarious because she dissolves into a fit of giggles and then leans across him, rubbing her covered boobs against his chest as she whispers in my ear. 'Don't be such a fucking wimp, babe. Just split and leave me to have my fun. Your face has been tripping you all fucking night. I shouldn't have agreed to bring you. You're too much of a goody two shoes.

Should've known you'd get all needy. Just fuck right off and leave me to have fun with Matty here, eh?'

I slide out from the booth, my hand tingling with the desire to slap her stupid pus useless. That'd teach her. What a bitch! *She* should've known better? Bloody cheek. It's *me* who should have known better. Should've known better than to break the rules and sneak out with Whitburn Academy's bad girl. Sod her. Just bloody sod her. I should've known better than to trust a skank like Jan Carmichael. As I storm across the threadbare carpet to the exit, the pair of them are at it again. Hands all over each other, tongues down each other's throats. Makes me feel sick. But maybe it's the voddy making my legs tremble and my head swim.

I stumble over to the door, uncomfortable in my unfamiliar footwear, and another wave of dizziness hits me. Before I leave, I spin round, my feet unsteady, and glare at her. Bloody cowbag. How dare she talk to me like that? How dare she? I raise my voice above the Ed Sheeran track on the jukebox and ignore the weird bloke whose head has jerked up to watch all the action. 'You know what, Jan Carmichael? If you end up on your back in a dark alley, with your throat slit, it would serve you right. You're nothing but a bitch. That's all you are.'

Chapter 48

Jan

The door slammed shut behind Ali as she stormed out of the Tartan Sporran. Jan scowled and pushed her amorous admirer away. She'd slipped the pill into Ali's glass as arranged, but after seeing Ali, so dishevelled and yelling like a banshee, she wondered if that had been a step too far. What if she got in real bother? Ali wasn't as streetwise as Jan, so she wasn't as equipped to handle the Bathgate streets at night. That thought made her snappy. 'Get that fucking dirty todger out of my face, ya minger. Nowhere in the deal did it say I'd to put up with that crap. Can't you control yourself?'

'Aw, Jan, darling, you're breaking my heart, you ken that? You can't blame me. Look at you.' Matty raised his index finger and thumb to his lips and kissed them before raising them in the air and releasing a hissing sound. 'Hot! That's what you are. Sizzling bloody hot!'

Jan tried to hide her grin behind a scowl and batted his hand away as she glanced towards the shadowy figure who had been sitting in the corner nursing the same drink since they'd arrived.

She'd sensed his eyes on them the entire time she'd been necking with Matty. Bloody pervert chancing his luck ogling her. Well, couldn't blame him, could she? But now he was off, slipping through the door. Good riddance, pervy boy. Turning back to Matty, she prodded him in the gut. 'Another drink, eh? All that necking's made me thirsty and we can't have that, can we?'

With an obedience born of stupidity and the false promise of getting his leg over, Matty slid from the booth and wandered over to the bar. As soon as he left, Jan got the burner phone out and, hiding it under the table, her fingers flew over the screen. Within seconds she'd sent her text.

She's all yours, mate. Where's the dosh?

The reply arrived within seconds.

Loos, cubicle nearest window inside cistern.

Grinning she returned the burner to her bag. As she waited for Matty, she considered what she'd done for the first time. Would Ali be all right? She shrugged. Course she would. Whoever wanted to play this trick on her wouldn't hurt her, would they? Not like he was a serial killer or anything. Jan laughed and shook her head. Don't get what he sees in that skinny wee bitch. I mean, I don't think I've met anyone as uptight as her. Bet her fud's as tight as a canary's arse. A grin spread across her lipsticked mouth as Matty returned. 'You know, Matty, that Ali's a weird one, eh? Maybe what she needs is a stiff one to loosen her up?'

Matty, struggling to focus now, grinned, his mouth a lopsided slit. Jan sighed. What a waste of space he is. 'Look, I need to go powder my nose, so let me out. I'll not be long.'

Sliding out of the booth, taking her handbag with her, Jan headed for the bogs. *I, for one, don't care what happens to that slag as long as I get the dosh I'm due and it better fucking be where it's supposed to.*

The women's loos in the Tartan Sporran reeked of piss and sick with ineffective undertones of lemon, which made Jan despair at the condition of the men's bogs. She headed straight for the

266

cubicle nearest the window and once sure she was alone, she locked the door behind her and lifted the cistern lid and peered inside. A huge grin spread across her face as she discovered the package wrapped in cellophane taped to the underside of the cistern. Her mysterious texter had come through for her. She ripped the parcel off, replaced the cistern, and plonked herself down on the closed toilet lid before tearing the wrapping off. Her grin widened when she got through to the contents.

Stuffing the wad of discarded wrapping into the sanitary bin, she ran her fingers over the wad of twenty-pound notes and grinned. All she had to do was sneak out without Matty clocking her, dispose of the phone, go home and decide how she would spend her hard-earned cash. Not that it was hard-earned. Apart from having to pretend to be friends with that drip, it was piss-easy.

Chapter 49

Mhairi

Hard to believe that a wee hoor from Bathgate could actually carry it off, but the wee cow did. Kudos to her for that, I suppose. Funny how anticipating payment can focus the mind.

This, right here and right now, is brilliant. Out of all my recent plans and accomplishments, this will be truly fucking brilliant. It'll really get to that stupid bitch Jazzy and boy, does she deserve it. I'd wondered about attacking her mum or her dad – maybe even that Queenie or the sprog grandkid, but all of that felt a wee bit too crude to me. Yes, it would destroy her, but mere destruction isn't enough. It needs to be drawn right out. Needs to make her suffer. Needs to pile on the guilt till it's more than she can take. After all, that's Jazzy's thing, isn't it? Guilt. She laps it up like a rat in a sewer.

I slip out of the pub and follow her. Nobody in there's paid me a blind bit of notice. I'm just another anonymous punter. It's almost like I'm invisible, but I won't be for long. No way, José. Soon they'll wake up and Jazzy will wish she'd never been born and she won't be the only one wishing her dead.

I take out the burner and reply to the money-grabbing slag's text, then focus on my prey. She's tall for her age and anger seems to have made her stride longer. She's at the taxi rank and I can't have that. I've got to sort it before she gets there. So, I speed up, and when I'm almost level with her, I swing one arm round her shoulder. 'Hey there, hen. Fancy seeing you here. Can we share a taxi home?'

She struggled – just for an instant – her eyes wide and fluttering. The faint smell of vodka on her breath makes me want to laugh, but I contain myself and then she slumps against me and her eyes flutter closed.

Chapter 50

Jazzy

'So? Plan of action?' Jazzy looked round Queenie's dining table at the motley group. They were all replete after downing the humungous lasagne Craig had left for them and, despite the circumstances, the evening had been light-hearted. With the dishwasher packed and the Eton mess demolished, Jazzy wanted to amalgamate the information the team had gathered. As she waited for a response, she fiddled with the burner phone on the table in front of her, torn between wishing it would ring and dreading it.

Guy pushed his chair back. 'I'll give you lot some privacy.'

But Jazzy halted him in his tracks. 'This entire case has disrupted your life. You've been uprooted from your home and work space. I think you deserve to hear this as long as whatever is said stays between these four walls.'

Geordie leaned across and linked fingers with his boyfriend. 'Besides, they have vetted you . . .'

Fenton, grinning from cheek to cheek, added, 'Besides which, Queenie would kill you if you leaked anything.' Then, realising that his words may be insulting, he shook his head. 'None of us believe you would, like.'

Queenie tutted. 'Trust you, Haggis, ya pillock. Always rely on you to upset the guests.' She turned her gaze to Guy, who had sat back down. 'We're aye happy to welcome a fifth Jazz Queen to oor wee group; that no' right, Jazzy?'

Whilst Guy, unfazed by the prospect, let loose one of his loud guffaws, Elliot cleared his throat and looked at Queenie, who scowled back at him. 'The jury's still oot on you, Elliot Balloch. Ye'll need to prove yourself before you're given a Jazz Queen accolade.'

Keen to avoid any dissent, Jazzy interrupted. 'Right, Queenie, you kick us off by telling everyone what you took away from Pollokshaws this afternoon and I'll chip in if necessary.'

'Aye, all right, hen.' Queenie took a slurp of water and cleared her throat. 'Well, there were two scenes, really. The first one gave us a concrete link between Mhairi, Simon, and the victim – David Paltrow. The second supplied the link between Paltrow's murder and those of Lewis Fletcher and Dwayne Taggart.' Excitement all over her face. She wiggled her eyebrows at her colleagues. 'But the biggest thing is that we – me and Jazzy, that is; not you two – have a meeting in Operation Birchtree HQ tomorrow regarding the bastard's funeral arrangements and this development. Anyway, I'm away to FaceTime Craig and Ruby. See yous the morra.'

As Queenie left, Fenton, Guy and Geordie pushed their chairs back from the table and, muttering excuses about catching up with their loved ones too, they left Jazzy and Elliot alone. For a moment or two Jazzy thought Elliot would leave too, but instead he lifted the nearly empty wine bottle. 'Might as well finish this off, eh?'

Jazzy relaxed back into her chair and nodded.

'You think this meeting tomorrow will be fruitful?' Elliot's expression as he poured the wine left no doubt as to his scepticism.

'Maybe, maybe not. But at least it's a foot in the door.'

For a while the two of them sat sipping their drinks and not speaking. Jazzy tried to remember the last time they'd shared such a comfortable silence and although she wanted to savour it, she had to take this opportunity to clear the air. 'Elliot?'

His eyes, impenetrable, bored into hers as he placed the glass on the table. 'You thinking I was a bent copper really hurt me you know, Jazz?'

With a tut, Jazzy leaned forward. 'For God's sake, Ell. How many times do I have to tell you that I never – not even for a second – thought you were on the take? I didn't take the job because I believed it. I took it to prove you were innocent.'

'Still, you could have told me?'

'Could I though? Could I really? If it was the other way around would you have broken protocol and told me?'

Elliot tapped his fingers on the table then finally gave a reluctant headshake. 'No, but I still can't shake the feeling that you don't trust me. That, even after everything we've been through, there's still that little bit of mistrust in your head, Jazz.'

'Rubbish! You're just acting the martyr now.'

'No, no I'm not. You keep things bundled up so tight inside that I've never felt you completely trusted me, even before this. Then along comes Queenie and suddenly you're best pals.'

Jazzy blinked, then threw back her head and laughed. 'You're jealous of Queenie? Oh for heaven's sake get a grip, Ell. Do you think I had a choice in being friends with her? She just barged her way into my life and took me over.'

Elliot blushed and inclined his head, his lips twitching. 'Yeah, that sounds about right. There's no denying the force that is Queenie, is there?'

They settled back into a contemplative stillness until Jazzy sipped the last of her wine and stood up. 'We good, Ell?'

'Yeah, Jazz, we're good. I'm still hurt, you know. But I'll process that. We need to be able to get on and I'll try not to be such an idiot.'

Although it was a step in the right direction, Jazzy wished she could erase the hurt that Elliot felt and things could just be the way they had been. There was no way she could apologise for doing her job and she reckoned that, deep down, Elliot knew that.

Inside Billi's room Queenie was tossing and turning on her bed, so Jazzy crept in, brushed her teeth and tried to fall asleep, but Queenie's restlessness made that impossible.

Being in Billi's bedroom, surrounded by her things, was really hard for Queenie. Every memory of her daughter's life and death was crystal clear to Queenie and the additional stress of this investigation and not having Craig as her counterbalance made everything exponentially tougher for her. Jazzy wasn't surprised when, huffing and puffing under her breath, Queenie, in as quiet a manner as she could manage, wrapped her duvet around her, grabbed her knitting needles and a bag of wool and vacated the bedroom. Jazzy listened for ten more minutes as the clack, clack clackety clacking of Queenie's needles continued, accompanied by low mumbles and grumbles and finally, when she realised she wouldn't be able to doze off either, Jazzy sat up, pulled her tablet onto her knee and by the faint light from the hallway began to review her notes on both Fletcher's and Taggart's murders and those written by Queenie after the Pollokshaws crime scene.

She was determined that by the time she attended the briefing after her meeting with Connolly she'd have a plan to find a course of action that might bring them closer to locating Mhairi. After an hour, Queenie slipped in, deposited a mug of coffee on the bedside table and left with a 'Well, if we cannae sleep, we might as well work, eh, hen?'

Within seconds, the clackety clack of her knitting started again and Jazzy knew her friend's amazing brain was working through the cases in its own unique way. Grateful for the distraction, Jazzy put her tablet down and picked up the warm mug. The smell of coffee was delicious and she savoured its soothing effect as she leaned back and allowed her mind to wander. She'd gone over the files and had noted a few follow-up actions for the next day. Now she wanted to think about her sister and what she knew of her both personally and through the huge files that had been amassed about her. 'Come on, Mhairi, what are you up to? What is it you want?'

She glanced at the burner phone charging beside her personal phone and, not for the first time since she'd taken ownership of it, she wished it would ring. It was frustrating knowing that her half-sister was nearby, yet not knowing exactly where. For all she knew, she could be outside Queenie's house waiting for one of them to slip up. The thought sent a shiver up her spine, and she had to force herself to remain in bed rather than go over and peer out the window. Afzal had a protection team on the house and she would have to trust in them. Besides, Mhairi was no fool. She'd not take unnecessary risks. Still, Jazzy wouldn't let her team slip up, wouldn't let them fall victim to Mhairi. She had to keep her wits about her and protect them. That was why it had been so easy to agree to all the measures they'd taken to safeguard their families.

As she rolled her shoulders to release the crick in her neck, she stroked Winky and let her mind drift further, plucking at a random memory and scouring it for any useful intent before discarding it and moving on to the next one. Something she'd thought earlier kept coming to mind. Something about her relationship with Mhairi, but whatever had prompted the niggle, Jazzy couldn't pin its significance. After all she wasn't the only one Mhairi had a relationship with, was she? Over the years there had been other significant people in her life. She found the list of names that had been linked to Mhairi since they'd been separated as children. Schoolteachers, therapists, her adoptive mother, social workers. Her sister had killed many of those on the list and those still alive had been questioned and interviewed many times.

Jazzy scoured the background details on each of the remaining people, looking for anything, a mere scrap of information that might just tug loose a clue. But there was nothing that Jazzy could see. She made a mental note to have Queenie employ her eidetic skills when going over the list again tomorrow. But, before she could give up on that train of thought she opened up the file on Elsbeth Tait, Mhairi's adoptive mum, who had died at her adopted daughter's hands. Elsbeth Tait, desperate to have a child of her own, had adopted Mhairi as a single parent. As she looked at the picture of Elsbeth and Mhairi together, Jazzy sighed. A simple twist of fate had sealed Elsbeth's future. She was pretty and the smile on her face as she looked at her new daughter spoke of high hopes for a fun-filled, loving future together.

The tragedy of it sliced through Jazzy, making her falter as she moved on to Elsbeth's family history. She had no idea what she expected to find; after all it wasn't like her eyes were the first to read this, but the coffee had revitalised her and she'd never get to sleep now anyway. Elsbeth Tait was the only child of Grace and Wilbert Tait and both her parents were also only children and both had died young, in their fifties, and were outlived by Elsbeth's grandparents on her father's side – Ena and Geoffrey Tait – both of whom had died before Elsbeth had adopted Mhairi. A note had been added saying that although Ena Tait had remarried briefly after her husband died, she and her second husband were both dead. Jazzy sighed. This had been a dead end too, but as she scrolled to the next page she noticed an addendum in red. Jazzy frowned for a second, wondering if she'd seen this addendum before, but then she noticed the date it had been added – three weeks ago by Clive Shanks from Operation Birchtree.

Three weeks ago? Breath held, Jazzy read the information and then leaned back, resting her head against the wall. Was this significant? At the moment she couldn't see how, but Clive had seen fit to add it, although the information predated Elsbeth Tait's death and Mhairi's killing spree. She reread the updated notes.

After Geoffrey Tait's death, Ena remarried within the year and remained married to a Stuart McCullough until her own death three years later. Stuart McCullough died on Skye the year Elsbeth adopted Mhairi. There is no indication Elsbeth and McCullough kept in touch and he died intestate. Action: None taken, none needed.

Jazzy gently banged her head on the wall as she thought. *Skye?* Was that relevant? Could it be the small insignificant piece of information they needed? After all, Mhairi had successfully evaded them for months and she had to hole up somewhere. Surely Skye was as good a place as any. Jazzy considered calling for Queenie, but as the sound of erratic snoring warbled through from the living room couch, she reconsidered. Queenie deserved some rest. She picked up her phone on the point of phoning Afzal with her thoughts, then stopped. Was lack of sleep and stress making her see things that weren't there? See clues that were irrelevant. Even if Mhairi had known of her step-great-grandad, would she have gone up to Skye? And even if she had, everything indicated she was no longer there. This could wait till the morning when she could get Fenton or Geordie to check with the Skye police and also find out more about step-grandad McCullough.

She shimmied under the duvet, pulled it right up to her chin, edged Winky over to the other side of the bed and closed her eyes as she tried to block out Queenie's less gentle snorts and wheezes. Which is of course when the phone rang. Jazzy blinked for a few moments, then as she sat back up the bedroom door burst open and four tousled heads poked through. 'Is it her?' Geordie, the tallest, squeezed past the other three, yanking on a dressing gown in Pride colours as he entered, whilst Queenie, yawning and rubbing her eyes, followed leaving Fenton in a pair of striped pyjamas buttoned up to the neck, and Elliot in a pair of Heart of Midlothian boxers taking up the rear. Her eyes went from one of them to the other as she picked up the phone, awaiting Elliot's signal to answer. The tech people were monitoring any activity so she had a moment to ground herself. Elliot nodded and she accepted the call and, breath bated, waited to hear what her sister would say.

For long seconds there was silence and Jazzy had to bite her tongue to refrain from initiating the conversation. She wanted Mhairi to speak first – it was the only show of resistance Jazzy was able to offer at this time.

'Did I wake you, sister dearest? Sorry, not sorry!' Mhairi's laughter echoed through the bedroom and Queenie's lips tightened. Fenton took a step forward, but otherwise everyone remained motionless. 'You not speaking, Jazzy? Well, it's up to you, but I won't tell you a secret if you don't say hi.'

Knuckles tight round the receiver, Jazzy, her voice deadpan, said, 'I'm all ears, Mhairi.'

Another burst of laughter from the phone, and sounding a little breathless, Mhairi said, 'Tomorrow's going to be busy for you, dear. But, here's a clue for you. The secret location is buried in the past.'

'What secret locat . . .'

But Mhairi had already hung up. Within seconds, Elliot's phone rang as the tech team contacted him. He listened, scraping his hand across his unshaven chin and ended with an 'Okay, do your best. Let me know if you find anything.' Shoulders slumped, he turned to the others, shaking his head. 'She wasn't on long enough to triangulate the call with mast towers, but they're going to try to isolate background noise, to see if that yields anything. In the meantime . . .' he lasered in on Jazzy '. . . any idea what she means by a secret location in the past.'

'No idea. Does she mean in Inverness, where we were born? That doesn't make sense, but it might be an idea to clue in the Inverness MITs, just in case. She's likely to be in West Lothian, because otherwise how can she be doing all of this? Plus, I'm here and Simon's funeral will be here; that's probably enough incentive to keep her in the area. On the other hand she's a tricksy cow, so, best cover all bases.'

A throbbing at her temple, made Jazzy blink. Tiredness seeped into her bones and as she glanced at her phone and saw it was almost four o'clock, she knew she had to get some sleep. 'All I can suggest is that we get some shut-eye and reconvene at the briefing tomorrow. I think we need to find other links she or Simon might have with this area, but that's another job for tomorrow.' As Queenie shut the door, Jazzy fell into a restless sleep filled with dreams of Mhairi dressed as Alice in Wonderland leading them into rabbit holes.

Chapter 51

Friday

Mhairi

It's the early hours of the morning and the last twenty-four hours have been hectic. Filled with non-stop adrenalin-fuelled activity. I'm running on fumes and can't deny my exhaustion any longer. Completely and utterly shattered. My head's spinning and my vision's becoming more fractured by the second as I try to go over the list in my head. Have I done everything I needed to? I check them off on my fingers:

Deposited sister's gift,

Located the Jazz Queens' bolthole,

Completed operation Intensify – I laugh at that one – it's a multi-pronged strategy designed to increase the pressure on sister dearest.

Tidied up loose ends.

Packed up Porty flat.

Relocated to safe house.

Taunted sister dearest with a cryptic clue.

That covers the main points, but have I been careful enough? I probably shouldn't have phoned Jazzy, but the temptation was too strong. She'll not get my reference. It's far too obscure for her; still a slight niggle remains. Have I covered my tracks? I'll have to shelve that thought till later, because I can hardly focus. The flashing lights and auditory disturbances impair my rationality. I have to trust that I did what I needed to. That's my skill. Besides, there's not much time left till the grand finale and I have more planned.

Jazzy, my sweet, evil sister, by the end of today, you won't know what's hit you. Sister dearest, I'm coming for you. I have to be prepared, though. This time I won't underestimate her and I need sleep to rejuvenate my mind and regain my focus. Even before I've unpacked my equipment, I take a huge slug of orange juice and pop a pill, spilling a few in the process, but I've got plenty. Then, stumbling over to the sofa, I allow the drug to perform its magic and drift into a welcome dream. The dream that encompasses one of my most treasured memories. The one that I can rely on to bolster me when I'm feeling at my worst. The one when great-papa McCullough came into my life . . .

As we walked along down the uncarpeted hall, I exhaled and sighed when my breath released puffs of arctic steam before me. Curious, I dawdled, my eyes veering from side to side as I peered into the two open doorways. One led to a kitchen with an old-fashioned, unlit Aga. A scorched wood table clear of any rubbish stood pride of place with four matching chairs stationed on each edge. There were no pictures or ornaments to give the room personality, but then I hadn't expected that. The only other room to the right was a bedroom with a large double bed, piled high with blankets and dated multi-coloured knitted covers. With the closed curtains and only the yellowing hallway light seeping into the room, it was difficult to make out the large heavy pine wardrobes and a dressing table.

Mum rapped her knuckles lightly on the door of the closed room and thrust the door open, ushering me in before closing it again behind us. Fire flickered in the grate between two massive armchairs, one of which was occupied by the oldest person I'd ever seen.

She thrust me forward, her hands resting on my shoulders, their tell-tale clenching and unclenching indicative of her emotional state as she propelled me forwards. 'Here she is. My daughter. Mhairi, this is your great-papa McCullough.'

Unsure of what to say, I blinked a few times. There was no need for words as curiosity sparked in his eyes. His frailty, accompanied by the inevitable stench of decay, told me he was dying. Everything about him, from his emaciated body to the frail legs covered by a blanket to his sunken cheeks and yellowy complexion to his skinny shoulders, hardly strong enough to hold his head upright. His green piercing eyes were the only thing that didn't speak of death. 'Come here, lass. Let me see you.'

I started. His rich, powerful voice surprised me. This wasn't the voice of a man ready to die. This was the strong voice of a warrior. A fighter. I raised my own eyes to meet his, and it was as if we forged a connection between us in that single second. My mum opened her mouth to coax me to placate the old man, but she had no need because I had already shaken off her hands and strode closer to him. The green of his eyes intensified in the flickering fire-light and as I stood before him, withstanding his stringent perusal, warmth fluttered through my limbs and into my gut. I smiled and with a slight nod, he smiled as well. As if all it took was that tacit acknowledgement of me, I dived forward and wrapped my arms round his body. For the first time in years, I felt seen.

No, that wasn't quite right, not merely seen, but also validated. Papa McCullough had looked into my eyes – right into my soul – and he'd seen me. Everything about me was paraded there before him and he wasn't repulsed. He accepted every part of me, the good, the bad, and the very, very ugly. I met his eyes again and for a fraction of a second, they narrowed. I swallowed hard, trying to work out what he was thinking. What that look had been. It wasn't fear in his eyes and definitely not disgust. What then? Sympathy? Concern? I couldn't work it out, but it didn't matter, so I pressed my cheek against the wiry wool of his jumper and closed my eyes, breathing in the heady mix of decay and old man sweat and firewood.

For the first time since we'd met, I looked at my mother, my lips turned up in a smile. Her fingers fluttered to her neck, her mouth a perfect 'o', her eyes alive with joy as she smiled. For a second Papa McCullough tightened his weakened arms around me and then he whispered, for my ears only, 'I see what you are. I know what you're capable of, and I know it's not your fault.'

We stayed four days with Papa McCullough. On the second day, he handed me a key. 'This is for you. No one else will want it. Not your mum, and there's no one else. I know your hate consumes you and your needs propel you, but when I'm gone, try to be kind to her. She's innocent in all this. Make your life here and you won't face many temptations. I did that for all these years and it mostly worked. You should do the same.'

Papa McCullough passed on the third day, and my mum gathered old photos from the bedroom dresser. Then when the funeral was over, we departed. I tucked the key safely in my pocket and held the memory of Papa McCullough and the way his eyes embraced the darkness in my heart like a living talisman.

Chapter 52

Jazzy

DCI Dick's face was all smarmy smiles and wiggling moustache as he buzzed them through the security lock and into the offices of Operation Birchtree on the top floor. With Queenie scowling behind her, Jazzy had no choice but to look at her old boss as he rocked back and forth on his heels, clearly ready to milk every second of his moment of superiority for all it was worth. 'Everything's top secret in here, you know, Solanki. Everything's on a need-to-know basis and . . .' he laughed, flinging his head back, mouth wide, revealing silver fillings and a wobbling uvula, which protected them from seeing what he had for his breakfast '. . . you two reprobates from D team don't need to know very much at all.'

Queenie's feet shuffled on the brand-new carpet and thankfully his laughter drowned out her snort.

He swivelled on his heel and began marching down the corridor, nodding and smiling at the officers he passed en route. With the scent of fresh paint lingering and the aroma of good quality fresh coffee making her salivate, Jazzy swallowed her annoyance and followed him.

'Classified. That's what most of this information is. You're lucky to be allowed on this level. I expressed my doubts as to the wisdom of this to DCI Connolly – after all, it was *you*, DS Solanki, who allowed your sister to escape.'

Jazzy's hands fisted by her sides as she bit down on her retort, but Queenie wasn't to be stopped from putting in her tuppenth worth. 'Aye, but I wonder who it was that failed to link the Clarks' murders with Jazzy's sister. Can you remember, sir?'

A flush appeared on Dick's face, but he brushed Queenie's words aside and sped up, continuing. 'DCI Connolly is a tad more lenient than me – and more forgiving. That said, she's nobody's fool. Don't for a second think that your presence in Pollokshaws signals a thawing in relationships. On the contrary. We have your mark and we will not let D team balls it up again. Uh-uh, no way.' He gestured to the windowless doors, each with an admittance keypad on the wall beside them, and lowered his voice to a hissing whisper. 'If for even a second you thought this invitation would give you access to information about your sister, then you're very much mistaken. This time the folk with balls are in charge and every precaution . . .' he indicated the keypad-protected rooms '. . . is in place to stop the likes of you leaking stuff.'

Jazzy took a deep breath, her fists tightening till her nails almost broke the flesh on her palms. The desire to retaliate was so strong that it took all her strength to refrain. Instead, she visualised herself smashing her fist into his overinflated gut and seeing it burst like a deflating balloon leaving him collapsed on the floor, his wiggling moustache wilted and lying on top like a dying hairy caterpillar.

She raised her head and met his amused gaze, refusing to back down from the silent confrontation. The dickless wonder would not get the upper hand. Not this time. His cheeks flushed even more and satisfaction surged over Jazzy as he swiped the back of his hand over his brow. She stepped closer and lowered her voice to make sure no one could hear. 'We all know who's responsible for Mhairi escaping. Every one of us downstairs is aware of who took their eye off the ball.' She smiled, allowing the very real pleasure she felt in saying what she'd been thinking for so long to chase the frown from her face as she delivered her final thrust. 'And believe me, so does my sister. She's already killed two people who threatened me . . . who do you reckon might be next on her list?'

A vaguely familiar masculine voice echoed down the corridor as Jazzy stepped away from an open-mouthed DCI Dick. 'Ah, so we meet again, DS Solanki. Welcome. You're here to be debriefed about the Pollokshaws crime scenes and to discuss the security arrangements for your brother's funeral on Monday and, lucky you, I'm the one in charge of that. When we're done discussing the security arrangements, DCI Connolly wants to meet with you both.'

As DI Clive Shanks, whom she'd first met at Lewis Fletcher's crime scene in Portobello, strode along the corridor, Jazzy couldn't help her smile deepening. Here, at least, if not exactly an ally, was someone who didn't hate her. Queenie nudged her and stepped forward, hand extended to the approaching officer whilst DCI Dick's expression took on overtones of a thunder cloud. Amused, Jazzy watched as Queenie all but genuflected in front of Clive. 'I'm DC Annie McQueen, but you can call me Queenie. How do you know our JayZee?'

Now it was Jazzy's turn to nudge her partner. 'Queenie, stop it.' Her eyes flashed at her friend, and Queenie responded with a wide, mock-innocent grin and a wiggle of her eyebrows.

'If you must know, Queenie, I met DI Shanks at the Fletcher crime scene. He was SIO until we discovered the note addressed to me . . .'

Clive, grinning from ear to ear, took Queenie's hand and for a second Jazzy expected him to raise it to his lips in a gallant knight in shining armour kiss, but he contented himself with a handshake and took up the tale. 'At which time, the burly and rather surly DI Balloch dispatched me from the scene. God, that guy's a case, isn't he?'

As Queenie giggled like a teenage girl, Jazzy rolled her eyes and, ignoring DCI Dick's tapping foot, turned to Shanks. 'Which doesn't explain why you're now part of Operation Birchtree?'

He shrugged, rubbed his hands together and gestured towards a door further down the corridor on the right. 'Thanks, Tony, I've got this from here.' He turned back to Jazzy and Queenie. 'Shall we?'

Clive Shanks's office space was generous and as he busied himself pouring coffee for them, Jazzy looked over at the diagrams, maps and plans that adorned the walls.

As she walked from left to right along the wall studying each map, she realised they were displayed in order of the route from the funeral director's – where Simon's body lay – to the cemetery.

Different-coloured string and arrows with cross-referenced written observations on risk factors and vulnerable points on the route, where Mhairi could stage something, trailed from the maps.

She plonked herself down on a chair and turned to Clive. 'Talk us through it.'

Clive sat on a table facing her. His intelligent dark eyes bored into hers until Queenie cleared her throat. 'For God's sake, do you two want me to leave you alone or something?'

Clive grinned and winked at Queenie. 'Now there's a thought, Queenie, but I'm afraid that'll have to wait till after the funereal, but believe me, it will be something I'll be pursuing.'

Jazzy's cheeks went hot, and she avoided looking at Queenie, whose deep-throated chortle told Jazzy that she liked Clive. God, Queenie would be unbearable now. For months she'd been yakking on about Jazzy needing to forget about Elliot – not that Jazzy thought about Elliot in that way, but Queenie wouldn't be convinced and told her, in her words, that she needed some rumpy-pumpy with a man with whom there was no desperately sad shared history. Jazzy looked at Clive. He was tall, he was attractive, he had a great sense of humour, and even Queenie's brashness didn't seem to faze him. Maybe she'd see where things went between them. He seemed keen, and she wasn't *completely* averse, but . . . She shook her head. 'Let's concentrate on the task, all right?'

For two hours, Clive led them through his proposals, outlining the security measures they had in place. Police Scotland would deploy armed response units around the cemetery and along the route. Police officers would replace the undertakers. The security personnel would check the route for booby traps and sightings of Mhairi.

Back and forth they discussed the benefits of alternate routes and additional surveillance units and so forth, until Jazzy yawned and said, 'I'm sorry, but I'm done in. I can't see any flaw in your plan, Clive, but I need a break. I'll consider it and contact you if I have concerns. For now, I'm content with the arrangements.'

Clive's professionalism and attention to detail appeared to calm Queenie to some extent, although she still vehemently opposed Jazzy's presence at the funeral. Jazzy's heart hammered at the thought that this funeral could go badly wrong and that even more deaths or injuries would be on her head. The only alternative was for her and the team to find Mhairi before the funeral, and that's what they would focus on for the next three days.

Queenie was first to the door, but as she got up to follow, Clive reached out and rested his hand on her arm. Voice low, he said, 'I'm serious about what I said earlier, Jazzy. When this is all done and dusted, you and I are going for that drink, agreed?' He held her gaze, his hand warming her arm and, despite her misgivings, Jazzy wondered what it would be like to have someone to confide in, like Queenie had Craig. She looked into his eyes and saw nothing but sincerity there, so she gave an abrupt nod and, ignoring Queenie's grin, left without a further word.

Chapter 53

Jazzy

DCI Connolly's office was an overheated study in various shades of green. Plants, some of which had leaves as big as dinner plates, whilst others had cacti spines that could have your eye out if you fell on them, dominated every available surface. A massive cheese plant with enormous leaves had pride of place in one corner. Queenie muttered something about 'triffids' under her breath as they took seats in front of her massive desk.

Whilst the DCI finished her phone conversation, Jazzy wondered just how much on her guard they should be for this meeting. Of course, they'd share every scrap of information they had. The stakes were too high to do otherwise, but Jazzy expected the flow of intel to be a one-way street, which was frustrating. Still smarting from Connolly's inference from the previous day, Jazzy struggled to quell the thought that this meeting might be a trap. She'd no idea who Connolly was talking to. Her tone was abrupt and incisive, her words delivered with slight sarcasm, as if the person on the other end of the line wasn't worth her time. Jazzy's eyes drifted round the room at the overabundance of plants and a comical thought occurred. Niamh Connolly, among her forest of triffids, *was* the Venus flytrap and right now, she and Queenie were the flies.

'Something amusing you, DS Solanki?'

Disturbed from her introspection, Jazzy diverted her gaze from a large cactus and met that of the senior officer. 'No, not at all.'

Connolly gave an irritated sigh, shuffled some paperwork on the desk, and glared at them.

'So, what do you make of your early morning communication with your sister, DS Solanki?'

'Half-sister.' Jazzy held Connolly's gaze and when she saw her acknowledge her correction she continued. 'I'm afraid I've come up with nothing. I don't know of any secret locations locally, yet I can't believe she's referring to something farther afield. Maybe your team will have more luck than I have. I am, however, a little concerned that her opening gambit about today being a busy day may be a threat of sorts.'

When Jazzy paused, Queenie took up the mantle. 'I agree with JayZee here, on that. That woman's toxic and nothing she says is ill-thought-out. I think it was a threat. Have the tech bods been able to retrieve anything that might hint at her location when she made the call?'

Connolly drummed her fingers on the desk and exhaled. 'Unfortunately, not. She's not daft, your *half*-sister. Okay, so that aside, let's move on. Time is of the essence. So, I presume you've done your thing . . .' she looked at Queenie and waved a hand in the air '. . . and have had time to process your thoughts, so spit it out.'

Although her lips tightened, much to Jazzy's relief, Queenie contented herself with raising an eyebrow before responding. 'Aye well, as you'll have seen from the report we sent yesterday, after scrutinising the bottle kiln scene, we discovered Mhairi appears to have adapted her MO regarding the eye mutilation, probably to toy with us. We believe that she's amalgamating her

289

use of religious symbols and icons as per her previous crime scenes with the eye mutilation. In summary, rather than physically removing the eyes as she did before, she is now leaving behind an eye-related religious "message". With Lewis Fletcher, the "eye for an eye, tooth for a tooth" scales were painted among the existing graffiti. Whilst in Dwayne Taggart's case, she incorporated the Eye of Horus on the signage on his van and with Paltrow, it was the fridge magnet depicting the Hindu God, Lord Shiva, who has a third eye on his forehead. We're still awaiting confirmation that the paint from the van and the graffiti match, but I'm confident it will.'

'You'll excuse me for saying, but it all seems a bit mumbo-jumboish to me. You seem to be stretching to find links where there are none and I'm not sure it's relevant. Didn't you get anything more concrete from Pollokshaws yesterday? Something we can actually use?'

Jazzy bit her tongue at Connolly's insensitivity. Didn't she understand how much processing that crime scene had taken from Queenie? Afzal had explained about Queenie's condition and how it worked – Jazzy had heard him – and here she was just dismissing her. It was intolerable. But Queenie had battled bigger demons than Niamh Connolly. 'My skill is that I can see at will and in minute detail every crime scene I've ever attended, and that means I am uniquely placed to see similarities between those scenes. I think with everything we already know about Mhairi Smith, my insights, although circumstantial until scientifically proven by forensics, are accurate.'

With an eye-roll Ivor would envy, Connolly folded her arms under her breasts and gave an elongated sigh. 'I don't have time for this. I've another meeting in ten minutes, so can you just finish up, Solanki?'

Although she wanted to slap the patronising look off Connolly's face, Jazzy bit her tongue and focused on the cheese plant. 'First, the long-range satellite phone in Paltrow's house indicates that

Mhairi has been communicating under the radar with him and possibly others. Did you obtain any data from that? It could be crucial to locating Mhairi.'

Connolly uncrossed her arms and leaned forward, resting her elbows on the table. 'DS Solanki, you seem to be under the illusion that we'll be sharing confidential and sensitive information with you. I'm afraid that's not happening. Your job is to offer insights that may help the task force locate your sister, then off you and DC McQueen trot back downstairs, you understand? Besides, it's nigh on impossible to track a satellite phone.'

Jazzy felt a tell-tale twitch by her temple as she decided how to respond. Using all her inner strength, she swallowed her anger and in a modulated tone responded, 'I appreciate that neither Queenie nor myself are part of the team, but we have in-depth knowledge of how Mhairi operates and, with all due respect, she sent this to me personally, not you or DCI Dick or anyone else on your team.' She held up the phone that Mhairi had sent the previous day. 'Delivering this and contacting me on it indicates that she is prepared to communicate with me. Doesn't it make sense to let us use our skills and knowledge of her? We're in a unique position to spot anomalies that may lead us to her door.'

Eyes flashing a warning, Connolly rapped her knuckles on the wooden desktop. 'Although we are erring on the side of caution regarding that phone and the *possibility* that your sister might let something pertinent slip . . .'

'Possibility? Possibility? The more she talks to JayZee, the more likely she is to slip up,' retorted Queenie.

Jazzy interrupted. 'DCS Afzal believes that Mhairi is in the vicinity and that sending the phone indicates an increased threat to my team. As such he has taken measures to protect us and our families. I think, considering my half-brother's upcoming funeral, which DI Shanks agrees could be the catalyst for my sister's return to the area, plus the three recent murders – two with links to me, and one a nurse who had access to Simon, it's pretty clear she's living locally and is a huge risk to the public. Have the house-to-house interviews in Paltrow's street thrown anything up? Surely someone saw something useful, or what about CCTV? If we can locate Mhairi on CCTV near Pollokshaws, we may be able to reverse-trace her movements.'

Connolly held her gaze for an uncomfortable few seconds. 'Operation Birchtree employs the best analysts, officers and scientists and has resources to expedite whatever information we need. Believe it or not, we have this under control without your interference. If you have nothing useful to add, I'd like to get on.'

Speechless, Jazzy couldn't refrain from tutting as she grabbed the burner phone and strode from Connolly's office, Queenie trailing behind. Once in the lift, Jazzy slammed her palm against the wall. 'Come on, Mhairi! Where the hell are you?'

Chapter 54

Jazzy

The entire team, including Elliot and Waqas Afzal, were waiting in the incident room for them. Queenie huffed and puffed her way to her desk, snagged a bag of prawn cocktail crisps from her drawer and, muttering to herself, stuffed them into her mouth as she glared at the others as if daring them to steal one. Jazzy followed more slowly and flung herself into the chair beside Queenie. Although she maintained a calm tone, her gut was clamped tight. 'That woman's a prize bitch, you know?'

Afzal cleared his throat. 'I take it she's still sidelining you?'

Jazzy shrugged. 'Yep, which is frustrating.'

'So, where do we go from here then, Jazzy?'

'Oh, I've got a few ideas. Couldn't sleep last night so I spent a while reviewing the files on Lewis Fletcher's murder and have identified a few gaps worth pursuing.'

'Gaps?' As he spoke, Afzal's phone rang. He glanced at the screen, scowled and declined the call, thrusting it back into his pocket.

'Yeah.' She shrugged. 'It's not much, but we should still check it out. The door-to-door team hasn't been able to speak with two individuals yet. In the flats overlooking the kiln. I want someone from our team to follow it up.'

Fenton jumped to his feet, grinning. 'If you want, Geordie and I can handle it. Plus . . .' he looked at his mate '. . . Geordie reckons we could try reverse-tracking on the local businesses and domestic properties' CCTV the person who met with Lewis Fletcher in the Black Swan car park. See if we can catch a vehicle or direction of travel, or perhaps a better angle, to confirm the ID.'

These were long shots, but anything was better than inactivity, so Jazzy nodded. What they needed right about now was more contact from Mhairi. Of course, the task force would have access to any communication, but they couldn't very well cut her out of the loop. She placed the phone on the desk in front of her and everyone's eyes locked on it as if willing it to ring again. So, when Afzal's phone's insistent ring filled the room, they all jumped. When he took it from his pocket and declined the call, they broke into scattered giggles, which broke the tension for a moment.

'There's one other thing, sir.' Jazzy looked at Afzal, hoping that he would agree to let her follow it up. If not, she would probably just do it anyway, but it would be better coming from him. 'I also spent a bit of time going over the files of Mhairi's acquaintances after we were separated and I found something had been added recently to the file on her adoptive mother.' Jazzy spent the next ten minutes explaining what she'd found out about Mhairi's step-great-grandad Stuart McCullough from Skye and her need to check if he had some property on the island that Mhairi could have used whilst she was in hiding.

Afzal shrugged. 'This is in the Birchtree files, I take it?'

At his words, Jazzy's heart sank. 'Yes. That's where I found it.'

'Well, in that case, I suspect it's been looked into already or else been discounted. I don't want us wasting time on that.'

Jazzy opened her mouth to reply, but Elliot spoke first. 'I know someone on Skye. It'll take me ten minutes to check it out, then we can tick that box and move on. Sometimes it's our distant relatives that we keep in touch with. Makes sense to be sure?'

Something in Elliot's words resonated with Jazzy but she couldn't put her finger on it. It was like a thought floating just out of her reach and one that she suspected was important. Experience told her not to push it. That it would come to her in its own good time. Meanwhile, Afzal held Elliot's gaze for a moment, then nodded. 'Okay, but then move on. Anything else, Jazzy?'

'Nothing more to report from me and Queenie.'

Queenie cleared her throat, her eyes glistening with mischief as she raised a finger in the air. 'Well, not quite all, is it JayZee?'

With a sinking feeling, Jazzy shook her head, her eyes lasering into Queenie as if she could shut her up by willpower alone. 'No, Queenie. Now would be a good time for you to shut up.'

'Ach, don't be bashful, Jazzy. I'm sure we're all on tenterhooks wanting to find out about your wee love interest. I mean, we've been saying for yonks now – haven't we, Haggis – that having a wee bit of romance would smooth off those rough corners of yours.'

Startled, Fenton blinked, then splayed his hands, his head going from side to side faster than windscreen wipers on fast. 'I've never ever spoken to anyone, far less Queenie, about your love life or lack of one. Honest, Jazzy.'

But he didn't need to tell Jazzy that. Nobody in their right minds would encourage Queenie on that subject. The woman was relentless all on her damn own. Feeling her cheeks burn, Jazzy wished the ground would open up and swallow her. 'Just shut it, Queenie. I mean it.'

But Queenie, insensitive as ever, blurted it out anyway, just as Afzal's phone erupted in his pocket again. 'She's got a date. Oor Jazzy's gone and got herself a date. That no right, hen? And not just wi' any auld loser. No, she's gone and snagged a date with DI Clive Shanks from Edinburgh. Now, isn't that good news?'

Thankfully, attention was momentarily diverted from Jazzy by the blaring of Afzal's phone yet again. His face blanched as he grabbed it from the desk and answered with an 'I'm at work. This better be important,' before storming from the office. Keen to avoid eye contact with the others after Queenie's bombshell, Jazzy's eyes followed her father through the semi-open door as he marched back and forth in short lines, his fingers raking through his hair. Guttural grunts drifted through the door, but Jazzy was aware of all eyes on her.

She wanted to wrap her hands round Queenie's neck and squeeze. Conscious of Fenton and Geordie making moves to exit the room, she sensed Elliot's searing sneer as he gave a humourless laugh. When he spoke, it was in a slow drawl. 'Well, well, well. Don't you think that's unprofessional, Solanki? Isn't he responsible for your brother's funeral arrangements? That smacks of conflict of interest to me.'

'Och away and raffle, Elliot. Shanks works in the Edinburgh division and when this funeral's over with, he'll be toot-tooting back there. Maybe you're just jealous.'

If Jazzy thought her cheeks could burn any hotter, she'd been mistaken. Queenie's words landed like an unexploded bomb between her and Elliot. Eyes on her, his lips tightened in an angry snarl. He spat out, 'As if. Good luck to him, I say.'

Jazzy's eyes scoured his face for even a remnant of the rapport they'd shared the previous evening, but all she saw was disinterested, cold dismissal. Unsettled and needing space, she turned and walked out of the room wondering what the hell had just happened back there. Once in the corridor, it took her a moment to notice DCS Afzal leaning against the wall, his expression blank and, without considering the consequences, Jazzy walked towards him. His eyes met hers and Jazzy almost shrank from the desolation within them. No matter her personal feelings for her biological father, the man before her looked broken, desolate and vulnerable.

Something was very badly wrong with her father and she strode towards him, resting her hand on his arm. 'What's wrong? Have you had bad news?'

Blinking, he gazed at her and then reached out, clutching her hand. 'That was my wife. My daughter's gone missing. She's been missing for almost twenty-four hours. Missed school, didn't go to her friend's as planned last night and . . .'

A chill ran up Jazzy's spine. *Shite.* They didn't need this now, not when they already had so much on their plate. Hopefully the girl had indulged in a teenage strop; after all teens did crap like this all the time.

He turned to Jazzy as if she alone could throw him a life buoy. 'She's gone, Jazzy. Aliyah's gone. She hasn't been home all night. What if . . .?'

He let the sentence trail, but Jazzy knew what he was really asking. *What if it was Mhairi?* What if Jazzy's half-sister had taken Afzal's daughter as an ultimate act of revenge? She slammed her palm against the wall, savouring the sting – deserving the sting. Then, after a deep breath, she spun back to her father. No longer the strong, suave, in-control man he normally was, he was now diminished. A shadow of his previous self. A man facing his worst fears, every demon alive in his perceived threat to his daughter. Something – jealousy perhaps, or hurt? – pierced Jazzy's heart.

With difficulty, she thrust away all the recriminations that floated like flotsam to the surface: *Where had he been when she needed him most? Why hadn't he loved her enough to want to save her? Why was she so unlovable?* Her stomach cramped in her efforts to douse the emotional flames that threatened to overtake her. She'd have time to analyse her own emotions later, but for now, a sixteen-year-old girl was missing. Her half-sister and that was hot on the heels of her other half-sister contacting her saying today would be a busy day. *Coincidence?* Jazzy didn't believe in them.

Along the corridor, the incident room door opened and Elliot strode out. 'Jazzy!'

Jazzy turned to Afzal and gripped his arm tighter. 'Come on, I'll take you away from here.' Ignoring Elliot, she manoeuvred her father down the corridor, her gaze focused on the elevator light indicating its imminent arrival.

'DS Solanki! Wait!' Elliot shouted down the corridor although she could hear that he was following them.

Jazzy hesitated, then heard Queenie's familiar feet thudding along the corridor too. She ground to a halt and turned. Queenie was sending daggers in Elliot's direction, but oblivious, Elliot was looking straight at her, frowning, his face ashen. 'Let's discuss what happened later, Jazzy. Now's not the right time.'

When he paused, Queenie jumped in. 'Damn bloody right, it's not the right time.'

She grabbed Jazzy's arm and dragged her back along the corridor, DCS Afzal, still unresisting, in tow. 'We're needed and, as for him . . .' She yanked her thumb in Elliot's direction, 'Well, Elliot Balloch will take a nosedive off the top of the Pentland Hills before he'll speak to you like that again.'

'Queenie, can't this wait? I need to speak with the super in private.'

Elliot took over. 'No, it can't.' He lowered his voice, but his words still sucked all the oxygen from the air. 'We've got a murdered teenager over in Bathgate.'

Afzal went rigid, colour draining from his face as he stumbled against the wall. Queenie's eyes shifted between Jazzy and Afzal, then back. 'What's up with him?'

Tight-faced, Jazzy blinked. 'His daughter's gone missing.'

Chapter 55

Jazzy

The overwhelming stench of stale beer and urine clung perniciously to the air as Jazzy and Queenie signed into the scene and suited up down the street from the Tartan Sporran. A tent shielded the body from the persistent smirr of rain and curious gazes from upstairs windows. Bloody ghouls!

Franny, the crime scene manager, her eyes unusually sombre, raised a hand in greeting. 'You can go in, Jazzy.'

Jazzy hesitated and counted to five before swallowing hard. Unable to speak during the ride, Queenie compensated with a volley of incessant garbled observations. If she'd had the energy, Jazzy might have yelled at her to shut up. But there were too many thoughts whirling in her own head for her to focus on anything other than the fact that, because of her, Afzal had probably lost his favourite daughter. He'd been broken. A shell of the vibrant, strong, decisive man she'd butted heads with over the past few years and seeing him like that made Jazzy realise how much, despite her determination not to, she actually cared about him.

The only thing she could offer him now was to find Ali's

killer – her sister? Well, all things considered, it seemed likely, but she couldn't be distracted until they had seen the crime scene.

'You okay, hen? You sure you should be here? I mean, we could get the driver to take you back . . .'

'Get a grip, Queenie. You think Afzal and his obnoxious wife want me there? She screamed that it was my fault when she arrived.'

'Aye, but that was seconds before she launched at the super and started battering lumps out of him. She's all over the place. Doesn't know what side's up.'

'I can do more good here.' She looked at Queenie, who, with her hood cinched tight round her bulbous face, looked ready to burst into tears. 'And so can you. You need to bring your A-game to this, Queenie.'

'Aye, you're no' wrong there, hen, and you can rely on me.'

They stepped over the treads and entered the tent. With the too bright forensic lights and the white fabric, it seemed huge and glaringly sterile. Despite the stink, Jazzy inhaled through her mouth and looked at the girl sprawled on her back with her knickers round her ankles and a pool of blood around her head from where her throat had been slit. Jazzy spun round, shoving Queenie aside as she barged back from the tent. Heaving in huge gulps of fetid air, she bent over, resting her hands on her knees as she tried to still her hammering heart.

Franny and Queenie approached, and the CSI offered her a bottle of icy cold water, but Jazzy, her chest filled to bursting, brushed it away. She looked up at Queenie. 'That's not Aliyah Afzal. That's not the super's daughter.'

Queenie put her hand on Jazzy's arm and squeezed. 'It's okay to be relieved, Jazzy. It's normal. I mean, Afzal's daughter is your half-sister, after all.'

'Aye, but it feels crap to be relieved that another young girl is lying on her back, dead in an alley with her throat slit. It's even sicker that I'm even more relieved that this looks unlikely to be anything to do with the Bitch.' She rolled her head to ease the crick in her neck and focused. 'We'll progress this as a murder inquiry. You get the usual protocols up and running, Queenie. I'll phone Afzal with the . . .' She stumbled over the word good and ended on 'news' instead.

Chapter 56

Ali

When I wake up, I'm warm. Too warm and my throat's scratchy and sore. I'm lying in the foetal position, my head bowed down to my chest as if to make myself as small as possible. But I know with a sickening certainty that it'll make no difference. I'm not hidden by an invisibility cloak. I've not shrunk to minuscule proportions. I'm a lump in the middle of this single bed in this darkened room. The same darkened room I'm vaguely aware of being thrown into ages ago. Was it only last night? As I realise I have no idea where I am or who brought me here, my heart speeds up. I yank at the duvet, thrusting it away from me, trying to catch my breath, but there's no air in the room. I scratch at my throat, as if I can gouge a hole for air to enter my lungs and still my heart thuds in double time. Black and white specks appear before my eyes and dizziness makes me squeeze them together. I begin to count to ten. Slow and easy, like that YouTube video showed, and as my heartbeat normalises and the dots fade, I open my eyes and despite my fuzzy brain I try to concentrate.

What the hell happened last night? I try to replay the events, but I can only get so far. It's like everything that happened is hidden behind cotton wool and only bits of it drift out to me at intervals and none of it seems to be in order. First, there's me laughing with Jan in her flat. Her bedroom's small, tiny in fact, with empty cans and sweet wrappers all over and piles upon piles of clothes tossed all over the bed and the floor. An overwhelming smell of alcohol overlaid with a too sweet fruity perfume cloyed in my throat. Although I'm laughing, I'm aware of an underlying anxiety pulling across my chest. What the hell am I doing with her? Jan Carmichael? I don't even like her.

Then the image shifts and I'm in a seedy pub with a vodka and Coke on a sticky table in front of me and Jan's got her tongue down some ginger bloke's throat and I think I want to go. Then I'm in the street, clattering about in a pair of heels I can't walk straight in and feeling drowsy and nauseous. No matter how hard I try, I can't remember what happens next. There're vague snappy sensations of being grabbed. Maybe a low laugh, maybe a car ride, but it's all half-formed snippets. Like a corrupted video, all jolty, with bits missing. My throat hurts and my head's pounding and I can't get rid of the metallic taste in my mouth. Is this a hangover?

I force myself to sit up, but as I stretch, every muscle in my body protests. Have I been in a car accident? No, that's not right. Why am I here and not at home or in the hospital? I glance round, ignoring the throb behind my eyes and try to make sense of things. I recognise nothing about my surroundings. And I can't see my phone anywhere. From the weirdly old lady floral wallpaper to the swirly burgundy and gold carpet that makes me feel dizzy. Or from the pine double wardrobe with its matching bedside table to the bedside lamp with its yellowy haze. Or the partially closed curtains, which reveal a shuttered window, to the sickly floral scent lurking on the bedding that hits my nostrils every time I move.

I'm certain I've never been here before, which makes my

circumstances stranger and even more worrying. A cough racks my body and I grimace at the pain in my throat, but there's a couple of bottles of water on the dressing table and I snatch one up. The seal's intact, so what the hell? I need to drink.

The water feels good as it trickles down my throat and after I've replaced the cap, I take a closer look at the room. Over in one corner there's a screen covered in multi-coloured peacocks and parrots and near the door are a couple of Morrisons recyclable paper bags. I edge myself over till my bare feet dangle from the bed, then I slip onto the garish fluffy rug that lies in front of the bed. My shoes – or rather Jan's high heels – lie to the side as if I kicked them off before lying down. Or maybe someone took them off. I wander over, first to the screen, and poke my head behind it. Yeuch! A commode with a roll of loo paper and a packet of wet wipes taunts me, and I shudder at the thought that I might have to use it.

With that fear plaguing me, I wander, on wobbly legs, over to the door yet, before I even reach out my hand to push the handle down, I know what I'll find. I've feared from the moment I opened my eyes that I'm trapped here. And I'm right. The door's locked. I press my ear to the wooden door. Is that someone moving about? Someone talking? I'm not sure. Maybe it's a radio or maybe I'm just losing it. I mean, who could blame me? I'm trapped in a room with shuttered windows, a commode, and a bed. My only supplies are some bog roll, a few water bottles and when I pick up the bag beside the door I find a bag of sandwiches, crisps and cereal bars.

My heart thunders against my chest and I wonder if it's going to explode. If it does, what would I do? Would I die here in this room with the commode and floral bed sheets? Would anyone ever find me?

Tears trickle down my cheeks and I flash back to Jan and my last unkind thoughts about her. That she'd end up in a dark alley, with her throat slit. Shite, I'll be the one who ends up dead. Now that image is in my head, I can't shake it. Why the hell didn't I just stay with her? Or phone my da'? He'd have come for me. Yes, he'd have been pissed off, but he'd have come and instead of being locked in this room, not knowing what's going to happen next, I'd be tucked up in bed at home with my mum taking my temperature and clucking about after me. I drag myself back to the bed and plonk myself down on the mattress. What an idiot I am. What a bloody idiot. I bang the palms of my hands on my forehead and try to yell, but all I can manage is a forlorn squeak. I can't even scream properly. With my eyes scrunched shut, I try to dredge up a memory of who brought me here, but still it's only shadow images and whispered unintelligible words that seep through.

All of a sudden, a wave of exhaustion floods me and I don't care where I am anymore. All I want to do is curl up and die. Curl up and sleep till it's all over. Despite my discomfort and my dislike of the scented sheets, I swing my legs round, shuffle under the duvet and drag it right up to my chin before tugging a second pillow closer and easing it under my throbbing head. A shiver racks my body and I tuck the cover even more tightly around me till I'm completely cocooned in its soft floral warmth. I shouldn't be shivering like this. It's summer, but all my aches and pains, my angry throat and my thumping head tell me that as well as being lost and alone, I am ill too. The thought that upsets me, more than my memory lapses, is that my mum's not there to look after me.

If I shut my eyes, I could almost imagine her warm hand smoothing my hair back from my face as she applies a cold compress to soothe my fever, but that's a futile wish and I can't waste my time thinking such stupid thoughts. I need to focus, because two persistent thoughts keep spinning in my head. The first is that I can't stay here because it might not be safe and the second is that I wish to hell I'd watched *Les Mis* instead of *Misery* with my dad at the weekend.

As the warm duvet chases away the chills, my head clears a little. I've no idea how long I've been here. No idea if it's days or hours. No idea if I'm in Whitburn or Bathgate or even still in Scotland and even less idea of why I'm here, so I'll just have to wait and see what happens. Logic tells me that whoever has locked me up here doesn't intend to hurt me right now. I mean, why would they provide bathroom facilities and food if their intention was to make me suffer? That reassures me a little and, as my eyes begin to flicker shut, a glint of something high on the wall in the opposite corner attracts my attention. A red light flashes. What the hell is it? A smoke alarm? Or is someone watching me?

Chapter 57

Jazzy

'In the name of the wee man, would you credit it, Jazzy? Look who's here, making the place look untidy.' Queenie peered round the bar, which was empty except for Shuggie Fratelli and the bartender.

Jazzy grinned at the lad. It hadn't been that long since he'd been caught up in another of their investigations into turf wars between organised criminal gangs in Glasgow and Edinburgh. In some ways she pitied him. He was trying so desperately to stay on the right tracks and had been taken advantage of by an old 'mate' of his dad's. He wasn't a clipe, but she hoped that their shared history might loosen his lips. If not, she was sure Queenie's powers of persuasion would do the trick.

Rubbing her hands together in fake glee, Queenie turned around and locked the door. 'No' sure, wi' a crime just round the back, that yous should be open.'

Shuggie Fratelli froze with his pint half raised to his mouth and slowly turned. His face paled when he recognised Jazzy and Queenie standing in the entrance to the Tartan Sporran. As he lowered his glass onto the beer mat, it slopped all over the bar's surface, earning him a tut from the bartender.

'Aw, no. No' you two again.'

'Aw, Shuggie, Shuggie, Shuggie, pray tell, were you in here last night?' Queenie's smile was anything but reassuring.

He lifted his chin in what would have been a hardman glare, if his eyes didn't flit to the door as if he was thinking of making a run for it. 'Aye, but I didn't do anything. Honest.'

Jazzy indicated a table nearby. 'So, in that case, you'll not mind spending a wee while telling us all about what happened in here last night.'

Left with no option, Shuggie sidled over and plonked himself down in one seat whilst Jazzy and Queenie sat on either side of him. 'Hey you, hen? You working last night, were you?'

The lassie with the red hair nodded and threw the tea towel she was using to dry a glass on the bar and, with a resigned sigh, joined them taking the fourth seat. 'Aye, I was working last night. Not very busy though, it being a week night an' all.'

'So, it'll be easy to remember who was in then, eh?' Queenie leaned her elbows on the table and grimaced as her jacket stuck to the wood. 'Christ, do you no believe in cleaning the tables, hen? A wee wipe-down with an anti-bac widnae go amiss, a scoosh of Fairy and a bit of elbow grease, hell, even just a dicht with an auld cloot.'

The girl shrugged and tutted. 'My name's Jeanie, no' hen, and that's not my job. Cleaner's supposed to do that, but she never turned in this morning. Lazy cow.'

Jazzy raised an eyebrow and Queenie leaned back letting her take over. 'This cleaner of yours, what does she look like, Jeanie?'

Jeanie studied Jazzy for a moment, her intelligent eyes appraising the woman. Then with a sigh, she said, 'You're no' telling me that wee madam's gone an' got herself killed, are you?'

'You're right Jeanie, we're *not* telling you that. All we're doing is asking for her name and what she looks like. And how old she is.'

Shuggie, huffing on the other side of the table, grunted. 'Her name's Jan Carmichael, and she's a wee hoor. She's young. Don't know why your dad gie's her the time of day, never mind a job.' He turned to Jeanie. 'She was rat-arsed last night, so she's probably shacked up wi' Matty somewhere sleeping it off.'

Jazzy turned to Shuggie and his shoulders retreated into his neck as he tried to avoid meeting her gaze. 'So, this Jan? The one who's not turned up for her cleaning job, was she in here last night? And, I'm assuming the Matty you're referring to is your partner in crime from that carry-on in Tarbrax with the gangs and drugs and all that?'

Red-faced, Shuggie shuffled on his seat. 'Matty's no friend of mine. He's a dosser and a druggie and I have nothing to do wi' him if I can help it. I haven't set a foot wrong since the last time I saw you guys. And you know, I was forced into that crime.' He sniffed, slouching further onto the chair. 'But, ye, Jan's the cleaner and she was in here last night. So was Matty, but again, he's no' my mate. He's an arse. But he was wi' Jan and the other lassie last night, too.'

Queenie rubbed her hands together. 'Now we're getting somewhere. So, what does this Jan look like, eh?'

Shuggie scrunched up his nose and Jeanie tutted. 'For God's sake, Shuggie, you should know what she looks like. She was all over you last night. Tits in your face and arms round your neck, dirty wee skank.' She folded her arms and glared at Shuggie.

'Aw, is that no sweet? Yous two are an item.' Queenie's eyes moved between the two teenagers. 'Is this your first wee tiff?'

'Queenie.' Jazzy's voice held a note of warning as she turned back to Jeanie. 'Description. Now.'

'All right, all right, no need to get tetchy. She's about five-foot-three, dark hair, one of those bottle tans, big tits, slutty dresser.'

'What was she wearing last night?'

'Mini skirt up to her oxters, a halter top doon to her belly button and too much knock-off perfume.'

Shuggie, keen to get on their good side, piped up, 'Aye, she reckons she's eighteen but we all know she's got fake ID and she's only sixteen . . .'

'Shuggeee, shut the fuck up. You want to get my dad in bother for serving under-agers?'

'Right now, we're not bothered about that, but just so you know, we *will* be telling the local bobbies to drop in here from now on to check IDs. For now, though, have you got her on social media?'

Jeanie huffed and, using her thumbs, brought Instagram up on her phone and then flicked through it before turning her phone so the two detectives could see. 'That's her profile.'

Jazzy took the phone and flicked through the images, which confirmed what they'd already suspected. Jan Carmichael was their victim. She had a lot of friends and was on social media all the time. Some of her posts verged on bullying and definitely targeted the 'not cool' kids. Jazzy checked her friends and saw she was friends with Ali Afzal. She went onto Ali's Insta profile and turned the screen back to Jeanie. 'This the girl she was with last night?'

'Aye, that's right. Not the usual sort of lassie Jan hangs out with. A bit stuck-up if you ask me. Looked round her like this joint was shite and then stormed off early, about half nineish, after giving Jan a mouthful.' Jeanie's face broke into a huge grin. 'That was well worth seeing, wasn't it, Shuggie?'

Shuggie grinned and nodded. 'It was a beaut of a catfight! That lassie right put Jan in her place. What was it she said to her, Jeanie?' He clicked his fingers, his grin widening. 'That's it. Something about how Jan would end up deid in a dark alley with her throat slit. It was brill. Then, she just stalked off.'

For a moment there was silence, then the grin faded from Shuggie's face as he looked at the two officers. 'Fuck's sake. You're not saying that's what happened to Jan, are you? That the wee posh bitch killed her, after all.'

Jazzy, heart thumping, glared at the boy until he stepped back. She wasn't for one minute suggesting that 'the posh bitch' had killed Jan, but she was inclined to believe that the way Jan had been posed in the alley was a deliberate ploy. Just the sort of head-fuck Mhairi would come up with. 'That's right, Shuggie. We most definitely are *not* saying that.' Still, as she uttered the words, a heavy weight settled in her chest and her earlier relief that the murdered girl was nothing to do with Mhairi dissipated. She didn't know Ali Afzal and now she regretted not making the effort. Although she couldn't see a clear motive for the girl to kill Jan Carmichael, stranger things had happened. Either way the burning question was where the hell had she disappeared to? In honesty though, Jan's murder and Ali's disappearance seemed more likely to be connected to Mhairi. So, the question still lingered. Had Mhairi killed Jan and taken Ali and if so, where were they? God how she wished that damn phone would ring. If Mhairi contacted her again, Jazzy could hopefully find something out.

Jazzy turned back to the two at the bar. 'So, you've never seen Jan with this girl before?'

'Nah, never. Jan's usual mates are slappers, just like her.'

'Anyone else in the bar last night?'

'Nope, just them four . . .'

'Ah, Jeanie, you're wrong. Mind that fella over in that corner? He left right after that lassie left.'

Jazzy looked over at the table in question, a glimmer of hope flickering in her chest. 'You didn't recognise this bloke?'

Both kids shook their heads.

'Describe him.'

Shuggie scrunched up his lips. 'He was weird. You know, like . . . weird.'

'Aye, son, that'll no' cut it. We're after something a wee bit more specific.' Queenie got right in his face, making Shuggie lean back.

Jeanie tutted and rolled her eyes at her boyfriend. 'He was tall and bald and fat, but to be honest, he didn't say or do much. Only bought one drink.' She gestured to the table where a half-drunk pint still sat. 'That's his glass. Then, like Shuggie says, he followed that lassie out and I've not seen him since.'

'And that table's not been cleaned or anything?'

'No, I told ye that was Jan's job.'

Gut churning, Jazzy stared at the glass. Too many coincidences, too much happening at once. It had to be Mhairi. That might even have been her in disguise. She turned to Queenie. 'Call in the CSIs. I want this pub processed, particularly that table and that glass. Jeanie, do you have a camera in the bar?'

'Aye right, that'd go down well with the punters.'

That was a bummer, but there was still the possibility of external cameras. Jazzy stood up, 'And get a couple of uniforms on door-to-doors here too. See if any of the properties have CCTV. I want to track where Ali went after she left here, and I want to see if this guy followed her.'

She paused. 'And send someone to drag Matty from his pit. We need to find out what happened after he and Jan left here.'

Chapter 58

Ali

I dozed off for a bit and woke up feeling better. My head's not so fuzzy and my throat, although still sore, is easing. I wonder who could have done this to me. Jan? Could she be responsible? Is this part of a plan to humiliate me? I don't think so. Jan has neither the patience nor the brains to work out something so complex. My only consolation is that my parents will surely be searching for me now. My father will have all his officers searching for me. All I have to do is hang on until they find me.

But what if they're too late? What if whoever has me locked up here decides to kill me before I'm found? That thought makes my skin itch and before I know it, I'm dragging my nails up and down my arms, raking into the skin until I draw blood. As always, the release calms me and I start to consider my options. I could just lie here and let whoever has done this kill me or I can be proactive. So, I have to come up with a plan. That's the only way forward.

But first things first. If that sneaky bastard's trying to ogle a cop of my privates when I use the loo, they can think again. I pull the case off the pillow and pull the chair out so it's just a bit away from the wall. Then, balancing on it, I throw the case, aiming for that red light. I want to cover it. It's hard to get the right angle, but I persevere. The very thought of some sicko watching me – spying on me – freaks me out. I don't know how many turns it takes, but finally the case hooks over the camera and although the red light still shines through, no one could possibly have a clear image of me.

Even that bit of activity has exhausted me, so I creep back into bed and pull the duvet under my chin. I try not to think of my friends or my mum and dad and that's when the tears start. As they pour from my eyes, I realise I don't want to be here. Not anymore. I've had enough. I'm done.

I roll onto my side and something digs into me. The underwire of my bra. I'm not used to sleeping in my bra, but I don't want to take it off. The more layers between my body and Mr Pervert the better, so I adjust it till it stops digging into my skin. That's when the thought takes hold. Dad's always banging on about crime scenes and the importance of forensics. Well, if that bastard moves me before they find me, the least I can do is leave something behind. My DNA. A message so they know I've been here. I inspect the room, trying to decide where to leave it, though. It has to be where it won't be seen at a casual glance. I have no idea when the creep who left me here will come back, but they can't see it. It's got to be hidden.

The easiest place would be on the wall, so maybe I can crawl under the bed and leave a message there. As I jump from the bed, the headboard crashes against the wall. I freeze and consider it. If I just pull the bed out, I can write something on the wall.

I take my bra off and use my teeth to make the hole where the wire is escaping bigger. And when it's big enough, I ease the curved metal through. I don't have a pen, but I'm well used to making myself bleed and that'll have to do, so I pull up my skirt and press the wire against my skin. The pressure feels so good and as I push the wire deeper; I feel my heart rate slow. And when the blood begins to seep out onto my skin, I'm at peace.

Chapter 59

Jazzy

Jazzy watched as Afzal, shirt untucked and hair awry, paced the floor of the incident room, barking out orders and generally getting in their way. Elliot had tried to get him to leave, saying he was too close to the investigation and should trust them to do everything they could. He'd lasered Elliot with dark, flashing eyes. 'That what you'd do is it? If it was your daughter, is that what you'd do?'

He hadn't been so hot on staying around when she had needed him, had he? Ignoring the brief pang of hurt that contracted her heart, Jazzy stepped in, offered him a bottle of water and guided him to a chair. 'You're setting everyone on edge. Just sit down and we'll go through every investigative strand we're following, okay?'

Afzal ran his fingers through his hair but complied, and Jazzy faced her team and the uniformed officers they'd drafted in. Elliot had suggested she lead the briefing, as she and Queenie had been at the Jan Carmichael crime scene. 'Right, we're working on the assumption that Ali's abductor returned later on and disposed of Jan Carmichael. B team are now pursuing that aspect of the investigation and are liaising closely with Fenton and Geordie, so both teams are fully cognisant of the others' findings.'

She nodded towards the officers from B team, who were huddled at the back. 'Ali's phone was found switched off and damaged in the alley where Jan Carmichael's body was discovered. The fact that the two girls were together last night and eyewitnesses saw a man leave the Tartan Sporran shortly after Ali left has escalated Ali's continued disappearance to a possible abduction. Ali's friend Isla confirmed that the "night out" with Jan Carmichael was planned as an act of rebellion against her parents. Further, Matty, who was with both girls at the Tartan Sporran last night, says that Jan told him she'd been paid to bring Ali to the pub. He says that payment was left in the female toilets at the Tartan Sporran and forensics are checking that out.' She spared a glance at Afzal and saw that although his head was bowed and his right leg juddered, he'd drunk most of the water and, for now at least, seemed content to absorb what information they had.

'Jan Carmichael earned some pocket money by cleaning the pub before school, but clearly that didn't happen today, which plays in our favour. Forensics are also processing the area around where the unidentified male sat last night. Door-to-door inquiries are ongoing, but CCTV from the bike shop opposite the pub picked up both Ali and her suspected assailant heading towards the taxi rank. A taxi driver remembers picking up a fare and says the girl was rat-arsed. According to Matty, Jan drugged her drink just before she left the pub, which would account for her becoming disorientated shortly afterwards. It would allow the assailant to manipulate her. The taxi dropped them off at an address in Whitburn.' She turned to Sergeant Hobson. 'Would you like to run us through that?'

Hobson stood up and cleared his throat. 'The homeowners of the house check out, as do the neighbours. They allowed us entry as did the neighbours and there's no sign of Ali there. Their home security cameras, however, did show the taxi parking up and a male figure helping Ali from the back. After the taxi left, the male hefted Ali further down the street.' He pressed a button, and the recording showed Ali and an unidentified person walking away from the house until they were out of shot. 'Uniforms are continuing to enquire about home security cameras or dash cam footage that might show what happened next.'

Afzal, eyes glued to the image of his daughter on the screen, nodded. 'Keep going with the footage, but my bet is he had another car waiting further along the road. He wouldn't want to be hefting her along like that for any distance. Get the cameras for the exit points at either end of that road and see if you can pick up their trail.' He clapped his hands together, laser-focused now. 'What else?'

Elliot stepped forward. 'We'd like to access both you and Humaira's digital footprint. We need to know if there's a personal threat involved or perhaps a work-related one.'

Humaira Afzal, who sat bundled in an oversized coat at the back of the room, shook her head, her eyes red and swollen. 'No way. I'm not letting you have access to my electronics. Some of that is sensitive work-related information.'

Afzal's words were like pistol shots. 'Don't be so fucking stupid, Humaira. Just give them your laptop and phone. This is Ali we're talking about.' He pointed towards Fenton. 'He's the only one who will have eyes on it unless he comes up with something that will give us a clue.'

Humaira opened her mouth, looking set to argue, then, as if the enormity of the situation was too much to bear, she nodded and, with tears streaming down her face, thrust her phone and laptop onto the nearest desk.

As Fenton retrieved the electronics, Jazzy said, 'So, the information we have is that Ali was targeted by her abductor. So far we have nothing concrete to indicate why?'

Humaira jumped up. 'That's not fucking true, is it? It's because of you and that fucking lunatic sister of yours. Ever since you

317

came back into his life . . .' she raised her chin in Afzal's direction '. . . you've brought nothing but grief. Why the fuck he has anything to do with you is beyond me. God, he doesn't even publicly acknowledge you as his daughter. Your mum was a sicko and so is your sister. Chances are you are too.'

Jazzy froze, her heart hammering as the surrounding officers took a collective breath. Although Queenie and Elliot knew about her relationship with Afzal, Jazzy hadn't told the others. Now, here it was out in the open and witnessed by constables she barely knew, some of whom would delight in sharing that with the entire station.

Afzal stood and glared at his wife. 'You are out of order there. I think you should leave. I'll get an officer to take you home and stay with you, but you're not staying here.'

She looked ready to object but instead, she glared at Jazzy as she strode out, leaving behind the disclosure of Jazzy's paternity, like a huge elephant in the middle of the room.

Chapter 60

Jazzy

Jazzy studied all the information on the incident board regarding Aliyah Afzal's abduction. *Are we missing something?* The phrase 'no such thing as coincidence' kept intruding and the continued weight of the silent phone in her pocket, taunting her, made her uneasy. Everything about Ali's abduction – the timing, the planning behind it, her father's relationship to Jazzy – all of it, particularly right now with Mhairi in the wind, had Jazzy on edge, but she'd learned that the only way forward was to follow the evidence and that's what they were doing. Still time was passing and they hadn't progressed much.

'Eh, Jazzy.' Geordie and Fenton approached. Their smiles made her heart rate increase and without thinking her fingers fluttered into her pocket to touch the glass Ganesh she kept there. *Please let them have something for me!*

'You got something, Geordie?'

'Well, not really related to this, but thought you'd like an update on our wee trip to Portobello earlier.'

Christ, in all the day's drama, Jazzy had forgotten all about that. They'd been retracing the early steps of the Fletcher investigation and hoping to catch up with some of the residents of the neighbouring flats who had slipped through the earlier door-to-door net. 'God yes. My mind's all over the place. What did you find?'

Fenton cleared his throat and took over. 'Well, we were lucky, really. One flat where uniforms hadn't got an answer earlier was lying open when we arrived because the landlord was about to clean it. The resident, an old bald bloke called Simon McCullough had apparently upped and left abruptly early this morning, bunging the landlord 500 quid and asking him to do a deep clean for his inconvenience.'

'Simon?' Hearing her brother's name was unsettling, and although it was yet another coincidence to rack up in this case, it was a common name. But then her frown deepened. *McCullough?* That was the name of Mhairi's great-grandad.

'Aye, we checked it out and got nowhere. Seems our Simon McCullough is a ghost. His references were false too, so suspicious, much?'

Mind still spinning, Jazzy tried to focus as Geordie took up the tale. 'Well, that made us curious, so we flashed our warrant cards and asked if he'd delay the clean-up till we'd had a poke around. And then we trawled the neighbours. Turns out this Simon McCullough didn't appear to live alone because some neighbours say they spotted a short fat woman entering and leaving the premises whilst others say they saw a tall, slender one going in and out. Nobody seems to have interacted with any of them. He's only held the lease for about three months.'

She held up her hand and turned to Elliot. 'Don't suppose you got the chance to check out that property belonging to Stuart McCullough on Skye did you?'

Elliot blinked at her then shook his head. 'No but something tells me I should now. Tell me.'

As succinctly as they could they brought Elliot up to speed

and, he marched off, waving his phone in the air and casting an 'I'm on it' look over his shoulder.

As Jazzy turned back to Geordie and Fenton, she could tell by the way they practically bounced on their feet that they'd got something even juicier, and she felt excitement bubble in her own chest. Could this be a breakthrough in locating her sister? 'Come on, spit out the rest, lads.'

'Bottom line is, we found a few interesting things in the flat itself. Enough for us to request Operation Birchtree to sanction bringing the CSIs in.'

Fenton handed over an evidence bag containing loose white pills. 'These are aripiprazole, which is an anti-psychotic medication. These pills are for 30mg, which is the maximum recommended dose. We found them scattered on the floor under a coffee table. Yet to find the packaging so no idea who they were prescribed to.'

That was frustrating, yet a very interesting find. However, Fenton wasn't finished yet.

'The place stank of urine and was mucky. A duvet on the couch was dry but smelled of wee, the bed was crumpled and although the cupboards were in the main empty, there were a few interesting finds scattered about. It seems that our man McCullough left in haste.'

'Yeah, but that's no' the best part, is it, Fent? Our guy left a chair by the window, which offered him a bird's-eye view of, guess what?'

'The bottle kilns?'

'You got it in one. All around it were crumbs and a couple of glass stains on the windowsill, as if he was treating it like a day out at the cinema.'

By now Geordie, usually calmer than his mate, was red-faced with excitement as he thrust another evidence bag at Jazzy. 'You'll never guess what this is?'

Jazzy prodded the contents of the bag, understanding dawning on her. 'A bald cap?'

'Yep, whoever Simon McCullough is, he appears to be going to extreme lengths to disguise himself or . . .'

'Herself?' Jazzy, brain working nineteen to the dozen, stood up. 'We need to access the cameras around the area again. This time looking for this Simon guy. Bring in the landlord and the neighbours who saw someone entering or leaving the property. See if they can identify whatever vehicle this guy has been using.'

'Done, done and done.' Geordie grinned. 'We just went ahead with it, but we wanted to update you because it's all been sent upstairs to Operation Birchtree now. But the analysis of that tweed cap Benjy found has come back. They found strands of hair on the hat, but it was synthetic wig hair, which indicates . . .'

'That whoever wore it might have been in disguise.' That didn't surprise Jazzy. She tapped her finger on her lip. 'DNA on the hat or the branch.'

'Blood traces on both. Not a lot – looks like the branch nicked the cap owner's skin and drew blood. They then appear to have wiped it off with the cap. Bit careless to have dropped it if you ask me, but they have sent it off for DNA analysis. Just a waiting game now.'

Jazzy nodded. This was to be expected. DNA rarely came back quickly even when expedited. Still, maybe Connolly would have more clout and work a miracle. The carelessness with the cap worried her. Mhairi wasn't careless, not by a long chalk, but then she was living on the edge and might be unravelling. But that was Operation Birchtree's problem. They had their hands filled with finding Ali, but it was reassuring that progress was being made regarding her sister, too.

'Good work, guys. Keep me updated if you hear anything.' She turned back to the board, then back to Fenton. 'Have you had a chance to go through the Afzals' electronics yet, Fent?'

Fenton's eyes slid to a point above Jazzy's shoulder. He swallowed, then shook his head. 'Nothing related to the case.'

Under Jazzy's scrutiny, his face reddened. What the hell has

Fenton found on those appliances? But before she could pursue that line of questioning, Elliot was back, Queenie running behind panting. 'Wait up. Ah've only got wee short legs, you know?'

Elliot ground to a halt in front of Jazzy. 'Highland and Islands are sending a team of CSIs over to Skye. Seems that McCullough left an old cottage, which has slowly been falling into disrepair. My mate says that gossip has it that a strange woman was sighted using it a few months ago.'

Spine tingling, Jazzy leapt to her feet. This was it. This was how it felt when things began to stack up. It was still a quagmire, but they were getting there – moving in the right direction. Now if she could only work out what the hell Mhairi's message meant.

Chapter 61

Mhairi

When I wake up, it's light outside and the absence of seagulls squawking disorientates me for a moment. Then I remember I'm not in Porty anymore, and I force myself to get up because I've got work to do. I study my reflection and think the old man's disguise will do for my plans today. Okay, it's not pristine, but I've learned that people don't tend to pay much attention to old fogies.

I take one of my other pills. The ones that electrify me and, as they kick in, I move quickly, setting up the laptop and linking it to the Wi-Fi. I need to check on the girl, but I'm not going in blind, especially as she found one of my cameras. Did she really think I'd have only one? No point in taking chances at this stage. The girl proved last night that she could be flighty – like her sister, I suppose. She's lying bundled up under the covers, not moving and for a moment I wonder if she's dead and my hands clench into fists. I bloody hope not, because that's not in my plan. She better not be dead. I was careful with the dosage I gave. Then she turns over in her sleep, her eyes closed, her face tear-stained, and

I take my chance. Jumping to my feet, I grab another Morrisons bag filled with food and hurry down the hallway to her room. She doesn't stir as I open the door and drop the bag just inside. She'll find it soon enough, no doubt.

Now, what's next? I feel the rage tighten my chest again. I'm furious that Jazzy left her house. I'd got quite used to my nocturnal visits there. I'm so angry that she's cosied up with her entire team at Queenie's, although to be fair, I suppose it was my sending her the phone that pre-empted that. Carting that phone around with her all the time, waiting for it to ring, must be like torture to her. That's why, although I've been tempted so many times and, much as I'd love to hear her voice again, I've resisted. Observation and idle gossip with a police officer who should know better has told me that all the Jazz Queens' relatives have been relocated and that makes it easier for me, because I've only got an empty house to contend with when I go in.

My hand's shaking again, and so are my legs, and I can't remember if I've taken my main meds or not. The shaking would suggest not, so I pick up the packet – stolen from a junkie in Glasgow – and pop a pill into my palm. Should I take two? Maybe that'll stop the side effects I'm feeling. I glance up at Simon, who's lying sprawled in a chair beside me, vomit trickling down his chin. 'What do you think, Si? One or two?'

I lean over, grab a tissue, as if I am going to wipe the trickle of vomit away. That used to be Jazzy's job. Wiping sick up, cleaning our arses . . .

'There, there, you'll be okay, Mhairi.' Her cool hand soothed my brow as I heaved, yet again, into the bucket she'd placed under my chin.

'I told you not to eat all of that tablet, Mhairi, didn't I? Now sip this water and curl up here beside me and we'll watch the rest of Lion King.'

'But I knew it wasn't the tablet that had made me sick. It was because I forgot to wash my hands after playing with that squirrel

325

Simon killed. I look at him and he reaches over and squeezes my hand. My brother, Si. My twin. He didn't forget our blood promise.'

I've no idea how long I zoned out for, but when I come to, Simon's gone – of course he was never there. And it's like a punch to my gut. I feel his absence like a searing pain. Knowing he'll never again hold my hand, or kill a squirrel, or watch *Lion King* with me or eat too much tablet has fractured me. Like half of my soul has been cut out and I know who to blame. So time for some more action.

The pill's kicked in and the shakes have receded as I bring up Google Maps and plan my route to Queenie's house. The bitch thinks I can't reach her there – that I can't reach any of her precious friends, but I can. I really can and especially now they're so distracted with everything else, it'll be a doddle.

By the time I get there – a doddery old guy out for a walk – I'm confident that no one will be at home. I do a couple of circles of the area and grin. Clearly, all resources are needed elsewhere because there's not even an officer out front. I pat my pocket to reassure myself that my Wi-Fi jammer – easily obtained from the dark web – is there. I want to leave a surprise for them. One they won't forget. One that'll drive a skewer right through the heart of the Jazzy Solanki fan club.

When I'm certain no one's paying me any attention, I circle round to the back of the house and, jamming the Wi-Fi, I edge closer, lock picks at the ready, and in under a minute I'm in the kitchen. The house smells of a weird combination of fresh coffee and a barrage of different perfumes. I stand still, head cocked to one side, soaking up the ambience, and that's when I hear it. A muffled curse, a chair scraping back, and footsteps approaching. Shit. How had I missed that someone was here?

I'm about to retreat when a huge barefooted figure looms in the kitchen doorway and we stand blinking at each other for a nanosecond. Then the yeti lunges towards me, emitting a feral growl from deep in his stomach and I grab the nearest weapon

I can – a knife from the knife block. Still, he comes at me and I thrust the knife, but he dodges and it slices into his upper arm. It slows him a little as I turn and flee through the back door and into the garden, but he's hot on my heels, his growls thundering after me and he's gaining on me. As I get to the gate, I grab the wheelie bin and push it towards him. He hurdles over it and grabs at my arm, his nails digging into my wrists, then he loses balance and lands on his knees.

I yank my hand away and escape through the gate, running like the wind with a memory at school sports day of Jazzy yelling, '*Run, Mhairi, run!*' and that's what I do until I get to my car and escape.

Chapter 62

Geordie

Geordie rushed through the door, pushing aside a uniformed officer in his haste to reach Guy, who was sitting feet up on Queenie's couch, a hot drink in hand and a bandage on the opposite arm. 'Shite, are you okay?'

Guy popped his cup down on the coffee table and patted his knee for Geordie to sit. Wrapping his arms round Guy, Geordie pulled Guy's head to his chest. 'God, if anything had happened to you, I don't know what I'd have done.'

The sound of a throat being cleared made Geordie pull back and roll his eyes at Guy, as Queenie descended on the pair. 'Hell's bells, can you pair no' get a room or something?' She peered round the room and wandered into the kitchen before returning with a coffee for herself. 'Thank God there's nae damage been done, eh?'

'Nae damage? Nae damage? Will you look at him? Guy was stabbed. Is that no damage?'

'Aye well, I spoke to the paramedic, and the lad said it was only a scratch.' She turned to Guy and winked. 'So, you'll not be getting out of doing the dishes tonight, son.'

Guy's laugh filled the room and with it the tension left Geordie's body. He pushed himself off his boyfriend's knee, straightened his shirt, and plonked himself down on the edge of the couch. 'We've got to take a statement. You know, description and that.'

Guy smiled at the officer hovering by the door. 'Already done. PC Brick took it, but I'll fill you in on the salient stuff.' He took a sip of his drink and frowned as he got his thoughts in order. 'The Wi-Fi went down and so I came through to faff about with the router, but in hindsight I reckon the intruder had some sort of jammer because, as per your instructions this morning, the alarm was on, yet it didn't go off when he or she forced entry.'

Queenie cut in. 'He or she?'

'Aye well, seemed to me they were wearing a sort of head cover thing to make them look bald, but the colour was off – didn't match their skin hue – and when I got close in the garden, I saw strands of hair escaping out the back. Plus, they screamed in surprise when they saw me and it was quite high-pitched.' He shrugged. 'Might have been a man with a high voice, I suppose.'

'So, nothing definitive, then?' Queenie pursed her lips in disappointment. 'Of course, the CSIs will print the place and we've got uniforms doing the usual door-to-doors and trawling for CCTV, so maybe we'll get lucky.'

'Or.' Guy grinned. 'Maybe the skin cells from under my nails when I scratched the fucker might give you an ID.'

Queenie glowered. 'Could you not have led wi' that?'

Chapter 63

Ali

I can smell myself. Jan's cheap perfume and stale sweat. Not a great combination. I've lost track of time too because I've been sleeping so much. It's light outside, but I've no idea how long I've been here. It feels like days, though.

I open the bag I found by the door and looking at the squashed sandwich and the Twix makes me want to throw up. My thigh has stopped bleeding and I'm chuffed with the message I wrote in my own blood behind the headboards. *Ali Afzal woz here!* At least when they find me, they'll know I tried to give them a clue.

That's if they even notice I'm gone. I thought they would but now I'm not so sure. Dad's always at work and she's so wrapped up in her new boyfriend – the one none of us are supposed to know about – that she won't miss me. Maybe Isla will have noticed I'm not at school. Would she raise the alarm though? Or would she be too scared of getting in trouble? I'm aware I'm going over and over the same things in my head. I'm losing it. My limbs shake and my chest's all tight again. The desire to hurt myself is constant and I'm not sure I can resist.

At the thought of nobody missing me, nobody caring enough to notice that I'm gone, my eyes well up again and although I try to get a grip as I brush them away, my heart races again. I can't focus and waves of dizziness blur my vision as the panic takes hold of me and my throat tightens. I yank at the scab on my thigh. That usually works, but not this time. I scratch the ones on my wrists, but my throat just gets tighter and tighter, tears stream down my face. My chest's about to explode and then I get it. Nobody cares if I'm here or not. If I live or die.

My fingers scrabble on the duvet until I find the wire from my bra. I grip it so tight it hurts, then I jab it into my wrist and pull it down. The sweet release of warm blood spilling onto my skin and soaking into the duvet calms me and the last thing I say as my eyes flutter shut is *'Ali Afzal woz here!'*

Chapter 64

Jazzy

In the incident room, Fenton jumped up and punched the air, making Jazzy turn towards him, hope blooming on her worried face. The knowledge that their safe house – Queenie's home – had been penetrated worried her, but she was thankful that Guy was okay. Of course, he couldn't ID his assailant as her sister, but the number of coincidences was building up too much to be believed. 'What have you got?'

Face scrunched up in concentration, Fenton flicked back and forth on his tablet. 'Well, that's weird.'

Jazzy snapped. 'What is?'

'Well, the CSIs have matched the prints from the flat in Porty . . .' He looked at Jazzy, a shadow clouding his eyes.

'For God's sake Fenton, just bloody spit it out.'

'They're a match for your sister. They're Mhairi's prints . . .'

Jazzy closed her eyes and exhaled, as Fenton continued. She'd expected that, but it was good to have her suspicions confirmed 'But that's not all, Jazz. They're also a match for the prints we took from that table in the Tartan Sporran.'

Again, Jazzy wasn't surprised. She'd suspected Mhairi had been the dodgy character observing from the side-lines – all the evidence had been pointing that way and now they had confirmation of her half-sister's culpability she was determined to keep up the momentum. Reassessing her sister's recent file had delivered her Mhairi's bolthole in Skye; what if looking at her earlier file – the one detailing information about Mhairi before they had been separated – had something to tell her. Jazzy slammed the heel of her hand to her forehead. Why hadn't she considered that before. Teachers, social workers, Mhairi and Simon's biological dad – all of those bore looking at again. Then it hit Jazzy. She'd assumed that Mhairi's use of the name Simon McCullough was a nod to her step-great-grandad and her brother, but now Mhairi's enigmatic parting words on the phone ran through her head: 'The secret location is buried in the past.' How could she have forgotten that Mhairi's twin wasn't the only Simon she knew. The twins' dad had shared that name with his son.

She yelled for Queenie, who rushed in, pulling up her zip and sliding to a halt before Jazzy. 'What?'

'We're going over Mhairi's early files. The ones from birth till she and Simon went into foster care. We're looking at any links to this area. Anything at all, no matter how obscure and . . . be creative. Think laterally. This might be our last chance.'

Nobody asked last chance for what. They didn't need to. Time was running out for Ali Afzal and they all knew it.

Chapter 65

Jazzy

Jazzy opened the file on Simon Smith, the twin's biological father. He'd deserted them when they were months old and, in all honesty, Jazzy couldn't entirely blame him because her mum was hard work. She'd paid little attention to his file previously because he'd died in a car crash soon afterwards and, if her memory of him was faint, then the twins' recollections of their birth father were non-existent. Still, the phrase 'blood is thicker than water' had to mean something didn't it? Just because they didn't *remember* him, didn't mean they hadn't researched their birth father and that's exactly what Jazzy set out to do there and then. She scrawled through records after records and database after database, which told her every living and non-living relative of Simon Smith senior. Then with dogged obstinacy she tracked each of them down, discarding any who lived abroad – two third cousins in New Zealand and narrowed it down until, finally, she hit the jackpot. Simon Smith deceased had an auntie on his mother's side who lived in Breich – in Blinkbonny to be precise.

Jazzy shot up and strode over to the map on the wall where pins showed where Ali Afzal had last been seen in Whitburn and the subsequent possible sightings of a vehicle exiting the Whitburn street and where they had headed. Her finger traced some and then when she saw how close one of the ANPR sightings was to Breich, she took a deep breath and turned round. 'Time to take a chance, folks. I think I know where she might be holding Ali. Let me phone it up to Operation Birchtree, but whether they're going in or not, we are. Agreed?'

'Hell yeah,' said Fenton, on his feet and grabbing his jacket before Jazzy had even dialled. Queenie and Geordie, jumped up too, and as Jazzy's call with DCI Connolly connected and she began explaining their findings and what she proposed they should do, they gathered round her. Their support seeping into her, making her voice strong and firm as she countered every objection Connolly put before her. Finally, in frustration, Jazzy blurted out, 'Well, have you got a better plan, boss?'

There was silence for a moment and then ice cold, Connolly's voice came down the line. 'You have a nerve, DS Solanki.' Then the line went dead.

Jazzy turned to her team, her heart thumping against her chest, sweat dotting her brow and her breath coming in pants.

'Fuck. I just did that, didn't I?'

Queenie nodded, then grinned. 'Yep, you did, JayZee. You were like a ninja, a panther, a rhinoceros and you handed DCI Connolly her balls on a platter.' Queenie slapped Jazzy's back, but Fenton frowned. 'Eh, but what are we going to do?'

The Jazz Queens looked at each other, then each of them grinned and punched the air. 'We're going to Breich; that's what we're doing. I'll text DCI Connolly and Elliot and let them know.'

As they grabbed their coats, Geordie thrust stab vests and extendable batons at each of them and, as ready as they'd ever be, they headed for the door, just as it flew open admitting DCIs Connolly and Dick accompanied by DI Shanks. 'Going somewhere are you?'

Connolly's raised eyebrow told Jazzy that although she might be smiling right now, her patience was on a tight leash.

Jazzy stepped before her team and nodded. 'Yep, thought we'd do a quick recce on a property in Breich. You know the one I told you about. Would be remiss of us not to, don't you think?'

As DCI Dick stepped forward his face flushed, spittle flying from the ends of his moustache, Connolly laid a hand on his arm. 'I'll take it from here, Dick. No time to waste. Jazzy's got a credible lead and, as she so rightly said, we'd be remiss not to follow up on it, particularly when a young girl's life is at stake.'

She shot a glance at D team and sighed. 'Against my better judgement and at the instructions of DCS Afzal, who is already en route with the armed response vehicle, your team will accompany us, but purely in an observational capacity. Let's get this show on the road.'

Chapter 66

Mhairi

By the time I calm down enough to drive, I'm shaking with rage and I'm not sure how much time I've lost. Minutes? Hours? It could be either. I pop one of my pills and set off up West Calder main street and back to the safe house, berating myself as I drive. How had I missed the yeti's presence there? I'd accounted for everyone bar him and it's frustrating. I'd meant to leave a wee bomb – not anything that would cause much damage, just enough to let them know I was there, but thanks to that hulking brute, I couldn't.

I got him with the knife though, so maybe he'll have succumbed to the wound, although judging by the way he tanked after me, that's unlikely. Regardless, this misstep on my part has meant I have to adjust my schedule for today if I want everything to go as planned at the funeral.

I slam my palm on the steering wheel as I turn into the street and, not bothering to even lock the car, I dash up the path, key at the ready and into the house. I've got things to do if my plan is to work. No way am I going quietly. My exit will be like a bomb detonating, causing as much damage as possible, inflicting pain on as many of her friends and family as I can. Not bothering to muffle my footsteps this time, I stomp along to the bedroom and burst through the door.

As I look at the supine figure on the bed with blood still dripping onto the carpet from her wrist, I scream 'Noooo!' and fall to my knees, head in my hands, allowing the anger to momentarily engulf me like flames. I stretch out a hand to her neck, feeling for a pulse, but I already know she's gone. The little bitch has thwarted me. Stolen from me the pleasure of killing her myself.

That's when I hear the noises outside and a glance along the corridor and through the open front door tells me it's time to leave. I jump up, aim a punch at the still girl's face and run into the kitchen, grabbing my backpack before, heart thudding as adrenalin floods through me, I scramble through the back door, grinning like a maniac. This is the last hooray and I'm ready for it.

Chapter 67

Jazzy

The row of ex miner's cottages in the stretch of Breich called Blinkbonny was, as the name suggested, a bonny area with smart houses and neat gardens. As they drew up outside, the ARV was already parked and the tactical arms officers were filtering up the path.

From where Jazzy stood, sweating buckets in the stab vest they'd given her, she observed that the front door of the property was ajar. Breathing heavily, tension making her spine rigid, she watched as they breached the front of the house whilst two armed officers filtered off down the side of the building. She grabbed Queenie's arm. 'Come on. There're enough bodies here at the front. Let's go to the back. She won't come quietly. She'll try to escape.'

As they scurried after the armed officers, a yell from inside the house made Jazzy hesitate. 'Paramedics needed now.'

She glanced at Queenie, who shrugged. As she continued to skirt the edge of the house, Jazzy saw her father barrelling inside after the paramedics. Her heart skipped a beat as she wondered what that could mean, but she stiffened her spine and put the thought of her half-sister's fate to the back of her mind.

Then the phone in her back pocket rang. She searched for someone on the main team to tell, but she could only see DI Shanks. 'Wait, Queenie. She's ringing me.'

She dragged the phone from her pocket, its jarring ring tone chilling her blood, but before she accepted the call, she waved it in the air and yelled, 'Shanks! Shanks! Over here, now.'

As Shanks sprinted towards her, his radio already out, she said, 'Tell Connolly she's on the line.'

Shanks connected to Connolly and, in hurried tones, updated her to the situation outside. Still the phone rang out, loud and clear and taunting. 'I'm going to have to answer. You know that.'

But DCI Connolly was already running top speed from the house. Yelling, 'Answer it. Answer the fucking thing. We're recording.'

Swallowing hard, Jazzy put it to her ear and answered. For a second, the only sound through the phone was of tortured breathing. Heart in her mouth, Jazzy scrambled around for something to say.

'Hi, sister dearest.' Mhairi's words were scarcely audible. Ragged wheezes filled Jazzy's ears and, for a second, she wondered if Mhairi had passed out. Moving towards the rear of the property, Jazzy focused on what she could hear through the phone line. The shouts of officers as they continued to search the property and police sirens at the front were audible, but faint. Jazzy signalled to Queenie, Shanks and Connolly and the three followed her cautiously as she breasted the wall and turned to survey the woodland that backed into the gardens. Behind her, Connolly whispered into her radio, alerting the armed officers who were now combing the shrubbery. Another two armed officers appeared and overtook them, joining their colleagues as they scoured the area.

At last, Jazzy, eyes darting everywhere, desperate to catch sight of her sister, spoke.

'Oh, Mhairi, this is a fine pickle you're in, isn't it? Don't you think it's time to give yourself up?'

Mhairi's voice was faint. 'Do you remember that day at the school fair when you stole money from Mum's purse and bought me and Si tablet? We watched *Lion King*. Do you remember, Jazzy?'

The memory sliced through Jazzy. Mhairi had presented her with one of those bittersweet memories she had suppressed for years. Now it lay before her in vivid technicolour. Jazzy blinked, trying to banish the memory of them at the school fair. Mhairi was trying to put her on edge, and she couldn't let her succeed. 'No. Can't remember that.'

A soft laugh, followed by a hacking cough, filled Jazzy's ears. 'Aye, you can, Jasmine. You wouldn't forget that. I know you.' Faint sounds of Mhairi moving through foliage or bushes drifted through the silence until Mhairi spoke gain. 'You found the girl yet? I wanted to kill her myself, but the stupid wee cow beat me to it. Looks like I'm the only sister you've got left. How does that make you feel, Jasmine?'

Ali was dead? She felt a sharp jolt of pain, but pushed it away. She couldn't allow herself to be sidetracked. 'Unfortunately, you're not one I can be proud of, Mhairi. Serial killer isn't really a glowing recommendation, is it?'

Mhairi's faint laugh, followed by an amused 'Touché' was accompanied by the faint noises of the officers searching the scrubland. They were close to Mhairi.

Eyes still scanning the area, Jazzy said, 'Surely, you know you can't escape, Mhairi.'

'Who says I want to escape? Maybe I've had enough. Maybe it's time for me to join Simon.'

Jazzy felt a chill as she heard her words. It was the first time that it occurred to her, that Mhairi had always planned for 'death by cop' if she was cornered like this. That she'd allowed herself to be cornered. Hadn't they all always said how smart Mhairi was? Had she planned for exactly what was happening right now? Holding the phone against her chest to muffle her words, Jazzy turned to Connolly. 'She's planning to end it here now. She's going to force them to shoot her. You need to order them to hold their fire. She can't escape so easily. She has to face justice for what she's done.'

Fingers tugging frantically at her hair, Connolly issued urgent instructions, but when the response came in a frazzle of static, the words were not ones Jazzy wanted to hear. 'You don't have the authority to issue orders, DCI Connolly. We are trained to respond to threats as they arise and that's what we'll do.'

In the silence following, Jazzy stepped forward, striding through the weeds as they clung to her legs, almost tripping her up. Her eyes bored into the depths of the darkest shadowy corners of the wilderness, seeking her sister out, determined to stop her from getting herself killed. 'Just give yourself up, Mhairi. Maybe we can spend some time together. Make up for lost time . . .'

Mhairi's laugh was gruff and when she spoke, laboured pants punctuated her words.

Again, covering the phone, Jazzy said, 'She's on the move! Can you see her?'

As all eyes scoured the field and into the woods beyond, Jazzy listened.

'I left something for you on the kitchen table. My last gift to you. Call it your last rites.'

Jazzy forced a scoffing tone. 'I want nothing from you, not a thing.'

'Oh, you'll want this, Jasmine. I know you'll want this.'

And through the line Jazzy heard a voice shout, 'Armed police! Place your weapon on the ground.'

With a sense of what was about to happen, Jazzy ran towards the officers, who stood on the edge of the woods, their guns braced against their shoulders. Barging through grass and discarded obstacles, Jazzy raced towards them, her chest on fire as she pushed herself beyond her limits. As she neared, she saw Mhairi, her bald cap awry, her hair escaping from beneath it and waving a gun at the armed officers.

As Jazzy ground to a halt, the inevitability of what was to happen seared on her brain. Mhairi released fire. Just once. Although the shot went wide, it was enough to seal her fate and, as Jazzy covered her ears with her hands, the armed officers fired back. Mhairi, looking right at Jazzy, a sweet smile on her face that reminded Jazzy of the toddler she'd once been, fell to the ground, a bright red bloom spreading across her chest.

Jazzy, her eyes glued to her sister, fell to her knees, and stayed there until Queenie appeared and wrapped her arms around her and cradled her there, letting her cry. Her sister was dead.

Chapter 68

Jazzy

'Death by bloody polis. Can you believe it? Bloody death by polis?'

It had been ten minutes since the fatal shooting and Jazzy, unable to move, had remained where she was, at first, just crying into Queenie's arms. Now, on her feet and trying to process her mixed emotions, she tried to block out Queenie's refrain. One of the armed officers had kicked her sister's gun out of reach, but even Jazzy could see it was unnecessary. Her sister lay, eyes open, a faint smile on her face as if she was mocking all of them.

Paramedics brushed past Jazzy, who continued to look down at her sister, then moments later stood up, shaking their heads. Jazzy wondered what she should do? What was the correct response to seeing your serial killer sister shot to death before your eyes? Should she fall to her knees and hug Mhairi to her like she had when she was a child? Only her own heartbeat assured Jazzy of its presence, relentlessly thumping in her chest. Shouldn't she feel something more than this all-encompassing numbness?

Strong arms circled her shoulders, guiding her away, and she heard, as if from a distance, Clive Shanks's voice, calm and reassuring, as he guided her through the horde of officers and medics gathered there. Then, from somewhere else, another male voice washed over her. One more familiar to her: Elliot. He grabbed her arms and studied her, his eyes scouring her face. Noticing the other man, he abruptly let go. Jazzy looked at him, trying to work out the play of emotions across his face, but he turned away before she could get a handle on them. 'Glad you're okay, Jazzy. I see you're in expert hands.'

Jazzy wanted to call him back. Wanted to feel his warm hand holding hers again, but he was gone and Shanks was guiding her to a car and thrusting a bottle of water into her hand, whilst Queenie followed behind, alternating now between 'I cannae believe it's over' and 'Thank God the Bitch is dead'.

Clive's radio kicked into action and he gave Jazzy a last hug. 'They need me. Don't go anywhere. I'll take you home, okay?'

Jazzy blinked and moved her gaze from his retreating figure to Queenie, who, enfolding her in her arms, nestled her head against her chest and gently patted Jazzy's shoulder. 'I know you, JayZee. You're blaming yourself for all of this, but that won't do. You need to let this go. You need to let *her* go. She's tortured you for the last time and now she's gone and it's good riddance to her.'

Jazzy pulled away from Queenie, and sounding nothing like herself said, 'This was too easy, Queenie. She gave in too easily.'

'Och, don't be daft. Having no other choices, she opted for the easy solution. Just be glad she's gone, and it's all over.'

Chapter 69

Saturday

Jazzy

The next day passed in a blur with Jazzy insisting she was okay and returning to work after being checked by paramedics for shock and a good night's sleep at Queenie's.

In a stable condition at St John's Hospital, Ali Afzal had lost a lot of blood from her self-inflicted wound, but the best news was that she was alive. Both her parents were with her, although the chief super had taken the time to update Jazzy before heading off to the hospital. 'She's been self-harming again, Jazzy. We had trouble with that a year or so ago and she had therapy. Clearly not enough.' He raked his fingers through his hair and blew his cheeks out. 'No doubt the continual arguments between me and her mum wouldn't help her either.'

Then he'd looked at Jazzy. 'I'm thinking of taking some time, so I can be there for her. This job takes a lot from us and it's time I put one of my daughters first. I failed you both probably. Terrible father.' He shook his head and looked away. 'Terrible husband too by the sounds of it. Look, I don't know, but . . .' Then he turned to face her again. He looked nervous. 'If there's a chance of you and Ali getting to know each other, then we could make that happen. You are my daughter and so is she. I don't even know why I've been denying that relationship to myself for so long.'

Jazzy smiled, but it was non-committal. She wasn't sure she was ready to take that step and she still had to sort out her own headspace after the events of the past few months. 'We'll see.'

He'd held out a hand to shake and Jazzy had returned his firm grip with a nod that seemed to signal a change in their relationship.

As the day progressed, additional details surfaced. A crucial one was Jazzy feeling well enough to find out what the gift was that Mhairi had promised. On the table in the house, was an envelope addressed to Jazzy with a note and an old key with a tattered address label attached.

McCullough House,
Skye

'That was the name she used to rent the flat in Portobello,' Fenton said as Jazzy studied it through the evidence bag. 'It all makes sense now.'

Dear Jazzy,
I found peace here a long time ago. Maybe you will too. But even if you don't, I'm sure you'll find something else and my last gift won't be lost on you.
Your dearest sister, Mhairi

Jazzy frowned and then a smile twitched her lips. Even to the end, Mhairi had to be enigmatic. She tossed the bag onto the table. She would never visit that place. Why would she? It meant nothing to her. The official investigation would scour it for additional clues to Mhairi's troubled life. The killings would stop now and that's all she needed to know. Her friends and family were safe.

By the end of the day, her mind turned to the last event she had to get through before she could finally take some time to explore her feelings: Simon's funeral.

With Mhairi dead, there was no need for the song and dance of protective measures and armed officers, and Jazzy was glad of that. This was a formality for her. Her final act of responsibility to her brother, and she wouldn't have to do it for Mhairi because she was to be cremated. She was relieved that Doc Johnston would lead the service and everything was in place. Mhairi's post-mortem had shown that Mhairi was taking large doses of the anti-psychotic drugs they'd found in the Portobello flat and, in addition, a concoction of uppers and downers. Fleetingly Jazzy wondered whether Mhairi was more or less likely to kill when she was drugged up. Is that why Ali had escaped with her life? But then she pushed the thought aside. It didn't matter anymore. The deaths were over.

Chapter 70

June 11th

Jazzy

'You okay, hen? You look a wee bit wabbit.'

Jazzy glared at Queenie and strode towards the loos. Much as she loved her friend, the last thing she needed right now was Queenie's empathy when she knew deep down that Queenie did not understand why she had agreed to most of her brother's death-bed demands.

Jazzy sped up, leaving Queenie trying to catch up as she headed along the corridor to her sanctuary. Once inside the toilet, she pushed the cubicle door shut behind her and plonked herself down on the closed toilet seat. Before the funeral started, she had to pull herself together and, judging by her hammering heart and the sickly volcano brewing in her gut, that would not be easy. Jazzy wanted to go in prepared to do her duty. No matter what he'd done, no matter how awful he'd been, Jazzy was determined to make good on the blood promise she'd made to Simon when they were kids, and that would take all of her reasoning and negotiating skills.

In the two weeks since Mhairi's death, Operation Birchtree had discovered that the McCullough premises on Skye was where Mhairi had holed up until her return to Lothian. However, that wasn't all they'd discovered. Apparently, McCullough who had been some distant grandparent of Mhairi's through her adoptive mother, had also been a serial killer. The land surrounding the farmhouse was dotted with graves – upwards of forty of them – and it would take the Highland and Islands police years to process and identify the victims, some of whose deaths went back over fifty years.

Jazzy found the coincidence of Mhairi and this old serial killer meeting too inconceivable to comprehend, but she hoped that the victims would be identified and their families would receive the closure they deserved. She'd already decided that she would never visit the property and had given permission for it to be razed to the ground when the police investigation was over. She'd always believed that there was no such thing as coincidence, but in this instance, she wondered if the natural gravitation of two like-minded deviants superseded her belief. Whatever the reason, she refused to dwell on it. With a surplus of personal memories, she struggled to process the actions of a long-dead old man from Skye.

She closed her eyes, popped her earbuds in and started the meditation recording on her phone. Over the past few months, she had increasingly been using it to calm herself and regulate her breathing and heart rate. Dr Johnston had recommended it and her therapist had agreed that this was a good habit to get into. Now all she needed was twenty minutes of peace to let the relaxing music and accompanying hypnotism soothe her frazzled nerves . . . of course, that was without Queenie. As soon as she heard the outer bathroom door slam against the wall, she knew who it was. Resigned, Jazzy pulled the earbuds out, stopped the recording, and, despite her frustration, grinned as she saw Queenie's head pop over the cubicle wall.

'What the fuck, Queenie? What if I'd been having a wee?'

Queenie tutted and rolled her eyes. 'I listened before I climbed up here. Was just making sure you weren't bawling your eyes out. Besides, they sent me to find you. We need to set off now.'

Chapter 71

Jazzy

Although the cemetery wasn't what you'd call packed, there were a fair amount of people there for Simon Smith's funeral and all of them were there for Jazzy, not her brother. She'd chosen not to wear black and nor had she got dressed up. This entire event was a travesty, and she wanted it over with a quickly as she could. Her own feelings about this afternoon's funeral were mixed. Far inside, a deep sadness lurked, yet somewhere closer to the top, rage was the dominant emotion. Since her brother's death her visions and nightmares had intensified. Even more memories from her childhood seemed to erupt every night and grip her so tightly she thought she would splinter into a trillion pieces. Besides her thoughts being so focused on the funeral, underlying frustration buzzed through her.

As she walked behind the funeral directors who carried his coffin, Jazzy made eye contact with everyone who'd attended. Uncle Pedro smiled at her, his enormous figure a reassuring mass as he stood, hands clasped lightly in front of him, Ivor by his side. Jazzy was glad Benjy hadn't come. Her work colleagues and their partners were lined up, smiling encouragingly at her, as she trailed alone behind the coffin. Even Afzal had come and stood next to her own parents and Crumble.

Heat filled with love for these people. She turned her gaze to the front where Dr Lamond waited. Once they lowered the coffin into the ready-prepared grave, Dr Lamond spoke. 'We are gathered here today to support a fine young woman who, through her enviable sense of responsibility, is fulfilling her final duty for her tortured soul of a brother.'

From the trees to the side of the grave, a flurry of movement distracted Jazzy. Someone was running towards them carrying something. *Benjy!*

Ivor darted towards him at an angle. 'Benjy. Noooo!'

Hot on her heels lumbered Uncle Pedro, his face a mask of confusion. Benjy reached the open grave with its cheap coffin and before anyone could stop him he threw the bucket of red paint he was carrying on to the grave yelling, 'Rot in hell, you murdering monster. Rot in hell.'

Everyone stood horrified, not knowing what to do. Jazzy stepped towards Benjy, who had fallen to his knees right at the edge of the grave weeping, and that's when it happened.

The explosion came from nowhere. Sharp and acrid and loud, hitting Jazzy like a freight train, robbing her of breath.

The momentum threw her into the air and as she fell, almost as if in slow motion, the screams of those around her became louder and more piercing. Then she crashed to the concrete ground, juddering every bone in her body. Yelled instructions, strident sirens, and flashing lights merged with the screams, penetrating her befuddled mind and filling her with terror as she tried to work out how badly she was hurt. Disorientated by pungent, belching black smoke, eyes streaming and her entire body one throbbing pulsating ball of pain and all she could think was: *How the hell did this happen?*

The piercing jaggy sensation under her eyelids was agony.

She tried to lift her hand to her face, but her arm wouldn't work. Her heart thumped against her ribcage as panic bubbled up, threatening to choke her. She tried one more time, but again, her arm wouldn't budge and as a wave of dizziness hit, she turned her head to one side and vomited. As her eyes fluttered and the light faded, images of those she loved swam before her and she longed to set eyes on them one last time. For auld time's sake.

Then something penetrated her woolly brain. Anguished cries, tears, and squeals of fear. A searing, caustic rage replaced her lethargy, the like of which she'd never experienced before. Scared to stir, trying to catch her breath and gather her senses, she breathed in deeply; but then a deep trembling began somewhere beneath her. At first, she assumed it was her body's reaction to the trauma. Maybe shock setting in, but then she realised it actually was coming from somewhere underneath her. She tried to roll over, to see what lay beneath her, and every move was agony.

Then someone was wrapping their arms round her – Shanks. Screams and moans echoed all around, and when her eyes cleared, she saw Dr Johnston sitting in a slumped heap on the other side of Simon's grave. He wasn't moving. Oh God. Her eyes skated everywhere, taking a mental inventory. Geordie and Fenton were scooping people together and moving them away from the area, Queenie was barking orders into her phone and in the distance, the sound of sirens became audible. Elliot? Where was Elliot? For a second her heart stuttered, then she identified him kneeling beside Uncle Pedro over by the grave, doing something to a bundle of rags on the ground. She frowned. Why was there so much red? Then it hit her in the solar plexus. *Benjy!*

Her heart plummeted, and she pushed Shanks away and crawled over to where the other two men kneeled. Uncle Pedro turned to her, tears pouring down his dirt-streaked face. As he shook his head, Ivor, who had broken away from Fenton, was right there beside them, looking at her cousin. Uncle Pedro tried to wrap his arms around her, but she shrugged him off, collapsing on the ground, her raw wail splintering the air.

'*Benjyyyy!*'

Chapter 72

Two weeks later

Queenie

Outside the crematorium in Livingston, the Stùrrachers fell in line behind Benjy's coffin. Benjy's dad and uncles carried him on their shoulders. For a long moment, they stood silent and still, heads bowed as the Argy Bargy pub landlord stood forward in full Highland dress and played 'Going Home', the pipes' haunting tones filling the air. Then, as the last strain of the haunting tune died, the villagers as one lifted their heads and sung 'Wild Mountain Thyme', replacing the word 'lassie' with 'laddie'.

By the end of it, only the Stùrrachers themselves remained dry-eyed as they took their son into the crematorium, closing the doors behind them, leaving the other mourners outside until they had said their own private farewells to the boy who meant so much to them.

Waiting outside in silence, Jazzy stood with Clive Shanks whilst the rest of the team stood to one side. Elliot notably standing on his own, a distance away. Fenton and Geordie edged up to Queenie. 'We took our eye off the ball, Queenie. Shouldn't have removed the officers at the funeral directors,' Geordie said.

Queenie nodded. 'Aye we did. We should have realised that

Mhairi would have something else planned. But hindsight's a wonderful thing, eh?'

Fenton nodded. 'Aye, but we found the lad who attached the device to the coffin. He did it the morning of the funeral. Told us it was a dare, but then tripped himself up and admitted that Mhairi, dressed like an auld baldy guy, paid him £500 to do it.'

'He'll go down for that, which is a good thing.'

'Aye, it's a good thing.' Geordie's tone implied it wasn't a severe enough punishment.

'So . . .' Fenton gestured towards Jazzy. 'That a thing, then? Those two?'

Queenie sighed and shrugged, her eyes resting on the two figures who so far hadn't spoken to anyone else. 'Aye, it seems so. He's there the whole time and Jazzy isn't objecting. Early days though, early days and if anyone deserves a bit of romance, then it's her, isn't it?'

Fenton shuffled his feet and Queenie turned laser eyes to him. 'Come on, Haggis, what's up? Spit it oot tae yer auntie Queenie.'

'Well, it's probably nothing . . .'

Geordie nudged him. 'It's not nothing, Fenton, so just tell her.'

Fenton closed his eyes and when he plucked up the courage to speak, his words came out in a rush. 'Well, I've heard he's a bit of a player.'

'A player? What the heck does that mean?'

Face flushing, Fenton shuffled his feet again, but finally blurted it out. 'You know . . .' He shuffled his feet some more. 'He's a, you know . . .'

Geordie tutted. 'For God's sake, Queenie, what he's trying to say is that Clive Shanks shags around.'

Queenie's eyes narrowed and all three pairs of eyes turned to Jazzy and Shanks, and Queenie took a step forward. 'I'll bloody strangle the wee bastard.'

'No, Queenie. We can't tell Jazzy till we know for sure. It's just rumours. Maybe they're not even true.'

As Jazzy and Shanks turned to join them, Queenie gave a quick nod. 'Aye, right, but I want to know for sure. Nobody takes any of us Jazz Queens for fools.'

A Letter from Liz Mistry

Dear Reader,

I can't quite believe that this is book 3 in the Solanki and McQueen crime series – doesn't time fly? In *Deadly Reckoning* I take the Jazz Queens from Portobello, to Glasgow and back into West Lothian again and like the others in the series, expect hard-hitting crimes, sensitive gentle moments, ones that will tear your heart out and, of course, with Queenie in the room, lots of lighter moments.

Some of you may recognise Portobello's iconic bottle kilns on the front cover, so let me tell you a little about why, almost by accident, they became such a feature in the book. A summer visit to Porty with my husband was supposed to blow away the cobwebs and clear my mind. It most definitely wasn't to research for *Deadly Reckoning*. However, I think we can safely blame my husband for that. Nilesh, a ceramicist and potter, was fascinated by the bottle kilns and spent an inordinate amount of time explaining to me how they worked, tapping the bricks, discussing the mechanics of firing in these kilns . . . meanwhile, as it so very often does, my mind wandered to darker places with those absolutely gorgeous kilns at the forefront of my 'what if?' questions and before you knew it, *Deadly Reckoning* was born.

As ever, I've had a whale of a time in the company of the Jazz Queens and in *Deadly Reckoning*, I resolved – perhaps in unexpected ways, some of the overarching story strands from *The Blood Promise*.

I hope you enjoy reading *Deadly Reckoning* as much as I enjoyed writing it. Of course, if you loved getting to know Jazzy, Queenie and the team, then please do leave a review, shout about it to your friends, sign up to my Mistry VIP club on my website, or talk about it on social media.

Until the next Jazzy and Queenie adventure, keep safe. Best wishes,

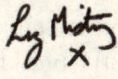

The Blood Promise

A DEADLY GIFT

Imogen Clark wakes up on her 16th birthday
to find her parents dead at the breakfast table,
along with a message from their killer.

A TWIST OF FATE

Detectives Jazzy Solanki and Annie McQueen join the
investigation, but the more they discover, the more
Jazzy suspects that the killing is a twisted message for
her. Jazzy shares the same birthday as Imogen, and
believes that this is more than a coincidence.

A RACE TO CATCH A KILLER

When Jazzy discovers the connection between the killer
and the stalker who has been following her for years,
she is forced to confront the dark past she was desperate
to keep hidden. She must stop at nothing to solve
the case, before she becomes the next victim . . .

The Revenge Pact

TWO DEATHS

Tommy and Markie Jones are discovered
dead at the side of a road in Scotland.

TWO RIVAL GANGS

Detectives Jazzy Solanki and Annie McQueen are on the
scene where the bodies are identified as the nephews of
Loanie Gibbs, head of a notable Edinburgh gang.

The turf war between the gangs of Glasgow
and Edinburgh has existed for years, but these
murders signal an escalation in violence.

ONE UNFORGIVABLE BETRAYAL

As the investigation unfolds, there's suspicion about a
leak within the police force, and to her dismay Jazzy
is asked to keep a watchful eye on someone close to
her. With distrust on all sides, can the pair uncover the
truth before the body count mounts even more?

Last Request

When human remains are discovered under Bradford's
derelict Odeon car park, DS Nikita Parekh and
her team are immediately called to the scene.

Distracted by keeping her young nephew out of trouble,
Nikki is relieved when the investigation is transferred to the
Cold Case Unit, and she can finally focus on her family.

But after the identity of the victim is revealed,
she's soon drawn back into the case. The dead
man is a direct link to her painful past.

As the body count begins to rise, Nikki must do
everything she can to stop the killer in their tracks
before anyone else gets hurt – even if it means
digging up secrets she had long kept hidden . . .

**For readers of Angela Marsons and LJ Ross comes
a gritty new crime series featuring bold, brave and
ferocious DS Nikki Parekh! This rip-roaring thriller
will have you reading long into the night!**

Acknowledgements

As always, I am amazed at how my ideas for *Deadly Reckoning* – from those tentative few ideas, to the first draft – have been whipped into shape by the fantastic team at HQ. The editing, publicity, and cover design team's attention to detail, enthusiasm and skill, as always smoothed off the rough edges of the story and made me raise my writing game. I am so proud of how *Deadly Reckoning* has turned out and it's all because of the team that work tirelessly behind the scenes to get it out there in the world and into the hands of readers. So . . . here we go with the thanks (and fingers crossed, I haven't missed anyone out). In particular, I'd like to thank my editor, Sophia Allistone, whose love of the Jazz Queens shone through in her detailed and perceptive feedback all of which has helped raised the quality of the book immeasurably. Helena Newton and Michelle Bullock also worked tirelessly to iron out my mistakes and catch my missteps – you have eagle eyes!

Many thanks to the cover designer, Anna Sikorska, who has truly excelled in bringing the Portobello bottle kilns to life with this amazing cover.

My agent, Lorella Belli, at LBLA and her wonderful team have worked tirelessly to promote the Jazz Queens. Thank you so much! Do you ever sleep?

My online crimey groups, especially UK Crime Book Club and Crime Fiction Addict, are a source of constant entertainment and provide a safe space to interact with readers and fellow authors. Thanks to the Admin teams of both groups who keep them running smoothly and for the readers who are so supportive of the authors in the groups.

My family too have, as always, been amazing. They know how much I cherish being a crime writer and see the joy it brings me and are always there for me. My husband, Nilesh, in particular, goes the extra mile to make sure I can do all the writerly things I want to do. Huge thanks and much love to them.

But, my most heartfelt thanks go to you, the reader, for without you there would be no reason to write. I have enjoyed chatting with you online, receiving your feedback, meeting you at events and festivals and generally spending time in your company. You are the absolute best!

Dear Reader,

We hope you enjoyed reading this book. If you did, we'd be so appreciative if you left a review. It really helps us and the author to bring more books like this to you.

Here at HQ Digital we are dedicated to publishing fiction that will keep you turning the pages into the early hours. Don't want to miss a thing? To find out more about our books, promotions, discover exclusive content and enter competitions you can keep in touch in the following ways:

JOIN OUR COMMUNITY:
Sign up to our new email newsletter: http://smarturl.it/SignUpHQ
Read our new blog www.hqstories.co.uk

𝕏 https://twitter.com/HQStories
𝐟 www.facebook.com/HQStories

BUDDING WRITER?
We're also looking for authors to join the HQ Digital family!
Find out more here:

https://www.hqstories.co.uk/want-to-write-for-us/

Thanks for reading, from the HQ Digital team